Broken Pieces of Tomorrow

A novel by
Soulla Christodoulou

Though some of the events mentioned in this book are based on the author's overall recollections over time, the overall story is a work of fiction and names and characters portrayed are of a fictional nature. Therefore, any resemblance to actual persons, living or dead, is entirely coincidental. Likewise, the views portrayed by certain characters throughout the novel are again, written within a fictional context and are not the views of the author or any other person connected in this publication.

All rights reserved. No part of this publication may be reproduced or transmitted in any form or by any means, electronic or mechanical, including photocopying, recording, or any information storage or retrieval system, without prior permission in writing from the author.

No responsibility for loss caused by any individual or oganisation acting on or refraining from action as a result of the material in this publication can be accepted by the author.

***

The front cover has been designed by Mya Glenister who can be contacted via
Facebook @ArtfulSilver or Instagram @artful_ginger

www.dragonrealmpress.com

*This book is dedicated to my three boys,
Christian, Alexei and Angelo,
who in my darkest days shone a light on my spirit
keeping me sane, strong and determined.
I love you all with my heart and soul, my everything.*

It is with heartfelt thanks and love that I mention the following friends and family who have supported my writing through what has been a turbulent, yet often exciting and exhilarating journey of self-discovery, wonderful creativity and many bouts of self-doubt.

To my mum and dad for believing in me.

To my partner, Alan Reynolds, for never once making me feel guilty about how much time I spent writing this book when we could have been spending time together, for your love and generosity of heart and for standing by me.

To my family, for all your love, support and encouragement and especially Lee Amoss and Angela Seaward who read my final manuscript.

To my creative writing buddies Louise Stevens, Mark Glover, Ian Grant, Judith Crosland, Tom Strong and Andrea Terroni. Your honest feedback, motivation and support helped me develop my own personal writing style with confidence and gave me belief in my writing ability.

To my wonderful beta readers from as far afield as Victoria, British Columbia; Leesa Lillis and the Book Club members whose positive words and feedback have stayed with me always.

To Mya Glenister for the design of my front cover. I can write but I can't draw!

Contents

Prologue 1
Chapter One 12
Chapter Two 31
Chapter Three 41
Chapter Four 64
Chapter Five 81
Chapter Six 88
Chapter Seven 97
Chapter Eight 129
Chapter Nine 140
Chapter Ten 160
Chapter Eleven 184
Chapter Twelve 205
Chapter Thirteen 225
Chapter Fourteen 245
Chapter Fifteen 257
Chapter Sixteen 277
Chapter Seventeen 294
Chapter Eighteen 301
Chapter Nineteen 322
Chapter Twenty 347
Chapter Twenty-One 367
Chapter Twenty-Two 378
Chapter Twenty-Three 389
Chapter Twenty-Four 401
Chapter Twenty-Five 419
Chapter Twenty-Six 430
Chapter Twenty-Seven 456
Chapter Twenty-Eight 469

Prologue

AS THE FIRST chords of the Bridal Chorus struck, Georgia intertwined her arm with her dad's. He patted her hand and she covered his with her other hand; his strength, his warmth, his love touched her. He wasn't a demonstrative man and Georgia knew from his touch all he wanted to say to her although a little part of her wished she could hear the words. She shook off the overwhelming temptation to say something and instead leaned in and gave him a kiss on the cheek.

'It's time Dad.'

'It is.'

The church, named the Cathedral of the Holy Cross and St Michael in Golders Green, looked beautiful swathed in all its wedding ceremony adornments and decorations. The usually inner sombre darkness of the solid wood arcade behind the altar bathed in the light coming in through the stained glass windows. Garlands of tiny gypsophila interlaced with pink and soft buttermilk roses in full bloom decorated the aisle and tall pedestal arrangements guarded the altar like two bridesmaids bursting with pride as they looked on at the proceedings.

The flickering glow of the lit candles in the sandboxes at the front of the church danced across the otherwise cold stone walls and columns lining the central seating area made up of long, heavy ornately carved wooden pews. In contrast, delicately painted murals of saints cast blue, red and green shadows across the church, reminding Georgia she was about to take her wedding vows in the eyes of God.

She took a deep breath in and exhaled in an effort to calm herself, the smell of incense and burning wax hitting her nostrils, making her slightly giddy. She smoothed the folds of her long gown and fingered the hundreds of handmade roses stitched across the front in pretty swags; pink, coral and dusky blue. She adjusted her veil hanging over her carefully made up face and took another deep breath.

Her sisters, Teresa and Katia and her brother Louis sat in the very front row with her grandparents, her mum's parents and her dad's parents. This was a momentous day for them all, the plans of the past eighteen months finally coming to fruition. She searched the crowd for Nicolas, the man she was marrying and saw the back of him stooped over talking to his *proto koumbaro*, Best Man, Miltonos.

Alerted to their presence by the music the guests turned round to face Georgia and her dad, many stood up and clicked photographs of her. Faced with a sea of smiles and waves and nods she smiled back, her nerves ebbing away with the warmth of the love she felt.

She urged her two six-year-old flower girls to straighten her train behind her. She looked ahead straight down the aisle, the gold edging either side of the dark red carpet mapping out the path to her husband-to-be. She tilted her chin up, fought against the tears of joy stinging the back of her eyes and took her first steps towards Nicolas and the rest of her life.

***

Walking back up the aisle, the Wedding March booming across the church Georgia and Nicolas came out into the sparkling sunlight holding hands. A surprisingly warm Sunday, May seemed to have kept its promise with an offer of bright spring weather on her special day.

The austerity of the Greek Orthodox ceremony over, cheers and whoops of joy and handfuls of rice and confetti instantly bombarded them as they walked out of the church hand in hand. Nicolas turned to her and brushing his lips against her ear he whispered. 'This is it Mrs Josephides.'

'It is, Mr Josephides. The rest of our lives starts now,' she said momentarily solemn as she spat out bits of sugar paper confetti stuck to her lip and shook the rice out of her bouncy curled hair and her cleavage. She laughed and waved at people she recognised; friends, family, family from Cyprus, Nicolas' aunt and cousins from Greece, and many distant relations she didn't recognise too. Her head fell back and she whooped, flinging her hands in the air, full of joy, waving her wedding bouquet high above her head.

'Come here.' Nicolas pulled her close, pushed the edge of her veil away from her face. He gave her a long kiss on the lips and as the cheers grew louder they both came up for air and their eyes locked.

***

The five-star banqueting suite, at the Royal Garden Hotel, in Kensington accommodated their four hundred guests with ease, spacious with tall light ceilings and painted in opulent creams and golds and the most luxurious carpet and exquisite wallpaper. Georgia had fallen in love with the room the moment she saw it.

The suite dazzled with crystal candelabra and flickering candles. Fresh flower displays of bud pink and ivory roses interspersed with soft ferny foliage and light catching crystals decorated the tables and raised top table on a curtained stage, beautiful balloon arrangements formed two interlocking hearts against the wall behind.

With the four course wedding meal almost finished and speeches done, although not traditionally customary at Greek Cypriot weddings, the celebrations got under way.

Georgia moved away the top table and danced around the open floor space ecstatically happy. Her long curled hair bounced below her shoulders; Harry and the Grecian Kings, one of the most highly paid and sought after bands for Greek Cypriot weddings of the 1990s, blared out the live music.

The four-foot train of her dupion silk ivory wedding gown swept the parquet flooring as she twirled and turned, dipped and moved her body to the rhythm. She loved the full skirt and the way it swished. The music seeped into every part of her and lost in her dancing which came as naturally to her as a pirouette came to a ballerina, she stretched out her arms to her side and clicked her fingers to the beat. She gave everyone her wide smile, revealing her pearl white even-spaced teeth and she could feel her dark brown eyes smiling too, mirroring the sparkle of the diamonds around her wedding ring.

The *chifdedelli* struck up, a popular dance to which the majority of Greek Cypriots and Greeks knew the basic steps. The dance floor brimmed with guests, some danced in small groups or in pairs; men with men, women with women. Georgia took a few steps around the dance floor like a swan, confident in her movements and in her skin for almost the very first time in her life; she had always been the 'chubby' one of her mother's three daughters and this had always thwarted her confidence.

She looked over at Nicolas, her new husband and felt her heart flutter with love and adoration. She thought how handsome he looked in his dark navy suit, his muscly upper arms showing through his cotton white shirt, now creased and edging out of the waist of his trousers as he kicked his leg out in front of him and slapped his thigh to the cheers of the men surrounding him in a circle.

'*Opas*,' called out Georgia's brother, Louis, as he joined Nicolas taking a step turn and kicking his leg out. He smacked his thigh with confidence as he dipped down in a squat and finished with a spring back onto both feet again to continue dancing opposite Nicolas, losing his rhythm but not caring as he kicked his leg out behind him this time.

'*Opas*,' chorused the melee of uncles, cousins and friends dancing around Nicolas and Louis. Georgia looked across in their direction and smiled again, laughing out loud. She continued to dance to the energetic rhythm, wiping the sheen of sweat from across her forehead and upper lip.

The music came to a natural stop and Georgia hugged her sisters, Theresa and Katia who'd been dancing with her. Georgia thought Theresa, tall and slim, with long straight hair, lighter than Georgia's dark curls, looked stunning in her figure-hugging floor length gown. The satin pink matched the glow of her flushed cheeks and painted lips. Katia, shorter than Georgia, hugged her back standing on tiptoe. Georgia could feel the heat coming off her as Katia stepped back and tugged on the sky blue bodice of her dress which had slipped down during the dancing. Katia's dark straight hair hung loose around her bare shoulders, the glitter of her hair clip matching the shine of the sequins scattered like twinkling stars over the fabric of her mid-length dress.

Georgia shuffled off the floor after another two dances and made her way to the raised top table. Miltonos, took a swig from his champagne glass as he chatted to one of her uncles who had flown over from Cyprus for her big day. Miltonos made a very handsome Best Man and she was glad Nicolas had asked his oldest friend to have the honour of holding the position of *proto koumbaro* on their wedding day.

Her eyes scanned the suite for Nicolas who had left the dance floor. She couldn't see him and proceeded to sit down, wiping her sweating brow. She sat for a few minutes taking in the atmosphere and felt a hand on her bare shoulder. She recognised Nicolas' touch.

'What a splendid day we're having,' she said stroking his face, before leaning in to kiss him on the lips.

'It's fantastic,' he said. 'The dance floor is packed. Everyone is up and dancing all the time. I can't believe the vibe. It's sensational. It's the best wedding I have ever been to,' he laughed as he waved to a group of friends dancing in a circle around Georgia's two sisters.

'Go girls!' Georgia jumped up and danced, arms in the air, taking steps to the left and then right. 'The band is incredible isn't it?'

'Yeah, worth every penny.'

'Wedding cake should be out soon,' she said. 'I hope they have remembered to keep the top tier for us.'

'They wouldn't dare forget.'

'Well, it's traditional to keep it for the first baby's

christening and I like our traditions.'

'What about in the church then?'

'Well that was different,' she smirked. 'I'm not going to allow you to dominate me just because I'm your wife now.' She re-called the moment in the church when Nicolas tried to stamp on her foot and she had just managed to pull it away. They were walking round the alter, Nicolas holding her hand, both of them bound together by the wedding bands on their fingers and joined together by the *stefana*, wedding wreaths, placed on their heads and tied to each other with an ivory sateen ribbon. Tradition dictated the groom stamped on his new wife's foot to show him as the dominant partner and the one to be obeyed in the marriage. The church had erupted in cheers as his foot came down instead onto the carpeted church floor with a loud thud.

'It doesn't mean anything,' he said.

'It does! It means you can't rule me, Mr Greek!'

'But I have all those *koumbari* on my side!'

'We'll see,' she said, pleased he hadn't quite managed it.

A line of women, *koumeres*, lined up on the bride's left and a line of men, *koumbari*, lined up on the right side of the groom. There had been over one hundred *koumbari* and equally as many *koumeres* who had come up before them at the front of the church.

A beautiful ribbon of matching ivory to her dress had been tied to each *stefano*, wedding crown, and placed on the bride and groom's heads. At a certain point in the ceremony, each person lining up wrote out a wedding message on the ribbon.

They then, in turn, a man and a woman at each time, took part in the traditional ring-swapping. This represented a life-long commitment on the part of each guest who took part to honour the new couple for the rest of their married lives. This tradition of the Greek Orthodox marriage ceremony created a special bond between the couple and their *koumbari*, male and female, for life. This element of the ceremony had taken over an hour to complete.

The dance floor began to clear as guests made their way back to their tables or stood chatting to each other at the periphery of the dance area. Within a few seconds the lead singer made an announcement.

'Ladies and Gentlemen, I now invite the Groom and his beautiful Bride to the dance floor for the wedding dance, Nicolas and Georgia!' The room filled with whistles and clapping, an assault of joy and merry-making.

Georgia stayed in the middle of the now empty dance floor and Nicolas walked over to her. She stood with grace, shoulders pushed back, standing tall, breathing in to tighten her tummy. She re-gathered the soft netting of her veil careful not to pull too hard or dislodge it from the pins holding it in her hair; laid over her arm, the folds cascaded down towards the floor over her skirt, a waterfall of soft layers.

The sound of the violin playing the first notes of the traditional wedding dance gave her goose bumps. Nicolas took a folded handkerchief out of his jacket pocket and shook it, waving it open towards Georgia. She took one corner and as the notes struck up they took the first steps of the dance together as Nicolas pinched onto the opposite corner. Georgia smiled as she looked at him but he didn't reciprocate. He looked down at his feet concentrating on the steps to the dance. She knew how nervous he had been. She, on the other hand, her confidence oozed, a natural dancer she relished the moment as she turned and swayed enjoying the attention of everyone now gathered around the edge of the parquet dance floor.

After a few moments Nicolas and Georgia's dancing was interrupted as both their parents came to drape garlands and swags of fifty pound notes across their torsos, securing them with pretty pearl-headed pins. Wedding gifts were not part of the Greek Cypriot wedding tradition but rather the gift of money to the Bride and Groom to start their married life together.

'Congratulations Georgia. Be happy and healthy always,' said her mother as she leaned in to kiss Georgia on both cheeks.

'Thank you Mum. Love you,' said Georgia.

The same wishes were repeated by her father and new in-laws. She looked over and beamed at Nicolas being smothered in kisses by his mother. Georgia's grandparents were next to come up to them and then all the guests, in turn, pinned their gifts of money taking pins from the little silk pin-cushion held by Theresa and Katia at each side of the dance floor.

By the end of the dance, Nicolas and Georgia were camouflaged with ten, twenty and fifty pound notes. As the guests moved off the floor they made a circle around the couple and clapped, cheered and whistled as Nicolas and Georgia resumed the dance, weighted down with garlands of notes, being careful not to get pricked by the ends of the pins sticking out.

Georgia danced, enjoying the attention. As the music slowed, she whooped with joy as Nicolas scooped her up in his arms and twirled her around and around as the music came to an end.

'I will always love you,' he whispered in her ear as he brought her back down to her feet.

'And I will always love you.'

As the happiest day of her life continued to unfold, she remembered to give thanks to God who had given her a loving family and a wonderful culture from which she gained so much. She vowed to continue following her family's traditions, to honour and love her husband and to uphold her wedding vows, as she entered this next phase of her young adult life.

Little did she know, as she smiled and laughed her way through the rest of her wedding day, it would prove far more difficult than she could ever have imagined.

Chapter One

AS GEORGIA DROVE home she didn't let the congestion wind her up and after sitting at a standstill through Whetstone and North Finchley, she weaved in and out of the traffic, singing You're beautiful with the front windows down. She swung by to pick the boys up from her mother-in-law's just off Nether Street and by the time she arrived home she felt exhausted yet energised at the same time, her dark curling hair tangled around her face.

Georgia recalled all the facts relayed to her during the interview; her first interview in eight years since giving up work to bring up the children.

The procedure, a formal one, involved the Head Teacher, two deputy Heads and the Director of Music. Queen Elizabeth's Boys' School, founded in 1571, moved to its current location in 1930. The school had a wide curriculum including Latin, Psychology, Politics, Ethics and Music. It had recently become a specialist Music College and needed a part-time secretary.

'The Music Department operates from a new purpose built building within the grounds of the school,' said the Head Teacher.

'But it's not visible from the main driveway onto the site. It's single storey, made of Old English Brindles,' interjected the Director of Music, Mr Liam Hemworth.

She remembered thinking how pompous he sounded using the exact name of the bricks but at the same time found his seriousness rather endearing.

After another half hour or so of questions, 'what if' scenarios and re-calling her strengths and weaknesses, Liam, as he told her to call him, showed her around the school site and the Music Block.

'The colours are always changing,' he said, pointing out the crowds of azaleas, hostas, hydrangeas and old fashioned roses with stripes and splashes of colour in their petals, 'a sea of technicolour.' Georgia followed the line of the deep border with her eyes, taking in the softest ivory whites to the brightest tangerine oranges and robust ruby reds.

'Beautiful flowers. And colours,' she said, recognising some of the names Liam mentioned but cringing inside all the same at her dull response.

The Music Block, in contrast to the main building, was a modern office block, with three large classrooms and eight peripatetic teaching rooms, each the size of a very large broom cupboard. She looked up the word peripatetic when she got home and was glad she'd worked out its correct meaning. The spacious office, had tall floor to ceiling windows on two sides, overlooking the grounds on one side and the smaller, over-flow staff car park on the other.

'So, it would be great if you could start on Monday week as we break up for May half term on Friday,' he announced, after a brief discussion on hours of work and main duties and responsibilities again.

'Oh, wow. Thank you so much. Yes, that would be perfect.'

'HR will email you confirmation. Shall we say 9.15 the first morning?' said Liam.

'9.30 will mean I can still drop off the boys to school. As I mentioned during the panel interview I have three boys at primary school. Would that be okay?'

'Oh, yes, of course. I don't see why not. A nine thirty start it is,' said Liam.

'Thank you. It was lovely to meet you. I will see you then and have a lovely half term break,' and putting her hand into his outstretched one she shook it, smiling.

***

'I got the job!' Georgia sang down the telephone.

'No way. You're joking, right?' said Nicolas and then as an afterthought, 'Congratulations!'

'They loved me. The Director of Music showed me around the school, it's magical. I said I needed a day or so to sort out the logistics of taking the boys to school and stuff but he agreed I can start after half term. Gives me a week to get things organised. I. Got. The. Job,' Georgia sang down the phone.

'Well, that's great! As long as you think you can keep up with it all. The cooking, cleaning, ironing, the boys, the Costco run for me...'

She remembered switching off at that point and thinking what a selfish demanding git he could be. Of course she could do it all – she was super woman! A secretary for the Music Department at Queen Elizabeth's Boys' School. Whoop!

After dinner and with the boys tucked up in bed, Nicolas broached the subject of her new employment again. 'What time will you start each morning?' he asked.

'Half nine,' Georgia answered, still not having sat down, having tidied the kitchen after dinner, bathed the boys and made Nicolas a mug of tea.

'I hope you're not going to be rushing off and leaving the boys on their own waiting for the school gates to open,' said Nicolas.

'Of course not, that's why I've mentioned and agreed the 9.30 start as opposed to the 9.15 one. I won't have to rush. There'll be plenty of time and I can still do the Costco run for you every Monday. And pick the boys up too. No-one will be inconvenienced if that's what you're getting at.'

'Well, I don't want you putting a part-time job first. The boys have to come first.'

'Of course darling, I know.'

'Well done again darling. That's brilliant news. I'm proud of you.'

'Thank you,' Georgia said, recognising his congratulations as insincere. But even his half-hearted words of praise could not diminish her mood of success and accomplishment based on her own merit, away from home. After eight years of bringing up the children she felt something within her say 2003 was going to be her year.

The few weeks since taking on her new job had flown by and the summer holidays were fast approaching despite the dreary weather. Georgia sat in her best friend's kitchen, one Saturday morning, enjoying a long overdue catch-up.

Thalia and Georgia had been friends since meeting at the baby clinic in Finchley. Andoni had been a few months old and Thalia's daughter, Sofia, only a few weeks. They had chatted and finding they had lots in common, both Greek Cypriot stay-at-home mums, living locally, they agreed to keep in touch. Thalia always looked ready to go out, dressed up, even when lounging at home. She had the figure of an athlete even though she didn't work out and the blackest shiniest hair which looked great down or up in a tight pony tail, left naturally curly or straightened. Her long dark lashes framed her smallish eyes and she had a small mouth with thin lips. She was unfailingly immaculate from her hair to her nails and from her clothes to her shoes. Thalia had that overall wow factor.

Georgia stared out beyond the kitchen window; the sky a muted, lead grey, the sun daring to take a peek from behind the low blanket of cloudy blurs and swirls. The clouds had been suspended there since day break, since getting up.

Hardly summer weather at all, Georgia thought. She pulled her chunky cable-knit Hollister cardigan closer around her feeling frumpy, a shiver ran through her. The back door had been left wide open after Thalia's lazy tabby cat had exited the warmth of the kitchen to wander round the garden at Thalia's insistence; a slice of cold air intruded on the cosy atmosphere. Georgia leaned over pushing the door to with a shove of her hand, but it didn't quite catch and remained ajar.

'How's work going then, hun?' asked Thalia looking down at her manicured nails.

'Good thanks honey.'

'You still enjoying it?'

'I am…still learning a lot but I've learnt a lot too, babe. I'm happy there. The school's a wonderful place. The grounds are just so National Park like.'

'Ah, how lovely to work in surroundings like that,' said Thalia.

'The other day the Head Gardener caught me walking up to the main building, which resembles a full-size model of Hogwarts in the middle of a Harry Potter film set by the way…just in case I haven't mentioned that before.'

'Yes, you have hun, like a hundred times,' Thalia said as she rolled her light brown eyes in an exaggerated manner before breaking into a smile.

'Ha ha! Anyway he nattered on, bless him, about his beautifully maintained deep herbaceous beds, blah, blah, blah and flowering shrubbery and rhododendron clumps that needed dead-heading, blah, blah, blah and how the reddish-bronze foliage was coming through, blah, blah, blah. I thought I was never going to get away when luckily another of the gardeners came over and I wandered off leaving them engrossed in their horticultural chit-chat,' said Georgia.

'How funny, but at least you're enjoying yourself, hun.'

'I am babe,' Georgia said, 'and it gives me a bit more freedom. Financial independence. Keeps me sane even though I hadn't realised, having not worked for so long how much I needed something. It's woken up my brain.'

'Well, you've been home a long time,' said Thalia.

'Yeah it has. Since having Andoni. And I had to put up with sarcastic comments from my mother-in-law about how good Greek mums stayed at home and cared for their children. And Nicolas, of course, agreed with her.'

'Oh, yeah I got that too from my *bethera*. But I was a lot younger than you. I was twenty-one when I had Sofia and twenty-three when I popped out Andreas.'

'Well, being at home hasn't been all bad has it? To be honest I've enjoyed it but the time was right for me to go back. The boys are getting older now. Can't believe they're already eight, five and nearly four.'

'I know what you mean hun, time doesn't stop still. I miss working but you know there's no way Tony would ever let me go back to hairdressing,' Thalia said, stretching her long slim leg out towards the door and pushing it shut with her foot.

'He's got used to you being at home.'

'And he likes to know where I am. He calls whenever he wants. It assures him to know I'm home.'

'And how d'you feel?'

'I'm used to it, I s'pose. I don't think about it much…too busy with the kids.'

'Well, to be honest, babe, Nico wasn't too pleased when I first told him but hey, I got the job. It was out of his hands once I'd accepted. And, he's enjoying the extra money coming in. It takes the burden off him a bit.'

'That's good.'

'And the job gives me a new focus and drive. It's re-ignited my ambitious side which I've had tucked away since giving up my career and I don't regret any of the time I've spent with the boys, but it was time to find some time for me, babe. A new purpose.'

'Do you think you'll stay there long, then?' asked Thalia.

'Who knows? The work opportunities are endless. It's great for now, fits in well with life. But I'd like to think my degree and all the studying haven't gone to waste. After all, if it wasn't for my mum persuading my dad to let me go to university in the first place, I probably would've ended up in a dead end job somewhere. Dad thought me going to university would be a waste of money. Well you know the story.'

'Yeah I remember you telling me when we first met,' said Thalia.

'You know, being a good Greek Cypriot girl he planned for me to get married, have children and look after my husband. End of.'

'Your dad doesn't seem like that though,' said Thalia.

'He's not now. He's proud of me although he's never said it to me. But he always smiles when Mum calls me her clever girl.'

'I bet he does. At least you got your chance. Look where hairdressing got me…straight to work in my parent's hair salon. The rest is history.'

'You're still young though, babe. You can still do something else if you want to,' said Georgia.

'Maybe, one day.'

'Of course you can.'

'You're lucky. You can escape the house, even for a few hours,' said Thalia.

'You a bit fed up, babe?' asked Georgia.

'No hun. I'm fine. It's this damn headache. I can't shift it. It's been squeezing the sides of my head all day,' said Thalia.

'Liam had a bad head yesterday too, must be the change in the weather.'

'And how's the gorgeous Liam? Have you got any pics?' said Thalia, rubbing her temples with her two forefingers in little circular motions as she squinted from the pain.

'No, of course I haven't. He's great though. I showed him my marketing ideas for developing the Music Department and, you know, increasing its profile across the borough. He loved it.'

'Of course he loved it. He loves you.'

'Don't go there, babe. He's just a nice guy. He's my boss. He has to be nice,' said Georgia.

'You are so naïve sometimes Georgi.'

'No I'm not. Why?'

'Because it sounds to me like he wants to be around you all the time.'

'It's not like that at all. All the staff are in and out all the time. It's a busy office. Stop it. You're going to make me self-conscious,' said Georgia, her cheeks flushing with embarrassment, but deep down she wondered whether Thalia could be right about him. But Thalia was right about one thing. She felt attractive working there and the job had certainly boosted her confidence. She thought about Liam…she did go a little bit giddy around him. He was a robust, well-spoken ex-army man, in his early thirties, she guessed, who also headed up the Territorial Army trips for the school.

'We'll see,' said Thalia.

'Stop it. You crazy girl.' Georgia's words caught in

a sigh as she twisted a curl around her finger.

The ringing phone interrupted their conversation. Georgia could hear Thalia speaking from the hallway, where she'd picked it up.

'Yes. No. It's Georgia and the boys. No. Yes she's staying here, till after lunch…yeah, I'll ask her, okay. See you later then. No, I won't. Okay. Bye.' She walked back into the kitchen. 'Tony. Wondering what I'm up to and who I'm with,' Thalia said. She took a swig of tea from the paisley-patterned mug. Her face told Georgia the tea had cooled too much while Thalia had been on the phone. Or was she annoyed with Tony for checking up on her?

'Thought it was. Is everything alright?'

'Yeah. Just seeing what I'm up to,' Thalia repeated.

'What are you going to ask me? Not that I was eavesdropping or anything,' said Georgia.

'Oh, Tony said come over for lunch one day. We haven't all got together for ages. Why don't you? It'll be nice for the kids to chill together while we all catch up.'

'I'll check with Nico and get back to you, babe. Thank you. That'd be nice actually.'

'Yeah, nice to have some company other than his family every weekend,' said Thalia.

'I know exactly what you mean, hun. Nico's the same although now I'm working the visits have become less frequent, which is a relief if I'm honest. It's tiring entertaining, especially when you have to put in all that effort for little appreciation, like it's expected.'

'Especially when your husband does nothing to help as well,' said Thalia.

'Well, Nico likes cooking so he does his bit in the kitchen but he's so particular about how things are done that sometimes I think it would be better if I was left to my own devices. He's always criticising this or that and just stresses me out so much I don't enjoy his family coming round anymore.'

'Don't knock it hun, at least he helps you. Tony won't even make a salad.'

'Well, I can bring a dessert over. Save you from having to do that too,' said Georgia.

'No. It's fine. I do it for his family and so having you over, in comparison, will be my pleasure.'

***

'Thank you, Thalia *mou*, for lunch. I'm glad we finally arranged it. It was delicious and those *melinzanes*...how d'you cook them? I always use aubergines in moussaka but I liked the way you did them.'

'So easy, hun, slice them, drizzle with olive oil, salt, pepper and a sprinkle of *rigani* and *koliandro* and in the oven they go.'

'I thought I could taste oregano and coriander. I'm going to make them next time your mum and dad come over,' said Georgia, looking at Nicolas and then back at Thalia who lowered her head hiding a little smirk.

'Yeah, good idea. Dad loves coriander especially on his pork kebabs.'

'Well, that's your domain, Nico, the kebabs. And we're a long way off from summer and barbeques.' Nicolas nodded. 'I'll help you clear up,' said Georgia, as Thalia scraped leftovers off the plates and stacked them one on top of the other.

'Stay where you are,' said Tony to Georgia, 'she's capable, aren't you my darling?' and he smacked her on the bottom as he continued sipping his wine. Georgia noticed he made no effort to get up and help Thalia himself.

'Tony, not in front of our guests,' said Thalia whose smile came out as a grimace Georgia noticed.

'They're our friends. They don't mind,' laughed Tony, squeezing one of her bum cheeks this time.

'Well, I do,' said Thalia, as she walked towards the kitchen holding the pile of plates, on top of which she balanced two empty bowls and held two empty glasses in her other hand.

'You okay?' asked Georgia, following her into the kitchen with the salad bowl and a few scrunched up napkins.

'Yeah of course, he's just so touchy-feely sometimes. It's embarrassing in front of people.' Thalia took the bowl holding shreds of limp and soggy lettuce, floating in olive oil and vinegar.

'Well, don't be embarrassed in front of me and Nico.

We know what he's like after he's had a drink or two.'

'Yeah, I know. Sorry, Georgi. Let's put the kettle on and call the kids down for dessert in a bit. I've bought a Waitrose American-style cheesecake with strawberries on top and my mum made *paklava* for us.'

'Ooh, how yummy. Can I have a bit of both?' Georgia asked laughing. She eyed the crisp folds of filo pastry layered with chopped pistachios and drenched in golden syrup. The smell of the cinnamon filled the air.

'We still talking about dessert?' teased Thalia, giggling.

'Stop it, babe. Of course I'm talking about dessert. What else could I possibly be referring to?'

'What are you two laughing at?' called Tony, from the sitting room.

'Nothing,' they both chorused and then fell about laughing again.

'Well, it doesn't sound like nothing,' he said from the kitchen door where he now stood.

'Where did you sneak from?' asked Georgia, holding her hand, palm side down on her chest, as her heart thumped from the shock.

'Well? What are you both laughing at? Share the joke.'

'Just something Georgi said, that's all,' said Thalia. She turned to the sink and filled it with hot water to soak her oven dishes and pans.

'Yeah, me and my work tales again, Tony,' said

Georgia, looking straight at him, with her biggest smile ever.

'Are you making coffee?' he asked. Georgia noticed his smile didn't reach his eyes. She took in his tall well-built frame and dark thick hair. He was a handsome man but not quite as relaxed as he portrayed.

'Yeah, kettle's on. Ask Nico if he wants one,' said Thalia as she ran her fingers through her long black hair.

'No thanks,' called Nicolas from the sitting room.

'He's getting comfortable for the match, Arsenal v Man City,' said Tony.

'Okay,' said Thalia.

***

Georgia could hear the men, both having settled on the couch in the sitting room, discussing Arsenal's latest conquest.

'The Champions League…game against Dynamo Kiev. I tell you that Henry, he's a legend. Amazing goal. Pure legend,' said Tony.

'Fantastic, well-deserved win, we definitely deserved it,' said Nicolas.

'Come on you two. We don't want to be listening to Arsenal and football for the rest of the afternoon, thank you,' said Georgia.

'Well, we're watching the match, the kids are watching too. You two will have to entertain yourselves for a bit. You don't mind do you, Georgia?' said Tony.

'Well, it's a bit anti-social but if the kids are watching as well, I'll let you off.'

'Arsenal is the greatest!' Andoni chanted as the match kicked off.

'Come on you Gunners!' shouted Zach.

'Man City are losers!' joined in Andreas.

'You can still come in and sit down girls,' Tony said, raising his voice in an effort to be heard.

'No don't worry. I'd rather sit and have a girly chat. You go ahead.'

'Me too,' said Thalia and they both wandered back into the dining room, Georgia with a very generous slab of strawberry cheesecake swimming in half a pot of fresh cream. Thalia carried through their mugs of peppermint tea.

'It's been so nice today. Thanks hun,' said Georgia.

'You're welcome. Sorry about Tony.'

'Is everything alright between you two?' asked Georgia.

'Yeah, same old, same old.'

'Maybe you should shake it up a bit babe. Same old, same old doesn't sound too good after being married for just over ten years.'

'Well, I know some things won't change hun, so I'm not even going to try to change them. But you, well...I know something good is coming your way!'

'You can look into my future can you?'

'No. Call it intuition. You're going to shine like a star.'

'Shining so bright like the star that you are,' sang Georgia, chorusing the words to one of her favourite Simply Red songs.

***

After the match finished and after another round of tea and coffee, Georgia gathered the boys together. She wrapped them up against the crisp September wind and drizzle, doing up their zips and buttons and pulling their hoods over their heads. Hurrying, they said their goodbyes and ran out to the car. Georgia held her jacket over her head, to keep the rain from frizzing her curls.

Nicolas shut the door behind the boys as they jumped into the back seat and Georgia strapped Kristiano into his booster seat before strapping herself in behind the wheel. Nicolas and Tony had almost finished two bottles of wine between them and so she drove home.

The windscreen wipers fought against the thrashing rain as they glided back and forth on double speed. Georgia stuck to the main road, driving at a slow, safe speed. The roads were already flooded and streaming with the downpour and she felt as though she drove through the ragged edges of the dark clouds. Distant thunder rumbled on and off and she jumped as a roll of thunder cracked overhead.

Georgia and Nicolas had a cordial conversation all the way home as the boys dozed in the back despite the grumble of the storm. Later than they had planned to leave, she knew she would struggle to get the boys up in the morning.

'Tony was cheerful today. The 'host with the most', said Nicolas, laughing at his little joke, 'I enjoyed his company.'

'Yeah, it was a lovely day,' said Georgia, 'but his behaviour embarrasses Thal' so he should back off, don't you think?'

'Slapping her bum? Yeah, I s'pose, but she loves it deep down. She loves all the attention she gets from him. She laps it up. Even last time we went out to that Italian place in Barnet…Prezzo he had his arm around her, and when the waiter made a comment about being in love, she enjoyed being in the limelight,' said Nicolas.

'Actually, it wasn't such a good night. You know when they both got up to use the toilet, which I thought was a bit odd, he had a go at her for flirting with the waiter.'

'No way, Tony did?'

'Yeah. Didn't you notice her eyes were teary when she came back to the table?'

'I thought she was just tired. She's always got red eyes.'

'No, she hasn't. He's just a control freak. I mean how can she have been flirting with the waiter, sitting with her husband, for God's sake?'

Well, I s'pose he just wants her to be a good and faithful wife.'

'She is. She doesn't go anywhere apart from take the kids to school and pick them up and meet up with me now and again. She has no friends. The only people she mixes with are either his family or hers.'

'Well, she doesn't want for anything. Tony earns a fortune. Wish I earned even a quarter of what he earns. D'you know he came home with near enough four and a half thousand pounds last week, in cash.'

'Money isn't everything, Nico. I don't think she's happy.'

'Has she said anything?'

'No, but I can sense it. Has Tony said anything to you?'

'Not a word. He always goes on about how good things are between them.'

'Somehow I don't believe him.'

'We'd know if there was something serious.'

'Would we?' she said, 'sometimes you can't see what's staring you in the face. Life throws curve balls when you least expect them.'

'You watch too much Eastenders.'

'Mark my words. Tony's hiding something. Thalia will tell me when she's ready.'

Chapter Two

ANOTHER TERM WENT by and a grimmer, colder January welcomed the New Year in. Georgia thrived in her role as Music Secretary and 'Marketing Guru' as Liam referred to her but she began to miss the demands of a more taxing job, a more responsible role, and reminisced about her days as a Hotel Sales and Marketing Manager. She remembered the buzz of securing a new corporate deal, the excited dizziness when she walked in and showed her boss the signature along the dotted line of a new contract and she began to wonder if she could do more than typing and pushing paper work around.

She began to hold the fort for Liam if he had to leave his lesson for something. Other times, if he arrived late for the beginning of a lesson after break, she would ask the pupils to line up against the wall outside the main doors into the building and file them in regiment-style into the classroom after they were silent.

'Thanks for doing that,' said Liam. 'The boys like you and respect you.'

'Well, they are pretty well-behaved aren't they to be honest?'

'Not always. You've got an authoritative presence and a firm hand. Some staff can't do what you've just done after teaching the same class for a year or more.'

'Well, thanks.'

'You're welcome Mrs Josephides.' Mrs Josephides…that sounded just like a real teacher's name she thought as she walked back down the corridor to her desk. She liked the way Liam said her name too; professional, but with warmth.

***

Winter gave way to spring and Easter arrived; a time when Georgia's family, like many Greek families, celebrated new beginnings and the start of new life. It was a huge event on the Greek Orthodox Calendar. Georgia made the effort to go to church with the children and persuaded Nicolas to come with them even though he didn't enjoy the prospect.

The children moaned and bickered, having to stand at the back of the overcrowded church, the stifled air heavy with the scent of burning candle wax and incense, the closeness of everybody increasing the temperature in the otherwise usually cool interior of the church. But Georgia hadn't wanted to let her parents down who were active church members; she knew how they would have disapproved if she wasn't there with the children.

The children bored after half an hour or so and Georgia heard their sighs of relief as they spilled out into the street for the Easter procession. The air cooled Georgia's flushed face as she walked out into the darkness of the late evening. She pulled her coat around her and wished she had worn more comfortable shoes. Her high heels were already causing her some discomfort and she winced as her ankle buckled over running to keep up with the boys.

'There's *yiayia* and *bapou*!' called out Andoni spotting his grandmother and grandfather, a few paces ahead. He pushed through the crowd to catch up with them. Georgia held onto Zachari and Kristiano as they walked along the now darkened street, flooded with intermittent pools of light from the street lamps.

'*Agabi mou*!' Georgia's mum scooped Andoni up as Georgia gave her a wave.

Nicolas walked beside Georgia and they followed the priest and the congregants who volunteered to carry the holy table on which the *epitaphio* was draped. The wooden ornate structure decorated with hundreds of cream, rose and pink flowers ambled ahead of the crowds which swarmed the pavement and road. The police on duty stopped the road traffic and ensured everyone walked within the cordoned areas.

The six men struggled under the weight of the decorated structure and at one point stopped as two men adjusted the weight of it on their shoulders. The low hum of the priest's voice echoed through the night air as he chanted prayers and blessings throughout the procession and anointed the street ahead with perfumed oil. The procession up the street and back lasted no longer than thirty-five minutes.

Nicolas held a sleepy floppy Kristiano over his shoulder and Georgia ushered Andoni and Zachari to the car. They waved good bye and blew kisses to friends and family from a distance and drove home after promising to catch up at Georgia's parents' Easter BBQ the following day. Georgia's parents hosted a BBQ banquet for the whole family each year and Georgia and she was already looking forward to it.

***

On Easter Sunday Georgia's parents' house burst with its usual hub of activity and joviality. As Georgia and Nicolas pulled up and parked along the side of her parents' corner property Georgia could already smell the sizzling lamb in the air. The boys banged on the side gate until their *bapou* unlocked it. It groaned as he opened it wide letting them spill in one after the other and kissing Georgia on both cheeks as she filed in behind the boys and Nicolas.

'Smells delicious, Dad. *Xristos Anesti*,' she said giving him a tight hug too.

'Jesus has risen,' he repeated back to her.

Georgia followed her dad down the path to the garden as she struggled with the two carrier bags; Easter Eggs for her nieces and nephews, a bunch of flowers for her mum. She smiled as whoops of joy from the boys filled the air when her sisters handed them a huge Easter egg each and then laughed when the other children echoed the same excitement and joy as she passed them her Easter treats. The children, like ants, ran around the garden in the sunshine, holding onto their chocolate treasures. Georgia's sister Teresa had three children and her sister Katia had two.

'Thank you, Teresa and *Xristos Anesti*.' Christ has risen, she said to her sister who was eighteen months younger.

'*Xristos Anesti*,' repeated Katia and Louis, her other sister and brother. One after the other Georgia kissed them on both cheeks. Eventually she made it to the kitchen where her mum was arranging platters of food and bowls of salad across the vast worktop under the open window, the net curtains fluttered in the cool breeze. Greek music burst out of the CD player on the window sill and her mum swayed to the rhythm of the beat.

Georgia handed her mum the bouquet and danced a couple of steps with her as the music continued.

'Ah, thank you my darling,' said her mum as she took the arrangement of pink gerberas, soft marmalade roses and parchment lilies interspersed with gypsophila and bright green foliage. 'They're beautiful just like you.'

Georgia laughed and gave her a big hug. Her sisters came in soon after and they added the final touches to the two tables; one outside and one in the kitchen diner. Between them they placed salt and pepper shakers on each table, a small bowl of lemons cut in half and a platter of traditional vegetable meze including radishes, fresh spring onions, pickled capers and fresh beetroot drizzled with olive oil, lemon juice and chopped garlic. Pride of place was a rattan basket filled with red-stained boiled eggs and a second flat basket piled high with *flaounes*; traditional baked Easter breads coated with sesame seeds and filled with a cheese, eggs, raisins and fresh mint mixture. Georgia breathed in the pungent smell of the cheese and mint as she tucked in the chairs and remembered baking the breads with her own *yiayia* when she was a girl.

Georgia chatted to one of her aunts as she continued to help her mum. She whizzed around the kitchen scooping out roast potatoes onto an oval platter and added olive oil and vinegar to the Greek salad her mum had already prepared. She gave it a quick toss with two matching serving spoons before placing the wooden bowl amongst the other dishes already crowding the buffet area.

'The meat is ready!' Georgia heard her dad's announcement from the garden and within seconds Louis walked in with a thermal bowl filled with chunky pieces of sizzling pork straight off the skewers. Her uncle followed in with another almost identical bowl filled with chicken pieces, golden and crispy. Cooked to perfection, thought Georgia.

Georgia and Teresa filled the children's plates first and once they were settled on the picnic blanket laid out on the day-old trimmed lawn, the adults began to fill their plates. The array of food, as always, was delicious and Georgia piled her plate up with a helping of each dish before plopping two scoops of houmous onto the edge of her plate before sitting in the garden.

She glanced over in the direction of the children who were always looked after first. It was a family tradition and food was a huge part of their culture. Heaven help anyone who visited Georgia's parents and didn't accept a plate of food! Not eating wasn't an option, ever! They were sitting cross-legged, eating and talking. Andoni sat on the rusty iron bench a little further away and Georgia watched him as he told Zachari off for talking with his mouth full and then clipped Kristiano across the back of the head for spilling his juice on the blanket. Georgia waited for him to retaliate but he didn't even though there were shrieks of laughter from the cousins. Kristiano carried on eating a chicken leg which he held with both hands unperturbed by the raucous laughter around him.

'Shove over Georgi,' said Nicolas as he sat next to Georgia. Teresa and Katia joined them within a few seconds too and so the jovial banter between them began. The sun beat down on the top of Georgia's head and she shifted her seat so she wasn't sitting in the direct line of the sun. She pulled her sunglasses off the top of her head, untangling her loose curls caught up in them and shaded her eyes.

'You okay?' asked Teresa. She looked over at

Georgia with her big almond-shaped eyes and tilted her head, the weight of her loose bun flopping it to one side as she did so.

'I'm getting a headache. It's this sun. Not used to it.'

'You're always headachy,' said Nicolas.

'You're tired,' said Katia. She ignored his comment and turning to Georgia she leaned across and patted her arm.

'Aren't we all?' said Nicolas.

'Well some more than others I'd dare say.' Georgia knew Katia was sticking up for her and saw the look of disgust cross her face as she took in Nicolas' insouciant comment. Georgia knew all too well Katia thought Nicolas was a demanding husband and nothing ever seemed to meet with his satisfaction but Georgia loved him and accepted his ways, much to the subdued annoyance of her mum and her sisters in particular. But he was well-liked having been part of the family since she was eighteen and in his own way he loved her and the boys and did his best for them. They were happy and fortunate too. They enjoyed annual holidays together and had nothing to complain about. So as far as she was concerned they had a good strong relationship.

His parents got on well with her parents too and this was an important part of their culture where families merged and became one, all the different family members welcomed each other into their homes and their lives. Greek families just got bigger and bigger as opposed to some families which broke up and saw less of each other as different members got married and had families of their own. Getting married was no excuse for not spending time with your family and Georgia continued to spend time with her aunts and uncles and her immediate family just as much as she ever did. She remembered someone at university commenting on her big family and saying how it was like being at a party all the time.

Georgia let out a quiet sigh. She put down her knife and fork and dipped into the blob of now congealed houmous on the edge of her plate. She tore off a piece of pitta from the whole one sitting in the basket on the table and dabbed at the dip not concentrating.

The teak garden table filled with more family members as they pulled up additional chairs and plastic stools. They squeezed in, elbows tucked close to their bodies so as not to poke each other as they used their knives and forks. The noise of animated conversation filled Georgia's ears. She filled with gladness. She knew to others it looked like she was non-stop running around the children, keeping the house tidy, cooking, cleaning and it was probable she was, to be honest. Her part-time job demanded more of her time and energy than she had anticipated too but Georgia enjoyed her time away from the house and despite Nicolas hinting at her to give it up if it was too much, she never once gave him reason to think she wasn't coping.

She looked down towards the bottom end of the

garden and watched Zachari and Kristiano as they kicked a ball back and forth to each other trying to avoid hitting Katia's younger two children who were waving bubble wands in the air. The little ones weaved in and out of the makeshift goals the boys had marked out with rocks from the garden's deep flowering borders and squealed with laughter as they caught up with each other.

Georgia loved the sunny Easter Sunday surrounded by her family and it was on this day on 11th April 2004 in the middle of the celebrations she wondered about her future and whether a second career as a secondary school teacher might be worth looking into.

She didn't mention it to anyone, not Nicolas and not her sisters. She didn't know anything about the training involved or the qualifications she needed. But she sat there, the pain in her head finally abating. She sat listening to the conversations around her with a big smile on her face. The decision to become a teacher would be one of the best Georgia ever made but she just didn't know it yet.

Chapter Three

AT THALIA'S, GEORGIA and Thalia sat at the kitchen table. Georgia played with what was left of her tuna salad, moving it around her plate. The clink of her fork on the china interrupted the silence. Thalia looked thoughtful as she sipped her iced tea to avoid the melting ice cubes floating around the edge of the tall tea glass.

Georgia had this awful hunch something wasn't right and didn't say anything to anyone, holding all her sentiments close for weeks. Then she just blurted it out. She was a typical Scorpio; all secretive one minute then hitting the closest person with it the next.

'Something's not right. Nico said something last week about people gossiping, that I shouldn't listen.' She slurped her tea. She felt her forehead scrunch up with worry.

'Gossiping? About what?' asked Thalia.

'I don't know. I questioned him but he didn't say anything else.'

'What d'you think it is?'

'I think there's something. He's moody, withdrawn. He's not interested in talking anymore. Maybe it's money or his health. I just don't know.' Georgia paused to take a breath. 'Maybe he doesn't love me anymore.'

'Are you still sleeping together?' asked Thalia, blushing at her rather gauche interrogation.

'Yeah that's not a problem. It's never been a problem but he's not here. He's somewhere else…'

'Fuck! How long have you been feeling like this? Why haven't you said anything?'

'I just didn't want to admit that things aren't going well. You know what it's like. My parents would be devastated if he was ill or had got himself into debt. In their own way, they love Nico. They know he's solid. You know reliable. He looks after me. Look at me waffling on…' Georgia avoided Thalia's eyes.

'Yeah but if you've been worried. Have you asked him what's wrong? I mean that's an odd thing to say about people gossiping. What does he mean?'

'I don't know. Money? I just don't know,' she said, thinking about the dark shadows in her mind but not wanting to verbalise them, make them real.

'Do you think he could be seeing someone?' Thalia said as if reading Georgia's thoughts.

'I don't think so. Who would he see? He's at the café all day. He works from six in the morning, six days a week. He's got no time to be messing around with anyone.'

'What about after work?'

'He's got football training with Andoni on a Tuesday after school and five-a-side with his mates on Wednesday evenings.'

'That's only two days hun. What about the rest?' asked Thalia.

'He's at Andoni's matches on Sundays.' Georgia was trying to convince herself as much as Thalia. 'I think he's getting depressed. He's hiding something. Oh God, do you think he's not well?'

'I don't know hun. You need to ask him. Keep asking him until he tells you. It's all very well being patient but you need to know.'

Georgia pushed her plate away and picked up her mug of tea. She looked down at her bulging tummy and wondered whether he didn't fancy her anymore. I mean sleeping together didn't mean a thing. It was a basic need. It could just be sex, she thought. Maybe he didn't want to be with her.

After dinner, Nicolas in his armchair, legs and arms stretched out; the Lord of the Manor, Georgia stood in the doorway drying her hands after washing up.

'Stay home tonight so we can talk. Don't go to football. I'm worried about us.'

'I can't let the boys down. We're two players down.'

'Well if it's okay for them not to show up why can't you?'

'No. I'm going. There's nothing to worry about. You're so dramatic!'

'I'll wait up then. Please don't be too late. I've got a busy day at work tomorrow.'

'Yeah, yeah. That little job in the music office. Yeah, hard work.'

'Bog off! I work hard and I pick the boys up from

school and still run the house and cook and clean.'

'Too right an' all. It's your job! They're your kids!'

'And yours. Not that you'd know. All you ever do is football, football, football.'

'Football with Andoni.'

'On a Sunday. Big deal! For God's sake I don't want a row.'

'I'm getting changed.' He stood up. Georgia watched him as he vaulted up the stairs two steps at a time as he always did and slammed the door to their bedroom. She felt annoyed she had risen to his taunting. She should have ignored him. She busied herself in the kitchen, filling the dishwasher and wiping down the table. The boys were such messy eaters. There was houmous down the plastic Cath Kidston table cover, strewn bits of squashed tomatoes and splashes of orange squash where they had overfilled their cups. She sighed. Thank God she had her 'little' job. It kept her sane.

***

She watched her usual mid-week entertainment of Emmerdale and Coronation Street and then, after emptying the dishwasher, sat down again to watch Sex and the City. She loved the box set Thalia had given her for Christmas and couldn't understand why she had not watched the series before now.

She washed her hair, giving herself a deep

conditioning treatment which made her curls silky soft. It was just past half ten and she was tired. She checked her phone. No text from Nicolas. Sitting up in bed for him, she went through her bed-time ritual of toning, cleansing and moisturising her face to remove her make-up, exhausted and with a heavy heart, her mind in turmoil, she turned the bed side light out at 11.20pm. She heard Nicolas come in but could not bring herself to talk to him at such a late hour. Her resolve had retreated into the shallow depths of her half sleep and deep inside, she knew she was being a coward, couldn't face what a conversation with him might reveal.

Her night's sleep was punctuated with heavy dreams and mixed up recollections of her life with Nicolas. She woke in the middle of the night remembering her dreams in broken fragments and she tried to piece them together like the shattered pieces of a smashed vase.

Her dream flashed on and off in her mind as she lay there in the dark, Nicolas snoring next to her, oblivious to her turmoil. Triggered by fragments of her dream she remembered with fondness and a huge bout of love their first meeting at a house party, she was eighteen and he was fifteen. Nicolas had stared at her from across the big square lounge holding her gaze until she had got the giggles and smiled back. She remembered the first time they'd made love and how he'd hugged her tight and how safe she felt around him.

Nicolas stirred and turned towards her, pulling at the

duvet.

'Nico,' she whispered, 'are you awake?'

'No. Go to sleep,' he mumbled back.

'Can we talk?'

Georgia shifted into a more comfortable position with her back to him; Nicolas's rumbling snores blowing on the back of her neck. She squeezed her eyes to hold back the tears but they spilled, filling her ear, running in streams across her face, down her neck.

She woke the next morning, to the sound of birdsong, and with bleary stinging eyes she padded downstairs. Her nostalgic, self-pitying mood plunged her back in time.

She pulled out old photo albums and leafed through them. Ah, Portsmouth. She remembered how they'd waved goodbye to each other at Waterloo Station, as she took the train to commence her four-year degree course. There was a photo of her hanging out of the open carriage window; she had waved at him until he was a tiny speck at the end of the platform. The train turned into a bend in the track and he disappeared from her sight. She looked forward to his visits most weekends, introducing her boyfriend with pride to her uni friends and then after four years of studying she was home again. She opened another album; their engagement party. She recollected how both their families were delighted with the news and excited about the wedding.

'What are you doing up?'

'Couldn't sleep.'

'So you thought a trip down memory lane at half five in the morning would be a good idea?' Nicolas said glancing over at the pile of photo albums.

'Nico…'

'Gotta go…can't afford to be late.'

For the rest of the day fragments of earlier blissful times floated in and out of her consciousness; their plush wedding at The Royal Garden Hotel, their honeymoon in Bangkok and Phuket, tarnished only by Nicolas almost losing his wedding ring in the hotel pool.

That afternoon after work she popped into Thalia's for half an hour. Their conversation turned out to be a little more serious than she had expected. Her friend was a mess and Georgia couldn't understand her mumbling through her tears. Georgia settled her at the kitchen table, and remained level-headed. She filled the kettle and flicked it on, passed Thalia the kitchen roll, hugging her until the tears subsided.

'I don't love Tony anymore. I'm asking him for a divorce.'

'What? Oh my God, Thalia. I don't know what to say. When did you decide that?' asked Georgia, voice cracking.

'Yesterday but it's been coming a long time…tell me it's going to be okay.'

'Of course it will be…'

'He's broken me. I don't have the energy to go on like this. He's demanding, controlling. I mean in all the years you've known me have you ever seen me in a skirt?'

'I don't know…no…no way! He tells you what you can and can't wear?'

'It's stifling, it's suffocating. I want to do things. I want to have fun and laugh at things without him looking at me, analysing my every move, my every thought.'

'Well I didn't see this coming. I'm shocked but not surprised.'

'I'm fed up of the claustrophobia…my daily routine and him.' She looked at Georgia blinking back the tears clinging to her lashes. Then she sobbed as her words came out in a high-pitched squeak like a chalk being scraped across a school board. Georgia looked at her from across the table, reaching out to hold her hand, her eyes already red and sore, her nose snotty, bunged up.

'He's arrogant Georgi. He sees only what he wants to see. He thinks the house, the money, the cars are all enough. That I'm ungrateful.'

'Looks like we're both in trouble.' Georgia saw Thalia deflate. 'Come on babe don't waste your energy crying…you've got to stay strong. This is a big deal.'

'I know. And you need to talk to Nicolas. Sort your mess out too Get the boys into bed and pin him down. Tell him you need to talk to him, that it's serious and you won't take no for an answer. Be insistent.'

Georgia didn't respond and their conversation hung in the air like something forbidden.

***

In the evening after dinner, the boys occupied upstairs, Georgia told Nicolas about Thalia and Tony's break-up.

'No way! I spoke to him earlier. He didn't say a thing.'

'Well she told me she told him yesterday.'

'He didn't say anything after football either.'

'Maybe he's embarrassed. In shock.'

'Shit! She's an ungrateful cow.'

'Nico! How can you say that? No-one knows what goes on between a husband and wife. We see the Victoria and David Beckham side to them; the glamourous lifestyle, the fun personalities, laughing smiling…but obviously it's not real. So you weren't home late because you were talking to him?'

'I said no didn't I?'

***

Georgia's dreams that night again took her to when she and Nicolas had bought their first house, eating Chinese take-away, by candlelight, out of the cartons as they sat cross-legged on the bare floor boards in the front room, sheets hanging at the windows to give them privacy.

She woke before dawn with the image of Andoni's birth like a moving photograph in her mind; Nicolas's face bursting with pride. Her parents' and his parents' joy at the birth of their first grandchild, the families rallying round. She remembered the relief that came from her mother-in-law's acceptance of her as she hugged and kissed Georgia on both cheeks. The births of Zachari and Kristiano. Giving up her career to be a full-time mum, scared but she loved taking on the role more than she had imagined.

Again on a third night she woke but this time her dream, her thoughts were punctuated with dark and twisted scenes she had forgotten or long since buried deep inside her head. Nicolas shouting at her for not cleaning the bathroom to his standards, yelling in her face about the bruise on Zachari's thigh, from rolling off the bed. The stress of summer holidays in Cyprus, Corfu, Zakynthos where the boys were always her responsibility. Nicolas telling her she needed to concentrate on her boys more when Andoni wandered off down the beach on his own. Nicolas called her a *jimismeni* over and over again. She accepted his criticism of being dopey and slow on the outside, but inside she screamed for him to shut up and the pain of his cruel words slashed at her heart like a blade.

Georgia woke heavy-headed, fuzzy and struggled to get out of bed. The boys were grumpy too, picking up on her mood. She struggled through the few hours at work, as she planned a Brass Band Concert. She dealt with timetabling issues arising as a result of extra sessions being requested by peripatetics leading up to music exams.

When the clock struck half past one she felt relieved and she made her way to the local swimming baths. It was the last thing she felt like doing, but she knew it would improve her mood. The monotony of swimming breast stroke and then front crawl, back and forth along the length of the pool, relaxed her mind and energised her spirit. The physical exercise soothed her tight, strained muscles and aching shoulders. She shook off the urge to lose herself in the past as she swam and thought instead of the happiness her job brought her.

She dawdled in the showers and then broke the speed limit all the way to Finchley, conscious of being behind schedule. She managed to find a parking spot close enough to the school to prevent the boys from moaning they had to walk too far and half walking half running she made her way towards the exit doors of the school. Her breath short, she spotted Thalia from across the playground waving at her from the main entrance.

'Well how did it go?' she asked, leaning in and kissing Georgia on both cheeks.

'I did thirty-two lengths in half an hour!' she said, reaching up to her damp hair tied into a ponytail.

'No with Nicolas. What did he say?'

'We didn't talk about us…shocked about you guys though. He got in late and I thought he might've spoken to Tony but he didn't. Tony didn't mention anything about your break -up or the divorce.'

'And nothing about his behaviour. About you being worried about him?'

'He's avoiding me.' Georgia's voice caught as she fought against her threatening tears. 'I think it's me. He's going off me.'

'No way. Please don't get upset. You'll sort this out. Don't cry. I hate it when you cry and you don't want the boys to see you like this.'

'I'm fed up with it all. You know how it is. It's tiring. It's exhausting trying to second-guess what's going on. I've got no idea what time he got in and he was out the door without even a kiss goodbye this morning.'

'Tell you what. I'll squash the boys into my car, take them home to mine. You go to the café and see him there. No interruptions.'

'You sure? I feel so hopeless. I feel like I'm drowning but I'm not sure why. I've been on auto-pilot all bloody day.'

'Yes go.' Thalia leaned in to give Georgia a kiss on each cheek.

***

She drove up to Barnet taking her time, sticking to the main roads all the way despite knowing the back roads would be quicker. She had a sense of foreboding and the knot in her stomach felt all-consuming. The beautiful denim sky of earlier had clouded over and the graphite formed low in the sky like solid lead.

She crawled past the café looking for a parking spot on the High Street and noticed the heavy metal shutters were pulled down – even those across the doorway. She indicated left into the petrol garage and eased into a spot reserved for shoppers at the Tesco Express. Pulling out her mobile, she checked the time. 3.18pm and searched his number – My Hubby – it flashed across the screen as the line rang. No answer. She tried again. No answer. On her third attempt she listened to the automatic message telling her the mobile phone she was calling was switched off.

***

'Hi. I'm home. What's for dinner?' Nicolas called from the hallway.

'*Makaronia tou fournou* and salad. The boys've eaten. Andoni ate all the macaroni and the mincemeat but scraped off all the cheese sauce. The other two loved it, even the grated halloumi over the top. Shall I warm it up for you? How was your day?'

'Yeah good.' He didn't ask how hers had been.

'What happened last night?'

'What d'you mean?'

'You were later than usual.'

'There was no booking for the pitch after us so we had another game.'

'Oh, right. You could've let me know. Nicolas didn't respond. He walked over to the kitchen sink and washed his hands. Georgia took out the plate of food warming in the oven for him. 'And you're home late again today. Were you busy?' she asked conscious of her heart racing.

'Not really, just a last minute rush. Five guys working on the roadworks came in at about half three. They all had the *kleftiko* so it was a bonus, an extra sixty quid or so. They loved the lamb and potatoes.'

'Oh yeah?'

'I told them I would get bacon sarnies ready for them in the morning so they'll be in tomorrow at half six.'

'I tried to call you,' Georgia said.

'Did you? My phone's dead. Stupid thing. Needs a new battery I reckon.'

Georgia looked at him, but said nothing. Why was he lying?

***

A week passed by and Georgia rushed around getting dinner ready before Nicolas got in. She just made it in time for the boys because she had worked an extra hour and didn't want to tell him as she knew how annoyed he would get. As a result, she hadn't had time to prepare the meal she had pre-planned before picking up the boys. Nicolas walked in just as she put the grill on for the salmon.

'Before you say anything I got held up at the boys' school,' she said. 'Mr Jones, was going on about support for the school fete next month and a couple of the other mums got involved in the conversation. They wouldn't stop talking. Then the boys disappeared onto the field and I had to yell at them to come off. Time just went. Sorry but dinner won't be ready for another half hour or so.' She rambled on but couldn't stop herself.

'Half an hour? You really are something! You can't even get dinner ready on time but I bet you can run around after your boss and make him a cup of coffee or get his typing done on time.'

'Look I said I'm sorry. Get cleaned up and it will be ready. Go outside with the boys for a bit. They're doing the puzzle your mum got them for Christmas. It's surprisingly still nice out there for April.'

'I need to go out.'

'Where?

'Just out.'

'How long will you be?'

'As long as it takes!' Nicolas grabbed his leather bomber jacket from the back of the kitchen chair, threw it over his shoulder. He turned his back on her as she followed him out into the hallway. Not wanting him to witness the tears welling in her eyes she returned to the kitchen. Georgia knew he'd yell at her for being too sensitive. But he didn't notice her tears. He didn't even look back or say good bye. The front door slammed and then the porch door closed behind him with a sharp click. She listened to the revving of the car and then the screech as he reversed off the drive, scraping the underside of the front bumper on the drop kerb.

She broke down and cried muffling her sobs with a tea towel so as not to alert the boys who had come in from the garden.

'Where's *baba*?' asked Zach.

'He won't be long, honey. He's had to go back to work for a bit.'

'Why?' asked Andoni.

'He forgot to take out some meat from the freezer. Now go and get cleaned up. Andoni help your brothers. Dinner is nearly ready.'

'I'm sitting next to mum today,' yelled Zach.

'No you're not. It's my turn. Mum tell him...' whined Kristiano.

'Enough arguing, you can sit either side of me. There. Both near me. Now eat!'

The boys piled food onto their plates spilling grains of rice across the table. Andoni used his fingers to pick out the broccoli pieces and baby corn he wanted from the earthenware bowl.

Any other time she would have admonished him but she didn't. She sat there looking from one to the other and she couldn't help thinking their dad didn't want to be a part of this anymore. Something or someone was taking him away from them, from her.

'I wanted that bit,' said Zach.

'Well tough. I got it first and I'm the oldest,' Andoni said pulling one of his mean faces.

'Bully!' shouted Zach trying to stab the broccoli with his fork and getting his hand slapped by his older brother.

'Bully! Bully! Bully! And Big Fat Pig!'

'Boys! Enough. Just eat your dinner. There's enough for us all. Think of the poor children starving in Africa.' The two older boys rolled their eyes and sniggered.

'They don't eat salmon and broccoli in Africa.'

'But they do eat rice. So be thoughtful please and don't behave like piggies,' Georgia said.

'Well it was him. Not me.'

For a brief moment Georgia imagined herself as a single parent. This is what it would be like. On her own. She shook the almost unbearable feeling away, a cold shiver replaced it.

'Enough bickering and complaining. After dinner it's homework and bed. Early! Zach has to be at school by quarter to eight tomorrow morning. You're going on your trip to Cadbury's World aren't you my honey?'

'Tomorrow? Wow! Yippee! I'm going to buy chocolate buttons and not get any for you,' he announced to Andoni, his mouth full of sticky glutney rice.

'I want choc-o-late bu-tt-ons,' squealed Kristiano, his hands all sticky from the orange squash he'd spilt onto the table and which he now patted with his hands with a dull thud.

Georgia sat with her legs tucked under her in the sitting room, looking through a couple of mini photograph albums. She flicked through bright happy photos of them in Cyprus, she could feel the light yellow sand of Limassol warm between her toes. Smiling faces stared back at her. The boys' mouths and chins were sticky with ice cream and their cheeks bright red. Nicolas's face was bright, his smile wide, his soft wavy hair longer back then flopping over his eyes. There was a picture of Nicolas pulling her into a hug. She remembered Andoni taking the photo; her long hair blowing across her face as the breeze came off the sea. Happy days. Life seemed so much less complicated back then.

'You frightened me,' Georgia said.

'Sorry. Didn't mean to make you jump. What are you engrossed in?'

'Holiday snaps. Cyprus two years ago.'

'The boys?'

'Asleep.'

'I'm going up.'

'Where were you all this time?' Nicolas didn't answer.

***

Georgia waved goodbye to Zach, who had pushed his way to the back of the sizeable coach which hogged the small cul-de-sac. She watched it move off, chugging up the steep hill towards Ballards Lane, all the while continuing to wave, her arm high above her head, until it rounded the corner and Zach's smiley face disappeared from view. She turned away from the sun and shaded her eyes with her hand. She had forgotten her sunnies.

She saw Thalia appear from around the corner. Georgia squinted against the direct sunlight, and noted she looked as glamorous as ever in her jet black leggings and wedge-heel converse. They reached out in unison to hug each other. Georgia felt too mumsy in her navy pencil skirt and plain navy T-shirt. I dress like a frumpy middle-aged woman thought Georgia looking down at her leather navy pumps; flat, practical.

'Things not good Georgi? You're not your usual bouncy bright self. You look tired.'

'Depends what you mean by not good. I didn't sleep too well last night. Nico went out and didn't come back 'til gone nine.'

'Where was he?'

'I don't know. I didn't ask. We just ended up having an…early…night.'

'As in an early night?'

'Yeah, as in an early night,' Georgia said.

'And?'

'It was like it always is. It was better than normal.'

'Blimey. You okay with that? Him out and then coming back for some.'

'Well, why should I deprive myself just because he's being weird?'

'Well, I'd want to hold back and teach him a lesson. I'd tell him no blow jobs or dressing up or anything until he was straight with me,' Thalia said.

'Would you? Or would you just let the lust take over?'

'Not anymore!' she laughed, her not so straight front teeth showing. Georgia noticed her friend's eyes were looking tired in the sunshine which highlighted their lacklustre further as well as reminded her she was not alone in having a hard time right now.

'And what's happening with your divorce?'

'I've got to organise a meeting to extend the mortgage on the house. Tony won't leave without his share. Like he hasn't got enough fucking money of his own!'

'I can't believe it Thal. He always seemed so generous. Gosh, how you get to know someone when you're divorcing.'

'Well they say you marry for love and divorce for money,' said Thalia, resignation in her voice.

'How sad. Anyway I need to work out what's going on with mine. I need to be in control. Win him over to open up.'

'And how are you going to do that?

'I'm going to play the perfect wife and see what happens.'

'You are the perfect wife already!'

'I'm going to control him with sex. Mind-blowing, crazy sex. He's always said my brain and sex are what he loves most about me. I've never thought about what that meant before but now's the time to use what I've got to my advantage.'

'You're mad Georgia.'

'And Liam will be mad if I'm late for work. See you later!'

***

Driving along, Georgia thought about how shocked, but not surprised, she had been about Thalia and Tony's separation. It had shaken her to the core knowing how unhappy her friend had been for so long, suffering in silence as Tony had chipped away at her. She vowed she wouldn't get so sad. She would sort things out with Nico. She had to.

***

Over the next few weeks Georgia did everything she could to make her husband happy. She cooked his favourite meals, made sure the house was extra tidy, the shower doors sparkled, the cushions were always plumped up on the armchair he sat in and she gave him the best sex ever. And her actions rubbed off onto him.

He massaged her feet and cleared the rubbish piling up along the side access to the house. She invited his parents and sister over for lunch at the weekend and took his mum to her hospital appointment. She avoided asking him questions. They didn't argue.

Georgia also made a bold decision too. She called her *bethera,* mother-in-law. Sitting in the car outside the boys' school she felt her stomach knot and tangle as she spoke to her.

'I just wondered whether Nico has said anything to you? Is anything worrying him?'

'No. Nothing. Why?'

'I don't know really. I'm just worried. He seems anxious all the time. Not wanting to be at home. Coming home later and later from work.'

'No. He's not said anything. I'll try and talk to him. I'm sure it's nothing. How are the boys?'

The conversation although brief went some way to placating Georgia.

***

It was a warm Sunday morning in June with a cooling breeze; her messed up curls swept around Georgia's face. She was in the park with Zachari and Kristiano, and Andoni was at his football match with Nicolas. Perching on the edge of the bench in the play area, as the rest of the seat was covered in bird droppings, she half-read her book and half kept an eye on the boys when her mobile rang. She rummaged around in her navy leather slouch bag, sat in a crumpled heap by her feet, but it rang off before she got to it. She looked down at "missed call" lit up on the screen, unknown number. For a second she wondered who it could be but went back to her reading, stopping to call out to the boys every few minutes as Zach played on the roundabout which looked like a big flower, painted in bright primary colours. Kristiano and another little boy bounced on the green caterpillar see-saw, its white, painted bulbous eyes staring out at Georgia unblinking. The phone in her hand rang again. This time she picked up before it rang off.

'Hello.'

'Mum! It's me! We won our match today! We beat Watford Town 6-2! It was wicked and I scored two goals!' said Andoni.

'Wow! How brilliant darling. Well done! Are you on your way home?'

'No, we're walking to the car. I'm all muddy. Dad says he won't put me in the car and I have to walk home.' She could hear his voice shaking and imagined how upset he felt.

'He's joking honey. Take the picnic rug from the boot and sit on that. See you soon and well done.'

Just as she ended the call the phone rang again and automatically and without thinking Georgia pressed the 'Accept call' icon. She wished she hadn't.

Chapter Four

GEORGIA'S HEAD REELED. She felt numb and uneasy. She picked up her book and grabbed her bag. She threw it onto her shoulder, her mind elsewhere as the bright colours of the park blurred in and out of focus around her. The sky darkened to an inky blue, matching her mood; the sun snuffed out by a trail of thick clouds. Her heart raced and her mind back-tracked. Everything she did next happened on auto-pilot. She felt like she was looking at herself through a frosted pane of glass, nothing clear, nothing making sense. A lump burned in her throat and filled her airwaves.

Georgia composed herself as best she could without alerting the boys to anything untoward. Their short walk back seemed, to Georgia, to drag endlessly and it took all her energy to keep calm and remain patient with them.

Zachari bumped up and down the kerb on his scooter looking older than his seven years and Kristiano, a typical five-year-old, pedalled like mad to keep up on his bicycle but it was stop-start, stop-start all the way as he paused to push his hair out of his eyes or whenever he came to a drain cover.

'We'll have to get you a haircut honey,' she said.

'Nooooo! I want long hair like Petit.'

'Well, you don't play for Arsenal and you look like a girl. So Dad will have to take you later. *Yiayia* and *bapou* won't recognise you next time we go to their house. *Yiayia* will say, 'I didn't know I had a granddaughter,' and she will chase you with the scissors.'

'You look like a giiirl! You look like a giiirl!' teased Zachari.

'Enough Zach. Come on *agabi mou*, my love, let's get moving. We're going so slow we might as well be going backwards.' Both boys laughed and she smiled at them even though her heart was breaking inside.

***

At home, the boys left their scooter and bike scattered across the drive, which would annoy Nicolas when he couldn't park but she made no effort to tidy them out of the way. They abandoned their trainers in the middle of the square hallway and ran straight out into the back garden to the trampoline.

'Be careful out there!' she shouted after them.

Georgia flicked on the kettle and tried to think. She made herself a traditional Cypriot tea, with soothing cinnamon and cloves, but it did nothing to take the edge off. She sipped at it, twisting and twirling her hair around her fingers as she looked at the boys bouncing from the open kitchen window, the light breeze cooling her down. Could it be true? She knew the woman, having met her dropping off the supplies for the café after the Costco run a few months ago. Thinking about it now, it had been odd that she had still been there when Nicolas would normally be on his own doing the last of the tidying before locking up. Bastard! Georgia sobbed, a shudder forcing her to stop.

She busied herself preparing *yiachni* for their late Sunday lunch, slicing onions, peeling potatoes, chopping up the tomatoes she had blanched earlier. She browned off chicken pieces in *Helea* premium Greek olive oil – all the while unwelcome thoughts flashed through her fuddled mind.

She finally sat down at the kitchen table, her mug of tea now cold, the cinnamon sticks and cloves half floating half immersed in the tea which had clouded over with a filmy residue of hard water. Her mind continued to endure the barrage of suffocating, jumbled thoughts.

***

'Mum, Mum! Dad says come and move the bikes,' shouted a sweaty, red-faced Andoni, helping himself to a swig of orange juice straight from the carton.

'Tell him I'm in the middle of something. He'll have to do it. And don't drink out of the carton. Get a cup please.' She moved away from the table and leaned up against the sink. Turning on the hot tap, she grabbed the sponge, soaked it with pink washing up liquid. She splashed water over the now dry crockery and pans she had done earlier and grabbing one of the frying pans she pretended to scrub away.

'For God's sake. You're so slap-dash! Can't you keep the drive clear? How am I meant to get onto it with their stupid bikes everywhere?' Nicolas threw his jacket over the back of the kitchen chair.

'Were they? I didn't realise. The boys must have left them there.' Georgia made no comment about his jacket which now lay on the floor, having slipped off the chair. She knew he wouldn't pick it up. That was her job. 'How was the match?'

'It was a really good game actually. Andoni's playing real good. And he's fast. What are you doing? Why were the bikes on the drive? I've had to faff about moving them before I could park.'

'The usual. Washing up, cooking. I took the boys to the park earlier for a bit. They loved it. They saw one of their school friends down there. They had a great time but were so slow coming back. I thought I was never going to get home. Like snails they were.'

'Stop moaning. If you didn't want to take them, why did you? Always complaining about something.'

'No I'm not. I'm just saying. What's wrong with you?'

'Nothing.'

'My mum called me earlier. My uncle phoned her.' She hesitated, waiting for his reaction. 'He told her you're having an affair with Roksana.' There, she'd said it. She'd said it even though she didn't want to believe it.

Even though it may be true.

'You are fucking joking!' The silence hung between them. 'Oh, what a laugh that's giving me! He's such a waste of space! It's that idiot who delivers the bacon and sausages for me. He's been making it up.'

'What's he got to do with it? And why would he make it up? Why would he say anything to my uncle? They're not best buddies are they? Uncle helps you out in the café now and again that's all. He's not going to be talking to the delivery man! Stop playing games and tell me the truth! Is that what these past few weeks have been all about? Are you seeing her? Are you sleeping with her? Are you fucking her? Are you?' Her voice a whisper now, she felt her eyes well up with tears again.

'Of course I'm not. He saw me at a coffee shop in Oakwood. I knew he'd put two and two together.'

'What were you doing there?'

'I was spying, you know, on the competition. To see what else I could do at the café to bring in some extra punters.'

'And?'

'Well, he must've seen me with her,' Nicolas said, running his fingers through his hair.

'With her? Roksana?'

'Yes. With Roksana.'

'Why didn't you tell me you? Why go to Oakwood, nearly 3 miles away from you? That's not competition there. It's too far. When did you go?'

'A while ago. I don't remember the exact date.'

'Tell me.'

'For God's sake! Everywhere is competition. Remember I told you not to listen to any gossip. I knew the delivery guy would say something. He's a slimy bastard. He's jealous. He's tried flirting with her before and she won't rise to it. He's a creep. I told her to keep away from him.'

'I thought you said she had a boyfriend. And why do you care whether she flirts back or not? What's it got to do with you?'

'Well, I want her working, not flirting with the delivery guy!' His face reddened. 'What's for lunch?'

'Work it out! Can't you smell it?' Georgia stormed off leaving him standing in the kitchen to cope with the boys as they piled into the kitchen one by one wanting a drink. She needed time away from him. She went upstairs to the en-suite bathroom. She kicked the door shut and plonked herself down on the toilet. She swore under her breath over and over again until she calmed down and then she ran out the house without a word.

***

Georgia sat on the velour couch with the gold fringing, in the lounge, not wanting to disturb her father-in-law, who had fallen asleep slumped in front of the television in the extension adjacent to the kitchen. Her mother-in-law, apron tied around her heavy waist from just having finished the washing up, sat in the matching armchair opposite.

'*Agabi mou*, it's not what you think. He's just worried about her. Your uncle's wrong to accuse him. How can your mum think it's true? Nico's a good man. He cares about you.'

'Are you sure he's not doing anything? Did you ask him?'

'I'm sure. He wouldn't do that to you, to us.' By adding 'us' to her response it re-iterated to Georgia her *bethera* believed her son would not do anything to bring his parents or the family into disrepute. This would be the ultimate betrayal.

'But did you ask him, *midera*?' Georgia asked, addressing her mother-in-law respectfully as mother. 'Did he give you a straight answer?'

'He promised me that he knew what he was doing and he's not sleeping with anyone but you. He cares for her, feels sorry for her. That's all.'

'So he's spoken to you about her?'

'Once. Only that she worked hard. Had no family here.'

'Did he say anything else? Did he tell you where he goes?'

'He didn't tell me anything. I don't know.' Her mother-in-law pleated and un-pleated the frilled edge of her apron.

'He says he's late because he gets last minute customers. But I know that's not true. I've driven up there and the café is closed as early as half past two.'

'I don't know what to say. But I believe him when he tells me he's not cheating on you. I'd be furious if he did that to you and the boys. I know you're a good wife, I can see it. You work hard. You put him first.'

'I do. I really do, *midera*. God, I want to believe you. I want to believe him. I haven't put in twenty-two years with him to throw it all away because of some infatuation. I won't let him break up what we have. The boys deserve better. This would break them and I love them so much.'

'I believe him. He wouldn't lie to me. And I know how much you love the boys. You are a good mum, Georgia *mou*.' Georgia's *bethera* showed a hint of ardent affection and support for her daughter-in-law. Something Georgia had not witnessed, from her, in all the time she had been married to Nicolas, yet Georgia detected angst across her *bethera's* brow. But for now Georgia would give Nicolas the benefit of the doubt. She understood how the phone calls could be explained. He could have fallen for Roksana's sob stories and just been trying to help her. He was a good man. She rationalised what he'd said to her and what his mother had said and, as Georgia went over it in her mind, the unease began to subside. She had to stay calm. Instead she looked forward to their holiday to Florida in August with enthusiasm and hope. Hope to save her marriage.

She drove home, much calmer, driving at a slow pace as she quietened the antagonist's voice in her head. She had to believe Nico. Otherwise what was the point of continuing?

***

Sitting round the kitchen table, lunch was strained but the boys didn't notice.

'This is my favouritest lunch ever!' said Zachari. The *yiachni* usually delicious, Georgia's paternal *yiayia* had taught her how to make it, stuck in her throat.

'Stop messing about boys. I don't have the patience for your nattering and bickering. Just eat.' That's all she said. She watched as Andoni shoved in a whole potato, the tomato sauce running down his chin, a stream of red juice making its way down his yellow Arsenal top.

'Georgia, look at Andoni…for God's sake,' Nicolas said. She reached across and wiped Andoni's front.

'Well, this is good. Lovely lunch darling. This afternoon boys, we'll watch the match live on SKY and leave *mamma* to do the washing up in peace.'

Georgia looked across at him. The man of the house. It was as if nothing had just raised its ugly head between them, or that things might never be the same again. In that instant she didn't recognise him. She hated him.

***

The sun moved on its trajectory and no longer shone through the kitchen window, shielded by the tall spiky fir tree in the neighbour's garden. The younger boys went straight to bed but Georgia could hear Andoni's whining echo across the relative silence of the house.

'It's not fair, I'm ten. Why do I have to go to bed at the same time as Zach? He's only seven!'

'Because your mum and I are going to have a quiet night in front of the telly,' Nicolas said. 'Because you all have school tomorrow. And you're Year 6 now which means you have to work harder. Set an example for your brothers.'

The odd thud and bump came from upstairs but at least, Georgia thought, Andoni was not up and down the stairs and in and out.

'Kristiano's fallen asleep,' said Nicolas.

'He was almost falling asleep in the bath. He didn't even want to play with his yellow submarine, the bubble-blowing one, or his octopus. He usually loves those stick on alphabet letters too. But he didn't splash about today and for once I didn't get soaked from head to foot.'

'Well, you did rush them a bit.'

'They were tired. That's why I filled the bath with just enough water for them to get clean in. Andoni insisted on a shower. He's growing too fast,' said Georgia. She let the silence fall between them, cold like a sheet of ice.

'So?' she said her tone brusque. She noticed

Nicolas's edgy, discombobulated demeanour, as he ran his fingers through his hair. She repositioned herself on the couch in the big bay window, her legs pulled up and tucked under her, arms folded across her stomach. She stared at him until his glare wavered.

'So what?' he said, from his armchair.

'Are you going to tell me the truth about what's going on?'

'For God's sake. I could kill your uncle and that idiot of a delivery guy. They've got it wrong. There's nothing going on. Listen to what I'm telling you.'

'Really? Because you know my mum will tell Dad and I need to know what to say to them when Dad asks me. And he will ask me.'

'Okay. I'll put them all straight.'

'So we're okay then? I don't need to be worried about anything?'

'No. Stop going on.' He flicked the TV channel back to SKY Sports. So much for a quiet night in front of the telly, she thought.

'So it's all rubbish. Just mindless gossip?'

'Yes. I've just said so haven't I?'

'As long as you're not lying to me. I just want the truth Nico.'

'You've got it. From me. Don't listen to anyone else, okay?'

'Okay.'

'You know I love you, don't you? We've got Florida

to look forward to, haven't we?' he said, tilting towards her, his voice gentler.

'Yeah, I know.' But deep down, where she didn't want to go, where she couldn't go because of fear, she wondered whether he was being unusually wordy to fob her off.

***

'I'm borrowing £100,000 against the house to pay Tony off. It's the best option and the Bank Manager has agreed to add this to the existing mortgage. The sooner he's my ex the better. Fucking pig! I can't believe he's putting me through this. Thank God I have the rental income from the house in Arnos Grove to keep me afloat. Otherwise the kids and I would be homeless,' said Thalia to Georgia.

They were sitting at a round lime green metal table in the window of Café Buzz, a jam jar overflowing with a handful of bluebells sat side by side with a salt and pepper shaker set and a plastic coated menu card.

'Babe, that's awful. But at least the finance is organised and he won't take the house from you. He can't now can he? The kids would be so upset to move. And anyway you would never be homeless. You've got your mum and dad, me, your brothers.'

'I know. It's such a burden though. I've never had to think about money before. Or bills. It's scary.' Tony continued to be as awkward as possible despite Thalia securing the money he wanted, questioning Thalia's every move. Georgia imagined a prison with twenty-four seven surveillance.

'Babe you're not on your own and you've done pretty well so far. And you've got me and your mum and dad. How are they by the way?'

'They're outraged that he's forced me to end my marriage. They're upset for me and everything I've gone through. My mum doesn't know the half of it and she would be even more upset if she knew it all, the way he treated me, the way I was made to feel.'

'Oh, hun. Well, my mum and dad are telling me to finish it with Nico. Dad's going mad since mum told him. Wants to have it out with him but I think I've persuaded him to hold back while I work out what to do. I wish my uncle hadn't said anything to them.'

'He must've been sure though to say something to you and to them.'

'I know that's what Mum and Dad both said. But the last thing I need is Dad wading in and then having the aftermath of that to deal with on top of everything else. I don't know though. He might've got it wrong.'

'Really? Do you think he would've said something to you if he wasn't sure?'

'I just don't know. I'm so angry with uncle for saying anything at all. I don't want this in my life.'

'He obviously felt bad for you, thought he was doing the right thing.'

'I'm too angry and upset to see how any of this can be the right thing.'

'Well, what's she like, this waitress?'

'Moody-looking, never smiles.' Georgia paused and then added, 'but then she's an illegal immigrant. Working for cash. Things must be hard for her.'

'Don't be fooled honey. She must be desperate. She will have an ulterior motive if she's making a move on him. And don't you dare make excuses or feel sorry for her!'

'I don't know. I'm so confused. Would he really do that to me? We've got three children, a beautiful home, a good life. Would he throw all that away to be with her? He'd be left with nothing. The house is in my name.'

'Solely?'

'Yeah, all legal and above board. He took out the deposit to buy the freehold of the café last year, against the equity of the house. He added the loan to the mortgage. So the house is in my name, the business in his.'

'At least you won't have to go begging for £100,000 to pay him off! The Bank Manager was a right creep!' They both laughed and then a warm silence fell between them for a few minutes.

'Just don't be naïve,' Thalia said, 'Be careful. Keep asking him questions. And pass by the café whenever you can and see what's going on. That's what I would do.'

***

Nicolas walked in after work whistling.

'You're happy,' called Georgia from the kitchen.

'I am,' he said coming up behind her, nuzzling her neck like he used to do. 'And these are for you.' She turned round and came face to face with a bunch of champagne and melon pink roses; the old fashioned ones that reminded her of her *yiayia's* garden.

'Wow! They're beautiful,' she said as she turned towards him. He wrapped his arms around her waist, kissed her on the lips.

'You're beautiful.' Georgia felt appeased.

***

That night after Georgia and Nicolas had gone to bed Nicolas's mobile vibrated on the bedside table. 11.30pm. He reached over and answered it. Within seconds he jumped out of bed and pulled on his discarded T-shirt, thrown over the pine rocking chair, pulled out a pair of boxers from the laundry basket.

'It's my mum. She wants to talk to me.'

'Now?'

'She's driving over.'

***

Georgia immediately recalled the conversation with her mother-in-law. That's what she must want at this late hour, thought Georgia. She didn't follow Nicolas downstairs as a light knocking against the porch doors echoed across the night's silence. Her limbs felt stiff and it took a few minutes for her to rouse fully. Pulling on a pair of cotton pyjamas, she sat huddled at the top of the stairs straining to hear the conversation between mother and son, carried out in hushed tones in the kitchen. Georgia caught most of the exchange despite the door being pushed closed. She listened, not daring to breathe.

'Georgia came to see me. She's worried. I'm worried too.'

'Oh Mum...'

'Where do you go after you've shut for the day?' said his mother.

The silence hung between them. Georgia listened but he didn't answer. So he's unable to explain closing the café early to his mother she thought. Either that or he couldn't lie to his mother.

'Do you love Georgia? Do you love the boys?'

'Yes, Mum...of course I do.'

'Then promise to my face there's nothing going on,' she repeated. Georgia could hear him faltering and then her *bethera* said in a voice as loud as a clap of thunder, 'You stop whatever it is before it's too late.'

Georgia heard the scrape of the old church chairs on the white American oak flooring of the kitchen, her mother-in-law's heavy steps as she crossed the hallway. Georgia tiptoed back to their bedroom.

***

Her sleep was disturbed, something she was getting used to. She lay awake for what she thought must have been half the night wondering if things would be okay for her and for the boys. She convinced herself it would be okay and then forced herself to face up to what might be happening. Her *bethera* would not have come round if she didn't have her own doubts too. Next to her Nicolas had taken up most of the bed, his arms unfurled above his head and his legs spread-eagled wide. She eventually fell asleep in a straight vertical line, her body in symmetry with the edge of the mattress.

Chapter Five

JUNE AND JULY passed by without any further arguments and their summer holiday to Florida came round. It was a dream come true for Georgia, who had imagined this holiday ever since Kristiano had been born six years before. She thought the hotel was sensational, a short drive from Disney and the other resorts. The boys got excited every time they took the glass lift which rose twenty-two floors up the middle of the hotel complex. They loved the kids' pool which easily matched the size of three tennis courts, with slides, a waterfall shaped like a mushroom in the middle and a tunnel, which they shot out of into an area embellished with a border of brilliant green tiles. Nicolas appeared more relaxed and patient with the boys and less snappy with her.

***

Disney itself delivered everything she had imagined and had wanted it to be for the boys. The boys enjoyed every second, when they weren't bickering or begging for something 'more' or 'again'. Rushing up to every Disney character they saw, they posed for photos, their Mickey Mouse Autograph Book filled up with scribbled signatures and personalised messages. Hair-raising roller-coaster rides forced them to scream their little heads off.

But Georgia, although chirpy and relaxed in the day, despite the almost unbearable temperature, became disconcerted with Nicolas. At two in the morning one night, half awake, half asleep, she turned round in bed and reached out to find an empty space next to her. She got up and noticed the bedroom door ajar she peered into the corridor through bleary sleepy eyes.

'What are you doing on the phone at this hour?'

'Um, I just needed to tell my dad something about the order for the café this week. Being out all day I didn't get a chance to call him.'

'Oh, okay. Say hi to him from me. I'm going back to bed.'

The following day the boys stuffed oversized pretzels dusted with sugar and cinnamon into their greedy little mouths, the sweet coating leaving sticky streaks across their faces. Georgia and Nicolas joined in being silly and Nicolas gave her a big sticky kiss on the lips which delighted Kristiano who cheered.

They held burgers in huge buns in both hands as they took messy mouthfuls out of them and the fattest fries ever and the skinniest fries ever and the curliest fries ever filled their plates every day.

'I'm going to get fat with all these chips every day,' said Georgia.

'Don't be silly darling. You're lovely. Isn't *mamma* lovely?' asked Nicolas giving her a flirty look. Georgia's heart skipped a beat. How could she have doubted

Nicolas loved her? Loved the boys?

But two nights later again, she roused from her sleep again to find him at the end of the corridor, his back to her. She called out to him but when he didn't respond she padded back across the cool tiles of the hotel bedroom and flopped back into bed, listening to the quiet humming of the air-conditioning.

'On the phone again last night?' she said over breakfast of blueberry muffins, syrup-soaked pancakes and crispy bacon.

'I just thought I'd give my sister a quick call, check she'd been round to the house and collected the mail.'

'And did she go?'

'Yeah, all okay. She watered the plants for you too.'

'That's nice of her. Hope you thanked her for running around. My mum could have done that,' said Georgia, although deep down something about the calls were giving her much umbrage.

The boys' skins glowed golden, Zachari's and Kristiano's cheeks highlighted ember red from catching the sun and Andoni's fringe became a bleached dark blond giving the impression he had highlights. Georgia thought they were the cutest trio she'd ever laid eyes on and she adored them so much. She watched Nicolas with them too and knew how their dad loved them too; he held their hands, queued for refreshments and sang Disney songs with them. The boys slept every night, exhausted from the long days and the sweltering heat and the excitement of all the parks they'd visited.

At the beginning of their second week again, the click of the hotel bedroom door opening woke her again.

'I just need to call home, check how my mum's hospital appointment went. You go back to sleep.'

***

The new school year began again and as September continued things carried on as normal or as normal as they could having accused her husband of cheating on her. Georgia threw herself into her part-time job and looking after the boys, she supported Thalia when things got nasty between Thalia and her soon-to-be-ex-husband. She enjoyed all the attention she got from her work colleagues who praised her for being efficient yet caring and warmhearted.

'Wednesdays and Thursdays…my two favourite days of the week,' said James, one of the peripatetics; a rotund man who looked older than his age because of his size, his once dark hair receded and he permanently had a mug of tea in his hand. He was a joker; playing tricks, flirting, messing around. Georgia liked the fun he injected into her otherwise serious work ethic.

'Really? Not Saturdays and Sundays?' asked Georgia.

'I see you on both days and I get to teach the trumpet and trombone to students who are committed.'

'You flirting with me James?'

'Would I?'

'Yes you would.' Georgia grabbed a pile of papers from her desk.

'Anything interesting in your in-tray today?'

'Not looked yet.'

'Oh, that's not like you. Little Miss Efficient with your infectious smile and bright white teeth!'

'Well, I like to keep you on your toes. Being too predictable is no fun!'

'So there's an unpredictable side to you?'

'Might be…'

'Well, I'm up for having some fun finding out.' James winked at her as he slurped his tea.

***

The attention she got from James made her feel invincible; she began to believe anything was possible. The attention empowered her; with more confidence, assertiveness and assurance she was appreciated and worthy of so much more. She collected the clothes from the washing line, which had dried too much, out in the late summer sun all day. As she folded them they felt like cardboard. She made a neat pile in the wicker basket lost in her thoughts.

'What are you smiling about?' Nicolas asked, as he sat on the garden bench watching her, a bottle of

Budweiser in his hand.

'Just something one of the music teachers said to me at work today.'

'Stupid bloody music teachers...who'd want to be a music teacher anyway? Bet they don't earn much either.'

'Probably not. How was your day? You were late home...again.'

'That lot from the road works came in last minute again. They're making a habit of it so get used to it. I can't turn them away. Looks like they're going to be around for months so it'll be good for business.'

'That's good. Is what's her name, Roksana working longer hours then?'

'For God's sake, you're not going on about her again are you? I've told you there's nothing going on. Your stupid uncle got it wrong. He's so bored with his own life he thinks it's okay to create a drama in ours.'

'I'm just asking. I'm allowed to ask aren't I? Anyway the boys keep asking why you're not home for dinner with us anymore.'

'I am. It's not every night I'm late. It's not even every other night.'

'Well, that's how they feel. They've noticed you're not around as often as you were. They miss playing footy in the garden and watching DVDs with you.'

'Well, work has to take priority. That's how we can afford the nice holidays and the nice dinners out and the nice house.'

Georgia picked up the basket of washing, tucked it under her arm and walked through the dining room and into the utility room, at the other end of the kitchen, to put it away. She knew full well Nicolas was lying to her. She'd driven past the café twice the week before and three times the week before that to find it shuttered up from half past two in the afternoon. Where was he going? And why, as she observed from the bedroom, did she witness him on his mobile phone as soon as he jumped in the car at half five every morning? She knew what she had to do now. She had her own epiphany right there and, bleary-eyed and sick to her stomach, she closed the door to the utility room.

Chapter Six

THE NEXT MORNING, Georgia pulled over into the car park at Queen Elizabeth's, and made a call. The automated system directed her to the correct department as she punched in one option number after the other. Eventually she got to speak to someone.

'Yes please. Can I have copies as far back as May 2004? My accountant's gone and mislaid the whole file I gave him.' She waited a few more minutes, her heart thumping in her chest and her pulse racing, as the woman she spoke to on the telephone actioned her request on the network.

'Your request has been logged and the documents will take between five to seven working days to get to you by post,' she responded, 'Is there anything else I can help you with today?'

'No, thank you for your help.'

***

After ten days, Georgia caught the post as she left for work. The bright red Vodafone logo on the white envelope jumped out at her as the postman, with his usual sullen expression mumbled a good morning to her. She hurried the boys and threw their paraphernalia into the car.

'Why can't we walk today? I want to take my scooter,' whined Zachari.

'Because I'm going to be late for work. Now come on...where's your book bag Andoni? Kristiano have you got your swimming bag? And goggles?'

She just made it in time for work, the traffic bumper to bumper along the lane approaching the width restriction. Georgia ran the short distance from the car park to the Music Office so she didn't arrive late. She didn't get a chance to look at what Vodafone had sent through.

***

The clock on the dash indicated one o'clock. Georgia staring at the envelope in her hand. She wound down the window to let in the fresh summer breeze and turned the radio on to KISS 100 to calm her nerves. Music always lifted her mood. She wished Thalia was there with her but with trembling hands, and a prickle on the back of her neck, Georgia slid a finger under the flap and tore it open. She let out a deep sigh and pulled out the sheets of paper. After a few minutes she called Thalia.

'Hi babe. It's me. Can you do me a massive favour? Will you pick up the boys for me and bring them home to me. I can't come to the school…I'm in a mess.'

'Are you okay? What's happened?'

'It's nothing…I'm not sure. Will you pick them up?'

'Of course.'
'Thanks Thal. I'll talk to you in a bit.'

***

Georgia hugged the children as they piled into the house one by one. She listened to their chatter about the bird which had found its way into the atrium and how the caretaker had to usher it out from one of the openings as he hung from a ladder. She listened to Zachari as he told Georgia about their Circle Time activity and how the children had all laughed at the piece of Spanish sausage a classmate had brought to 'Show and Tell'. Georgia laughed with him, her tears a mixture of joy at her son's excitement about what had happened and the misery of her own predicament.

Finally, Georgia scooted the children out into the late afternoon sun with an ice lolly each. She sat in the dining room relishing the last of the rays pouring through the open french doors and handed Thalia the wad of folded papers from her bag.

The tall trees fringing one corner of the garden gave the children welcome respite from the angry sun. Georgia looked up and across at the wispy cirrus clouds looking down on them from a powdery blue. The scene before her, one of calm and contentment, jarred with her knotted stomach. The children were taking turns bouncing on the trampoline while Andoni kicked a ball up against the back of the folded tennis table, the rhythmic thump-thump echoing off the solid table. The sound of a tube train chugging into Finchley Central Station could be heard in the distance and the slamming of the doors reverberated across the open void between the garden and the train track below at the far end.

Thalia glanced through invoice after invoice, month by month, noticing the same number, which Georgia had noticed too, her red scribbled lines under each one a give-away…Sunday mornings, most mornings mid-week as early as half past five and in the evenings after ten…the night he played football she guessed.

'The bastard,' said Thalia.

'I feel so damn stupid. Even while we were in Florida.' Georgia's heart sank again, her voice shaking. He'd made a fool of her. He'd promised her nothing was going on. And she'd always been so proud of her marriage. Of what they had together.

'Oh my God….' said Thalia. 'What are you going to do now? Have you called the number?'

'No. I'm too scared it will be who I think it is. I'm scared it will be her voice on the other end.'

'You have to call it Georgi. It's the obvious solution. That way you'll know for sure. Look, put it on loudspeaker and we can listen together.' They edged back from the dining room doors, to escape the noise of the children shouting and calling to each other and to avoid them overhearing anything.

Georgia dialled the number. 'Ha-llo,' answered the strong Eastern European voice.

'The fucking Romanian *katsela*! The fucking Romanian cow! I am going to kill her. Then I'm going to kill him. That bastard…'

'Georgi…hold on…calm…'

'I don't believe he's doing this to me! Oh my God what am I going to tell the boys? They won't understand all this. They won't understand infidelity. They'll want him to stay. What am I going to do?'

'Calm down Georgi. You don't know anything for sure. Yes, it's her voice but that doesn't mean they're at it. And you can't confront him with the boys at home. Not in this mood. Let's take the boys to mine and you can pick them up when you're ready. That way you can talk to him and get the answers you want. There might be an explanation. And stay calm. Stay in control.'

'Yeah, you're right hun. Sorry. But I'm calling again to make sure.' She hit redial; the same voice, the same monotone accent. Georgia hung up. Her heart felt like a dead weight in her chest.

***

Nicolas strolled in a few minutes before six o'clock and went straight up for a shower. Georgia waited in the kitchen shifting from one foot to the other until he eventually came back downstairs.

'Of course I've got her number. Why wouldn't I? She works for me doesn't she?' said Nicolas.

'What do you need to call her for?'

'If she's running late, if she's not well enough to come in, if she's missed the bus to work…loads of reasons. What's with all the questions?'

'I'll tell you why! Because her number is all over the Vodafone bills like a rash! Her number is there every fucking day! You made call after call after call to her. Sometimes five, six times a fucking night. In the mornings. On Sundays. On. Sundays. When you should be watching your son play football you're on the fucking phone to her for an hour, for two hours!'

'Oh come on. How do you know that?'

'Because, darling, I have seen the bills.'

'Look I can explain. There's nothing going on. She's been doing extra shifts what with those workmen coming in at the end of the day. I couldn't cope on my own. And she's having a hard time with her boyfriend. He's possessive. She just needs someone to talk to. I've done nothing wrong. I promise. I've promised your mum and dad. I've promised my mum too. On the boys' lives I haven't done anything with her.'

'Don't you dare swear on the boys' lives!'

'I promise!'

'And my mum and dad aren't stupid! They don't believe you and neither do I.'

'I promise, Georgia please…'

'I don't believe you. You just said it's because she's late or ill. Now you're saying something different. And if nothing's happened, you want it to. She wants it to. The fucking cow! She knows you're married. She's met me. She's met the boys!'

'Look I care for her. She works for me. She's on her own. She's here without permission. Imagine what that's like for her.'

'What it's like for her? You are joking, right? Why do I want to imagine what it's like for her? I've been out of my mind with worry. I've been thinking the worst; you were ill, you might be in debt, having a break down or something. And you want me to imagine what it's been like for her? You imagine what it's been like for me. Just for one fucking minute!'

'You're such a drama queen. It's not about you or me. It's about helping her out. She's in trouble here. She's without her family. She has no-one. We have each other and the boys and our families. You've got me. I'm working my arse off to give you the life you want. To give us the life we both want.' He ran his hand through his hair, nervous.

'Liar!' Georgia wanted to bash his big fat head on the kitchen wall behind him, but instead she turned and stomped out. He didn't follow her. Grabbing her car keys, she walked out, slamming the porch door behind her.

***

Georgia didn't have the energy to weave in and out of the evening traffic and apologised to Thalia for being so late; she'd got there past the boys' bed-time. She rushed back home, promising to fill her in the following day. At home, after a quick hug from their dad, the boys were tucked up in bed.

She made herself and Nicolas a mug of tea.

'Where were you? I was really worried,' said Nicolas, reaching out for the proffered mug.

'I just needed a bit of space. Clear my head.'

'And are you okay now?' his tone calmer.

'Yes. I think so.'

'Good.'

***

In bed, Georgia snuggled into him, the mattress holding the contours of her body, and she did the thing she knew would turn him towards her. It worked every time. It took a while that night but finally, just as she began to doubt herself, wondering whether the strong physical connection they'd always experienced had waned, she felt his hard-on between her legs. If she could still do that to him, for as long as she could, Nicolas wouldn't go anywhere. They fucked and she was the whore in the bedroom he liked her to be. It was fast and furious, without the usual foreplay and teasing. She felt somewhat appeased yet a niggling little thought at the back of her head taunted her; was he really capable of cheating on her?

'I love you. You know that?' Nicolas whispered, his breath hot on the top of her head, as his fingers traced her collarbone. She nestled further into the crook of his toned arm, a tiny smile settled on her lips. Although spent from the emotional exhaustion of the last few hours, days, weeks, she knew she had won him over.

Chapter Seven

A FEW MONTHS passed and their trip to New York was almost upon them. Thalia had been very persuasive. Georgia had discussed it at length with Nicolas and her mum and, with Nicolas's permission albeit somewhat half-heartedly at first, Georgia had agreed to take the four-day trip, in celebration of Thalia's thirtieth birthday, the following Easter.

In the final few weeks leading up to their departure Georgia wondered whether she made the right decision but knew she could not back out. On the one hand she looked forward to escaping the everyday and on the other hand she worried about leaving the boys and leaving Nicolas. Her mum had wholeheartedly said she would rally round and help with the boys and to be fair, Nicolas's mother had said she would have the boys for a day too. She knew deep down they would be in good hands but she still felt like she was abandoning them all. That niggly voice inside tugged away subconsciously at her like a subliminal advertising message, telling her she was being irresponsible. She also wondered whether she could trust Nicolas to look after the boys. To be committed to them in her absence.

Although he seemed more connected with her as the months passed by, more attentive, less critical than he had been over the past couple of years she still couldn't shake off the nagging voice in her head, the antagonist, planting doubts.

'Hey. Let's get a takeaway tomorrow. Save you from cooking.'

'Ooh, lucky me,' said Georgia leaning in to kiss Nicolas on the lips.

The following evening Nicolas came home with a bunch of roses, bursting with the vibrancy of a rainbow.

'What are these for?'

'Does there have to be a reason?'

Georgia smiled. She tried to stop herself from analysing his every move over the previous few days to discover if anything didn't sit right. She enjoyed the attention and the affection and less criticism from him. He hugged her and gave her good morning kisses and good night kisses.

Thalia had talked about nothing more than what an amazing time they would have and delighted with the planned short break, her excitement overflowed whenever they had a catch up. Thalia, more selfish in some ways than Georgia, relished the thought of being child-free for a few days and talked about shopping trips and nights out and drinking in bars and dancing in clubs. All this excited Georgia too but she still felt guilt-ridden about leaving her family behind.

Georgia slept badly the night before their trip and the next morning a road accident diverted their taxi through picturesque villages and past quaint pubs, adding half an hour to their estimated journey time.

When Georgia and Thalia finally arrived at Gatwick Airport they ran along the main concourse towards check-in conscious of how late they were. Georgia stifled her giggles as she watched Thalia struggling with her big bold animal-print suitcase.

'Bloody hell, Thalia, we're going for three nights!'

'I couldn't decide which shoes to bring and then I thought I might need my boots as well and then I thought if we go clubbing I'd need my high heeled ones as well. Better safe than sorry hun.'

They queued for less than five minutes when a chirpy blond ground steward summoned them to the check-in desk. Georgia handed over her compact navy Samsonite suitcase, placing it on the scales with ease unlike Thalia who struggled to lift hers onto the conveyor belt.

'You're lucky he didn't charge you excess baggage – you were overweight by four kilos!' Georgia said as they walked away from the desk.

'Darling...I've never been over weight.' Thalia's laughter attracted the attention of all the men in another queue as the girls walked past.

'I can't argue with that. You look like an athlete and you never exercise! It's not fair.' Georgia placed her arm across her bloated belly.

'Well, I do exercise actually,' said Thalia, 'just not the traditional form.'

'Well, listen to you. No more than me so how come

I don't look like an athlete?' Georgia smiled to take the sting out of her comment. She knew Thalia struggled with 'no sex' since her separation.

'Show off!'

'Just saying it as it is, babe. You know me,' said Georgia.

'Yeah, sex mad and insatiable.'

'Not quite insatiable. I'm going without sex for four days to be with you, my honey.'

'Such a sacrifice, thank you my darling. Will make it up to you. This holiday will be worth it.'

***

They both looked up at the departures board, scanning row after row of information for their flight number.

BA227 New York (JFK) B32 08:25 Go to Gate 27

'Come on, babe. It'll be miles away,' said Georgia, looking across at the huge yellow sign, a black arrow pointing the direction to Gates B1 to B32.

'We've plenty of time yet,' said Thalia, up-dating her Facebook status with an airport selfie.

'The plane won't wait for us. You can do that later.'

'It's done. Look already got four likes and one comment.'

BROKEN PIECES OF TOMORROW

***

Waiting for their boarding numbers to be called up they babbled, Thalia already flirting with the older gentleman sitting opposite them in the Departure Lounge.

'You girls are going to make this an interesting flight for sure,' he said to both of them.

'We will indeed,' said Thalia, 'Where are you sitting?'

'Up front. I always travel Club World when on business,' he drawled, his American accent booming at them.

'Well, we will make an excuse to come up front and see you,' said Thalia.

'Don't worry about her. I'll keep her strapped into her seat,' said Georgia. 'It's me you have to worry about,' she said, giggling.

'Yeah, the quiet ones and all that,' said Thalia.

'Sounds like you are both quite a handful,' he chuckled.

'Well, Georgia's more like two,' said Thalia, tilting her head towards her bosomy friend.

'Can't argue with that,' drawled the American a mischievous twinkle in his eye as he winked at them both. 'And I'm Bobby by the way.' He leaned across and shook their hands in turn.

'Thalia and Georgia,' said Georgia, trying not to lean too far over as she became conscious of her buxomness.

'Well it's my pleasure. If you'll just excuse me.'

Georgia and Thalia watched him walk off and carried on chatting, Thalia's laugh like a brass bell clanging across the relative quiet hustle of the waiting area. An announcement over the public address system shushed them both.

'Passengers Mrs T. Ellinas and Mrs G. Josephides,
Flight BA227 to New York,
please make yourselves known to the airline staff at
the check point with your boarding
passes and passports.
Passengers Mrs T. Ellinas and Mrs G. Josephides,
Flight BA227 to New York,
please make yourselves known to the airline staff.
Thank you.'

'That's us,' said Thalia, looking at Georgia.

'Bloody hell. It's got to be your overweight luggage.'

'Attracting more attention, eh?' Bobby said as he walked back towards them, lowering himself into his seat.

They walked over to the staff checking passengers' boarding passes clutching onto their hand bags and made themselves known. They both handed over their travel documents.

'Really? No way? You're joking?' said Thalia. Georgia just looked from the stewardess to Thalia and back again, not saying a word.

***

'I am gob-smacked,' said Georgia on the plane. The air steward, took her hand luggage from her and positioned it in the overhead locker. 'I still can't believe this is happening.'

'It had to happen like this,' said Thalia, 'it's my birthday, after all!' she shrieked, handing over her bag and already making herself comfortable in her very wide seat.

'If it's your birthday, ma'am, we will make sure you get an extra special gift,' he said.

'Why thank you, Jake,' said Thalia, reading the name on his badge, 'and my friend too…we can't leave her out, can we?'

'They will not believe it when I tell them back home. It's like a dream come true,' said Georgia, 'I've got a good feeling about this trip. Not that I didn't before. But this is just awesome!'

They both fell about laughing at her very bad American accent. The excitement didn't fade the whole flight.

'Smells gorgeous,' said Georgia, rubbing the Elemis lotion into her hands, 'needed that. My hands are dry today.'

'It's cos you're getting old hun,' said Thalia, 'I'll make you young again on this trip.'

'Shut up, you cow. I'm a mere seven years older than

you. What else is in our 'complimentary amenities bag'?' she said in her dreadful American accent again.

'Anti-wrinkle cream.'

'Love you too.'

'Love you more,' said Thalia, as she squeezed her friend's hand.

***

Before they knew it, they were making their lunch choices. They chose the same starter of Smoked Shetland salmon tartare with pickled cucumber and a radish salad. Georgia selected the roasted corn-fed chicken with summer truffle and wild mushroom sauce, herb mashed potatoes, baby fennel and honey glazed carrots and Thalia dithered before finally opting for the penne pasta with red pepper pesto, basil and chilli sauce, courgette and piquillo peppers.

'We didn't order those,' said Georgia as the steward handed them two sparkling flutes of bubbly pink champagne.

'They are from Bobby with compliments,' Jake said.

'That's it,' said Georgia looking at Thalia, 'The upgrade. It was Bobby. Oh. My. God.'

'Those boobs babe, who can resist?'

Georgia felt her face redden as a slow panic filled her. She wasn't in a position to do anything and she hoped Bobby wasn't expecting anything from her. Her mind raced. Fuck. What a situation to be in. If she had realised sooner, he was behind the upgrade, she wouldn't have accepted. Economy class would have been fine. She forced herself to have the dark chocolate fondant with caramel sauce in front of her, all the while a sickening sensation increased with each swallow.

'You're quiet.'

'I've got my mouth full.'

'Bet Bobby wished it was full with something else!'

'Stop it Thalia. It's not funny anymore. I'm still married for goodness sake.'

'Relax Georgi. He's not going to jump you on the plane is he?'

'That's not the point.'

'I am so full,' said Thalia in her silly American accent again. She stretched her legs, rotating her ankles. She pushed her head back into the memory foam headrest. 'Absolute heaven. It's what we deserve hun.'

'You're right. We do,' said Georgia as she tried to shake Bobby and his possible looming attention away. 'I still can't believe it.'

'I'm telling you. The next few days are going to be incredible. New York here we come!' yelled Thalia, not caring about disturbing the other passengers.

'I'm taking a nap.' Georgia closed her eyes. If she didn't talk she could hide her sudden lack of enthusiasm from Thalia. Georgia didn't want her own mood which had shifted from flirtatious to cautious to dampen

Thalia's.

'I don't think so,' said Thalia, pressing the service button on her arm rest, 'I'm just getting started.'

Georgia had a snooze and an hour before landing Thalia persuaded Jake to allow her into the World Class section of the plane to thank Bobby. Georgia refused to go, asking Thalia to tell Bobby she was sleeping off the champagne.

'He can't argue with that, can he?'

'Bet he does.'

***

They touched down at JFK and collected their luggage within twenty minutes of strolling into the reclaim baggage area. Georgia kept an eye out for Bobby but didn't even glimpse him and with relief they hopped into a yellow cab for the hotel. Cars, trucks and buses raced along the streets, corn yellow cabs, just like in the movies, dotted along the highways and wide streets. The traffic noise and roar of engines came at her from all angles and Georgia slipped another two headache tablets into her mouth taking a swig of the last drop of water in her bottle.

***

At the hotel, an American flag blew in the light breeze above the huge brass-trimmed rotating doors, which sparkled in the mid-day sun. The porters assisted them with their luggage. Their smart uniform with the Radisson Martinique logo, across the front right-hand side of the jacket, stood out against the inky black fabric, in deep contrast to Thalia and Georgia's casual attire.

Behind a high-shine mahogany counter two efficient-looking receptionists checked them in and before they knew it Georgia and Thalia were walking across the marbled lobby, following the porters, who carried their luggage for them. As one of the porters inserted the key card into their bedroom door, he waited for the green indicator to light up and pushed it open with his foot. Thalia swept past him as he lent against the door, holding it open with his back and she flopped, with a ceremonious plop onto the bed's king size mattress which dominated the room.

'Darling, however will I find you in this big bed!' she exclaimed, before she winked at Georgia. The porters had already put the luggage down onto the racks either side of the huge mirrored wardrobe. As they backed out of the room Georgia waved goodbye and thanked them as she tried to stifle her giggles.

'The look on their faces,' said Georgia, as the door closed. 'You really are mad! Happy Birthday honey! May all your wishes come true in New York! This room is fantabulous. Look at the size of the TV screen and that sofa. You sure this isn't a mini suite or something?'

'They like things big in New York.'

Georgia threw herself onto the bed next to Thalia. They both sighed, looked at each other and then rolled around laughing and screaming, 'We're in New York!'

***

Sitting in a Bar and Karaoke Lounge, walking distance from their hotel, the girls toasted their awesome trip with a cocktail each. The atmosphere was one of sophistication. The polished bar gleamed and the mirrors sparkled. Georgia thought the muted lighting just right and she didn't have to fight against any overhead glare. The bar filled by the minute, men in suits, women in high heels and short skirts, men in jeans and shirts. As they chatted, the barmen were busy plunking ice cubes into glasses, un-corking bottles of champagne, refilling the coolers, adding a splash of this and a splash of that to all colours of cocktails.

Both Thalia and Georgia were laughing, excited to be out, and getting looks from all directions, from men and women alike.

'Well, the men want to be with us, instead of their boring wives,' said Thalia.

'And the wives wish they could be having as much fun as us, instead of being with their boring husbands,' said Georgia laughing and then almost choking on the cocktail the barman had recommended. He looked over and smiled at her.

'Well, you should've stuck to the non-alcoholic one you chose first missy,' said Thalia. 'I mean mescal and peppercorn what's-it Cointreau?'

'And Lillet rosé and cilantro,' read Georgia off the cocktail list, pulling a face as she took another sip, still not quite sure of the taste which hit the back of her throat as she swallowed.

'Anyway, cheers honey,' said Thalia, clinking her tall glass of 'Beaten Gypsy' against Georgia's.

'Fuck,' blurted Georgia out of nowhere. 'I think those two are coming over.' No sooner had the words come out of her mouth, Thalia had already responded with a perky 'Hi.'

'Hi,' repeated Georgia, putting out her hand to introduce herself while she tried to re-position herself on the bar stool which, covered in soft Nubuck was rather slippery to sit on. She bit down on her lower lip realising she'd come across a little bit tipsy as she tried again to balance herself on the seat.

'You're from England?' said the taller of the two dark-haired guys, his jeans so tight Georgia was surprised his voice could be that deep.

'Yeah, from London actually,' said Thalia, re-adjusting her posture with her back straight, sitting tall.

'Oh, that's awesome. You don't look British,' chipped in the second guy, his voice smoky, his T-shirt stretched across his tight muscle bound chest.

'We're of Greek origin. Greek Cypriot,' said

Georgia.

'No way. Jeeez. We're Greek too. We live here in Manhattan. Our parents are Greek.'

'Both of you?' said Thalia.

'Yeah. We're brothers. I'm John and this is Panos.'

'I don't believe this,' said Georgia, 'I knew there were lots of Greeks in New York but to meet Greeks...'

'That's got to be a coincidence for a reason,' chimed in Thalia.

'How long are you here for?' said Panos.

'It's our first night,' said Thalia.

'Well, let's make it a first night to remember,' said John, reaching out to stroke Thalia's upper arm. She beamed at him, enjoying the attention. Georgia thought maybe Nicolas was right about Thalia enjoying the limelight. Without warning she thought of him and missed home. She felt a long way away from him and the boys and wondered if they were all okay. She wondered whether allowing Thalia to persuade her to come to New York had been such a good idea.

They ordered more drinks and as they moved to a secluded corner, Georgia leant into Thalia and whispered in her ear, 'What the hell are we doing?'

'Having fun, Georgi...we're not doing anything wrong so just chill,' said Thalia.

A 'reserved' sign perched on the low rattan coffee table surrounded by an emerald green velvet sofa and four tub chairs in a turquoise and cream stripe.

'You must be more than regulars if you have reserved seating,' said Georgia, as she lowered herself into one of the tub chairs, always the observant one.

'Well, we are what you call big in New York.'

'Oh, yeah? How big? What do you guys do?' asked Thalia.

'You know the New York Yankees, right?' said Panos.

'Well, we've heard of them but don't know them,' said Georgia with a sarcastic tone.

'Well, we do all their catering - every game, every function, every event, every PR session.'

'Wow, that's amazing. You must be rolling in it,' said Thalia. Georgia knew the money impressed Thalia.

'Yeah, we live the high life here, don't we bro?' Panos nodded in agreement.

John sat on the couch just big enough for two, his broad shoulders taking up almost half the width of the sofa and chatted to Thalia next to him. A bit too close, Georgia noted. She listened while Thalia told him everything about her separation and how awkward Tony was being, not believing how open Thalia could be with a complete stranger. Panos sat and listened too for a while, sipping his drink straight from the bottle. He made polite small talk with Georgia who chatted without thinking too much, careful not to be drawn into a situation, whatever that might be.

'Yeah, how about we get out of here now. Where do

you two want to go? Anywhere. We'll take you. We have a limousine outside,' said John.

Thalia looked at Georgia. 'Oh, my God!' she screamed. 'It's like Pretty Woman.'

'We can go up west, there's a great Lap Dancing Club.'

'Lap Dancing?' said Georgia.

'No funny business. We'll just have a drink,' said Panos. He seemed to sense her awkwardness, the edge to her voice. Somehow Georgia didn't believe him. He looked almost as nervous as she felt.

'And I'll pay one of the girls to dance for you,' said John, eyeing up Thalia and running his tongue over his lips.

'Let's do it,' said Thalia jumping out of her seat and dancing to the tune being pumped across the bar. 'Whoop!'

'God help me,' said Georgia, but she forced a smile and jumped up too, swaying her hips and waving her arms around in the air to the beat. She wondered where this was going.

'Told you I'd need the high heeled boots,' shouted Thalia, to be heard above the music, as she carried on dancing.

'Go, girl,' said Georgia, smiling, but her mind was full of panic.

***

They sat in the back of the white stretch limousine, quiet at first and Georgia wondering what they were getting themselves into and more importantly if they would manage to get themselves out of it. They both sipped at the bubble pink champagne which had frothed over the edge of the glasses as Panos poured for them and leaned in towards Georgia. 'You deserve to be treated like a lady. Total respect.'

Thalia and Georgia looked at each other, and then both screamed at exactly the same time. 'We love New York!'

'Wow!' John high fived Panos. He looked like he was enjoying himself too, as he sang along to the music. The girls shouted at the tops of their voices as they stood precariously on the back seats, waving from the open sunroof. Georgia laughed as she tried not to slide across the leather seat and into Thalia every time the car turned a corner.

Georgia couldn't quite believe it. It would never have turned out like this in her imagination and although pleased for Thalia, who deserved a birthday to remember, she couldn't help thinking about the boys again, and Nicolas. The boys would have jumped with joy in the limousine, Andoni pretending to be a famous footballer. She flopped down into the luxurious leather seats and grabbed her phone. She had no idea of the time in London but she wanted to let them know she was thinking about them all. She sent a text.

***

The lap dancing club was more like a strip club and Georgia felt uncomfortable although she went along with the evening's entertainment, trying to hide her embarrassment by exaggerating her enjoyment and giving the impression she was tipsier than she actually was. This meant she could laugh and flirt and be a bit silly without coming across too naïve or ill at ease. It meant she could let her barriers down, just a little, and enjoy herself just as much as Thalia appeared to be, even though Georgia wasn't eligible to. It was her way of protecting herself because she wasn't relaxed in the brassy, sweaty-smelling bar; the faded velvet seating and curved wooden tables scattered in no particular order opposite the open stage in front of their seating area.

There were two gleaming chrome poles and Georgia watched a girl, probably no older than twenty, writhing up and down one of them. Her fuck-me-pink leather skirt was the width of a wide belt and her fishnet stockings topped with a row of diamante beads sparkled in the lights flashing pink and white in turn from the other side of the floor. Georgia stared at her high heels and wondered how she could even walk in those let alone dance in them and then remembered she could boogie better in her heels than she could walk, and burst out laughing. She couldn't stop.

'Hey, what's up?' said Panos.

'Nothing, just having a great time. How often do you

come here?' asked Georgia.

'Twice, three times a week,' said Panos, looking apologetic. He gave her a puppy-dog look which reminded her of a picture that used to hang in her *yiayia's* hallway which always made her soppy inside.

'Really? That's a lot. What about work?'

'We check in in the morning and then again in the afternoon. Our management does the rest.'

Panos leaned into the seat and his body slumped against Georgia's side. She felt a bolt of electricity run through her. Fuck she thought. And then he leaned in and kissed her. Not wildly. Not shyly. Panos kissed Georgia on the lips, a slow lingering kiss which passed her lips, his tongue probing hers. She momentarily kissed him back and then coming to her senses pulled away.

'Where did that come from?' asked Georgia, stumbling on her words, the sensation of his kiss still fluttering inside her. She looked over to Thalia who, thank God, appeared oblivious to what had just happened between her and Panos.

Panos laughed, his dark eyes resting on her cleavage. 'Order more drinks for the ladies, John.' Georgia shifted in her seat, sliding over towards the arm where she rested her elbow, her hand hiding her face. But she didn't want to run. Her reaction to the kiss confused her.

John ordered the drinks and signalled to one of the girls draped over a cream leather bar stool to dance for Thalia. Georgia forced a smile. Thalia gave Georgia a strained smile in return. Thalia was not enjoying the obvious attention from the dancing girl as much as Georgia guessed she would. But she noticed Thalia didn't push John away as his fingers brushed up and down one of her legs. Perhaps she's embarrassed thought Georgia as John squeezed her inner thigh as she felt her own cheeks glowing like red embers after Panos's kiss.

Georgia coughed in the direction of Thalia and gave her a look which she ignored. Georgia was in turmoil. Conscious this trip was all about Thalia's thirtieth birthday she didn't want to say or do anything to spoil it. She sat back in her seat and crossed her arms. She knew Nicolas would be furious with her if he knew where she was let alone two random guys had brought her here. She kissed a man she knew nothing about.

But oddly the place excited her, Panos excited her. It reminded her of her uni days where no-one knew her background or her sworn commitment to Nicolas. She could pretend to be an ordinary university student and a single girl out for some fun.

She watched the dancer and could feel Panos's eyes on her. She liked the way that made her insides somersault. Georgia looked over at John who watched the dancer, his eyes bright with desire, with lust. It had been a long time since Nicolas had looked at her like that. Made her believe she was desirable, wanted, sexy.

Her mind wandered back to the days when all they wanted to do was have sex. In bed she could be whoever she wanted to be. She imagined herself thinner, prettier. It was easy to create the perfect fantasy and get lost in it. Her reality was different though. Deep down she wasn't the confident girl everyone saw and she had become a less confident woman with conflicting feelings, views and ideas about who she was and how she should live. In New York, vibrant, bright and loud, Georgia began to question her beliefs and values.

***

The next day after a huge breakfast of waffles with syrup and bacon and a chocolate muffin the size of a birthday cake, Georgia and Thalia took a carriage ride across Central Park. Their slim Philipino tour guide, Edwin, had a crooked smile showing white teeth too big for his mouth and a high-pitched voice. They listened and laughed and giggled marvelling at the sights he pointed out.

Georgia craned her neck to look down the hill at the Wollman Rink and imagined it in a snowy white park with skaters and how the boys would love to skate there. The carriage trundled gently down the path and through a red and white brick archway to a beautiful carousel.

'This is the favourite attraction in the park. It has 57 horses and runs every day in the summer. Tourists with children come here for fun rides,' said Edwin.

Above the thick canopied foliage of the tall trees Edwin pointed excitedly to The Dakota Buildings and specifically to the apartment where Yoko Ono, the wife of John Lennon, now lived. Georgia wondered how she could live there after losing her husband and a wave of sadness washed over her.

'You okay?' asked Thalia, squeezing her hand.

'Yeah. Just thinking how sad she must've been when he died.'

'You soppy thing, you.'

'Now you see the Bethesda Fountain with the Angel of the Waters statue. This is the fountain you see in the American sitcom Friends.'

Georgia clicked away with her camera wanting to catch everything to show the boys and Nicolas. She wondered if Nico missed her.

The temperature dropped and they shopped along Fifth Avenue. Georgia strutted up and down the shop in a pair of high heeled sling back shoes from Guess. She felt sexy in them and threw caution to the wind as she punched in her pin number and smiled at the young model-like girl serving her. In DKNY she bought a blue and silver glass beaded necklace. Thalia bought two tops in a slinky stretch lace fabric; both left nothing to the imagination, one in black and one in red from Armani.

***

The following morning, they took a visit to the top of the Chrysler Building. Georgia looked down on the busy city, cars, people, buses, taxis…dots of every colour moving around frantically like twinkling fairy lights flashing on and off. She thought about how small she felt. How small they all were in this universe. She found the thought overwhelming and wondered what life was all about. Was it about getting things done? Was it about finding love or happiness? Was she happy? Did she really love Nicolas? Did he really love her? He used to…in the beginning. She was sure of it. She remembered the look in his eyes after they made love; glazed over, full of love. What was she doing here? She should be home with her boys, her husband. She brought her fingers up to her lips remembering Panos's kiss. Guilt consumed her. She felt her temperature rise.

'Awesome view,' said a tall American in a baseball cap and white Lacoste polo top next to her.

'Incredible,' Georgia said dreamily.

'Makes you wonder how we can feel so big when actually we are but specs.'

'I know what you mean. I was just thinking the same.'

Thalia nudged her in the ribs. 'Flirting again?'

'Stop it. I was just talking. You know, an intelligent conversation...' Georgia poked her in the ribs with her elbow; they both giggled and moved around to another viewing point but the words of the American played over in her head. Was she now only a small part of Nico's life, his thoughts?

Back on solid ground Thalia pounced on a group of

police officers.

'Come on Georgia. Don't be shy.' Georgia cautiously allowed the stocky blue-eyed police officer closest to her put his arm around her. 'Closer big boys,' urged Thalia. The other three officers crammed in around her as Thalia clicked away and then grabbing a lycra-clad jogger, Thalia jumped in and had her photo taken too. Georgia scooped loose coins from her purse and fed the change into the benevolent association collection tin being shaken by one of the officers as she waved goodbye, Thalia's enthusiasm igniting her own.

'This has turned out to be one of my best birthdays ever. Thanks for sharing hun.' Thalia bit into her Ham & New York Cheddar sandwich at lunch time.

'Wouldn't want it any other way babe,' said Georgia, reaching over to the counter to grab a pile of napkins stamped with the Starbucks logo.

'Shame about the crap at home. Arguments in front of the kids. It's really winding me up.'

'No way, that's so not good babe, for any of you.'

'Tell me about it hun.'

'He's still refusing to move out?' said Georgia.

'Yep, said he won't move out until he's holding the final divorce papers in his hand.'

'Even though he's got his £100,000?'

'It's made no difference,' Thalia said.

'What about the kids?'

'Confused. He's still living with us like we're

together. I'm still cooking, doing his washing, sleeping in the same bed…'

'Why don't you sleep on the couch, or go in with one of the children?' said Georgia, her voice registering dismay.

'Because I can be just as stubborn,' said Thalia, a trace of weariness showing around her eyes, strain colouring her features. The silence sat between them for a few seconds.

'What about your thing with Steve?' said Georgia, changing the subject. Thalia perked up. Steve owned a discount furniture store and had wooed Thalia when she had been looking to buy a new kitchen table a few months before.

Georgia had met Steve a few times and liked his generosity, good looks and charm.

She liked the way he put a smile on her friend's face and his easy-going nature.

'Well…the other day I thought Tony'd seen him leaving the house. He'd delivered the new pine storage chest for me and well…' Thalia stopped, her cheeks reddening, her eyes sparkling just a little too much.

'And what? Oh my God…you didn't end up…no way! Tell me you didn't! I mean tell me you did!'

'I did. We did. It was a fumble and embarrassing but God I was gagging for it hun. It's been seven months!'

'Oh my God! Wow…I can't believe you haven't told me this.'

'I didn't want you thinking badly of me.'

'Never. No way. You're separated. You're free to do what you want, babe.'

'I know, but it's weird.'

'I can't imagine sleeping with anyone else. Nicolas's the only guy I've ever slept with. I don't even know if I kiss properly.'

'Well, I thought that, but you know what, once you're in a situation, you don't think about it.'

'It's alright for you. You're slim. You've got no extra bits. I'd never take my clothes off in front of someone new. Thank God Nicolas and I are back on track.'

'Never say never babe.' Thalia checked her phone.

'No, honestly. We're good.'

'Well stay alert Georgi. Don't let him off the hook that easily,' said Thalia.

'He's made a promise babe. To me and his mum. I'll drive myself crazy wondering all the time. I have to believe him.'

'You won't believe who's just texted me.' Thalia had completely switched off; her focus now on the text message in front of her.

'Who? Not John?'

'Yes, John. He wants to meet up. What shall I say?'

'It's your call, babe, but I haven't come to New York to hang out on my own and he's obviously only after one thing. Look at what happened last night. And what about Steve?'

'Steve's not here. And John's okay. I didn't mind the kiss.'

'It's not the kiss I'm talking about. He was all over you in the club. It was embarrassing.'

'It was dark. No-one could see us.'

'I could.'

'Jealous, were you?'

'Course not, babe. But you don't know him.'

'That's why it's fun. Why I can do stuff I wouldn't normally and not be worried someone will see me and report back to Tony.' Georgia couldn't argue with that and Thalia was unattached now.

'Just be careful. I don't think you should go out on your own with him but if you do go, meet late, in the hotel bar, after eleven when I'm tucked up in bed. And don't you dare bring him back to our room.'

'Okay. Fair enough. We can go out for dinner again tonight and I can meet up with him afterwards if he's up for it.' Thalia texted him straight away.

'Oh, he'll be up for it alright,' said Georgia, 'Just stay in the hotel where I know you'll be safe.'

'He's texted back already. Panos is coming too.'

'No way,' said Georgia, incapable of hiding her surprise and excitement.

'Problem solved. A foursome it is.' said Thalia. Georgia ignored her last comment. 'What'll we wear?'

'We've bought half of Fifth Avenue!'

***

They dragged themselves out of bed, Georgia bouncier than Thalia.

'You shouldn't have drunk so much, Thal. I've got Anadin if you want a couple. You'll feel better after breakfast.'

'I don't care how I feel but look at my eyes. They are so sore and my hair mimics an advert for Best Bed-head 2005.'

'Or best Just Got Fucked the Night Before,' said Georgia.

'That obvious…' said Thalia, perking up.

'Come on, we're going to miss breakfast if you don't stop whining.' Georgia, despite her banter, couldn't accept her friend's behaviour and yet held back saying anything out loud to her. Thalia had actually slept with John; John who she had only just met, Georgia had seen his hands all over her. Then another voice in her head taunted; New York was the city of opportunities, of taking chances. Georgia knew that. She had watched enough films. But to be here and breathe in the air of freedom around her was just too much when she was unsure of her own situation and emotions. She had to stay grounded, forget Panos's kiss and his advances last night. Thalia seemed to float further away from reality like a helium balloon in never ending blueness but Georgia had to stay grounded.

'Yes Miss. It was worth it though, wasn't it?'

'I'm sure it was for you,' said Georgia, and then regretting her words, she added, 'Yeah, it was. Panos was charming. He's lovely to talk to. Really sensitive and he really listened to me.'

'Yeah, course. He didn't take his eyes off your boobs, that's why. At one point I thought if he stares any harder he'll give himself a hard-on. Honestly hun, he's definitely a boob man.'

'Stop it. I can't help it if he was looking. I certainly didn't encourage him.'

'No you didn't, but your low cut top did,' Thalia said, laughing, and then holding onto the side of her head, 'it hurts.'

'Not my fault then.' Georgia chuckled quietly and handed Thalia the fob of tablets, her mind glazing over with the heady sensations she felt as Panos had kissed her with a passion and urgency she hadn't felt from Nicolas in a long time. Panos was sure of himself. Did the money and status make him come across like that? What was wrong with her? This wasn't real. She had to snap out of it.

***

At Ground Zero, Georgia cried and then felt guilty because she realised she sobbed for herself and for Thalia more than for those who had lost their lives. Georgia stood there amongst the throng of people, mainly tourists, dishevelled. The still derelict expanse stretched in front of her beyond the wire fence, the air heavy with the smell of death even after nearly three years since the destruction of the Twin Towers.

Georgia's thoughts drifted off to Nicolas and their marriage. It was a good marriage. He might be demanding and brusque but he had high expectations and to be honest his expectations were no higher than what she demanded of herself. She wanted to be the perfect wife and mother and for the main, enjoyed the roles. She loved Nicolas but something kept niggling at her. What if their adoration had reached its expiry date? What if all love comes to a natural end and theirs was nearing? She knew however difficult it might be she would have to accept it. Perhaps that's why the kiss with Panos felt so good.

She had been with Nicolas for twenty-two years. Who was she to stop him from finding passion, if that's what it was, with somebody else? Or her with someone new? She vowed to talk to him when she got back home. She needed to know he wanted to be with her and wasn't just staying because it was the right thing to do. Because his mother had made him stay. There was always a choice even if it was a hard one.

***

For the rest of the two days both Georgia reverted to being

her younger self and flirted unashamedly with every man she came across, from the lift attendants in the hotel and in Bloomingdales and Macy's to waiters in cupcake cafés and Mexican restaurants and shiny New York bars. She liked being away from her family and community in London; the taste of freedom gave her an edge of daring, of pushing her boundaries away from her usual comfort zones.

Georgia and Thalia dallied with shop assistants and taxi drivers and chatted to cashiers, bus drivers and bank tellers. They ate whatever they wanted, Tennessee whisky marinated ribs, giant burgers, Mexican fajitas, Waldorf salads, fries and deep fried onion rings the size of basketball hoops. On their last evening, Thalia fobbed off John and Panos' offer of clubbing, wanting to avoid anything heavy. Georgia relieved, didn't say so to Thalia. Lying in bed, knackered and not even being bothered to take her make-up off, Georgia listened to Thalia nattering on.

'I've had the time of my life. John's gorgeous. And loaded.'

'He is, babe,' responded Georgia, already half asleep.

'And Panos really liked you. John said so.'

'And I've got a husband back at home. I have behaved impeccably, unlike you.'

'Impeccably misbehaved.' Thalia yawned, pulled the sheet over her head and fell asleep.

Georgia felt the palpitations in her chest, tasting

Panos's lingering kiss on her lips.

***

The flight home wasn't as exciting as the flight out or the time they had in New York. Although cramped into economy seats, tired and going back to the hum-drum of life in London, Georgia looked forward to being with the boys and to seeing Nicolas again, although with trepidation.

'I've got to admit, I've missed the boys,' said Georgia.

'Well, I've not missed mine. They've been so demanding since we announced the split. They're rude, they're arguing with each other, with me,' said Thalia.

'Well, they don't understand what's going on, hun. They're only kids. Don't be so hard on them. It's not their fault their dad is a grade A arsehole,' said Georgia.

'I want to be in New York. I want to do it all again.'

'Get real, babe. We're going home. Nothing you can do will change that.'

'But I can dream, can't I?' said Thalia.

'We can all dream,' said Georgia, smiling.

Chapter Eight

GEORGIA HAD ALREADY been back almost two weeks and enjoyed spending a few days with the boys. However, she still hadn't plucked up the courage to broach the subject of love and Roksana and Nicolas.

'Do you think that's what's happened to us?' she asked, as she watched an episode of Eastenders with Nicolas.

'What?'

'You know that we've reached the expiry date for the love we have for each other?' Georgia looked toward Nicolas, waiting, her heart in her mouth.

'What d'you mean?'

'Look, if you think you love Roksana and you think you'll be happier with her than with me then go. I love you too much to force you to stay with me if it's where you want to be,' she said. Nicolas looked over at her, incredulity all over his face.

'It's not like that. I love you Georgia. But I think I love her too. I'm confused. But I promise I haven't done anything with her. We just talk.'

'Why don't you talk to me? We used to talk all the time, d'you remember? We used to lie in bed and talk for hours before the kids…making plans…' she said, tears welling up in her eyes.

'Don't cry. For God's sake, I'm not going anywhere.'

His brash attitude riled her and she thought of Panos and his kind eyes, lingering kiss, his hands on her skin as he stroked her neck.

***

'You're glowing,' said Katia when they all met up for lunch at their parents' one Sunday in June. 'And you've lost weight.'

'Well, I've been carrying all that extra weight around since having the boys so it's about time,' said Georgia. The truth was her lack of guilt over kissing Panos addled her and it was this unfamiliar feeling which dampened her appetite as opposed to an effort to lose weight. She knew she wouldn't tell Nicolas about the kiss but at the same time agonised over it.

'And your bum looks sex-ee in those jeans,' said Katia, pulling on her dark hair tied in a high pony tail. 'You don't normally wear fitted stuff.'

'Got them in the sale at Zara. The lady at the changing rooms said they suited me and convinced me to buy them.'

'Good for you.'

'Well, with my own money now, not that it mattered before, the joint account was exactly that, but I'm buying clothes for work so feel better spending my own cash. I got this really gorgeous shirt with pearl buttons from Banana Republic and a peplum pleat top.'

'I bet that really shows off your curves,' said Katia.

'It fits really well with this pencil skirt I got in like an inky blue colour. Finishes at the knee about here,' Georgia used her hand to indicate the length of the skirt.

'That's a good length on you, darling,' chipped in her mum from the kitchen sink, where she was washing apples and nectarines for dessert, 'reveals your shapely calves and slim ankles.' As opposed to my not-so-pretty face thought Georgia and for a moment she annoyed herself for spoiling the happy moment.

'As opposed to my fat belly and fat arms?'

'Of course not. You're lovely darling.'

***

At work, she became a different person; confident, professional, capable. Every day she left 'mum' and 'wife' at home and it felt good putting on the persona of Music Secretary.

'Good morning, Georgia.'

'Good morning, Liam. How are you?'

'Good thanks. You?'

'Fine thank you. It's not very nice out there,' she said, shaking the muggy summer drizzle out of her hair.

'But lovely in here,' said James, one of the peripatetics.

Georgia laughed, half embarrassed and half pleased she was appreciated.

'Stop it, James,' she said.

'Nothing wrong with showing our appreciation and support for all your hard work and loveliness. Is there, Liam?'

'Certainly not.' Liam, smiled at her with a 'we just have to put up with him' look.

'When you've got a moment I'll show you the plan I've been working on for the Musical Brass Band and String Quartet Soiree,' said Georgia to Liam.

'Already? For November? That's very efficient of you. Well done,' he said, looking over her shoulder at the word documents on the screen, as Georgia scrolled down through them.

'Well, I thought if we plan ahead we can perhaps charge for the tickets and include a welcome drink and nibbles on the tables. That way we can make it a more formal occasion and attract more of the parents, Governors, maybe even the Mayor of Barnet and other big wigs from the local community.'

'Genius. I think it's a brilliant idea. What would I do without you?'

'Plan a very ordinary soiree?' she said, smiling.

'Not anymore. I am absolutely thrilled with what you've proposed. Do you have any figures?'

'Yep. They're all here. Three columns. Food and drink from Costco, Waitrose and a private caterer. Figures based on fifty, eighty and a hundred guests. And I have already spoken to the caretakers about setting up, room plan and timings.'

'I don't know what to say.'

'Just say thank you and tell me I can join you on the night,' she said being cheeky.

'Of course you can. You've got to be there after all the thought and planning you've put into it already, with pay of course.'

'In that case I'll be there. As long as hubby is okay to look after the boys. Thank you, Liam,' said Georgia.

***

She continued to flourish in her job noticing Liam, always thanking her for something or other, spent more time in the music office and less time in his own office, at the other end of the Music Block. Georgia didn't mind at all at first and looked forward to their quiet chats. But when she began to notice Liam instigated situations so they could be alone she wondered whether he was making a move on her. Part of her was flattered but the other part was tormented not wishing to complicate her life any further. Thankfully, since her heart-to-heart with Nicolas things at home flowed beautifully although she could understand how working with Roksana all day, every day would put temptation in Nico's way. After all she was younger than Georgia and perhaps she was like this with Nico. But for Georgia, although flattered the men at work wanted to be around her, she knew she would be true to her marriage vows, to her commitment to her husband and her children.

To this end Georgia pulled away from Liam making excuses not to be alone with him when he approached her with a proposal or other to discuss together in his office. She didn't want to offend him and yet remained conscious at the same time of not giving him any messages that could be misconstrued as interest in him.

***

'The boys are going to grow up and one day the boys won't need me so much anymore,' Georgia confided to Jessica, another of the peripatetics. The stuffy summer months had come and gone and the term edged towards the end of the academic year. Georgia wanted to do more with her life.

'I know what you mean…you don't want to be one of those lost souls, stuck at home, with an empty house and too much time to fill.' Jessica was nearing retirement age, tall, slim with strawberry blonde hair, heavily streaked with the silver grey which comes with aging. She always wore her flat red lace-up shoes with long flowing patterned skirts and cardigans she knitted herself from odd balls of wool she picked up in charity shops. She was like a walking multi-coloured dream coat and on this dark cold afternoon in early October she brought colour and joy to an otherwise bleak day.

'I know. And this might be pie in the sky but I've been secretly wondering if I could train as a teacher. I haven't said anything to anyone.' Georgia took the mug of tea Jessica had just brewed for her and cupped her hands around the mug of tea in an effort to warm up.

'Well why not?'

'I don't know really. I don't know anything about what I need to do or how long it would take.'

'I have a friend of a friend who's one of the admissions officers at Middlesex Uni. I'll find out a bit more about the PGCE for you.'

'PGCE?' asked Georgia.

'Post Graduate Certificate in Education. I think it's a one-year course, a fast track programme into teaching,' said Jessica as she swallowed the last of her coffee in one gulp.'

'Oh Jessica you're so kind. Would you really do that for me? Thank you,' said Georgia, already half-nervous, half-excited at the prospect of becoming a teacher. Since taking on the job something had ignited within her. She loved the boys but wanted more for herself. Domesticity suited her for a long time but she now gravitated towards professional achievement once again. She wanted to feed her mind and her soul.

***

Boys tucked up in bed, the flames from the open grate

cast amber and orange spice shadows across the room and the radiator pipes clanged as the central heating kicked in. Georgia broached the subject with Nicolas.

'A teacher?' he asked, taking a gulp of tea and pulling a face as it burnt the roof of his mouth.

'Yes, a teacher. Secondary school. Probably teaching business studies although I haven't properly looked into it. Jessica, one of the music teachers, is going to ask someone she knows for me.'

'Business studies?'

'Well it's the closest subject to what I did at uni. You know, the business side of Hotel and Catering. Business was a big part of the whole degree.'

'It's up to you. That's a lot to take on. But yeah, good for you.' Nicolas sprawled out in his armchair and, turning to watch the news, he glanced down at his buzzing mobile phone.

'Who's that?'

'No-one. Just one of those random Vodafone texts,' he said, looking back at the TV too quickly, his face flushed crimson.

'So you think it's a good idea?' asked Georgia, relieved the conversation she had dreaded appeared to be moving in her favour.

'Your choice, but yeah. You'd make a great teacher,' he said, looking down at his phone. 'When would you start the training?'

'Next September I'm guessing, so there's lots of time

to think about it.'

'Well, at least you'd earn decent money,' he said, reaching for his phone again.

Georgia didn't reply or ask about the text again but she felt a spiralling disappointment building up in her heart. A dull cramping sensation in her stomach dampened the earlier excitement she'd felt talking about becoming a teacher.

***

At work, Georgia received advance reservations for 87 tickets for the musical soiree and on the day of the event she took a number of calls for last minute reservations which brought the total to 98.

Once the caretakers had set up the room as per her room plan she spent most of her day setting up the tables and decorations in the hall with a handful of sixth formers. She made sure the table nearest the stage reserved for key staff and guests; the head teacher, Liam, three school governors and the Mayor of Barnet whose promised attendance she was secretly chuffed about.

'Everything is in place. Double and triple checked,' she said.

'Caterers?' asked Liam.

'Delivering food at 6.30pm so I will be here to meet them.'

'Wow! You've thought of everything. Thank you.'

'Of course. See you tonight.'

***

Georgia knew the soiree was a great success. Liam publicly thanked her at the end of the evening. She curtsied enjoying the applause from the parents and the students on stage as she stood next to him looking out at the sea of smiling faces. She walked back to her seat hitching up her floor length skirt, the periwinkle fabric giving off a soft sheen in the light of the spot lights. She suddenly felt she was where she should be and feeling Liam's eyes on her she looked across at him and smiled.

She bid everyone goodnight, overwhelmed by the number of compliments and thanks she received. She waited until the last guests and all the performing students left and turned to James who gave her a huge hug and kiss on the cheek. As she pulled back from him her cap sleeve fell loosely down over her arm, pulling her bra strap with it. James very gently pushed the strap back up sending goosebumps through her.

'Amazing night. Amazing you,' he said.

'Georgia tonight was incredible and the Press being here was just so unexpected,' said Liam coming up behind James.

'Well, I kept that detail back just in case they didn't show at the last minute but yeah them being here was amazing.' Georgia smiled and as Liam bent in to hug her their noses bumped and he clumsily brushed his lips against the side of hers. The attention Georgia got made her realise she made a difference at work; she was capable of so much more and her confidence had grown and with it the empowerment it gave her.

***

Christmas overflowed with family time and catching up with the boys' friends, play dates and meet ups. The house became a toy shop with all the action figures, board games and science kits the boys got for Christmas and Georgia did as little tidying as possible wanting the boys to enjoy the freedom of no routine. Nicolas closed the café for a few days and they spent time together.

They had an early lunch at their local Chinese restaurant two days before Christmas Eve and took the boys to The Chronicles of Narnia late afternoon. Georgia enjoyed having Nicolas around. He relaxed not having to rush around and he looked happy to be at home with Georgia, closer to her somehow. Georgia missed working but relished the time she had to be with her family and the boys and enjoyed the attention Nicolas gave her; the compliments, the morning kisses, the love-making in the middle of the night, she, careful not to wake the boys and Nicolas not caring.

Chapter Nine

THE FIRST WEEK after the Christmas holidays, Jessica bounced into the music office proffering a glossy, but rather dog-eared brochure into Georgia's hands. 'It's the PGCE courses prospectus. My friend has even found out the name of who you need to speak to. The Course Leader for Business is a man called Slav Pou-na-no-va,' she read from the booklet. 'She said he's really amenable. He's already said to contact him for any further information. His extension number is scribbled on the back here.' Jessica pointed to the back of the prospectus.

'Oh, Jessica, thank you, really. I think I'm going to do this. I will call him today. No point in wasting time.'

'Call who?' said Liam, as he walked in, catching them mid-way through their conversation.

'I'm thinking about training to be a teacher at Middlesex Uni. What do you think?' said Georgia.

'She'd be great, wouldn't she?' said Jessica.

'Undoubtedly. But we'd miss you around here.'

'Well, it's not definite and I haven't even applied or had an interview yet.'

'When does the course start?'

'September I'm guessing. But as soon as I know for definite, I will give as much notice as I can. I won't leave you in the lurch,' she said, embarrassed at him finding out her plans like this, with no pre-amble or formal discussion.

'That's not the issue,' he said, looking a bit disappointed, and then quickly added, 'You'll blow them away.'

'Who's Georgia blowing away this time?' James walked in and went straight over to the kettle.

'The admissions board at Middlesex,' said Liam.

'Oh?'

'I'm thinking of applying for a teacher training course.'

James didn't have to say anything. A disappointed expression clouded his face.

'She might not be with us after the summer,' said Liam.

***

The grounds of Queen Elizabeth's froze and January's dipping temperatures made everything hoary like winter in an old Christmas movie. She uploaded her application on line, sent off the fee and prepared for her interview. She planned her ten-minute lesson on Price, Product, Place and Promotion; the key elements of the marketing mix with the help of one of the business teachers.

Tuesday 18th February 2006 came around quickly. She felt nervous. On the morning of her interview her mobile phone didn't stop burring, alerting her of incoming text messages from friends and family, wishing her luck. Even Nicolas called her as she arrived at Middlesex University's Trent Park Campus just after 8.30am.

'Good luck, Georgi,' he said.

***

Georgia zigzagged her way back to the visitors' car park, avoiding the puddles lurking in the potholes along the muddy path. She shielded her eyes from the sudden burst of sunlight dappling through the trees bowering the waterlogged pathway, her head aching from the stress of getting through the day.

'They didn't like me.'

'You're winding me up,' said Nicolas.

'No, they said I was too old,' she said in a subdued voice.

'Bastards!'

'Only joking, the leader of the course loved me. He said it was great being a mature candidate with children of my own. He liked the fact I'd worked in industry too. He said it gave me a 'rounded' experience which 'undoubtedly' would make a marked difference in my, quote 'attitude, commitment and success'. I'm in!'

'I knew it. One thing I can say is you're clever. Congratulations Miss. Let's see how you cope with it all.' She ignored his last comment. Nothing would dampen her excitement.

***

Overjoyed, every morning, Georgia's candescent face looked back at her in the mirror. A 'new' helpful, unselfish Nicolas emerged and she welcomed his support unquestioningly as he offered to do all kinds of chores for her and share the running around after the boys too.

When invited out with the music staff at work he willingly said, 'Go. Have fun. You deserve it.' Great on the face of it, she realised much later it was so she wouldn't complain at the frequency of his tardiness. Focusing on her new planned career meant she had been increasingly preoccupied but then she began to grow wary although she didn't want to face up to her niggling thoughts. She didn't question him at first. She didn't antagonise him by asking questions. Then, one night, she couldn't ignore the constant burr of his mobile and the complicitous whispering on the phone. She shied away from confronting him. She needed evidence, something concrete to fight with. She would bide her time and if anything was not right she had to rely on God to help her find a way out of whatever this turned out to be.

***

After one such call in April, convinced of his hushed conversation with Roksana, Georgia planned what to do. She would have to catch them out somehow. She worked out they often went to the local shopping centre in High Barnet having heard snippets of Nicolas's exchanges. She negotiated an early finish from work one afternoon and she made her way up there, certain she would catch sight of Roksana there. She would catch them out for sure. Yet she hoped with all her heart and all her might she would be wrong. That she would glimpse her there with someone else. All the way there her head felt fuzzy with a debilitating anticipation of fear and anxiety.

She headed off to the Spires, a tiny shopping centre with a Waitrose, a Carphone Warehouse, a couple of coffee shops, a pizza place and a WHSmith. Always quiet and it offered a convenient run-in for mid-week shopping items like bread and milk and the odd hostess thank you gift if invited to a dinner party. Today she embarked on a different mission.

She hurried across the concourse, towards the coffee shop; tables spilled onto the main concourse. All the while Georgia looked around her, alert, like a leopard waiting for its prey. She stopped momentarily. Was that her just ahead? She picked up her pace and pushed past an elderly gentleman ambling in front of her. It wasn't her. She breathed a sigh of relief. But it was short-lived and a gasp choked her as she recognised a voice.

Her heart thumping, her hands sweaty, she looked over slowly expecting to witness Roksana with Nicolas but she spied her there alone talking loudly into her mobile. Roksana stood directly in front of Georgia, her back turned to her, not even three feet away. She's on her own, thank God, he's not there, Nicolas's not there. The relief almost stifled her.

But Roksana turned, her face lit up. Looking in the same direction Georgia saw him, his mobile to his ear, one arm stretched out in front of him to take Roksana's hand.

Georgia blanched, edged back, just a few inches and froze, wide-eyed, the diorama unfolding. She stood listening carefully yet barely taking in the scene in front of her. It wasn't real, was it? She was swiftly shaken out of her reverie conscious people walking past her would notice her eavesdropping. She sat heavily onto a metal chair outside the coffee shop. Georgia wanted to say something, to shout, to scratch her face, to scratch his face. She instantly felt nauseous, the taste from the garlic bread at lunch smothering her sense of smell. She almost vomited, but instead gagged horribly. The dull ache in her abdomen turned into a stabbing pain.

Bleary-eyed she got up and ran back to the car, her sprint ungainly, almost knocking an old lady over as she went crashing past her. She then tripped over the front wheel of a buggy and stumbled into one of the mobile phone 'pop-up stalls' positioned in the middle of the concourse. Her breathing came in short sharp gasps, she was hot, sweating. Her mind fogged over and her head felt heavy. If she hadn't witnessed it with her own eyes she would never have believed or imagined this. Not this.

Not ever. A different sensation bubbled within her and she let it grow, pushing up towards the top of her skin until she thought it would blister.

***

In the car, her heart pounded in her chest. Georgia let out a scream. It left her lips and filled every inch of space inside the car. She felt detached from it. But she knew it came from her. She brushed her hair away from her face, her hands clammy, shaking. She allowed the tears to come hard and fast, drip down the front of her jacket and into her lap.

She sat in the car her scream still ringing in her ears for what seemed like forever. Time had stood still. And then she telephoned her mum.

'Mum?'

'Hello darling…what's wrong?' she asked detecting the whimper in Georgia's voice.

'I've just seen Nicolas with her. With that bloody waitress who works for him!'

'Oh Georgia. No! Oh darling I'm so sorry. I'm going to kill him. I'm going to absolutely kill him!' ranted her mum.

'Not before me!'

'What do you want me to do Georgi darling? Tell me. Anything at all.'

'Can I bring the boys over after school. I need to have

it out with him. Tonight.'

'Of course. There's plenty of food. See you soon darling.'

'Thanks Mum. Love you.'

'And I love you more than you'll ever know,' her mum said, the squeak in her voice giving away to tears.

***

Georgia collected the boys from school and as they walked to the car she took a deep breath, only just trusting herself to speak without crying.

'You are going to stay at *yiayia's* house tonight. She's making *kiofdethes* for you, baby meatballs, just how you like them and *bapou* said he has got you the biggest pot of houmous ever.'

'*Kiofdethes*?' said Andoni.

'Yes, your favourite.'

'Are you coming?' said Zach.

'What about our pyjamas and toothbrushes?' asked Andoni.

'All packed for you and ready. I've got everything in the boot.'

'And my *oushi*?' asked Kristiano, who wouldn't sleep without holding tightly onto his baby blanket, which his *yiayia* had knitted for him when he was born, nearly five years ago.

'And your *oushi*.' Georgia's voice quivered slightly

as the rawness of what she had witnessed and heard earlier echoed in her mind.

'*Mamma*, are you coming?' asked Zach again.

'Maybe later, darling. I just have a few boring things to do at home,' Georgia said, straining to smile as naturally as possible, the boys oblivious to the undercurrents, 'and *yiayia* and *bapou* have really missed you. I've put the Toy Story in the bag, so you can all snuggle up and watch it after dinner, if you're good for *yiayia*.'

'What about my nintendo DS?' asked Andoni.

'In the bag, too, honey.'

***

Georgia couldn't relax. She took a shower. She tied her hair into a loose top knot and then un-tied it. She put in two grips to hold her hair away from her face and then took them out again. She made a mug of tea and left it sitting on the kitchen table while she made the boys' beds; her brew an insipid mud when she returned.

Eventually, in the sitting room Georgia snuggled in front of the TV, not really watching anything but needing a distraction from her thumping headache. She waited for Nicolas to come home. She flicked through her Country Living magazine and skimmed through a short article on coastal erosion and another one, mainly pictures of the lush green countryside on a Cumbrian farmhouse refurbishment. She lacked concentration and the words began to swim in front of her eyes, her headache getting worse. All the while she wondered how to confront Nicolas. Should she ask him straight out? Should she tease a confession out of him? Was she ready to face the truth? The truth had presented itself to her that day but like a scene from a drama on television; unreal.

She heard his car pull up on the drive and the key as he jiggled it in the lock. He poked his head into the sitting room as he toed off his trainers and abandoned them by the doorway. He then quickly disappeared upstairs to get showered and changed like he always did.

***

'I saw you today,' she casually said as he sauntered into the sitting room. She stopped her thunderous mood filling every inch of her from spilling into her voice.

'Oh yeah? Did you drive past the café?' His face blanched.

'No.' She waited for a response. It didn't come, so she carried on, enjoying herself as she toyed with him, like a kitten with a ball of wool.

'Guess who else I saw today.'

'Who?'

'You'll never guess,' she continued, prolonging her announcement, which took every bit of control she could muster.

'Where are the boys?'

'They're having dinner and staying at my mum and dad's tonight.'

'Since when?'

'Since I realised you really are the biggest liar, the biggest cheat going!'

Nicolas looked at her, dumbfounded, his face reddening, his hand reaching across to touch his sweating forehead. 'What?'

'You heard. I saw her today and you! Together! And either she's been taking advantage of the free food she gets working at the café, because she looked like a fucking fat whale, or she's pregnant!' Georgia spat the words out and jumped up from the sofa. She charged towards him her fists screwed up tightly. She hammered them down on to his chest, face, head. She didn't care whether she hurt him or scratched his eyes out or battered him.

'You've got it wrong,' he managed to say, deflecting her punches, which eventually subsided, as she lost her strength and gave way to impotent tears.

'Don't you dare lie to me again. Don't you fucking dare! It all makes sense now. You being so helpful and amenable. You just wanted time with her!' Tears rolled down her face.

'It's not mine. I promise you.' Georgia took in the dull flush creeping up his neck to his face. She knew he was lying.

'I heard her on the phone. Yeah, in her stupid Romanian accent. 'O-K Nico. I will be careful. I know. I know. Yes. Yes. I wait.' Why would she be talking to you in the middle of the day when she should've been working at the café and clearly wasn't?'

'She felt unwell.'

'But well enough to go to Barnet and traipse around the shops!'

'That's her choice. I didn't know where she was.'

'She was talking to you! On the phone. Then you were there. I saw you!

'I…I…' He tried to arrange his features into a confident expression. He stroked his chin, etched with a few days' worth of stubble. He sat in his armchair and then stood up again.

'You know damn well the baby's yours and if it's not yours, why the hell have you not mentioned she's pregnant. In all these months you've not said a word!'

'It didn't come up in conversation. She didn't want people knowing.'

'Why not?'

'Because she's not with her boyfriend anymore and she doesn't want him knowing.'

'Rubbish! It's you who didn't want anyone to know. I've been so stupid but not anymore. You can pack your stuff and get out.'

'Come on, it's not like that. I promise,' begged Nicolas, panic settling across his eyes as he avoided looking at her.

'You bastard. How could you do that to me? To the boys? You've lied over and over again to your mum, to my parents. You have no respect.' Tears streamed down her face.

'Look…'

'While the boys are still at school one day this week, you come in and take whatever you want to take. By the end of the week I want you out of my house,' said Georgia, sobbing loudly, 'how could you do that to me?' she said again her voice burning with hurt. She wiped her constantly running nose with the back of her hand, the tears making a wet soggy patch on the front of her blouse. 'I have loved you with all my heart! I gave everything to you. You stupid, stupid man.'

'Look, it doesn't have to be like this. She can go back to Romania. We can keep the baby and bring it up as our own. It's a girl. You've always wanted a girl,' he said, crying now too.

'You are unbelievable. You said it wasn't yours!'

'I…It's…' struggled Nicolas.

'You think I'm desperate for a girl. Have so little self-respect I'd take her baby and bring it up as my own?'

'Why not? We could do it. I know I could persuade her to go back,' he said, running away with the idea. 'You're a good mum. A daughter would complete our family.'

'You're a monster! You'd take her baby from her and

send her back to Romania? You're inhuman. You've no feelings. I don't know who you are any more.' She couldn't believe how he could be so disingenuous. 'You're mad! You think I'd destroy the boys' lives to save you?'

'Think about it, please,' he begged, 'I've made a mistake. I felt sorry for her. I love you.' But Georgia, so distraught, couldn't tell whether his words were truly genuine or just plain facetious.

'You are selfish and manipulative and I feel sorry for her. But you both deserve each other!' She grabbed her mobile phone from the coffee table and dialled.

'Who are you calling?'

'Roksana? It's Georgia here. You know, Nicolas's wife. You know Nicolas don't you? Your boss, my husband, your lover! Well he's all yours and good luck, cos you're going to need it!' Georgia ended the call. She grabbed a cushion and held it tightly across her front, her body scrunched in pain. Her sobbing sounded alien to her; coming from a desperately sad soul. Nico stood there. Still. Rooted to the rug as if he'd trodden in a gooey mess. Eventually Georgia's sobs quietened. 'I meant what I said. I want you out by the end of the week.'

'No you don't. You love me. Think about the boys.'

'The boys? The boys! That's rich. Thinking about the boys now. The boys will stay with me, their mum, and I will adore them and cherish them and do everything I can to bring them up to be men who respect women, their wives and their marriage vows. They will grow up to be the opposite of you!'

'Where will I go?'

'That's your problem…don't you dare guilt trip me!' she screamed, before breaking down again, allowing the tears and the anguish of the past few months to flood through her. Georgia knew how undignified she must've looked but she didn't care. She wondered how she would tell the boys. She imagined their little faces in front of her and little pieces of her heart broke away bit by bit. She knew the absence of their dad would be raw and painful and every beat of her aching heart now sang in a lower key.

'Look Georgia, I love you,' he said and without warning, Georgia saw an agonising look cross his face for the first time and he looked tired, his forehead streaked with frown lines.

'And I love you. But this isn't love anymore. I deserve more. I deserve better than you,' she said as she drowned in her own heartache.

'Give me another chance,' he said and instinctively held out his hand to her.

'No…it's over…you've ruined everything!'

'Look if we love each other we can get through this.'

'It's too late. I'm sorry. Sorry for all of it.'

'Please Georgia,' he beseeched, 'let's not throw all this away,' gesturing around the room, a melancholic expression on his face.

'You're the one who's done that. You. Not me.'

'Where will I go?'

'I don't know. I don't care! Just get away from me. I loved you with all my heart. I can't believe you've done this.' She stormed out of the room and up the stairs. She slammed the bedroom door, the force sending her wedding photograph on the wall next to a framed one of the three boys in Florida, crashing to the wooden floor. The Venetian frame splintered instantly, minute stalactites of glass everywhere, broken like her marriage.

She fell asleep with the shadow of Nicolas's sleeping head imprinted on the empty pillow next to her.

***

'No, Mum why? Where are you going Dad? Why can't you just stay together? What about us? Where will we live?' The questions came at her from all directions as the boys huddled on her double bed as she sat upright against the brass bedstead.

'I don't have all the answers my darlings. It's complicated. But for now you have to believe me when I say I really love you, we both do, all of you with all our hearts and this will not be horrid. You will see Dad all the time and…' her voice trailed off as she couldn't utter the words forming in her head and her heart struggled to accept.

'What about football on Sundays?' Andoni had tears

in his eyes.

'Dad can still pick you up and take you. That won't change. I promise.'

'And summer holidays?' asked Zach.

'We can take it in turns and you might even get two holidays a year. How's that for something to look forward to?'

The boys continued firing questions simultaneously and she felt bombarded and out of her depth, her insides felt bruised, unexplained guilt consuming her. How could she answer them honestly? How could she tell three boys of eleven, eight and seven their dad had been having an affair? They wouldn't understand. And so she just cried with them and held them. Zach looped his arms around Georgia's neck and sobbed into her shoulder; his body rigid at first, and then as she cradled him, she felt him go limp on her, shrinking into his little eight-year-old body. Kristiano stared from Georgia and back to Nicolas again.

'I don't want you to worry. It's going to be alright. Nothing will change apart from Dad won't be living here. You can still see him all the time.' She hugged Andoni, her hands rubbing his back gently as he bravely fought his tears.

***

Nicolas seized any opportunity he could, coming back to the house, to try and persuade Georgia not to split their family. She saw how the weight of his mistake, the affair, weighed down on him and he cried, brushing the tears on his cheeks away brusquely; his eyes rimmed with dark circles looked haunted. Guilt does that to you thought Georgia. It sucks the life out of you. Part of her, her heart, wanted to reach in and take away the hurt, but her head told her to let him go and so she cried herself to sleep almost every night, aware of the heavy guilt surrounding her decision, their lives changed forever.

The day she heard about Nicolas's baby being born she was at home with a migraine. The news couldn't have come at a worse time. She closed her eyes, curled up in the darkness of her room, and cried. She cried tears of regret, tears of shame, tears of humiliation. Nicolas had the one thing she had always wanted with him. A daughter. And as if nothing could make her feel any worse she heard they had chosen the name Helena for her. She had always wanted the name Helena Evangeline if she had a daughter. And now he had not only taken that chance away from her, he picked at her badly healed scars causing her to bleed again.

But Georgia didn't talk about the baby girl or her torn dreams or her shattered heart, each broken piece now smashed into a thousand pieces again. She held it all inside and on the outside carried on the only way she could. She focused on the boys and her studying; she put everything into it, every last ounce of energy.

**

Saying her goodbyes at Queen Elizabeth's was another emotional and traumatic ordeal but deep down she knew the timing of her departure couldn't have come at a more apt time.

Even on her last day Liam's attention played havoc with her emotions and even more so since her marriage had broken down although she hadn't told him or anyone at work. Her personal life and work life were strictly separate. Georgia didn't want the lines between home and work to become blurred. She remained professional and dedicated.

Liam made a lovely speech in the office, all the peripatetics and a couple of the staff from the administration office gathered into the small space and they handed gifts of chocolates and flowers and many cards as well wishes passed her way.

'If you need anything let me know Georgia. I'd be glad to help.'

'Thanks Liam I will.'

'You've been amazing and I'm…we're all going to miss you.'

Georgia could have succumbed to him guilt-free; he was an attractive man and she liked the effect she clearly had on him, she saw the longing in his eyes and the way he stuttered and jumbled his words. But she held onto her resolve deep down knowing she wouldn't cross the line; she wouldn't even call him and as he hugged her goodbye she knew why. It was because she still loved Nicolas in spite of everything, her heart aching from longing and from being broken.

James helped her carry all the presents and her personal belongings from her desk to her car and after a hug and more tears she drove home exhausted, emotionally spent.

Chapter Ten

DURING THE NEXT nine months, the PGCE course took up every waking moment outside of caring for the boys. Georgia, with the help of her mum, juggled their care and well-being, studying and holding everything together.

Her life went by in a blur, and with not enough hours in the day she found herself studying late into the night more frequently as the course progressed.

Georgia benefited from one of the most positive aspects of the training being that she had the same holiday and half term times as the boys; keeping things going for them as normally as possible her priority. She also made every effort to ensure they didn't feel excluded from this new part of her life and often practiced her lessons in front of them as well as sharing her simpler resources such as word searches with them. Andoni and Zach, now twelve and nine competed against each other ferociously to find all the hidden words.

As she worked late into the night the snatched words of a conversation with Thalia, earlier in the week, played on her mind.

'And the boys are playing up. Zach is being a little shit at school. He's lashing out. Getting into fights. Arguing with his teacher. It's chaos. The Deputy, called me last week, asked if I would be happy to enrol him into this Anger Management Programme,' said Georgia, pulling at her mascaraed lashes, still wet from the tears.

'So what if he's angry? Let him be angry. He's got to express himself.'

'I know. But anger management for my usually sweet-natured Zach? What have we done?'

'Enough of the 'we' please. It's him. He's done this to Zach. To you. All of you. You just remember that.' Thalia leaned over and hugged her friend tight.

'I'll try. But it's so hard. I can't help feeling guilty I didn't see his cheating earlier. I believed him over and over again…all those bloody lies.'

Exhilaration and enthusiasm unleashed within her, energising and motivating her, the adrenaline pumping as she worked on her lesson plans and planned new resources for her lessons. She often retired after midnight, or closer to one o'clock in the morning to find one of the boys in her bed. She found comfort in this and her heart warmed every time she saw one of their huddled bodies under the duvet.

The new lease of life forced her to focus on the course and meant she pushed aside the break-down of her marriage, the pain of having to leave her old life. But she didn't think about this much in the day, being far too busy. Her life became punctuated with new and often unforeseeable moments. The course became her life-line and she focused on getting through it and securing a teaching job for the following July. The energy to do this flowed through her veins like a turbulent stream, hurried and rushed. She managed to hold things together, emotionally and physically. She was grateful her life regained a new purpose, a new rhythm and focus.

At around the same time as the start of her course Andoni started at his new secondary school. Thankfully there were no problems and he became the 'man of the house', as he often referred to himself, almost overnight. He looked out for his brothers and took the responsibilities of his new-found position in the family seriously, taking the changes in his stride now he had turned twelve. But Georgia's heart broke a little more every time he said those words to her, a reminder Nicolas was no longer with them, a reminder the situation was forcing Andoni to grow up before he was ready. Before he should have to.

Thalia remained Georgia's staple companion and kept her sane, her solid rock. Georgia's mum and dad who were not only coping with Georgia's emotions but battling with their own emotions of betrayal and dishonour did everything they could to support her and the children. Her sisters and many friends rallied round, some were more helpful than others but every single one, with no exception, voiced their shock at what Nicolas had done. Georgia often sat quietly and listened as some slagged off her soon-to-be ex-husband and, unable to voice her real emotions, would often defend his character; as after everything, he was still the father of her children.

Deep down she battled with her love for him and she missed the routine of their marriage. In truth Georgia continued to sleep with Nicolas when he visited the boys; snatched urgent moments, hungry, rushing. To her it represented the act of sex, a physical need and she needed it with him.

***

On one of those surprisingly hot days during the Easter holidays, even the weather forecasters didn't predict, Georgia and Thalia threw a picnic together.

They met in Friary Park, a formal Edwardian open space, with lots of soft rolling banks of grass. The trees shimmered and whispered. The warm breeze gently danced pushing the clouds, curling and translucent across the dense blue in a higgledy-piggledy pattern. It felt like summer.

The children ran off ahead to the play area in the periphery of their vision. Thalia screwed up her eyes against the sun and Georgia noticed a fretwork of fine lines appeared at their corners as she followed Thalia along the gravelly winding path into the park. Five pigeons ahead of them took flight as they approached them and despite Georgia's bunged up ears she could still hear their wings flapping. She admired the fronds of purple flowers climbing the crumbling wall of the bowling green and the scarlet poppies scattering the edges of the path, the sweet musk of the grass floated up her nose and made her sneeze.

They wandered across the emerald carpet of grass Georgia holding her sandals by the straps; she savoured the cool grass tickling her bare feet. They laid out a patchwork of picnic rugs and blankets not too far from where the children played in clear sight of them and could be kept an eye on easily. They sprawled out, in the semi-shade of a huge oak.

'My hay fever is bad today.' Georgia sniffed and blew loudly into an already used and crumpled tissue she had found in the inside pocket of her handbag and struggled to fold it over as it disintegrated in her hand, soggy. 'It's gradually getting worse, attacking me from all angles – red eyes, runny nose, itchy throat. I'm a wreck.'

'Probably stresses and strains making it worse too hun.'

They both sat there companionably for a few minutes. Georgia flipped her hair over one shoulder. She peered up at a nest half camouflaged by deep sage-green lobed leaves thickly covering the branches of the sturdy oak tree. She looked way into the distance as if there might be something more edifying up there to guide her, something to give her hope, to make sense of everything which sometimes just felt too much, far too much for her to cope with.

Thalia broke the silence between them. She

rummaged amongst the amorphous pile of cool bags, Tesco shopping bags and the children's sweatshirts 'just in case it got cold', for a bottle of water. She held one out to Georgia, who leaned over and took it.

'Thanks babe,' she said raising her voice, to be heard over the high-pitched wails of a screaming toddler. A woman nearby ranted loudly in a cockney accent into a mobile phone wedged between her shoulder and her ear, paying little attention to the red-faced child who now thumped the woman on the legs with her tiny clenched fists.

'Anyway how are things with you?' Thalia asked, unscrewing the cap and taking a few gulps of the cool water. 'That's done the trick,' she said, smacking her lips.

'Okay, you know. The course is going really well,' said Georgia. She pushed her glasses into her hair as the sun disappeared behind a crocodile-shaped cloud, and hitched her gypsy skirt further up her thighs to cool down. 'I'm loving it. It's like it was meant to be.'

'I'm so glad for you, babe. Strange how things work out,' said Thalia, nodding knowingly.

'I know. Me? Nearly a teacher.'

'And Nicolas? How's he been since the break up?'

'Okay most of the time. You know a bit uppity when I've asked him to baby sit, wanting to know where I'm going and with who, like he still has a say,' Georgia said, raising her eyebrows heavenwards, 'but otherwise I keep out of his way and don't rise to his silly accusations.'

'Accusations?' Thalia let out a dramatic sigh.

'Oh, babe it's been awful actually,' Georgia burst out, tears filling her eyes and her hands shaking. 'He's been accusing me of neglecting the boys, of not looking after them properly because I'm not always able to pick them up from school, going out at weekends more,' she said, wiping the tears from the corner of her eyes with the back of her hands simultaneously, smudging her black mascara down the side of her flushed cheeks.

'Gosh I'm so sorry. I had no idea.'

'I don't want sympathy babe. I'm so fed up with him.'

'I'm just concerned about you. Worried about you'.

'I'll be okay Thal. It just gets on top of me every now and again.'

'For fuck's sake. He's got no right. Pointing his dirty finger at you? He's the one who put it about. Had a baby. And now he thinks he can tell you what to do and accuse you of that? Don't cry.' Thalia also couldn't hold back her own fury. 'Well, Tony's latest is he's not going to move out until the divorce is final. So I'm stuck with him, in the house, til then. It could be months, years.'

'Oh, babe, that's awful. How uncomfortable. Where will he stay? You know sleep?' asked Georgia, the tears sticky under her eyes.

'Well he refuses to sleep anywhere else but our bed so we're both in the same bed,' said Thalia, pulling a cringy face.

'Bloody hell! Are you really putting up with that?'

'What choice do I have?' Thalia sighed heavily.

'They are both such idiots. I mean Nicolas thinks he can still tell me what to do. It's so upsetting and really makes me angry. I know I should let it all go over my head, but it still hurts, and him wanting to upset me even more. It's too much. Like he hasn't done enough to me already.'

'He's jealous you're getting on with your life without him. He's realised his mistake and can't live with it. That's why he's being a jerk. That's why Tony is being a jerk too. Two jerks!'

'Yeah, I know. But it still hurts and as for moving on I don't know if I am. The course is great. It's given me focus. Something to aim for and only a couple of the girls I'm friendly with know my personal situation so I don't have to explain myself to anyone but it's still painful. I don't think I'll ever get over him, the bastard. I still love him.'

'Well of course you love him, hun. The love's not going to just disappear from inside you. Your situation's different to mine. I ended it with Tony because I didn't love him anymore.

Georgia thought about her situation and had to admit, at least to herself, she had low days, where she cried for the loss of her marriage and the life she'd planned with Nicolas by her side; days when the tears came from nowhere. The all-encompassing, suffocating encompassed her. She felt the all too familiar ache in her lower abdomen and it spread to her heart, pulling until she thought her arteries would rip away; her physical pain real.

Thalia tried to reason with her, to stop her from falling into the abyss of dismal misery she recognised.

'You ended it because you were forced to. You had to put your sanity first. Your self-respect.'

'I used to be so proud of what we had. I know it wasn't perfect but it was my perfect, the house, the husband, the children, the holidays. It wasn't all bad.'

'I know Georgi, but you have to move on. You don't want him back do you?'

'No babe, no. But I just miss what we had, what my life was. It was all planned out and now I feel like I'm in one of those fairground rides with all the funny mirrors. I don't know what I'm going to find in front of me anymore. It's all distorted, bent out of shape.'

'You'll get through this. I promise Georgi.'

'Yeah I know. But I feel so let down. Our marriage vows meant nothing to him. All those promises we made to each other,' she said repeatedly twisting her wedding ring. The wedding band now representing Georgia's broken marriage, broken vows.

'I know it's hard hun. Fucking hard. But it will get easier.'

'At least you're not in the same bed any more. I woke up the other night, sweat dripping from me, thinking I'd just stabbed Tony. Convinced there was blood everywhere. Took me a couple of seconds to realise he was snoring his head off next to me. The bastard!'

'Oh babe. I know what you mean. I don't know how you're doing it.' Georgia managed a small smile and then they both burst out laughing, a nervous laughter tinged with sorrow, but laughter all the same.

***

With June, and the summer definitely here to stay, Georgia accepted an invitation out on a girls' night. She was excited about going out somewhere new with the three other girls she most got on with on her course and organised the boys' sleepover at her sister's house. The village, home town of one of the girls house-sitting over the weekend while her parents were away, sat off a junction of the M1 near Luton. Since they could all drive they decided on a night out further afield than Enfield, Finchley or Southgate where they lived. Somewhere new would be fun, thought Georgia.

'Look, it's not a problem. I'm happy to have them and if you decide to stay over then you won't be worrying about them. Honest…go…have fun,' said her sister, as Georgia dumped the boys' overnight bags in her hallway.

Georgia felt relaxed, free and as she drove back home to get ready she blasted up the music in the car and sang loudly to George Michael's *Outside*, attracting the attention of two guys in the Audi next to her as she stopped at the lights. She laughed, and then embarrassed looked straight ahead until the lights turned green and she shot off ahead of them.

She climbed into her navy jersey dress, with sheer chiffon sleeves which hung like bells to her elbows. She gently tugged at the zip at the back, just managing to pull it all the way and smiled at herself as the hall mirror outside her room, reflected her image back at her, the dress hugging her curves perfectly. She put on a pair of sheer tights and the high sling-back shoes she'd bought on a whim when in New York with Thalia. Her make-up was understated but the smoky blue eyeliner she'd used really stood out against her dark eyes and complimented the blue of her dress. She felt oddly nervous, but wasn't quite sure why. She had printed out her route; she knew exactly where to pick up the motorway and where to come off. But jittery all the same she wondered if it was because she was meeting the girls outside of their usual environment. She had to admit being a little worried they would have nothing in common with her; all being in their mid to late twenties, with no dependents, unlike her, who carried an airport load of oversized and overweight baggage around with her like a huge tag marked 'damaged goods' or 'heavy heart' around her wrist.

She shook off the feeling and smiled at herself, catching a glimpse of her reflection in the dressing table mirror, bright white teeth shining back at her, cheeks glowing peach from her light touch of blusher. She would be fine.

***

The tiny village had one main high street running through it. She drove tentatively, mentally noting the 'speed camera' signs. She passed a fire station, a Post Office, a Co-op, and a one storey building brandishing a glaring carrot-shaped sign, 'Bunny Hop Nursery', across the front of it. Around a bend she spotted an ornate 'The Indian Marquee' restaurant sign. She pulled neatly into the first available parking space on the left hand side of the road, careful not to bump the unusually high kerb.

Getting out of the car, the fresh, still air hit her. She could hear the twitter of bird song in the trees on the opposite pavement, the low branches weighted down with masses of powder blossom. A row of tiny cottages, painted in a range of pastel tones, lined the opposite side of the narrow street enclosed by picket fences painted in soft pastels. She noted the pretty window box, on the sill of one whose wooden frame, splintered with peeling paint, once white, now sat faded and yellowed by the sun. A brass plaque glinted and reminded her of the brightly painted doors of tall townhouses in Hampstead.

She locked the car with a click of the ignition key and with a spring in her step, walked up the three steps leading to the main doors of the restaurant. As she pushed the heavy, glazed door of the restaurant, a waiter pulled it open at the same time, and the welcome coolness of the air-conditioning hit her. She walked in, with her best smile.

Two of the girls, already seated at a table situated almost opposite the doorway, looked up and waved. Paula had long straight hair which cascaded past her shoulders, ebony black eyes and small tight lips which hardly moved when she spoke. Jade's hair, highlighted chestnut and shiny, shaped into a feathered bob softening her otherwise rectangular cheek bones and pointed chin in her elf-like face.

'Hi,' said Georgia, as she bent over and kissed both of them in turn, on each cheek, 'Greek style,' she joked, as they hugged her.

'Hi, you. You look lovely,' said Jade, as Georgia shrugged off her Levi's denim jacket and handed it to the waiter, loitering behind her. 'Thank you. Wasn't sure what to wear but hey, it's stretchy so I can eat as much as I like. Smells delicious.' Georgia breathed in the aromatic smell from the food being served to a couple seated at an adjacent table. 'And the truth be told, I'm so hungry. I didn't eat lunch, too busy finishing our assignment.'

'Oh, wow. I've not even started it,' said Paula tossing her hair over her shoulder.

'Really? Oh, I couldn't leave it any later. I'd be panicking about not getting it done. You know it's for Wednesday right?'

'Well, I s'pose with the kids you need to plan ahead more than we do,' said Jade.

'Well, I've always been a planner. But yeah, you're right.'

'Hi. Sorry I'm late,' said Julianna, interrupting them, hair in a chignon and the highest thigh high boots in black leather covering light blue jeans so tight they looked sprayed on. Georgia smiled at her guessing she intended to make an entrance; of all of them she loved being in the spotlight.

'Hi,' they all echoed.

'I haven't been here long, so don't worry,' said Georgia, 'Really easy to find wasn't it? I hardly looked down at the directions. And the village looks cute, all those quaint little houses.'

'Yeah, looks lovely. What a great place to grow up in.' Juliana said to Jade as she pulled out a chair and sat down but not before scanning the restaurant.

'Hope you don't mind but we ordered poppadums and all the bits while we were waiting,' said Paula.

'Not at all,' said Georgia, tucking in, 'suits me fine.'

'I like the look of that guy over there,' said Julianna.

'What guy?' asked Jade. 'We haven't noticed anyone…too interested in the food.'

'That guy. And who's with him…hiding behind the pillar?' asked Julianna, peering across the restaurant more carefully at a guy who appeared to be talking to a huge potted palm across from him.

'Not noticed,' said Georgia.

'Well I'm sure we could find out.' Julianna rummaged around in her bag asking for a pen and paper. Georgia pulled a page out of her notebook and a pen.

Who are you with? Georgia wrote out in her neat writing.

'Fabulous Georgia. Let's have some fun.' Juliana's eyes sparkled as she spoke.

'You're never going to send it to him?'

'Yep that's exactly what I'm doing.' Georgia looked straight at Jade who almost choked on her poppadum.

Georgia folded the piece of paper in half and called the waiter over. 'Can you please hand this to the guy over there?' She pointed in the direction of the pillar and taking the note from her, Georgia noticed he walked off with a smirk on his face.

'So what do you recommend? It's your local after all.' Paula took hold of her hair and placed it over her shoulder again.

'Well, everything really. I've been here so many times over the years I think I've eaten or at least tried everything three or four times.'

'Don't look up but he's just looked over.' Juliana kicked Georgia under the table gently.

'Let's see if he responds,' giggled Georgia, being the most carefree she'd felt in a long time and geared up for a good laugh.

'Now let's focus on ordering,' said Jade as she

opened the leather-bound menu in front of her.

The girls took their time choosing from the menu but eventually, through giggles and lots of laughter, they ordered a mish-mash of starters and mains to share, a bottle of still water and a bottle of sparkling water, a diet coke for Paula and a G&T for Jade. Jade was the only one drinking.

'Do you think we've ordered enough?' asked Paula, when the waiter came over.

'I think so,' he said, nodding politely as he read out their order from his pad.

'And one portion of that, please,' teased Georgia as he walked off, pointing to his derrière. The girls were in fits.

'You are just too mad. I think I've met my match.' Georgia picked up a hint of uncertainty in Juliana's voice and Georgia wondered if she didn't like not being the centre of attention.

The girls talked for a while, filling the time with banter and easy chatter which Georgia really enjoyed, nothing heavy and nothing about divorce or settlements. The waiter deposited the drinks, careful not to lose the balance of the metal tray he held and he handed a note to Georgia.

'It's a reply,' she whispered conspiratorially to the girls, getting flustered as she tried to make out the scribble in front of her.

'Here let me look.' Juliana grabbed the note and read

out loud, '*Who wants to know?*'

'Damn. What do we say to that?' asked Jade.

Georgia, the pen ready in her hand, turned to Paula and thinking for a moment, grabbed back the note and wrote, '*The brunette*'.

'But we're all brunettes, kind of,' said Julianna, looking up from her mobile phone distractedly.

'Exactly,' said Georgia, laughing. 'That'll confuse him.' The girls roared with laughter but not Julianna who had a strained smile etched on her face.

They ate their meal passing dishes back and forth between them.

'And we were worried about not having ordered enough. Look at all the rice still left,' said Paula. She leaned back in her seat unbuttoning the side clasp to ease the waist band of her trousers. 'Oh what a relief. I thought I was going to pop.'

'That's why I wore this dress,' piped up Georgia, and she shifted from left to right and back again as she sat in her seat, twisting her body back and forth inside her stretchy dress. The waiter appeared and Georgia noticed how he made an effort to hide the smirk on his face, as he placed another note on the table avoiding the splats of curry sauce and mango chutney.

'Sorry about the mess.' said Georgia, 'My friends aren't used to eating in public.'

'Oh stop,' said Jade giving Georgia a playful shove.

'With a mate. Going to the Plum of Feathers after

this. See you in there?' read Paula.

'I think he means plume.' Jade sniggered.

'Good speller then,' said Georgia, before she burst into a fit of giggles too. 'Which one of us do you think he's interested in?' She looked up to find him staring straight at her; a wide grin across his face. Julianna caught Georgia staring and looked in his direction too but his gaze remained transfixed on Georgia and she felt herself flush crimson.

'Who says he's interested in any of us?' Julianna shifted in her seat, pulling at her boots with splayed fingers careful not to break her painted talons.

'Well, he wouldn't have responded if he wasn't and he wouldn't have said he was going to the 'plum' either,' said Georgia, almost choking on her glass of water as she laughed at her own joke.

'Count me out,' said Julianna, 'I've got to make a move. Sorry. Had a great evening though.'

'You okay? You've been a bit quiet tonight,' said Jade to her.

'Yeah, just tired and I'm not too sure of the route home so don't want to leave it too late.'

'You're more than welcome to stay over with the girls. It's not too late to change your mind. My parents' Laura Ashley couch is really comfy.'

'I'd rather get home tonight but thanks for the offer. Right, night darlings. See you at college on 'deadline' Wednesday,' Julianna said, before handing over £30.00

cash. 'This should cover my meal and drink.'

Julianna waved back at them from the open door and disappeared. The guy they had been exchanging notes with followed her out. His mate close behind him looked over and gave Georgia a smile.

'He's with another bloke,' said Jade, 'Come on, let's go to the pub. See what happens.'

'Well, it had to be another bloke,' said Georgia, laughing, 'he was hardly going to be asking us to meet him in the pub with his girlfriend.'

'True. But he could've been chatting to the palm all night,' said Jade.

'Ha, ha,' said Georgia, 'come on, let's hit the pub but I'm not drinking a thing. I am so full.'

***

The next morning, Georgia woke before the others and used to getting up early with the boys, she decided to make breakfast for everyone. She took eggs, cheddar cheese and mushrooms from the fridge and cooked up a huge one pan omelette. She had just put the bread in the toaster when Jade padded in, bare foot, with her bright fuschia-painted toes at odds with the cool grey of the kitchen units and pale stone-coloured flooring.

'You've been busy. How long have you been up?'

'Not that long, half an hour.' She didn't reveal Nicolas had sent her a text demanding to know where she was and why she wasn't picking up the house phone. 'You don't mind me doing breakfast, do you?'

'No of course not. It's nice not having to make my own for a change,' said Jade as she stifled a yawn. She grabbed a pencil from the pot on the counter and poked it into her Chinese bun. 'Nice not to have to eat it on my own, too. Thank you.'

'You're welcome, hun. If I'd thought it through I could have brought some bits with me.'

'Don't be silly. Heard anything from Sean?' asked Jade.

'Actually yes I have. A couple of texts.'

'And?'

'Asked if we could meet up but I've fobbed him off.'

'Why? He seemed really nice last night and he lives near you. I knew it was you he was after. His face lit up when we walked into the pub; he couldn't take his eyes off you.'

'Stop it.'

'No really. I think he's lovely. He was chatty. Offered to buy us all a drink and his eyes are just the most amazing colour…brown one minute and then green and then in between…and that thick hair. Ooh bet you could pull on that!'

'Stop it…I didn't notice. And anyway what about the boys? And he seems really young. Bet he'd have a heart attack if I was to mention the three boys and up-coming divorce.'

'You don't have to say anything yet. Go with the flow. Have a bit of fun.' Jade, being the only one of the uni crowd who knew about her situation, showed her both discretion and empathy, having a cousin gone through almost an identical break-up.

'I'll see. Not sure I want to get involved.'

'Your call,' said Jade, 'but why walk away?'

'Not walking away…just not sure yet.'

'Take a chance. You deserve it. Now shall I wake Paula?'

'Yep. All about ready, just need to butter the toast,' she said, as the toaster popped.

***

Later in the week, after handing in her completed assignment and finishing from uni at mid-day, she called Thalia and arranged to meet up in Café Buzz on the High Street a few miles from where they both lived. Just as she locked up the porch Mark, the gardener, pulled up onto her neighbour's drive. The sun broke through the clouds and she pulled her sunglasses from her hair as she clicked her car open.

'Hello you,' he called out.

'Hi Mark,' she replied noticing the way the shafts of light crossed his face. He adjusted his cap to keep the brightness out of his clear blue eyes.

'Doing your garden today if that's okay with you.'

'Yeah of course. I'm going out now and don't have cash on me but maybe pop back if you have time.'

'Thought you were. You look nice.'

'Oh, thanks.'

'If I don't make it back this way today I'll be back later in the week,' he said as he winked cheekily at her. She immediately flushed and wondered if he could feel the heat blasting off her face.

***

In the café Georgia filled Thalia in on the events of Saturday night. They sat at a round metal table on the pavement under the awning and ordered something to drink and a couple of pastries to share between them.

'No way. You dark horse, you,' said Thalia, as Georgia recounted the events with her. 'Are you going to meet up then?'

'We're meeting up in Hampstead Friday night. Nicolas is being a pig refusing to look after the boys when every other time he's falling over himself to be with them. I think he's guessed I'm going out with someone. But Mum said she'd have them for me.'

'He's changed his tune, one minute all obliging and the next back to being a selfish git.'

'Stuff him, I don't care,' said Georgia liberated.

'What will you wear? You have to look sultry and sexy, hun,' said Thalia.

'I always look sultry and sexy,' laughed Georgia, pouting her lips and throwing a kiss to Thalia.

'You do hun. But I'm talking extra sultry and extra sexy. Have you told him about the boys?'

'No. But I'm going to. What about you and Steve?'

'Well…we're still, you know.'

'Well, you're getting more than me,' she lied.

***

'Oh hi Mum. Dad stopped by earlier,' said Georgia, pulling at the tangled telephone cord.

'Yes. I know, He's home now. Did he say anything to you about Sean?'

'No, he didn't. We just chatted about the allotment and what's growing well over there. You know…nothing too serious. Why?'

'Well when I told him only this morning you had met someone he said he was so happy. That Nicolas wasn't the only one who could make you smile again and after what you've gone through he wants you to be with someone else, someone kind and loving.' Georgia's eyes teared up and she couldn't speak without a high-pitched squeak.

'Thanks Mum,' was all she could say. She knew with her mum and dad's approval she could enter the relationship with Sean with an open heart, guilt-free. She didn't want the break-up with Nicolas to hurt her mum and dad any more than it had already and she had thought meeting Sean may have.

The Greek Cypriot community could be a tough one to live in. People not only judged everything you did and said but judged your parents for everything you did and said too. She didn't want her parents to be the focus of idle gossip or mean-spirited comments and she knew having their blessing, especially her dad's, showed her parents were ready to re-buff any such remarks. Knowing Georgia had her parent's approval to meet someone new lightened the burden of guilt she carried, the guilt of having let them down, the guilt of having caused them so much sorrow.

For the first time in ages, Georgia felt the first shafts of light penetrating the darkness within her and the wave of emotion swiftly threatened to break into fresh tears at any moment, tears of relief and happiness.

Chapter Eleven

GLAMMING UP FOR her first date with Sean didn't turn out to be the fun session Georgia imagined. She ran out of conditioner but remembered only after she was already in the shower, so she made do with just shampoo.

In her bedroom, she towel-dried her hair and then generously ran some John Frieda serum through the tangly knots with her hands, scrunching the roots to give her hair more lift and hoped for the best. She put on her music, extra loud. Listening to music would normally have psyched Georgia, even excited her but not on this night. She pulled out her cream slash-neck top and almost cried when she noticed a dirty stain on the shoulder of it. Damn! She remembered Thalia's make-up rubbing off on it as she gave her a hug the last time she'd worn it. Why hadn't she put it in the laundry basket?

As she drew the dark blue liner under her eyes her hand shook and the lines ended up too thick, uneven, making her look like an over made-up Cleopatra. She ended up smudging the blue under her eyes as she rubbed at the lines. Her mascara looked a mess; her hand shook as she layered the thick black make-up onto her eyelashes and then she blinked sending a spattering of black across her upper eyelids.

Everything was going wrong. She wanted to cry and wondered whether it was all worth it. She looked in her triptych mirror, dark circles around her eyes and her hair already a frizzy mane, frown lines etched on her forehead. She thought she looked more like fifty than forty. Who was she trying to kid? She was a woman with three children. Her life was complicated enough without adding a new boyfriend to the equation. She could always call him, no text him, and make some excuse about one of the boys not being well. Then she remembered he didn't know she had children. She sat heavily on her bed and lowered her head into her cupped hands.

Her gut instinct tugged at her to check her horoscope online. Maybe Russell Grant will give me a sign, she thought, as a shiver of hopeful anticipation ran through her veins.

'You are ready to kick up your heels and start the party early.
Clear out your major responsibilities and then take off and enjoy a frolicking weekend.
Seek out fun with friends who can not only offer you a great time, but also a renewed sense of spirit and enthusiasm.
Share moments with those who have a positive impact on you and prepare for some wonderful opportunities which are coming your way soon.'

She knew it was silly but the reading helped to reassure her, and less worried, she shook away her nerves.

***

Having spent many happy days and nights in Hampstead in her late teens and early twenties she reminisced the time spent with friends drinking cups of tea and eating hot buttered raisin toast at the Coffee Cup on Hampstead High Street and the many raucous nights partying and laughing at the Old Bull & Bush.

She drove up and down the high street twice. She eventually, nosed into a space between a red Peugeot and a white pick-up truck outside Hobbs. There will be more good days to come, said a little voice in her head.

She texted Sean to say she had parked at the bottom of the hill. He texted back straight away.

```
Walk up towards the station
```

She felt awkward, her shoes were too high. She tried to walk uphill gracefully; an almost impossible feat and her ankle went over a second time. Bloody hell, she thought, I'm going to kill myself. As she straightened up she literally bumped into Sean. She looked up into his sexy hazel eyes under rows of soft long lashes.

'Thought I'd walk down and meet you half way,' he said, smiling.

'Oh, hi,' said Georgia. She took a sharp intake of breath and looked down at her shoes desperate to shy away from his penetrating stare.

'You smell lovely you do and look lovely too, you sweetheart.'

'Thank you.'

'The pub's back this way,' he said and very lightly he put his arm around her waist. He guided her up the hill; Georgia's head spinning with the word sweetheart. He towered over her, taller than she remembered, maybe nearly six foot. 'So, how are you?' he asked.

'Good, thanks. You?' She avoided his eyes and instead glanced at his hair taking in its thick mousy brown wave and the way it flopped seductively over his forehead; she breathed in the amber aroma of his aftershave.

'Busy week to be honest but knowing I was seeing you tonight made it bearable like. I couldn't wait to see you again,' he said, his eyes a mixture of muted greens and glossy golds.

'To be honest, I've been really nervous. I almost blew you out.'

'No way. I would've been really disappointed. Really disappointed.' His voice cracked with emotion and he leaned in towards her, their hips knocking as they walked in tandem towards The Holly Bush.

***

The pub heaved with punters. Sean pointed to an unoccupied table piled high with empty pint glasses.

'Grab that table. I'll get the drinks.'

Georgia made her way over to a square mahogany table, its surface a mosaic of sticky glass rings of spilt beer and cider. She pulled out one of the ladder-backed chairs and sat down, facing the bar.

She surveyed the alcove in the adjacent wall painted dark terracotta and bare apart from a painting of a girl in a heavy dark ornate frame, gilded in gold. The lower part of the wall housed a fixed bookcase with a panoply of old leather bound books, market finds and knick-knacks, the kind her *yiayia* used to have on her mantelpiece. It smelt musty and of alcohol. It buzzed and Georgia appreciated the noise which helped mask her awkwardness, giving her something else to concentrate on other than the fact she was not sure how to behave on a first date. Totally different to the first time she had met Nicolas at a friend's birthday, surrounded by her sisters and friends from Greek school, nerves strangled her.

'Lemonade and lime,' Sean said, pushing three pint glasses away with his hands as he put down the drink in front of her.

'Thank you,' she said, quietly impressed he remembered what she'd had to drink the first time they had met just under a week ago. 'Lucky we got somewhere to sit.'

'That's why I thought we'd meet up early,' he said. 'It's always busy in here and I hate standing all night.'

'Me too.' Georgia looked down at the honey-coloured flagstones, fiddling with the strap of her handbag. She touched her hair and quickly pulled her hand away; it felt dry and wiry.

'Look, I know I've already said this to you but I don't want you to think I pick women up in restaurants all the time. It was a one-off last week. I couldn't take my eyes off you and when that waiter came over with the note I really hoped it was you who was interested.'

'Really? Wow…I don't know what to say.'

'Say you'll go out with me. You're not still nervous are you?' It was all happening so quickly Georgia felt like she was on the outside looking in. It felt surreal.

'Look, Sean. I don't know what to…'

'Just say yes.'

'Look, you have to know that…' Just then one of the barmen leaned across them as he collected the empties. 'Know that…'

'Don't tell me anything. I don't need to know anything. Let's just enjoy this…us.'

Georgia hesitated for a moment, embarrassed at the open adoration he expressed towards her. 'Okay,' she said, eventually. 'One step at a time.'

'Cheers,' he said. He lifted his pint glass clinking it against her tumbler. 'Here's to going out with the most adorable woman I have ever met.'

'Cheers,' she said, hardly feeling beautiful, and conscious the knotty mess of her hair matched the twisted knot in her stomach. She looked at Sean and recognised an immature quality about him but she couldn't quite work out what exactly made her think that. He came across confident and bold and sure of himself yet an underlying boyishness shone through too. She wondered if this was a good thing; after all she certainly wasn't a young girl.

***

Georgia chatted about work, her PGCE course, her new planned career. Sean filled her in on his job as a Section Manager at Marks & Spencer, holidays, growing up, Ireland and his siblings. His light eyes fizzed with laughter as he spoke and Georgia giggled like a school girl. Sean intermittently stroked her arm sending tingles throughout her body and they knocked knees together under the table once too, him so close making her hot. As the evening went on Georgia felt more and more charged with excitement. Sean, a great raconteur, had her laughing out loud with his banter tinged with a hint of an Irish accent. But he also listened carefully to her and when he looked at her intently she felt her cheeks glow cherry-red.

There on the street, pushed up against the side of her car, Georgia shivered involuntarily as Sean kissed her, his hand almost touching her as it brushed against her hair and the back of her neck. Georgia couldn't remember the last time she had kissed like that. Nicolas had never been one for kissing and so the anxiety as Sean moved in to kiss her consumed her. Doubts coursed through her mind.

What if I don't know how to kiss? What if he thinks I'm an awful kisser? What if I don't do it right? The kiss seemed to last forever. But as soon as Sean pulled away and looked straight into her eyes, she knew everything was going to be alright.

She knew Sean was lost in her from his dreamy light-dancing eyes and from the tilt of his head as he looked at her.

'Wow. I'm so lucky to have found you,' he said, his voice unwavering.

***

During those first few weeks, Georgia had to cope increasingly with abusive text messages and threats from Nicolas. She tried hard to ignore his barrage of insults but sometimes she couldn't back down and they ended up having the almightiest rows, leaving her shaking and crying.

Despite this negativity, she continued to absorb herself in her course and the practical teaching element and Thalia gave her all the hugs and support she needed. Finding themselves in similar situations meant they could empathise with each other. Georgia's emotions yo-yoed, up one minute and down the next; up when around Sean and then down when not. She didn't know where or how Nicolas was going to get at her next, and it made her edgy. But one thing she knew for certain. He knew about Sean and she knew she would have to tell Sean her situation. She couldn't hold back any longer.

***

Georgia looked forward to meeting Sean's friends in Islington and to finding out more about Sean through them. His friends, mainly couples, were already at the restaurant when Georgia and Sean walked in, Sean gripping onto her hand. She immediately lapped up the attention she got from them all and felt relaxed in their company.

'Didn't think Sean had it in him to pull a real woman,' joked Tom, his oldest friend from school.

'Ah come here, tell me this 'n' tell me no more…' Sean said, his Irish accent stronger than ever.

'What does your mother say about it?'

'His mother?' asked Georgia keeping the alarm out of her voice.

'Sean is still attached to his mother's apron strings. His father living the life of Riley in Ireland, getting up to God knows what.'

'Oh get away with you! Ignore them. I live at home with my mum that's all they mean. Dad visits when he can.'

'And I always thought he had eyes for no-one else,' joined in Fabio, his Italian mate with a long Roman nose and long slender fingers. 'Wink, wink,' he continued, nudging Sean playfully in the ribs.

'Be quiet, you lot.' He turned towards Georgia and reached for her hand under the table, squeezing it tight. 'Ignore them, they're eejits, they are.'

'Only joshing mate. She's lovely, your Geor-giii-aaa,' said Tom.

'Enough. You're embarrassing her,' said Diana, Tom's girlfriend and she turned to Georgia and mouthed 'sorry' from the other end of the table where she sat with Mary, Fabio's fiancée.

Georgia could not help but notice Sean was mesmerised by her. He hung on her every word like a love struck teenager. She quickly relaxed. They forked food into each other's mouths, Thai fried prawns and feta stuffed chicken breast. He laughed with his head tilted right back and she giggled like the giggle pot she used to be at school. They shared their dessert of raspberry crème brûlée and Georgia held tightly onto Sean's hand under the table. She imagined this is what it felt like to have an affair. Every fibre in her body stood on end, soporific emotions engulfing her. A shadow however hung over her; she knew what she had to do before their relationship went any further.

***

Sean's mates ordered a taxi and at half past eleven, the bill paid up for their meal, they all spilled out onto the pavement outside, still laughing and joking. Sean had his arm around Georgia's waist. They all kissed each other goodbye.

'If you had less edge you'd evaporate,' said

Tom to Sean as he disappeared into the taxi.

'Yeah, yeah,' shouted Sean after him. The taxi did a U-turn and disappeared up the road as Georgia and Sean waved after it.

'Less edge?' asked Georgia.

'He means I'm relaxed, you know chilled.'

'Oh right.'

'So,' said Sean.

'So,' said Georgia.

'What now?'

'I need to tell you something,' said Georgia. 'Is there anywhere we can go and sit a while?'

'Yeah. We can sit…we can dance…you said you like dancing.'

He pulled her up the road to what looked like a sleazy pub, a small raucous group of people spilling onto the street as Georgia and Sean pushed their way in. But once inside, although small with just enough cramped stools and tables for no more than forty or so people, it bubbled with activity, the resident DJ knocking out old seventies tunes. Throwing her bag and jacket down at a table Georgia let Sean guide her to the empty floor. Georgia relaxed as the music washed over her, rattling under her feet, pulling at her limbs, setting the gaudy lime walls buzzing. Within minutes she lost herself in the music. She waved her arms in the air, above her head, she teased Sean, rubbing her body up and down his and pressing up against his crotch. She turned round and round and laughed as he tried to stop her from losing her balance as she fell against him, she dipped down low and shimmied and belly-danced. Completely mesmerised by the atmosphere and her attention, Sean's eyes flickered brightly staring at her and she knew he was taking in every bit of her. On a sudden impulse, she pressed her lips hard up against his. He responded kissing her deep, his tongue searching urgently, persuasively for hers. She was hot, wet between her legs and her body quaked. She pulled away, her breath wheezy.

'I need to sit down,' she said, holding on to him for support, feeling his well-developed muscular shoulders under his shirt. 'And I need a drink of water.'

Sean disappeared to the bar.

'Here you are,' he said back within seconds.

'Thank you. And sorry.'

'What are you sorry for?' he asked, perplexed.

'For what I'm about to tell you. And I want you to know whatever you decide it's okay with me.' She felt her stomach tighten.

'Okay…'

'I've had the best few nights with you ever. And if you walk away I won't blame you. I won't think any less of you.' Sean tried to say something but Georgia carried on, holding up her hands to indicate she didn't want him to interrupt her. 'I'm separated from my husband. We've been separated for a few months now.' Sean's hazel eyes widened and he became very still, serious. Georgia fingered the necklace hanging between her cleavage as her heart pounded. She looked down catching a glimpse of her skin as it shimmered with perspiration.

'Go on,' he said.

'I've got three children, boys. They're twelve, nine and seven. That's why I only see you now and again, when I can get someone to look after them. They are amazing and I love them so much. I would never give them up not for anybody, not even you. So there you have it. That's my story. Messy, complicated.' Georgia spoke quickly, almost tripping over her words as they tumbled out and then burst into floods of tears. She hid her eyes with her hands and waited for Sean to respond.

'Oh Georgia. You silly girl. I love you. I don't care about you being separated. I don't care about you having children. You're the love of my life.' Georgia said nothing, crying into his shoulder and staining his shirt with make-up and mascara and tears. He stroked her hair and held her until she finally pulled herself away, looking up at him through her teary-stained face.

'I love you,' he repeated. Her skin tingled as she took in his honeyed words again and adrenaline spikes coursed through her veins, not only from surprise but from the shock of him being so deep, so heavy early on in their relationship. She pushed the negative sentiments aside and focused on her deliriousness. This man who she had known for a couple of weeks had just told her he loved her. She couldn't believe it. She had the urge to touch him, his skin. She boldly unbuttoned his top three buttons and slid her hand across his taut belly and played with the hairs on his chest. Sean didn't stop her.

***

At home, as Georgia lay in bed she went over Sean's reaction and his words over and over in her head. Every time she thought of those three little words her heart somersaulted and the butterflies in her stomach fluttered so hard she actually felt pain, a beautiful all-consuming one. But she had to get a grip. She wondered how someone she'd only just met could say he loved her? Utterly insane. It was flattery. Nothing more and she had to accept Sean was being a 'nice' guy. She couldn't afford to get all mixed up in anything other than a bit of fun.

Nevertheless, she battled with her emotions. Sean was just what she needed. She needed to be loved after the way Nicolas had treated her. Nicolas had made her feel ugly, unlovable and as much as she hated to admit it she secretly needed a man to validate her womanliness, her sexiness, her worthiness to be loved again. She knew his affections were highly untrue but didn't care she just wanted to feel special.

***

Georgia and Sean's relationship continued to blossom although Georgia held back and didn't sleep with Sean.

'I know what a big step all this is for you.'

'Do you?'

'No pressure.'

But things between them were physical all the same. They touched, they teased, they pulled away from each other, until in the private underground car park of the Crown Douglas Hotel in Cricklewood, Georgia succumbed to Sean's attentions and her own longing for him. The risk of being caught in a public place heightened her excitement to a whole new level.

Kissing in the front of the car, both leaned across the gear stick towards each other awkwardly. Georgia reached for the seat's lever and pushed her seat back into a reclining position.

Sean looked deep into her eyes, full of yearning for her, anticipation fluxing behind them. She settled back and he came round to the driver's side, opened her door and knelt on the concrete floor. He hungrily drew her flowing, cotton skirt towards her waist and ran his fingers urgently up and down her inner thighs. Then he stopped. Georgia held her breath in anticipation and moaned with pleasure as he rested the tips of his fingers just there. She bit on her lip to stop herself from calling out, the electricity from his touch an unbearably sweet. He touched her through the silk of her underwear. He pulled the soft material to the side and teased and probed with his tongue. Then he yanked the silky material all the way down her legs and she impulsively shook them off so they lay hanging around one ankle.

She closed her eyes and felt herself brimming with the predictability of the moment. She let herself go, biting down onto her hand to stop her screaming and she rode along with an intense sexual pleasure she hadn't ever experienced before. Sean drank her up and then she lay there, breathless as he put his head in her lap and she lovingly stroked his sweat-matted hair.

***

Georgia's energy levels were boundless. She had an abundance of patience around the boys and found herself humming merrily around the house and down the school corridors. She arrived extra early for her university lectures and seminars and effortlessly completed her final assignment. Nothing eradicated her happy go-lucky mood.

The following week Sean invited Georgia over to his place on his day off. Georgia admitted to herself she would sleep with Sean that day.

'Thanks Thalia,' she chirruped down the phone after confirming arrangements for the boys with her and then left a message on her lecturer's answer machine. 'Hi Slav.

It's Georgia here. I won't be in today as one of my little boys is unwell and off school. I will email you to re-arrange the feedback for my school placement if that's okay. Thank you and sorry.'

She hung up excitement running through her but also guilt about missing uni. She was being a bad girl but didn't care. Driving over to Sean's Georgia felt a bolt of panic hit her. It was one thing fumbling around and kissing but making love? What if Sean thought she was old? She was after all seven years older than him. What if he didn't get excited making love to her?

Sean opened the door to her and bundled her into the living room. Before she knew it, almost without thinking, they ripped each other's clothes off, discarding them randomly onto the old fashioned deep pile rug. Sean pushed her back onto the brown couch and within seconds pushed against her as he moved on top of her. She laid back, her legs wrapped tightly around him, as he pushed his condom-hugged hardness into her. At first he was gentle but he soon writhed above her, pushing in and out faster, deeper until she could hold on no longer, squirming with anticipation and as she let go they both came together.

Sean lay spent on top of her, one of his hands cupping her protruding breast.

'Hello, Sean,' she smiled.

He got up and came back with a pale blue sheet and wrapped it around her as she lay on the couch like an open flower.

'Thank you,' she said and she moved up against the back of the sofa facing outwards, him snuggling in next to her, their legs entangled.

They remained there, not saying anything. Sean stroked her belly, her arms, her breasts. All the while Georgia thought about how the act of making love with another man actually made her feel. She floated in the clouds. She felt weightless, ecstatic.

They made love three times more and then Sean disappeared into the kitchen to make sandwiches and tea. This was no bachelor pad. There were trinkets covering every space on the mantelpiece and the three shelves built into one of the alcoves. She noticed a pair of brown reading glasses taped around one side on the coffee table and a pile of washing folded neatly in a plastic laundry basket. Georgia suddenly panicked. What if his mother, came back home and found her like this? She hurriedly threw her clothes on and wandered into the kitchen at the end of the long hallway, noticing the damp smell coming up from the worn carpet as she padded across it.

'Hey. Sandwiches are ready. Hope you're hungry.'

'So this is your parent's house?'

'My mum's house. Dad shipped out to Ireland four years ago. Still married but you know, does his own thing. He's a bastard.' She remembered his friend's comment about Sean's dad and suddenly panicked.

'Oh…um…I'm sorry Sean but I really have to go.'

Sean followed her along the hall, grabbing at her arm as she opened the front door.

'Say you'll come again.'

Georgia didn't answer him and her head spun again as he kissed her sending lightning bolts to every part of her.

***

'Oh, well done you. So you're not a divorcee virgin anymore,' said Thalia teasing Georgia, as they sat at the new table, in Thalia's kitchen, waiting for the kettle to boil later in the afternoon.

'And you've had another visit from Steve,' said Georgia, tapping her fingers.

'We're not talking about me.'

'Okay. No, I'm not a divorcee virgin anymore. But I tell you something I didn't realise men's you know could be so big.'

'Stop showing off,' said Thalia.

'I'm not. I'm being serious.'

'Well, you're never too old to make new discoveries,' laughed Thalia and they both fell about laughing, tears rolling down their faces.

'Enough, enough.' Georgia doubled over trying not to wet herself. She crossed her legs, as she poured water all over the worktop, missing both mugs as she continued to laugh.

***

After that, Georgia was insatiable, as was Sean. Every time they met they made love and it didn't matter where they were or what the risk. She metamorphosed backwards into the rebel teenager she never dared to be. Something had awoken in her.

'I can't get enough of you,' Sean said. He told her over and over he loved her. Their relationship relied on Georgia having childcare for the boys and so they did not plan anything too far ahead but he always accepted and understood this. Georgia also avoided going back to his home not wanting to bump into his mum; the thought of it embarrassed Georgia no end.

'Hey. I'm sorry about tonight,' said Georgia down the phone.

'Look, it's okay. I understand.'

'My mum is just not feeling up to having the boys after that stomach bug she's had the past couple of days.'

'You can make it up to me next time.'

Georgia liked the control she had over her relationship with Sean, which meant she could, for once, do what suited her. She could however feel herself becoming more selfish and the more she saw of Sean the more she wanted him, like an addict she craved him. She began to spend more and more of her free time with him and less and less time with the boys. And every time she saw him they made love. She pushed his home situation to the back of her mind; for now, it didn't matter where he lived.

On Sundays while Nicolas took the boys to watch Andoni play football, she met up with Sean in Hampstead. Nicolas, she knew, had spent hours at a time talking with Roksana during Andoni's Sunday matches and she now did the same thing under his nose and even though they were separated she felt smug about it; getting one over on him. They took a different route each time, Georgia breathing in the fresh scent of nature and avoiding the banks of nettles as they walked hand in hand. They made love behind huge green bushes and brambles, camouflaged by the shady woodland and the thick canopy of petalled branches casting pink and red shadows along her skin. Georgia lay on the soft lichen covered ground of the forest, the damp earthy scent filling her nostrils, the heavy drone of insects filling her ears as Sean fluttered her name against her lips.

They never got caught and the risk of getting caught, of doing something daring, dangerous, added to the intensity of their love-making. Georgia didn't care though. She took Sean in her mouth, writhed up and down on him, her bra hanging around her waist. Sean loved her hard and she saw fire in his eyes as he loved her harder still. She felt invincible.

Chapter Twelve

GOING OUT WITH Sean gave Georgia a renewed lease of life, carefree and happy, at least on the outside, despite the continued barrage of abuse from Nicolas. She went out with Sean whenever she could, the boys didn't complain about staying at Thalia's or their yiayia's and they enjoyed the time their dad now spent with them; making up for all the lost hours he'd chosen to spend with his mistress instead of his family.

***

One Friday evening, in July, Nicolas, in a foul mood, brought the boys back home after dinner at his mother's house. She noticed him becoming more and more riled as she ignored his barrage of questions and his temper escalated when Georgia refused to tell him where she had been the weekend before.

'Get out, you complete and utter idiot!'

'No way, you tell me where you were!'

'I don't have to tell you anything anymore. Or have you forgotten what you did to me?'

'Don't bring that up again…' he started.

'Again? You really are stupid. You're in denial. Trying to make me look like the bad guy here.'

'You're the one leaving your kids to go out with

whoever the fuck Sean is!' With two wide strides, he stood in front of her. He lashed out and grabbed her by the hair. He pulled her across the hallway.

'*Boudana*!' he yelled as he shoved her up against the wall. His eyes were wild. He spat in her face, the warm sticky spittle spattered across her eyes, cheeks and lips.

'How dare you call me a whore!' Georgia shocked at his foul language, defiantly wiped her face with the back of her hand. Although visibly trembling her mind sharpened. She pulled her mobile out of her jeans pocket, punched in 999.

'Police please,' she said through the sobs now engulfing her. She tried to hug Andoni who having heard the commotion from his bedroom snuggled up to her.

'For fuck's sake!' said Nicolas. 'You're kidding me!'

'Dad stop,' said Andoni, his bottom lip trembling as he squeezed his eyes to stop the tears from falling. Nicolas ignored him, pushing him away roughly as he loomed over Georgia.

'24, Greenwood Close, N3 OAY. In London. Finchley.'

Nicolas snatched her mobile and smashed it against the wall. '*Boudana*! You fucking tart!'

'Stop it. Stop shouting Dad!'

Georgia, heard the sirens above Nicolas's continued yelling, ranting and swearing, and flung the porch door open to two police officers. She tried to pull Andoni towards her but he wriggled away, choosing to hover by the foot of the stairs.

'We've received a 999 call to this address,' one of them announced as Georgia stepped aside to let them in. Nicolas looked at them incredulously and then at Georgia who recognised the fury darkening his eyes. Georgia took in a deep breath and exhaled slowly in an effort to slow her racing pulse. One of the officers spoke to her in the hall. She focused on him to block out her panic; tall with a mop of strawberry blond hair, cropped short, carroty freckles dusted the bridge of his nose. He explained Nicolas would be cautioned based on the complaint received.

'We'll take him away in our patrol vehicle. He will be hand-cuffed and only if absolutely necessary; if he resists arrest. He will be required to come to the station for further questioning.' His lips moved in an odd way as he spoke as if swallowing the air he breathed in. His grainy voice wafted over Georgia making everything seem skewed like a dream to her.

'It may be upsetting for the children to witness,' he explained looking over at the boys who were stunned in silence, all huddled together at the bottom of the stairs, 'so I suggest you take them upstairs preferably to a back bedroom so they don't witness what's happening.'

The second officer, shorter with broad shoulders and black hair which stuck up in tufts when he took off his hat, indicated to Nicolas to step to one side. As he had a quiet word with him Georgia strained to listen to what he said but struggled to hear anything over her pounding heart.

What happened next felt oddly surreal. Georgia ushered the boys upstairs into the back bedroom. They all sat on Zachari's bed, Kristiano hugging her tight as he sat on her lap, his slim legs dangling over the side of the bed. Andoni however agitated, insisted on knowing what was going on and kept asking questions. He disappeared into his bedroom without warning. Zach and Kristiano followed him. Georgia rushed in after them. As she looked on at the scene unfolding at the front of the house, she realised with a heavy heart Andoni had just witnessed his father being handcuffed, his hands held out in front of him.

'No, no,' Andoni called, pounding his fists on the window pane, 'the police are taking Dad away in the police car.' Zach stood on tiptoe to get a better view and Kristiano had pulled himself up onto the bed lined up with the window, straining his neck to glimpse something of the scene unfolding outside.

'The police just want to talk to *baba* about shouting at *mamma*,' she said, her voice splintering with emotion as confused tears ran down Zach's face. 'You can see *baba* tomorrow, come on. Move away from the window boys.'

Zach held tightly onto her hand and Kristiano reached up to her to be picked up again as the four of them cried, their tears like the crashing waves of a turbulent sea.

***

After finally settling the boys, who fell asleep in her bed, Georgia called her brother, Louis. He would be the one to panic the least when she recounted what had unfolded and having taken over their father's electrical contracting business she knew he had lots of contacts.

'I need to get the locks changed, so he can't just walk in and out whenever he feels like it,' she said, 'I need a locksmith tonight. I can't wait until the morning, Louis-Lou,' Georgia said using his pet name. 'Do you know anyone?'

'I'll call Billy. He's reliable, does a 24 hour call out emergency service. I've used him before. And don't worry about paying him I'll sort it out. He owes me.'

'Thank you,' she said, her voice catching, relieved her brother could help her. 'It's been awful. I still can't believe he could do this to me after everything he's done already.'

'Do you want me to come over?'

'No, no… it's okay. The boys are sleeping. I need to make sure he can't just walk in. I know he'll be back…Oh, Louis there's a knock at the door, hold on will you?'

Georgia walked across the hallway and hesitantly opened the front door. 'Who is it?' she asked.

'You stupid cow! How could you call the police on my brother?' Nicolas's younger and only sister, Angelina, dressed in her usual Juicy Couture bright bubble gum track suit, her hair tied in a messy knot and face devoid of any make-up, yelled at her.

'Look, Ange. It wasn't my fault. He hurt me. He pulled my hair. Spat in my face.'

'No more than you deserve. He tried to keep your marriage together but you wouldn't have it.'

'How dare you? I couldn't go on like that. Has he told you he's had a baby with her?' Georgia spat.

'Liar!' Georgia saw the confusion and self-doubt creep across Angelina's features as she desperately tried to re-compose herself. She stomped down the drive and revving her car, screeched off leaving Georgia standing in the doorway, shell shocked.

'Don't worry Louis, it was his sister, she's gone off now,' she said as she resumed the call with her brother. Her body began to shake involuntarily, delayed shock catching up with her.

'Angelina? What did she want?'

'Blaming me for everything. I don't believe it. After her brother had the affair.'

'Look, are you sure you're okay on your own?'

'Yes. Sorry, Louis. I'll wait up for the lock smith.'

'I'll text you when I get through to him. Give you his ETA.' She didn't bother telling him Nicolas had smashed her phone and she wasn't even sure if it still worked.

'Thank you darling. Love you.'

'Love you too. I'll call you in a bit, make sure you're okay.'

'On the house phone, yeah?'

'Okay, Georgi.'

'Thanks and please don't mention any of this to Mum and Dad. They're upset enough by the separation as it is.'

'I won't don't worry. Speak to you in a bit.'

'Okay. Bye Louis *mou*.' Georgia put the phone down. She sat in her front room, she felt alone and desperately woeful. Nicolas was never going to leave her be. He couldn't let her go.

***

Within the hour, the locks changed and safer at least for the night, Georgia crept into her bedroom. She carefully tried to get into bed next to Kristiano who had one of his legs splayed across Andoni's as they both slept intertwined. She gently nudged Kristiano over to make room for herself. The movement woke Andoni up. He stretched, looking smaller than his twelve years.

'I'm all squashed.' He pulled himself free of Kristiano's web of limbs and slipped off the bed wandering sleepy-eyed to his own bedroom. Georgia followed silently and tucked him in, pulling the duvet over his shoulders. He was growing up; almost a teenager.

'Love you, *agabi mou*,' she whispered to an already

asleep Andoni. 'I'll always keep you safe. Sleep tight.' She watched him for a few minutes as his chest rose and fell under the duvet, an almost imperceptible whistle leaving his parted lips with each breath. The light of the moon coming in through a gap in the curtains shone around the top of his head like a halo.

Back in bed, Georgia couldn't get comfortable with the other two boys still in with her. She crept back downstairs and made herself a mug of tea. She picked up her mobile phone from the hallway where it still lay on the floor. Despite the cracked screen it otherwise worked. She saw the message from her brother too. Bless him, she thought, I'm lucky to have such a supportive and caring family.

She sent her brother a kiss. She hoped it would go through. She then thought about Sean and sent him a text even though she knew he'd been working a late shift at a building depot for extra cash and would be asleep. Within a few minutes her mobile vibrated and she pressed 'Accept call'.

'What happened?' asked Sean.

'He pulled me across the hall by my hair and then spat in my face.'

'The gobshite!'

'And the kids saw it, heard all the shouting.'

'Hope you called the cops?' asked Sean, agitation in his voice. She could imagine him clenching and unclenching his fists, his hair sticking up in tufts from sleeping.

'I did and he got arrested. They've taken him to the station.'

'Well don't let him in if he comes back. I'll bust his cranium! I'm coming. I don't care if the boys are there. I won't stay long. Just a couple of hours till you feel better.'

Georgia reluctantly agreed and waited patiently, until almost an hour later, a rapping at the window made her jump. She got up and went straight to the front door.

She threw herself into Sean's arms, there on the door step, not caring if anyone saw them. She sobbed quietly into his shoulder.

'You okay?' she asked. 'You're trembling.'

'Yeah darling. Just worried about you. Want you safe.' His eyes were full of concern and something else but Georgia couldn't work out what before he looked away. They sat entwined in each other on the sofa. Georgia drifted in and out of sleep. She woke up with a start, hearing Zach's cottony voice as he called out from upstairs. Instantly overwrought with worry he'd come down and find Sean, she held up a finger to her lips to hush Sean and she groggily left the room. She found Zach in the hallway outside her bedroom door.

'Is *baba* still with the police?' he asked, his eyes red and sticky with sleep and she saw tears brimming behind them.

'No, *agabi mou* he's gone back to his flat now and he's sleeping,' she lied, 'which is what you should be doing.' She ushered him back into her bedroom. She crouched down beside the bed as he snuggled under the cotton duvet and Georgia sang a Greek lullaby to him which her *yiayia* used to sing to her. Georgia's hushed smooth tones echoed across the stillness of the room. Before she finished Zach's eyelids closed tight and his breathing became rhythmic indicating he had fallen asleep. She kissed him lightly on the forehead and then walked to the other side of the bed where she gently stroked Kristiano across the cheek. While upstairs Georgia changed into her nightwear and wrapped her dressing gown around her.

Downstairs, Sean dosed on the couch and as she watched him an overwhelming gush of emotion swept over her and she realised she had come to care for Sean deeply. He had come into her life when she was feeling unloved, ugly and worthless. She needed him in her life. She needed to feel loved and adored. She shook an involuntary shiver away.

The land line rang interrupting her thoughts. The female officer, from Colindale Police Station, spoke quickly, her voice spiky.

'Mr Josephides has been cautioned but not charged. He has clear instructions not to come back to the family home within the next twenty-four hours. He's not allowed in the house without your express permission thereafter. If you feel threatened in any way, call the station immediately.'

Georgia thanked her and scribbled her name, PC Emma Richards, on the note pad she kept by the telephone and hung up.

'Who's that?' asked Sean, stretching his arms above his head and yawning loudly.

'The police station. He's been cautioned and released.'

'Gobshite.'

'He has to stay away for a day minimum.'

'He shouldn't ever be allowed back full stop,' said Sean, his tone brusque.

'Well the locks are changed so he can't use his keys,' said Georgia.

'You should've changed the locks a long time ago.'

'Well I didn't in a million years think it would come to this,' said Georgia.

'I know babe. I know,' he said pulling her towards him.

***

Rousing from her groggy sleep it took her a while to realise where she was. A banging pricked at her mind and she registered a thumping coming from the front of the house. She pushed herself up from the sofa. She squinted, focusing on the Laura Ashley clock; the hands indicated ten past eight. She did a quick mental calculation in her head. She'd only had four hours sleep and realised she'd fallen asleep on the couch after Sean left.

She steadied herself and tied her robe tightly around her waist. She padded across the hallway still not quite fully awake, the early rays of the sun coming through the hallway window, sending beams of light bouncing off the huge antique mirror. She squinted as her eyes adjusted to the brightness, illuminated dust motes dancing around the space.

'Alright, alright,' she said quietly under her breath. 'I'm coming.' Probably the postman, she said to herself. Or a delivery for one of her neighbours.

She pulled open the front door and she peered out across the porch. She couldn't move. She couldn't speak.

'Go away,' she said quietly hoping the boys wouldn't wake but she feared his knocking which got louder and stronger might alert them anyway.

'No way. You have me arrested and then you change the locks. You're not getting away with this.'

'Go away,' she repeated, 'or I'll call the police again. You're not allowed to come here.'

'Says who?'

'The police told me. So just leave,' she said not wanting to make eye contact with him; to see the sadness and desolation she knew would be there. Georgia closed the front door behind her, leaving him in the porch banging, the thumping getting louder with each crash on the wooden frame. She sat on the other side of it shaking; her knees drawn up protectively. She wrestled with what she should do. If she called the police, the boys may see their dad being taken away again and it would break their hearts. Sure they wouldn't forgive her, she decided to wait until she could call Thalia.

The hallway clock struck nine. She gave a sigh of relief as the banging subsided and the boys, unusually, slept on. They must be exhausted after all the commotion last night, she thought. She knelt up from her sitting position and could still distinguish Nicolas's outline through the coloured glass.

'Don't move. I'm just dropping the kids off to Woodhouse Saturday Camp. I'll be with you in ten minutes. Fifteen the most,' said Thalia, no questions asked.

Georgia waited now slumped against the dresser like a rag doll and thought how only a few weeks ago she had still been sleeping with Nicolas.

She remembered how she had initiated the sex, all on her terms, something that hadn't been typical of their sexual relationship while married. She couldn't explain it other than she needed sex and sex with him she had fathomed to be better than no sex at all. Georgia hadn't cared how it would make Nicolas feel. She suspected, on more than one occasion, Nicolas thought sleeping together meant she would forgive him. She wouldn't, she couldn't. It was quite simply loveless and emotionless for her. And she knew it made her feel better, but she couldn't explain that to anyone. Not Thalia. Not her sister. In an odd way she felt dirty and ashamed yet liberated and in control too. But since meeting Sean she had stopped not wanting to cheat on her new boyfriend. She wasn't going to cheat on Sean nor stoop to Nico's level.

She waited for Thalia, listening to her breathing naturally rhythmic with the ticking of her *yiayia's* old fashioned wind-up alarm clock in the hallway.

***

Thalia arrived and hearing her pull up onto the driveway Georgia tentatively walked into the hallway. Certain Nicolas had left the porch, she opened the front door a crack.

Thalia and Nicolas faced each other. Thalia gave him one of her penetrating stares.

'I don't know what's gone on Nico,' she said, 'but this is not the way to sort it out. The boys are asleep. You're going to wake them up and they'll be upset if you're arguing again. Come on.' Her tone severe but calm, had just the right amount of sympathy to avoid riling his temper.

'She's changed the locks to our house,' he said pathetically and then more aggressively, 'she's not getting away with it. I've worked hard to get her the house she always wanted.'

'Well, strictly speaking it's her house now.' Thalia hesitated and then continued. 'You don't live here anymore so she has every right to change the locks.'

'What do you know?' he snarled at her, finding a renewed level of spite, his spittle landing on her lower lip.

'I know you can't do this to her. You've done enough,' Thalia said and she wiped her mouth with the back of her hand, looking him up and down.

He turned and walked down the drive taking long purposeful strides. With no warning, he looked back towards the house.

'It's not over. You can't play a dirty trick like that and get away with it!' His words were directed at Georgia, who peering out from behind the half-open front door, clutched at her robe. Thalia ignored him and walked into the house.

Georgia hugged Thalia, the relief of him leaving left her deflated and lethargic. She pulled agitatedly at her hair bands which were coming loose, her long waves wispy around her cheeks.

'He's in a bad way. He looks like shit. Gosh, better off without him if he's going to let himself go. Not shaven, stubble. He looks so much older. And who does he think he is, saying you've played a dirty trick on him? He's played the filthiest trick of all on you and almost got away with it.'

'I know. I'm so stupid,' said Georgia. 'Pig! I can't stand the thought of him being anywhere near me.'

She filled Thalia in on the saga of the night before. Thalia mostly listened, said nothing and every now and then stroked Georgia on the arm or held her hand.

'Look, it's bad. I know. But he's got the message. It's over. You two are not getting back together again. And if you need a phone, I've got my old Blackberry at home.'

'Well, the phone seems to be working for now. The screen's cracked but that doesn't bother me although I can't read my texts properly. But you know what? He's not just going to disappear, babe. He's mean. I don't think I ever really knew him.'

'You've got Sean now.'

'Yeah, I know. But it's not real with him Thal. It's not like being married and having your family unit. It's like I'm playing a part. It's like I'm leading two lives – the loving mum who's working hard to look after the boys so they don't miss out on anything and the girlfriend who doesn't have a care in the world. It's not real at all, you know?'

'It's not meant to be like being married. No responsibility. You don't owe him anything.'

'I know…'

'Just enjoy it for what it is, hun. And it is real. You're real. Where're boys?'

'They're still sleeping, surprisingly. It was gone midnight, maybe even one o'clock when they finally settled. Lucky it's a Saturday. They won't be up yet. Well, at least I hope not or they'll be really grouchy.'

'So you and Sean are okay?' asked Thalia.

'It's a bit of fun. I'm not going to marry him. I mean

sometimes I think I've got four boys not three. You know, instead of buying three pairs of trainers when I'm out I keep thinking I will have to buy a fourth pair for him too.'

'Oh, babe. That's funny.'

'And he's still living at home…it's a bit awkward.'

'I bet it is.'

'And listen to this. It'll really make you laugh. The other night, I was on the phone with him, just chatting, well talking dirty actually, and I hear this frosty voice, 'it's getting late and Sean really should be getting to bed, he's got an early start in the morning'.'

'Who was it? Not his wife? Don't tell me he's married?'

'No. It was his bloody mother! She'd picked up the other extension. We were on the house phone, his mobile was dead. She butted into our conversation. I was mortified. I mean, for fuck's sake. I don't even know how long she'd been listening in.'

'No way!'

'Yeah, honestly. How mad is that? Stupid cow!'

'Oh fuck,' said Thalia. 'What did you say?'

'I just kind of apologised pathetically as I stifled the giggles.'

'Time to find a real man, hun. Honestly. His mother?' Thalia burst out laughing as she rolled her eyes exaggeratedly.

'Oh stop it Thal'. I'm so at ease with him and he makes me feel good. Makes me feel pretty, young.'

'Young might be too optimistic, babe, if not near impossible!'

'Oh shut up…' said Georgia, pulling a face at her friend in jest, to hide her hurt ego.

'I'm joking babe. You're lovely, you don't need a man to do that.'

'No, I do when my husband has cheated on me and I keep wondering is it because I put on weight? Is it because I'm not pretty? Is it because I'm getting older?'

'Georgia, stop that. You're amazing. You're clever. You're a teacher for fuck's sake. You attract men wherever you go and your boobs are 'awesome'.' Thalia put on the American accent they were both prone to doing since their trip to New York. 'And if you do need a man, and Sean's not right for you, there're lots more out there.'

'Not with as big a cock, I bet!' laughed Georgia, in an effort to lighten the tone of the conversation and her mood. She was tired, as knackered and as weighed down as a village donkey carrying baskets of figs and grapes.

'Well, depends how spoilt you are now,' said Thalia.

'Very,' said Georgia.

'That's better. Keep laughing, babe. It's the only way we're both going to get through all this shit.'

They moved from the lounge to the kitchen, with its hand-built cupboards, painted a washed blue, the decorative, ornate columns enhancing its luxuriousness. They chatted together for another hour or so. Georgia made a round of toast which she buttered thickly and served with chunky slices of halloumi and wafer thin smoked ham. Georgia sat there with her friend. The tranquillity of the house wrapped itself around her but she couldn't shake off the hopelessness and desperation of earlier and it crept up on her again like a dark angel. She resolved not to break down again because of him.

She forced herself to eat, more from nerves than from hunger. They sat in comfortable companionship for a few minutes longer when the doorbell rang.

'Oh, God, will you get it?' Georgia felt her face turn the colour of a porcelain doll.

'And if it's Nicolas?'

'Tell him to go to hell.'

***

'Is this a bad time?' asked Mark as he stood up against the jamb of the kitchen door. Thalia stood behind him making faces and mouthing "cor".

'Oh no not at all.' Georgia relieved it wasn't Nicolas, or his ugly sister, beamed with a stupid grin she couldn't subdue. She handed him thirty pounds from her stash in the kitchen drawer and shifted from one foot to the other as she waited for her change.

'Sorry I've only got coins,' he said as he counted the loose change into her hand, touching it momentarily. 'So how have you been?'

'Okay thanks. Busy, you know.' She felt herself

blushing.

'Well look after your pretty self and see you next month,' he said as he gave her a wink.

'My gardener,' she explained to Thalia as she walked back in.

'Mine doesn't look like that!' she teased.

'Are you serious? Mark? He's just Mark.'

'Everyone is just someone until you see another side to them,' she winked.

Georgia nibbled at the last slice of halloumi when the doorbell chimed again. Her heart stopped and she felt the colour drain from her face, sure it would be Nicolas this time.

Chapter Thirteen

'WELL, IT'S LOVELY to meet you Sean,' said Thalia, as she shook Sean's hand. He was standing in the hallway rather awkwardly, after Thalia had answered the door expecting to see Nicolas. Georgia, hearing his voice, appeared from the kitchen.

'Call me later,' Thalia said to Georgia as she grabbed her handbag. 'I'm going babe.' She bent in close to Georgia and whispered in her ear. 'He's cute. Go girl.'

'Well, this is a surprise,' said Georgia to Sean, giving Thalia one of her looks. Georgia was slightly unnerved; Sean had turned up uninvited and without warning. What about the boys? She had no intention of telling them about him, not yet, but at the same time she had to admit she was pleased to see him.

'I missed you,' he said, groping her bum and pulling her close. He pushed her robe open, her full breasts burst out of her baby-doll nightie.

'Did you? You were only here last night,' she began, getting flustered, only to have him stop her mid-sentence. His mouth closed over hers and he kissed her hard, the heat trailing from his mouth to hers, leaving her senses with the lingering smell of his aftershave and the sharp mintiness of his breath. She felt her soft nipples harden, the wetness between her legs. Before she could stop him, they stumbled into the sitting room and slammed down onto the sofa. Sean just stopped the table lamp, as it wobbled precariously, from crashing to the floor. His hands were all over her. He pulled at her dressing gown and she wriggled out of it. She pulled his sweatshirt over his head, dug her nails into his back.

'I love you,' he said, before locking his lips onto hers, his fingers teasing both her nipples. She fought to stay in control but her emotions came in huge tidal waves, washing over her, drowning her, like a ship lost at sea. She could see he knew exactly what effect he had on her and she felt intoxicated. Wanting to gain control of the situation, she pulled away just before she gave way to an orgasm and scrambled into a kneeling position on the floor, in front of him. She tried to hoist his jeans down but couldn't. Finally, he helped her and she yanked down his boxers, and freed him, hard and erect. He pushed her down towards him, pulling and twisting her hair as he did, into a tight knot behind her head. She knew exactly what to do to make him come. It didn't take him long. 'God, I…lo…ve… you,' he called out, in a strained voice, as he released himself.

No sooner had she wiped her mouth clean she heard footsteps, muted by the coir carpet cross the landing upstairs. She mouthed to Sean to hurry up and get dressed. He frantically pulled on his sweatshirt, pulling at the sleeves to straighten them out. He hopped into his jeans and almost lost his balance as he pushed one leg in after the other. He fell back onto the sofa and leaned back, one arm stretched out across his knee, trying to look relaxed.

'*Mamma?*' She heard Kristiano calling out.

'Coming *agabi mou*,' Georgia answered, still breathless, her heart thumping hard. She stifled a nervous giggle as she kicked her nightie under the couch, pushing Sean back onto the sofa from where he had jumped up to kiss her. She tied her robe around her and noticed with horror it was inside out. She realised too her hair ties had fallen out. She snatched a rubber band from Zach's elastic ball sitting on the mantel piece and swept her hair up, wincing as her curls got tangled in the stretch of the rubber band. Sean made out he'd just taken a swig from the half empty mug of tea from the night before. Multiple footsteps padded down the stairs and the door opened.

'*Kalimera* my darlings.' Georgia found her breezy voice and said good morning to the boys as they huddled together in the doorway. 'This is Sean,' she managed as she introduced the boys one after the other to him.

'Hi,' Sean said, looking like a teenager with his matted hair everywhere.

'Who's that?' Andoni eyed Sean up, not getting too close as he surveyed him from the door his arm protectively around the shoulder of Zach. Kristiano came over to Georgia and buried his face in her tummy.

'He's a friend of mine,' interjected Georgia, her cheeks flushing crimson as she ruffled the top of Zachari's head as he scrambled onto her lap as she flopped back into the armchair.

'What's he doing here?'

'He came to see if I was okay,' mumbled Georgia.

'Why? Who is he?'

'Uh, we met a few weeks ago. At a restaurant,' said Sean.

'Stop all the questions Andoni. It's rude,' said Georgia and still panicking about her robe she got up and ushered them out towards the kitchen. 'Let me just go for a wee and I'll make you all some breakfast. Go on, go into the kitchen.' Georgia's heart raced. She hadn't wanted the boys finding out about Sean like this. She didn't want them thinking any less of her or to be confused after everything that had happened. She suddenly wanted to cry.

Sean followed her into the kitchen, smiling cheekily at her. Georgia realised he had noticed her robe now the right way round. Panic spread through her as she prayed the boys, especially Andoni, hadn't noticed. None of them remarked on it though.

After an unusually quiet breakfast of Coco Pops, Shreddies and a round of toast she packed the boys off upstairs to get dressed.

'Help Kristiano get dressed *agabi mou*,' Georgia persuaded a reluctant Andoni to go up.

'Why do I have to do it?'

'Because you're the eldest and I need your help.'

'I'm going to clear up down here.'

She shrugged Sean off, who had come up behind her as she stood at the sink. He slipped his hand inside her robe and groped one of her boobs. 'Stop, it,' she flirted, 'the boys. They might come down again any minute.' He ignored her and carried on. 'Stop it, Sean,' she said more aggressively. He pulled away and sighed. 'Come on,' she said, splashing Fairy Liquid suds all over the front of her robe, 'They don't know who you are. They're confused and I'm really upset they've seen you like this.'

'Like what?' asked Sean petulantly.

'His trousers are in the bottom drawer of the wardrobe folded up,' she called up to Andoni, ignoring Sean. 'The khaki green ones. I'll come up and find them in a minute.' She finished the washing up and leaving Sean sat in the kitchen she ran upstairs to find the trousers. She gave Andoni a hug and said, 'Sean's just a friend darling. I promise. Nothing's going to change.'

She took a quick shower and smothered her skin in body lotion. She threw on a white cotton skirt with a Cinderella hem line, which lay draped over her rocking chair and moss green T-shirt, with silver italic script spelling 'Mademoiselle Butterfly' stretched across her chest.

She nimbly rushed around the bedrooms and pulled the duvets across the beds while the boys each brushed their teeth, making a mental note to tidy up the bedrooms properly later on in the day. She could hear Andoni and Zach arguing over who would use the sink first. Andoni's tone aggressive.

'One of you can use the sink in my bathroom,' she called out. 'So stop bickering.'

***

Standing in the hallway, eventually ready to go to the park, Georgia held onto the canvas bag filled with bottles of water and the football retrieved from the old stone pot in the garden. As they piled out onto the drive, Sean turned to Georgia.

'I'm off now.'

'Where? You not coming to the park with us?' Georgia said, quietly relieved.

'No. You know, need to get home. Check up on Mum.'

'Does she need checking up on?' Georgia asked, incredulously.

'Well, she's not been well.'

'Probably all those midnight conversations she's been eavesdropping on,' she said sarcastically, 'Must have forced her blood pressure right up.'

'Yeah, Yeah. Ha, ha. Hysterical. Will see you later.'

'Well only if the boys are going to their dad's tonight,' she whispered as she leaned in towards him.

'Oh okay,' he said and he turned towards the boys, 'Bye boys. Good to meet you all. See you soon.' Sean gave them the thumbs up. He leaned in to give Georgia a kiss on the lips but she turned her head and he brushed the side of her face awkwardly.

'Bye,' they chorused back at him but Georgia didn't fail to notice Andoni hadn't replied.

'Bye,' Georgia said, as she ushered Sean off the drive and onto the pavement, mortified at the sheer discomfiture of Sean being observed by someone who knew her, or worse still, knew Nicolas.

***

At the park, the boys played football with some friends from school, there with their nanny who looked relieved at not having to kick the ball around any longer. Georgia, on the other hand, relieved Andoni hadn't questioned her any further about Sean still caught him looking at her a couple of times with a sideways look of suspicion.

Laid out across the blanket she had grabbed from the boot of the car at the last minute, she stretched out her bare legs in front of her, breathing in the smell of honeysuckle which hung in the air. She took out her damaged mobile to text Thalia and sat up. A text from Sean blinked at her from her messages received box; she could just make out the message through the cracked screen.

```
Hi. I'm home. Thinking about u and … body
x
```

She smiled and texted back,
```
Oh, yeah?
U bet. Can't wait to … later x

OK xxx
And u r so gonna … again x
```
Damn screen, she blasphemed.

```
Yeah?


Like never before x
```

The boys came running over to Georgia and Andoni stretched up for the ball sitting wedged in the hedgerow a few feet behind her.

'Nearly knocked my head off,' she said, 'be careful boys.' Zachari threw his arms around her, his sweaty forehead and red cheeks, rubbing the side of her face.

'I liked Sean,' he said.

'And Sean liked you,' she said.

'He has a big head,' said Kristiano. She laughed her head off at the irony of this.

'Why are you laughing?'

'Because I think it's rude to say that,' she said, through her giggles, and she reached out to tickle him. He fell about squirming on the blanket next to her while she tickled and tickled him. Georgia felt happier and relieved the younger two at least weren't upset by someone they didn't know being in the house, but she still wasn't sure about Andoni. She'd have to handle the situation sensitively. She didn't want to spoil the trust between them or create any further uncertainty for him.

Zachari and Kristiano ran off towards the enclosed play area with their friends and their nanny and this gave Georgia the opportunity to talk to Andoni. He refused to sit close to her and instead sat on the dry yellowing patch of grass opposite her.

'Look Andoni *mou*,' she began, 'I'm not going to lie to you about Sean. Are you listening to me?' she asked. He sulkily poked the hard ground with a stick and then tore at a tuft of grass. He ignored her, refusing to make eye contact. 'He's a friend I met when I was out with Jade and Paula and Julianna. He's been nice to me. I'm lonely when you go to your dad's and when Sean is with me it makes the time go faster and it means you're back home before I know it. You and your brothers mean the world to me and I love you to the moon and back,' she said, using their special little saying, to soften him up. 'Do you understand?'

'Why was he in our house? We weren't at Dad's today.'

'He came because he knew I was feeling upset...after the fight with your dad. He didn't want me feeling sad on my own,' Georgia said gently, tears pricking the back of her eyes.

'You weren't on your own,' he said stubbornly, 'we were home with you.'

'I know my darling. But he didn't know that. He was just being kind.' Andoni looked up at her, his face all screwed up and furrows of anger scrunched up across his forehead.

'Dad doesn't need anyone else,' he blurted out.

'Well dad has a friend too,' she said carefully.

'No he doesn't.'

'Why would I lie to you? When have I ever lied to you?'

'You're making all this up because you feel bad about Sean.'

'Now look, Andoni. I don't want to argue with you. There are things you don't know. Things you won't understand. You're still young but your dad hurt me. He lied to me about lots of things and I'm the one left to look after you. I'm the one trying to do the best I can to keep things going.'

'Well Dad wants to come home. He told me he loves you but you won't let him come back. It's you who's done this.' Georgia watched him as he got up and skulked away, his shoulders hunched, scuffing his trainers along the footpath as he disappeared towards the park exit gates miserably trailing the stick he still held behind him.

'Don't leave the park without me, Andoni!' He didn't seem to hear her and carried on walking.

Georgia hesitated, unsure whether to follow him or leave him to calm down. He was twelve years old and went to school and came home on his own. She would let him have his space to calm down. She looked up as she heard an airplane and watched the powder trail in the sky above her as it magically disappeared in front of her eyes. That's what she had to do, she thought, make the messy situation go away. She had to be honest with the children about her break up with their dad. She had to tell them about Roksana and the baby. She was no longer prepared to look like the bad one here. She was not prepared to continue with this façade. By not being honest with the boys Nicolas remained protected and Georgia as a result looked like the reason for the boys' parents not being together. With Sean on the scene it was getting messier. That morning proved it.

***

Back home Andoni sat on the iron bench outside the porch. She gave him a hug and although stiff and unresponsive at first his body gave way to her and he sunk into her as she held him tight. She promised him everything would be okay and he nodded reluctantly.

The boys were going to their dad's for the night and although she didn't want them to go she couldn't face arguing with Nicolas after she received his text. She knew the boys would want to be with him and she would never stop them from spending time with him. She texted her agreement and then decided, on a whim, to send him another text.

```
I'm telling the boys the truth. They need
to know.
```

He didn't respond.

***

Angelina pulled up onto the front drive, hooting to alert the boys. She made no effort to say hello staying seated in the car and avoiding eye contact with Georgia. Georgia didn't care. She didn't want to get into another row and Angelina's surly face momentarily put a dampener on her otherwise excited mood, as she anticipated the night ahead with Sean. Hugging the youngest boys tight, she kissed them, lots of silly light kisses all over their faces, on their noses, their foreheads, their eyes, their ears, their cheeks.

'Stop, *mamma*,' complained Zachari, but he made no endeavour to pull away and neither did Kristiano as she kissed him playfully, in turn.

'Bye my darlings, love you, see you tomorrow after lunch. Be good!' she said.

She tried to catch Andoni's eye but he didn't look up at her. He sloped away quietly grunting an ungracious goodbye.

***

She only just managed to hold back the tears while she waved them off and broke down after watching them disappear up the road. She hated them going and leaving her. And she hated the way things had been left with Andoni.

She missed the boys and she knew they found it difficult too; the backwards and forwards between homes. She could see it on their little faces and the way they ran into her arms when they came back home as her heart filled with regret; regret for a broken marriage she knew could never be fixed and for the life she had imagined herself living which had been ripped apart, like her heart, by the man who she thought she would grow old with and be married to for the rest of her life.

***

Georgia needed to unwind before Sean came over and went up for a shower. She took her time and languorously lathered herself all over with her favourite shower wash from The Sanctuary. She let the steaming water splash over her. She massaged herself with the matching body mousse and the stress of the day left her more relaxed, her tight shoulders and neck loosened under the shower's hot spray.

Once dry she massaged all over with the matching body mousse. She threw on some clothes dabbed on some blusher, ran a smoky grey liner across her lower eyelids and finished off with a thick layer of black mascara. Her curls dried naturally as she ran around tidying the upstairs hallway, throwing socks and discarded vests and Spiderman boxers into the laundry basket on the upstairs landing. She smiled at the plaque on the wall above it: *'LAUNDRY – drop your pants here'*.

She padded downstairs to the kitchen realising she had not eaten anything since breakfast. Her stomach growled at her echoing her thoughts. She buttered a handful of crackers, sliced some red Leicester cheddar cheese and cut half an apple into wedges. She gobbled down a piece of cheese as she took the plate into the sitting room.

Her jeans felt loose around her bum and the low cut top, although a bit tight, accentuated her buxom breasts and dwindling waistline. Losing weight gave her a sparkle and biting into her cracker she flicked on the music channel, blasting the volume up. The music almost instantly lifted her spirits, the thrum riding under her pulse. She danced in front of the mirror and as she looked closely she didn't recognise the woman staring back at her; peppy on the outside, her dull eyes told a different story.

She looked over at the PGCE graduation scroll sitting on her dressing table. It had been handed to her by the Dean a few days before. It had been a wonderful celebration for her and although her parents had been unable to attend the Graduation Ceremony, Thalia and

Zach had been there to cheer and wave as she walked up the steps to receive her accolade. It had been a proud moment for her.

***

Sean arrived just before nine o'clock. Georgia by now engrossed in a new drama on ITV found his insouciance selfish and although he apologised for his lateness, she felt the agitation mounting inside her. He blamed the bus. For God's sake, Georgia said to herself, bloody excuses, bloody bus. How old was he?

'Hi,' he said indifferent to her mood. He sat next to her and tucked one of her loose tendrils behind her ear, as he ran his fingers across the back of her neck lightly. His kiss tasted of mouthwash and she shivered with sexual anticipation as he continued to graze the back of her neck gently. He tilted her chin up towards him and he kissed her again, harder this time.

'Hi,' she gasped, her voice powdery. She licked her lips and tasted his minty saliva and a hint of something else too.

'You okay?'

'Of course I'm okay. Just been enjoying the quiet without the boys,' she lied, leading him into the sitting room.

'Yeah, I know what you mean. They're typical boys aren't they?'

'Full of energy and questions and drive. Just how I want them to be,' Georgia enthused.

'Just like their sweetheart of a mother,' he said, pulling her down onto the sofa on top of him so Georgia sat astride of him, 'and I know she's got a lot of energy.'

'Stop it, you're embarrassing me.'

'No, I'm not. You're blushing 'cos you know it's true.'

'What's in the carrier?' she asked, leaning over to have a peak at the brown bag on the floor.

'A couple of beers. And a WKD for you.'

'Ooh, we can party.' She switched channels and increased the volume. '*Give It To Me*' blasted out across the room and she flirtingly writhed up and down on his lap.

'Come here, you amazing woman,' he said and kissed her on the lips. She felt herself melt as his tongue probed hers and their tongues entwined and flicked and teased. They kissed deeply. They kissed hard. She pulled away from him, running her tongue over her lips seductively. He felt for her bra strap and he undid it in one quick movement. '*I Wanna Love You*' filled the room followed by 'The Way I Are'. She loved the music being loud. His hands were all over her and her lips were on his, his hardness pushed up under her. 'But together we can be the perfect soul mates, *Talk to me girl*,' sang Sean and then Georgia joined in, '*Baby if you strip, you can get a tip, 'cos I like you just the way you are*'. They laughed and kissed and drank each other on the couch, across the coffee table, on the rug, clothes strewn everywhere, until they were spent and Georgia yawned, dark shadows falling over her cheeks.

**

'You fell asleep,' he told her as she roused.

'What's this?' she asked, pulling at the knitted throw tangled around her.

'You looked cold.'

'How long have I been asleep?'

'About forty minutes. You kept calling out. Crying too.' He hugged her tight. 'You had a nightmare.' He took two swigs of his beer.

'Did I?'

'Yeah, you did to be sure…crying you were my sweetheart.'

'Well, it's probably because… I slept awkwardly. I feel stiff,' she said, rolling her neck to ease the tension out of it. She pulled herself up from where she had been lying and re-positioned herself snuggling back into him. She hoped she hadn't called out Nicolas's name. How embarrassing, she thought.

'Not the only stiff thing round here,' she said groping him under the blanket. 'And we can't ignore this, can we?' Her eyes sparkled with anticipation, now wide awake. Her breathing quickened and she disappeared between his legs. She worked on him until he almost stopped breathing from sheer excitement, and just at the moment before he came she pulled away and finished him off with her hand.

'You're absolutely amazing. The most amazing sweetheart I've ever known.'

'Oh, yeah? And how many have you 'known'?' she teased.

'Hundreds,' he teased back, 'and not one of them even comes close to you and how you make me feel.'

'That's because there's no-one else like me.'

'You're telling me,' he said. She listened to his breathing becoming shallower and then quieter as his heart rate slowed.

'I'm really hungry,' Georgia said.

'Have I not filled you up?'

'I mean food. My stomach is hurting I'm so hungry.'

'What would you like?' he asked her, stroking her breast.

'Pizza. With pineapple, pepperoni, black olives and mushrooms. You can pick one up.'

'Is that what you want? Pizza?'

'Yes please.'

'Then pizza it is for my sweetheart Georgia,' he said. Georgia watched him as he went from naked to fully clothed in a few minutes.

'I prefer you naked,' she said, pulling at the front of his shirt as he bent down and gave her a slow, deep kiss, his tongue exploring hers, filling her mouth.

'After pizza you can have me… any…way… you… like,' he drawled in his Irish accent.

***

The next morning, as the birds tweeted and chittered in the trees in the central reservation opposite the front of the house. It was Sunday and little traffic noise came from the High Road. Georgia woke and looked over at Sean. He looked like a boy angel with a stream of early morning sun hitting the top of his head as he slept, but she knew he was no angel. She remembered last night after the pizza and the beers and the WKD. Sean had been insatiable and she had experienced a night like no other. He was gentle but powerful, he was kind but hard, he was loving but passionate to the point of possessing her. He excited her. He unleashed in her all those things a 'good' girl shouldn't do and she loved it. She turned away from him and closed her eyes. She wanted to remember every moment of last night forever. She drifted back into a dreamy sleep.

***

The ringing of her mobile woke her up. It must have been an hour or two later. She answered it, groggy, half-sleep.

'Hi, it's me.'

'Nico? What d'you want? Are the boys okay?' she asked sleepily.

'Yeah of course they are!' and then more calmly he continued. 'Look, I'm not going to take all this lying down. I'm seeking the advice of a solicitor.'

'On a Sunday?' She sat up and dangled her legs over the side of the bed.

'Don't be so sarcastic. I just wanted to let you know.'

'Advice? What about?' she asked more alert now.

'I want full custody of the boys,' said Nicolas and he ended the call before Georgia could say anything more.

Chapter Fourteen

'IF YOU CAN'T move on babe, if you can't work it out why don't you come and see Warren with me?' said Thalia down the phone as they chatted a week later.

'Warren? Oh, I don't know Thal I'm not into stuff like that and my mum would go mad if she found out,' responded Georgia, 'playing with the devil and the unknown spirit world.'

'Look it's nothing weird. He's so good–accurate–and he'll give you peace of mind which you don't have right now.' Peace of mind, what Georgia desperately craved.

'Look it's not for me.'

'But he could make all the difference to how you feel. How you look forward,' insisted Thalia. Georgia doubted it. No-one could take away her inner turmoil and regret and anxiety, ever present. Mostly on the inside those feelings crept out on her when she least expected it and that's what she couldn't deal with.

'If I decide to go, will you come with me?' she said after a few minutes' silence.

'Of course I will. I'll book our sessions back to back. You wait for me and I'll wait for you. Or I can sit in with you if you want me to.'

***

At home, Georgia looked up her horoscope:

You will come across someone a little strange or eccentric
They will show you have the strength to face your problems
You will get your self-confidence back
You will face your inner anxieties and fears head on
Someone new will show how much you should appreciate your wonderful qualities

Encouraged by the horoscope and mulling over Thalia's suggestion from every possible angle Georgia called her back.

'What will this guy ask me? Anything, you know…weird?'

'No he's really ordinary, plain really, small. The sort of person you probably wouldn't notice in the street.'

'And you'll come with me?'

'Yes of course I said I would, didn't I? Are you going then?'

'Babe I'm going to do this. I've got nothing to lose.'

'And everything to gain,' said Thalia delighted her friend already sounded lighter. 'I'll make appointments for us. You won't regret it Georgi. Promise.'

***

Georgia followed Thalia up the concrete cement steps to the second floor of the council-estate housing block after being buzzed in by Warren. The stair well smelt damp and dirty. Litter carpeted the stairwell; fragments of broken beer bottles and empty scrunched cigarette packs strewn everywhere. The walls smeared with dirty smudges closed in on Georgia as she followed tentatively up the stairs behind Thalia. The smell suffocated Georgia who screwed her face up in disgust as she spied a used condom two steps ahead of her.

They reached the tiny square landing and Georgia waited nervously with Thalia for the scuffed magnolia-painted door to open. Georgia noticed layers of paint peeling off in thick strips and the gaping hole where the door handle used to sit. For a split second she wanted to run and hide. What was she doing here for God's sake? Warren pulled the door wide to let them both in.

Standing in the tiny, rectangular vestibule, Georgia peered into the darkened room opposite her lit up by a shaft of light shining through the gap in the mottled brown curtains, which had seen better days. What am I doing here? she said to herself again. She took Warren's proffered hand and shook it. It felt damp and sticky in hers and she wanted to pull away. Her hands were soft and moisturised and as she followed Warren she wiped her hand on the outside of her jacket as she looked him over. Warren was shorter than she had imagined him. Not that she had spent much time thinking about him. His suit jacket drooped off his skinny shoulders and the cuffs of his shirt hung longer than his suit sleeves. He needs a new wardrobe, thought Georgia.

Georgia sat upright on the beige padded kitchen chair Warren brought into the room for her from what looked like a bedroom coming off the narrow hallway. It reminded her of the corridor which lead to the Head mistress's office at Moss Grove School, her old primary school, shadowy grey and uninviting. She pulled the chair up to the plain table with legs shaped like the spindles she remembered going up the stairs in her *yiayia's* house. She nervously traced the geometric patterns in its turquoise Formica top with the tip of her forefinger.

Warren settled opposite her and explained he would tape the reading for her. Georgia nodded at him. Her gaze landed on the fluted glass vase on the coffee table holding a small bunch of faded plastic flowers trapped under a layer of dust. The rest of the room stood bare other than the shabby mustard-coloured three seater pushed up against the wall to her left; its presence domineered the rickety coffee table in front of it. He definitely doesn't live here, thought Georgia; it's too echoey, too unloved, empty. She shivered as the cold of the room seeped through her silk blouse into her skin.

'I don't keep a copy,' he said, interrupting her thoughts. He leaned across towards the tape recorder, the dusty lead trailing off towards the floor. 'Ready?' he asked as he pressed the play and record buttons together.

Georgia's mind flashed back to age seventeen, staying up on a Friday night to record the Lyceum Live from the radio at midnight, hiding under her bed covers so the clank of the buttons wouldn't be heard in the silence of the house.

'Ready,' Georgia said nervously.

'So first choose a medium.' Georgia looked from the crystal ball to the deck of tarot cards. The ball teased her with its shiny, smooth curves. The pile of giant lavender edged cards somehow beckoned her. She looked from one to the other and pointed more assertively than she actually felt to the deck of cards.

Warren nodded in acknowledgment of her decision and picked up the card deck. He expertly shuffled the cards. He put them into three piles, face down, and asked Georgia in turn to pull out a card from each pile. He fanned them out in front of her, again facing down. He then turned each one over and placed them in front of him, one next to the other. He looked at each card carefully. Georgia studied his face as he did this. He had bushy wild eyebrows which sat low above his blue eyes almost giving the impression he had no eyelids. The hairs poked out in differing directions. His hair revealed flecks of ash over his ears and his head shone with purple-blue veins running across it in a pattern of rivulets.

'This card here...I can see you are experiencing real trauma in your life right now. This is something to do with a man. A man who has been in your life for a long time…there's a long line showing you have been together for a long time…it stretches far and long. And yet you don't really know him. You must not trust what he says to you. He is manipulative. He is calculating. He's betrayed you and you're deeply offended and upset by this. He will try to gain your trust again and he will poison anything kind and loving you give him. The card here urges you not to go back to him.

Georgia swallowed, trying to keep herself from crying even though a ball of sorrow ascended towards her heart where it sat, heavy and painful. The pain physical.

'This man, his initial is N and he is looking back. He is in reverse. He is faceless. He cannot be trusted.'

'That's my husband,' said Georgia quietly, her voice almost a whisper.

'He is looking back and he is not to be trusted. He has been playing away for a while and he has been living a double life which has left you confused and vulnerable. I can see he walks forward and doesn't look back which shows he has no regrets. He's living the double life. It says you forgave him a great deal in the past but he's broken the rules again. He's in the reverse again. It says you don't want to be with him now. There would have been a time you would've overlooked his shortcomings. But it shows the lies are no more. You are saying it's over but you're entangled in the happier times of the marriage. You want a change in the marriage and the ring you have taken off is shown to be with solicitors.' Warren paused, closed his eyes.

'Yes.' Georgia could trust herself to say nothing more, her voice strangled by her tears.

'Your troubles will pass and you mustn't be afraid. I see a house with a big red ribbon tied around it. Tied around it like a bow on a present. It's bright. It's red. This is a good sign. This means you will hold onto any property you want. It will be yours to do what you choose.' Georgia swallowed again. 'I think you will keep it for a while but I also see a new set of keys.' Georgia shifted in her seat, fingered the ends of her hair nervously.

'I see three boys. Young boys. Do you have any sons?' asked Warren, looking up at Georgia for confirmation.

'Yes, three.'

'One is far more upset than the other two. His name begins with an A.'

'That's my oldest. His name's Andoni.'

'He is partly hidden behind the others. That's why I almost missed him. They are with you and want to be with you. I see a courtroom but you will go there determined. You will be strong. Love is all around. They feel safe with you. I can see your arms spread wide around them. You are protecting them. An argument will take place but you will leave smiling.'

Georgia's tears rolled down her face, the relief she felt overwhelming her. The room remained silent apart from the sound of her sniffling, as she tried to stop her nose from running, and the quiet whirring of the tape recorder. She looked across the room and focussed on a picture hanging crookedly, on the scuffed plain wall. A sheep dog in a green field and a bright blue sky stared out at her. Hope, she thought.

'I don't mean to upset you. I'm sorry,' Warren said. 'Would you like me to stop?' Georgia shook her head, too afraid to speak.

'I can see the grief coming to an end soon and you're stronger than you think you are. Someone will test you but they are not themselves. They will be sorry. Someone new in your life. They're not bad. The number three may indicate three months from now or a number combination of three. Remember the number three,' he repeated.

Georgia smiled through her tears.

'I see the letter D. There's a man in your life whose name is…Dave. David. He has a strong presence and influence on you. Do you know anyone called David?'

'No. I don't,' Georgia said. 'No, I don't think so.'

'At work, a friend?'

'No there's no David at work...'

'Well the image is perfectly clear. I can see the name David in big gold letters flashing brightly which means David is already in your life. He is someone you know. So look out for him.' Warren, dropped his arms to his side and he shook them loosely. After a few seconds, he raised one hand to his forehead and scratched at the furrowed lines across it and then again at the hairline behind his ear.

Georgia noticed a light flurry of dandruff against the charcoal of his jacket as he itched away.

'He genuinely adores you and has a great deal of love for you. David is facing you head on and is a strong man. He will be there for you no matter what. He is not the man you see yourself with but he will prove himself to you. He will be loyal and loving and supportive. Adoring of you.'

'There's a lady in your life with a letter T. Do these mean anything to you?' he asked.

'Well, my friend with me today is Thalia. She's one of my best friends. She's the one who persuaded me to come to see you.'

'There is a big room with lots of people in it. You're smiling and talking to a girl who isn't feeling well. She will leave the room, there's a party but you will stay. Something will keep you up late when you get home. I can see you smiling. This is a good reason to stay awake. It's your phone. There's a call. You normally go with your head. I can see the heart in recess and the head is big and bold. You will listen to your head. So look out for an invite to a party or a celebration of some sort. I think it's in a house. It's a room, a long room.' Georgia smiled. She liked parties.

He paused for a few minutes and cleared his throat, reaching over for his glass of water. Georgia watched his Adam's apple bob as he swallowed; his shirt collar too big for his scrawny neck. 'There's a lady trying to get through to you from the other side. She's just sat down on a chair. One you were close to though. She ... who is Anna please? Your dad's mother. She's waving to you. Two ladies are watching over you. They are watching over you and the children and will protect the four of you. There's something about a child who didn't survive. Not to upset you but there's a lost child. Anna's giving you coffee in a little cup and she wants you to drink it. She wants you to drink it with your father. It's good for your chest and gets rid of all the bad colds...oh they've decided to sit quietly now. They are just watching now...'

***

On the drive home, Georgia felt lighter and somehow excited. Georgia tumbled everything out to Thalia and then she listened to what Thalia had to say about her reading too. Georgia held tightly onto the tape Warren had given to her. She went over and over what Warren had told her. The boys would be safe and happy which gave her such a sense of relief. But then who on earth was David? When would he show himself? Georgia wondered how much of what Warren had told her would turn out to be true and what was just pure guesswork.

Georgia's head reeled with everything and as they approached home her *yiayia's* request to drink coffee filled her mind. How was she going to drink coffee with her dad? She hated coffee and her dad knew it too.

BROKEN PIECES OF TOMORROW

***

A few days later Georgia's mum called her. Georgia walked to her car with her weekly shopping, surrounded by the twilight migration of commuters spilling out across the road from the station as they headed for home.

'Your dad's home for a change. Come over *agabi mou*, my love, and have a cuppa with us,' she insisted.

'Okay Mum. I'll see you in ten minutes.'

Georgia hurriedly unpacked her food shop and grabbing her mobile phone and sunglasses drove to her parent's home.

Sat round the scrubbed pine table in her mum's kitchen her mind went back to what Warren had said about the coffee.

'Actually Mum I'll have a Greek coffee with Dad.'

Coffee? Really?'

'Well, I had the oddest dream a few days ago,' she lied, 'and *yiayia* Anna told me to drink a cup of coffee with Dad.'

'Oh darling, that's lovely. She's looking out for you. Coffee is good for you, keeps you healthy,' Georgia's mum said, tears filling her eyes. Georgia looked at her and felt a ball of scrunched up emotion and pain building up in her throat. She hugged her mum tight and together they cried. Georgia released her mum and then pulling themselves together Georgia's mum began to make the coffee on the stove. She stirred the coffee patiently as she waited for it to rise and just before it over boiled she took the little brass coffee pot off the heat and poured.

'What's happened?' asked Georgia's dad as he walked in noticing their red eyes. 'Are the boys alright? Has something happened?'

'They're all okay Dad. You know the usual arguments and fighting but nothing major,' she said as she gave her dad a kiss on both cheeks

'So you're not crying?'

'I just had a dream about *yiayia* Anna and she wants me to drink coffee with you.'

'Yes? Come on then,' he said. 'Let's drink coffee together.'

And they both sat and drank the strong black Greek coffee together from the little demi-tasses with a map of Cyprus painted on the side of them. Georgia took baby sips at first. She felt warmth and an odd fuzziness run through her as she drank. She knew her *yiayia* would look after her somehow and she snuggled warmly in her closeness fighting back the overwhelming urge to cry again as she looked over at her dad.

Chapter Fifteen

ONE MONDAY EVENING, Thalia busied herself preparing dinner for them all. Thalia, in her granite grey onesie, had her jet-black hair swept back off her forehead into a tight shiny pony tail. It swung from side to side as she moved around the kitchen. Georgia quietly envied how she looked so glamorous even at home cooking. In contrast she felt too prim in her pencil skirt and blouse. Her legs, clad in navy sheer tights felt sticky from the heat. Her long lacklustre waves, tied back from her face with plain brown Kirby grips, fell messily around her shoulders as she tucked them behind her ears again.

'He can't do that,' Thalia tried to reassure her as she stood by the sink, peeling potatoes to make *badades me d'avga* for dinner. The fluffy eggs, already whisked filled a Pyrex bowl ready to add to the small cubes of potato to shallow-fry.

'Well, he's spoken to some lawyer and he must think he's in with a chance if Nico's saying it,' replied Georgia, somewhat more aggressively than she had intended. Sitting at the kitchen table she loudly chopped and viciously sliced tomatoes, red onions, cucumber, white cabbage and lettuce to make a Greek salad.

'Listen. He's bluffing. He's trying to scare you,' said Thalia, and then hesitantly added, 'watch yourself with the knife babe. A trip to A & E is the last thing you need on top of all this.'

'Sorry babe, yeah I know. I'm just so wound up!'

'He's trying to control you.'

'Well, it's working,' she said, putting the knife down. She took her third chocolate bourbon from the open packet. She looked down at the washed vegetables she still had to chop and picked up the knife.

'You have to stay strong, focussed. Right, let's think. Why would a court give him full custody?'

'Because he will convince the judge I can't look after them…'

'He can't do that. He's not clever enough,' said Thalia, keeping her voice calm and low, conscious the children were next door watching Pokémon.

'But his top notch city lawyer will.' Her voice prickled again, panic rising within her.

'Nicolas works six days a week, including half terms and holidays, he lives in a crummy flat, he has no way of getting the boys to school when he has to be in work by six in the morning.'

'The boys say the flat above the café's nice. They told me he's done it up and bought bunk beds for them.'

'So what? He can't compete. You're a teacher, have half terms and holidays off with the boys, you already have someone lined up to walk Kristiano and Zach to school and pick them up for you, you still live in the family home, near their friends, family, familiar surroundings, regular routines. No judge is going to give him full custody,' said Thalia assertively. 'I promise you.'

'So in the meantime I just have to wait.' Georgia stuffed another biscuit into her mouth greedily. What was wrong with her? Her mind wandered to Warren's words about the red ribbon round her house. Maybe he was referring to her family, the boys, as opposed to the physical building. She hoped against hope the home as she knew it would remain in her life; for her and the boys.

'No. You just have to carry on being the mum you are; the best mum those boys could have. The judge'll recognise how you're putting them first as opposed to Nico who's clearly putting his need to control you and his fucked up situation before the welfare of his sons.'

'I hope you're right, babe. I will die without… the… boys.' Georgia burst into floods of tears. Her voice trailed off into a strangled sob and she ran to the downstairs cloakroom to compose herself. When she came out she gave Thalia a weak smile.

'Better?'

'Yes darling. No more tears. He's not going to beat me.'

'That's the spirit babe. Now tell me about work. How's it all going?'

'Well my Faculty Leader's offered me a job from July which means I have a permanent job at The Ravenscroft School and I get paid over the summer!'

'No way! How lucky are you?'

'So lucky! It means I can complete my NQT year there, where I'm familiar with the staff and practices and the classes. It couldn't be better hun.'

'What's NQ…?' asked Thalia.

'NQT. It stands for Newly Qualified Teacher. Basically my teaching practice is observed and judged against a list of Teaching Standards and once I've evidenced these, over the course of the school year, I'll be signed off so to speak which means I'm awarded Qualified Teacher Status, QTS.'

'Sounds complicated.'

'Not really. It's just a way of making sure I'm ready to teach my subject and deliver to the professional level expected. It will be hard work but it won't be difficult. I am on it!'

'So proud of you, Georgi. You've taken everything negative and used it to make something of your life, something positive, something for you.'

'Having something to focus on has definitely made it easier. I would've gone mad otherwise. It's been a distraction and it's got me through this…this…turmoil and sadness.'

'Good for you,' said Thalia.

'And it's meant I haven't been dwelling on him and her!'

'Exactly. Instead of sitting there all bitter and twisted and thinking about revenge you've done something for yourself. Stuff them!'

'Exactly babe. Stuff them!'

***

June disappeared and the month of July went by just as quickly and before she knew it the summer holidays had arrived. She calmed down about the prospect of going to court and harnessed her emotions by focusing on preparing her case. She wasn't going to lose the boys. Sean remained a constant in her life too and she always felt thrilled spending time with him, thankful to have him in her life. Sex was heavenly with him and she enjoyed playing out his fantasies for him. It gave her control. The sort of control she hadn't always had in her marriage and she liked taking the lead. She liked the way she felt more confident and happy around him. He didn't question all the time or criticise her. She knew how much Sean adored her and everyone who saw them together could tell.

***

Home alone, one evening, Georgia sat with a mug of camomile tea thinking how she already missed the boys who were staying with their dad for a couple of nights. She tried to fill the time and kept busy; she worked on a Scheme of Work for September, in front of the telly. However, she lacked the productivity she normally would achieve, already horny at the thought of Sean coming over. She couldn't concentrate and gave up after planning a mere five resources and two activities which took her up to Week Four of the autumn term.

Putting her laptop aside, Georgia stood up and breathed in the fresh summer air coming in through the open window. She faced the mirror above the mantel piece and adjusted the zip of her soft jersey hoodie, pulling it down, the top of her cleavage just visible. She ran her fingers through her curls. She then took a step back and standing with her legs apart she tipped her head down towards the floor, fingering and teasing her roots to add more fullness. She threw her head back as she stood upright and the bouncy curls settled loosely around her shoulders.

***

Sean arrived half an hour later than she had expected him but she didn't say anything. He strolled in and put the pizza he had picked up on his way down onto the kitchen table and turned towards her. He roughly pulled her close and she felt his intake of breath.

'Hello there, my sweetheart,' he said, with joviality in his voice. Georgia noticed his red eyes and how he slurred his words.

'Hi, babe,' Georgia said. She could see Sean delighted in seeing her. He gave her a lingering French kiss. It left her breathless and with an odd after-taste.

'You pushing me away, Georgia?' he teased.

'I can't breathe,' she said, slowing her breathing as it came in short, hard gasps.

'Well, that's what love does to you. It takes your breath away.'

'So this is love is it?'

'Yes. I love you,' he said, clearly earnest and with such seriousness she wanted to laugh, but knew she would offend him if she did. She didn't think she loved him. Not in the way she had loved Nicolas with every bit of her, every thought, every action. She lusted after him, yes, but that wasn't the same thing. Not in her book anyway.

'What pizza did you get?' she asked, steering the conversation away from the subject of love.

'Your favourite,' he said, pulling her close again.

'Why not your favourite?' she asked.

'Because my favourite is right here,' he said, edging the zip further down on her hoodie to reveal the top of her breasts.

What happened next became a heady blur of touching, stroking, arousing. Sean physically turned her around. She shuffled her bum back across the smooth waxed surface of the pine, her legs hung over the table's edge. Sean grabbed the pizza box and threw it insouciantly. It collided with an empty tumbler. She heard the shattering of glass but she didn't care. How unfair she thought for a split second if it had been one of the boys she would have shouted at them for being clumsy. Then her head spun. Sexually aroused, her desire oozed from every pore.

Sean pushed her back across its length. Lifting her feet up she spread her legs as he leaned between them. Slowly he pulled down the zip of her top, stopping at her décolletage. She blistered with want; her cheeks burnt flame, her palms clammy as she throbbed with desire for him, his hands, his touch. He stroked the top of her breasts, the back of her neck where he grazed her lightly with his fingers. He pulled at her hair and kissed her softly, gently.

Georgia wanted him inside her, his pace agonisingly slow crashed with her need for fast and furious. She looked at him, her eyes begging him, willing him to release her. He carried on taunting her. He exposed her breasts. He rubbed her nipples, teasing each one in turn. She moaned and played the game. Close to exploding Georgia held it together not wanting to succumb just yet seeing how this turned him on. He leaned back away from her and pulled down his jeans. He stepped out of them and pulled off his Calvin Klein boxer shorts. As he stood up against the edge of the table she leaned forward, moved in close and urgently took him in her mouth as he moaned her name over and over again; his need becoming stronger. Just as he came he pulled away and she licked him up. She edgy, ready to explode. He satisfied, his eyes sultry, lost.

Then her turn came. She wasn't disappointed.

***

'Why aren't you eating?' he asked, his jeans still on the floor where he'd dropped them not twenty minutes earlier.

'It's cold,' she said.

'Haven't I warmed you up enough?' he said.

'No. I mean yes. I'm talking about the pizza.'

'Put it in the microwave,' he said.

'You've got me all tizzed up now.'

'Well, if I were you I'd eat because you'll need all the energy you can get tonight.'

'Yeah?'

'Oh yeah.'

'Why's that?'

'Cos I haven't finished with you yet,' he said, leaning across and stroking her face, his hazel eyes holding her stare.

Half an hour later, she remembered she'd left her mobile upstairs when she'd gone up to shower. She began to make her way up the stairs when Sean followed her and took her hand, forcing her to turn around. She stood on the steps which just turned up and around the corner to the top landing. He pulled her down right there and then and she gasped in anticipation. He slipped off her bottoms and unzipped her hoodie, fully exposing her. He pulled it down over her arms and left it there, restraining her movement. She arched her back and he released her bra strap losing himself in her full breasts as he kissed and sucked hard on her nipples. He entered her, the condom swiftly on him and there on the stairs, he made her come with such all-consuming force she cried, the emotion too much for her.

'Did I hurt you?' he said.

'No, not at all. I'm just overwhelmed by what you said earlier.'

'What did I say?'

'You said you loved me,' she said, the tears welling up in her eyes again.

'I do, Georgia. I love you.'

'How can you love me? You don't know me.'

'I know you're amazing. I know you're the best lover I've ever had. I know you make me wild with happiness.'

'Really?'

'Yes. Really. You're my sweetheart. I love you.'

'What if you get bored…find someone else like Nicolas did?'

'I won't. I'm not going to stop loving you.'

***

Georgia rose early two days later to take a last look over her Scheme of Work before putting it away and switching off from school for the summer. Summer she thought. Yeah, right. An overcast, colourless sky hung low, the wind squally and the heavy drizzle thrashed against the window panes making the old, thin glass rattle in their paint-blistered frames. The August weather matched Georgia's mood; edgy, nervous, unpredictable. She wondered if she missed the physicality of having Sean near her. She craved him and her mind wandered back to when she hankered for Smarties while pregnant with Zachari and pepperoni pizza with Kristiano. That all seemed like a long time ago. How things had changed. Her life had become unrecognisable to the life she imagined as her destiny.

She heard the clatter of the post box and padded over to the porch. She scooped up the mail from the Victorian tiled floor, and shuffled through it absent-mindedly. She stopped as her eye caught the blue franking of the solicitor's postmark on one of the envelopes.

Abandoning the other letters on the top of the shoe cabinet in the porch, she walked over to the kitchen and sat down heavily. She leaned her elbows on the reclaimed pine of the table top and held the envelope out in front of her. She felt instantly cold and her heart raced. She tore at the envelope, knowing too well what she would find inside and yet still hoping against hope Nicolas would have changed his mind. The letter, short and succinct, outlined Nicolas's intention to apply to the courts for full custody of the boys.

SOULLA CHRISTODOULOU

Grange, Johnson and Donovan
Solicitors & Advocates

Mrs G. Josephides
24 Greenwood Close
Finchley
London
N3 0AY

5th September 2007

Dear Mrs Josephides

We have today been instructed to act on behalf of our client, Mr Nicolas Josephides, to pursue full custody of the three minors, your sons jointly, named Andoni Louis Josephides, Zachari Nicolas Josephides and Kristiano James Josephides.

As Mr Josephides' solicitor we have applied formally and in writing to the Barnet County Court for a mediation meeting with a view to securing full custody of the children. Once a date has been confirmed the court will contact you directly with details of the hearing.

Should you require any further information or clarification of anything contained herein, please do not hesitate to contact us on the number at the bottom of this letter.

Yours sincerely
Alvin C. Gregory, LLB (Hons)

BROKEN PIECES OF TOMORROW

Grange, Johnson and Donovan
Solicitors & Advocates
68 Great Eastern Street, 3rd Floor, EC2A 7PY
020 7235 5679/0207 235 5680/020 7235 5681
Email: acgregory@gjd.co.uk

Georgia's breaths came in short nervous gasps as she read the letter over and over until the words were a blur in front of her and tears fell in big wet drops over the page. She couldn't believe it had come to this. She couldn't believe his actions against her. She had to talk to Nicolas, to make him see sense. She got up, flicked on the kettle and breathed more slowly in an effort to calm herself. She turned to make the call to Nicolas when the land line rang.

'Hello,' she said.

'It's me. You're likely to get a letter in the post today,' Nicolas announced in a cold voice, detached of emotion.

'I already did. How could you? How could you do that to me after everything you've put me through,' yelled Georgia giving in to the rage within her.

'Now hold on a minute. You started this. Changing the locks. Getting me arrested.'

'Because you hurt me. You dragged me across the hall by my hair. You spat at me in front of the boys. You're disgusting!'

'And you can't keep the boys from me.'

'And how am I doing that exactly?'

'You're turning them against me and I couldn't stand not seeing them,' he said.

'Well, you know what? You did that all on your own when you slept with that whore and then decided to have a bastard baby with her!'

'Don't bring her into this. It's nothing to do with her!' he said.

'Oh, really now? So she had a baby all on her own. The cleverest most amazing Romanian in the world! Aren't you lucky to have her!' Georgia slammed the phone down, shaking and swearing over and over again until she finally burst into tears again powerless to control her emotions. She had to get in touch with her solicitor.

***

The weather progressively worsened moving into September and Georgia, back at school, continued to dedicate her time to planning and delivering her lessons with the highest level of detail and creativity. With the uneasiness of the impending court hearing bearing down on her she battled as she neared burnout, energy draining from her as if she were wounded.

God only knows how but Georgia got through her lesson on cash flow forecasting after yet another broken night's sleep while everything crowded her head. Her termly lesson observation addled her usually composed calmness yet surprisingly she received positive feedback.

'A great lesson Georgia. Innovative and well-planned which had the students engaged and yearning for more. The pace was good and students asked questions and clearly enjoyed the group activity. Well done,' said her Faculty Leader.

'Wow, thank you,' Georgia said completely gobsmacked.

She smiled in response to the applause from her colleagues when she told them but all the while Georgia wanted to get home as soon as possible to phone her solicitor, Madeleine Stone. The after school staff training typically over-ran. Eventually she got home, and had to prepare dinner by which time she missed the opening hours in which to make the call. Georgia sighed as she recalled Madeleine's watery response to her questions the last time they had spoken.

The next morning, she waved Andoni goodbye as he sauntered off to school with two of his new secondary school friends, looking more assured than she knew he actually was. She dropped Zachari and Kristiano to St Mary's Breakfast Club and just made it to school on time. She made the call to Madeleine during her morning break from the privacy of the Faculty Office which nearly always accommodated Georgia alone. The other teaching staff of the department preferred to use their own classrooms during their planning and non-teaching time.

She should have been exhausted and yet she felt strangely energised and more alert than ever despite, at most, only getting five hours sleep a night for weeks. She often lay awake staring at the time on her mobile - 2.17am, 3.22am, 4.32am - time standing still, dragging, things going round and round in her head…she wasn't going to let Nicolas wear her down or take the boys away from her. She was their mother, their mum, their life line. Quite oddly Georgia felt on the verge of a nervous breakdown and yet she found the energy to keep on going. She refused to let negative thoughts about losing the boys frighten her, not after everything she'd been through.

On the way home from The Ravenscroft School, weaving in and out of the traffic expertly, she planned her counter strategy. The solicitor had been about as much use as a fish net with holes in it to a fisherman. She pulled onto the drive hardly remembering her homeward journey but with a clearer plan of attack in her head. She vowed to build a case for herself and she would discredit Nicolas in the process without looking vindictive or selfish or unhinged. That last word kept repeating itself over and over in her head like the nursery rhyme tune built into a child's toy in a horror movie playing over and over again. Unhinged. Was she unhinged? Was she losing the plot?

***

Towards the end of September, the evenings began to close in from as early as three o'clock, the hollow chill in the air signalled the first hint of winter and it quickly became darker and colder than ever. On the morning the letter from the Barnet County Court came a curtain of flint rain shrouded the house and darkened the windows. It felt gloomy, the clouds graphite steel grey.

The hearing was scheduled for the morning of Friday 27th October 2007, at ten o'clock. A photocopied leaflet accompanied the letter too, 'Conciliation in the Barnet County Court, A Guide for Parties'. She read through the leaflet word for word not once but twice, the second time highlighting key points she needed to be mindful of. She had to approach this strategically – like she would have a marketing proposal or an assignment for University or a lesson plan. From then on, she spent every waking moment either planning her lessons and resources or scribbling notes in a blank exercise book from school that might be useful leverage in discrediting Nicolas and showing her in the good light Georgia deserved.

As the date approached, Georgia also considered how to broach the subject of Andoni needing to be in court with her. She knew this would be one of the hardest things to go through with him. One evening, with the other boys tucked up in their beds and asleep, Andoni came downstairs for a glass of water and she called him into the dining room, where she worked diligently on her lesson plans for the following week.

She pulled up a chair, patting the seat for him to sit down, 'I need to talk to you about something,' she said quietly, looking him straight in the eyes, 'It's about you and your brothers and who you are going to be living with,' she began, noticing how young and vulnerable he looked in his pyjamas. She took a big breath in and bit on her bottom lip, to stop the tears from forming.

'*Baba* wants you to live with him. And I want you all to carry on living with me. Now because it's a such hard decision to make we have asked someone clever who works in a court, who knows about families, to help us decide.'

'Like a judge?' asked Andoni, his eyes as wide. She saw his intake of breath as he steeled himself.

'Kind of, yes. It could be a lady or a man but they won't be wearing a curly white wig like you see on the telly, at least I don't think they will be,' Georgia continued.

'Will the judge want to ask me questions?' he asked, sounding surprisingly excited about the prospect of being interviewed in a court.

'It's possible, yes. And I want you to know there is no right or wrong answer. You just have to answer honestly and as best you can. There will be no trick questions and I don't want you to be worried about anything.'

'Will Zach and Kristiano come with me?' he asked.

'No, they're too young and the court has only asked to speak to you because you are twelve years old,' said Georgia, her heart breaking as she listened to Andoni being brave and grown-up beyond his age.

'Will Dad be there?'

'Yes, we will both be there but the Children and Family Reporter, the judge, will speak to you on your own.'

'Will I miss school?' he asked.

'Yes, you will,' she answered as she gave him a big hug.

'My friends won't believe it when I tell them I'm going to court,' he beamed, appearing again not in the least worried or fazed by her announcement.

'Come on, off to bed, my big clever boy.'

'Night Mum,' said Andoni.

'Good night, *agabi mou*. Sweet dreams.'

'Love you.'

'Love you more,' said Georgia.

***

Georgia sat up for another hour or so thinking. Her boy may be called up by the Children and Family Reporter because of her idiot husband. She hoped it wouldn't be necessary. She also knew how stubborn Nicolas could be. She knew the process would help the court decide how to move the case forward if an agreement acceptable to both of them could not be reached. The court's main concern would be the best interests of the children. Georgia's only concern too being the children. Nicolas's however, she believed to be one of revenge because Georgia had refused and still refused to listen to any of his continuous pleas to have him back. She recognised the court case as astronomical in terms of what her life would turn out like. She knew also, again, there was no turning back.

Chapter Sixteen

SEAN AND THALIA both wanted to accompany Georgia to court. She refused Sean's offer knowing his presence would cloud her mind and also rile Nicolas.

'Andoni might not be called in hun and you can't leave him on his own while you fight it out,' Thalia argued.

'S'pose not, it makes sense you being there. For him. For me. Thank you babe,' conceded Georgia reluctantly.

Georgia felt bad having to rely on Thalia knowing the turmoil she suffered too but knew also without any ounce of a doubt Thalia would be her rock. No questions, no expectations, no demands would be made on her on what she anticipated would undoubtedly be a trying day. Thalia's presence would be assuring and Georgia knew she could rely on her to get Georgia and Andoni through the inevitable ordeal. Georgia's family didn't know anything about this and Georgia didn't want an escalation of ill-feeling around her so she had kept quiet about Nicolas's intention. She didn't need any distractions either and needed to focus on the facts of the situation and not on anything or anyone else. She needed to keep a clear head. She had opted to represent herself in court. She was intelligent. She could communicate eloquently and passionately. She knew she had to keep calm and level-headed. She had to avoid getting personal and avoid getting dragged into anything that would make her look petty in front of the judge or whoever would be making the decision today.

As she sat up in bed she went through the green folder she had marked 'custody case' and further annotated her notes and the letters she had received over the weeks leading up to the hearing. Barnet County Court in Finchley operated as a civil and family court centre. She knew its location but never ever had imagined she would be summoned to go there. She tried to shake off the suffocating premonition haunting her since the day she had received that damn call from Nicolas. She focused on the practicalities. She could easily walk there with Andoni. Thalia coming with her proved a blessing. Reading through the information again she realised without Thalia, Andoni would otherwise be left with a warden of the court during the mediation. She felt overwhelmed with sentiment for her friend. She was lucky to have her on her side.

***

The morning of the court hearing, Georgia quickly walked Zachari and Kristiano to the top of Dollis Park. She waved good bye to them as she stood for a few minutes watching them disappear on their scooters in the direction of their primary school.

Agitated and her nerves frazzled, she had to get a grip

and stay focused. She tried, but couldn't dissipate the anger she felt running in her veins at the thought of Nicolas playing the loving father with his now one-year-old daughter.

She had to keep calm. She breathed deeply as she meandered around children on scooters and bikes, parents with buggies and professionals in suits and high heels. Her slow pace contradicted the speed of those around her at that time of the morning and one man bashed his briefcase up against her thigh as he pushed past to get round her. In no hurry to get back, she collected her thoughts, composed herself and got home without even realising how she'd got there. She couldn't remember crossing any roads or waiting at the pedestrian crossing where it always took forever for the green man to light up. She felt a huge pressure around her head, like someone squeezing her temples.

Back home, Georgia swallowed two paracetamol to take the edge off the fuzzy headache she had woken up with and the pain of the bruise on her leg. She called to Andoni to get dressed who jumped around excited about missing a day off school. Thalia arrived in good time and hugged Georgia tightly sensing her agitation.

'Keys,' Georgia said to herself as she rummaged through her hand bag. 'Damn! Where are my keys?'

'Key rack?' said Thalia, 'Don't panic babe. We've plenty of time. It's only just gone 9.30.'

'And my mobile...where's my mobile?' Georgia

dashed around downstairs almost running from room to room as she called up the stairs to Andoni. 'Check if my mobile is by my bed *agabi mou.*'

'What Mum?'

'My mobile…is it next to my bed?'

'Yeah.'

'Bring it down for me please and come on we have to go. You ready?'

'I need the toilet.'

'He always needs the toilet at the most inopportune time,' said Georgia to Thalia who laughed.

'We've still got twenty minutes,' said Thalia, bundling out of the house as the three of them made their way to the court house.

The school-run traffic along Ballards Lane had tailed off and the road had become less noisy than earlier. Andoni gloated about his brothers being at school while he had a day off although Georgia sensed his jangling nerves. He kept tying and untying the cord to his hoodie, his fingers twisting and untwisting it over and over.

'All set?' asked Thalia as they all walked through the sliding entrance doors at the front of the building.

'I think so.' Georgia fought back the wet salty tears welling up behind her eyes and changed the subject. 'Can you believe this used to be St Mary's School years ago? We had friends who used to come here. Odd to think it's now a court.'

'Look you'll be fine.'

'I'm nervous. My stomach is churning up.'

'You're good at talking, you're a loving mum and anyone can see that.' Thalia slipped her arm into the crook of Georgia's and nudged up against her reassuringly.

'I just want it over with. I'm a wreck.'

'Well it will be soon.'

Andoni's nerves evaporated as he whooped with joy at having to put his DS into a flint-coloured plastic tray for scanning. He visibly straightened up and pushed his shoulders back as he walked through the body scanner as directed by the burly security guard in a dark navy uniform. Georgia noticed the guard's torn left jacket pocket and his shoes had Velcro straps across the front, not laces. She followed Andoni through the scanner, pausing for a few seconds before being ushered through. It bleeped and a red light flashed.

'Bloody hell,' Georgia said.

'Walk back through and remove your cardigan please.' Georgia had chosen to dress 'mumsy-ish' with a pair of wide-leg jersey trousers in navy, a white T-shirt and her favourite Hollister chunky-knit cardi in pebble grey.

'For God's sake,' she said getting wound up, 'what a palaver. Probably the buttons.' She took off the cardigan and placed it loosely folded in a plastic tray.

'Okay. Try again,' said the security officer with a sigh. Georgia passed through bleep-less this time. Thank

God, thought Georgia, agitation building to a crescendo inside her. She looked up at the old metal school clock on the wall opposite; two minutes before ten. The three of them followed the signs to the upstairs waiting area taking the short escalator up to the first floor which opened out into a bright, open space with doors coming off at different intervals around its perimeter.

Georgia, Thalia and Andoni sat in a row on a leather padded banquette. Georgia saw Nicolas settled on a similar bench a few feet away. Nicolas and his solicitor, Georgia noted, wore formal suits and ties. 'The Krays' she laughed to herself. The light from the window behind Nicolas shone across him. She smirked at the thought of him being an angel. Absolutely no way, she said to herself. Andoni spotted his dad at the same time and rushed over to him, leaving Georgia alone with Thalia.

'It's like waiting for a bus.'

'Only worse,' said Georgia morosely.

'I'm telling you it'll be okay. I promise.' She looked at her lopsidedly giving her an encouraging yet sympathetic smile.

'Of course it will be,' said Georgia.

Georgia watched as a tall woman in a dark trouser suit and flat gold pumps on her feet strolled over in her direction after having spoken with Nicolas and his solicitor. The Mediation Officer allocated to their case introduced herself as she shook Georgia's hand warmly.

A few minutes later the surname Josephides sounded

over the tannoy. Georgia bit on her lower lip as she followed the usher to a support room off the main concourse. Andoni followed her right up to the door and she bent down to hug him before going in.

'Don't you worry about anything *agabi mou*.' Georgia straightened up and faced the solid door in front of her. Just before she entered the room she turned round to give Andoni a wave. But he didn't notice; his head, already bent down in concentration over his DS.

Georgia stood for a second in front of the door; a column of six square glass panes ran from the top to the bottom on the right hand side. She pushed the heavy beech door and walked into the warm room wishing she had worn her high heels. Instantly she felt her body temperature rise, the back of her neck sticky under her long dark curls.

They were asked to sit down around an oval beech table, chipped around the edge and revealing the squashed sawdust of MDF underneath the plush finish. Georgia pulled out the chair nearest to her and shook off her cardigan. She sat down heavily, surveying the room from her sitting position. She could see the Barnet County Court crest with the words '*Unitas Efficit Ministerium*'. She guessed it meant something about fairness and unity. Her eyes kept focusing on the two gold wings coming out either side of what looked like a rounders bat standing upright in the middle of the crest, at the top. It reminded her of something out of Harry Potter and the game of

Quidditch. She wished Andoni was with her; he'd like this being a Harry Potter enthusiast she thought. Against the same wall stood a huge mahogany desk with three drawers at either end. It looked solid and heavy. It had stood the test of time. Its sustainability somehow gave Georgia strength and she shook off a shiver.

Georgia took the cardigan from her lap. She folded it neatly and placed it on top of her hand bag, on the floor next to her. She quickly focused her attention on the woman sat at the other end of the table. A blond shoulder length bob framed her soft face and she had a button nose. Georgia guessed her age as mid-fifties which pleased her. She concluded this meant she likely had lots of experience, probably as a mum too so she would be inclined to be more sympathetic towards Georgia; a mother with a cheating husband. She noticed her finger nails too, almond-shaped, painted a pale nude colour; neutral, not gaudy. Georgia overjoyed with the vibes she got, breathed in and out slowly to steady her nerves.

'Mr Josephides, Mrs Josephides thank you for attending today. The purpose of today's mediation is to establish the custody options for your three children,' said Claire Walden, the Family and Children Reporter allocated to their case. She continued reading out the boys' names, in a hollow voice, as if reading out a shopping list, and not the names of three children who meant everything to Georgia. 'I would like to remind you this is a mediation session, not a court hearing, and if you do not reach a mutually agreeable way forward for the children then we will proceed with a formal court hearing at a later date. However, it is in the best interests of all parties we settle this today, here and now.' Georgia looked over at Nicolas as he fiddled with the button on his shirt cuff.

'Yes,' said Georgia, her voice quivering. She reached up to her hair and tweaking the ends she flicked the curls over her shoulder. She looked down at her copious notes, ran her fingers over the pages and picked up her pen.

'Mr Josephides, I understand you have legal representation today. If you'd like to start with your position,' she said, looking directly at Nicolas and Alvin Gregory. 'However I will not require Mr Gregory to intervene at any point during this meeting. This meeting is between parents only at this stage. Mr Josephides, do you understand? Mr Gregory I'm sure you're familiar with the way a Family court works.' The solicitor dipped his chin and nodded his acknowledgement. He looked over at Nicolas, giving him permission to talk. Georgia took a deep breath.

'I don't think my children should be with her. She can't look after them properly,' Nicolas began. 'She's not a fit mother. She can't look after the boys properly. She's...' Nicolas stalled, losing his trail.

'Let me stop you right there, Mr Josephides. I will not have you referring to Mrs Josephides as 'she'. 'She' is the mother of your children. I would ask you to refer to her respectfully or I will not continue with this Conciliation Meeting.' Nicolas, shifted in his seat, his face reddened, as he mumbled an apology.

'Now, if that's clear, please continue Mr Josephides.' She spoke curtly yet remained poised, professional.

Georgia listened to his plan to look after the boys full-time, not only stunned at what he proposed but also surprised he had considered it all in such detail. It must have been his top-shot lawyer. As Nicolas continued, Georgia began to doubt herself and her ability to represent her argument on her own. Maybe she should have hired a solicitor to represent her after all, to advise her at least. She felt unanticipatedly small and insignificant; like Alice in Wonderland, shrinking not in size but in confidence.

'I would like to point out that Mr Josephides… I mean Nicolas lives in Barnet temporarily and starts work at between 6.00am and 6.30am every week day, including Saturdays. How does he propose getting the boys to and from their schools in Finchley Central and East Finchley if they live with him?' asked Georgia, her confidence growing. She spoke without erring or stumbling on her words.

'Mr Josephides, can you please respond?'

'Well, I haven't got anything finalised yet, but…'

'And yet you say Mrs Josephides will be unable to take the children to school which is true. But she has put in place an alternative which, in the eyes of the court, would be deemed more than acceptable and most responsible, given the ages of your children,' said Claire.

'She's mad. She goes out all the time and the boys don't know where she is. I don't know where she is,' he cut in.

'You are now separated as I understand it Mr Josephides and therefore where your wife is should be of no concern of yours. From the point of view of this meeting today, Mrs Josephides has explained, that in her absence from the family home, her mother, father or immediate family members look after the children. Do you have any reason to believe the children are not safe with the members of Mrs Josephides' family mentioned?' She referred to the completed forms from Georgia, copies of which had also been made available to Mr Gregory prior to the meeting.

'No,' Nicolas said, 'but they are being passed from pillar to post.'

'Can you further explain what you mean?' said Claire.

'She's never home.'

'I go out at the weekends that's true,' intervened Georgia, 'but I need a break too. I'm working flat out working full time. I have recently completed a PGCE at Middlesex University and being a new teacher means having to work late into the evenings after the boys are in bed. I don't stay late at school. I fit what I have to do around the boys and their care.' Georgia paused and then, adding as an after-thought, 'If I didn't get any time to myself I'd be no good to anyone.'

'Where do the boys stay?' asked Claire.

'Mostly at home so they have their games and can follow their routine with the least disruption. I'm lucky my parents are well and able to look after them and they do it willingly, with no complaints.'

'Andoni was up till half past eleven last weekend. That can't be good for him,' said Nicolas, the agitation in his voice and his manner becoming more evident. His face flushed. He tugged at his tie roughly eventually pulling at the knot until it unravelled and undid his top button.

'It was Saturday night. He did his maths home work until eight and when Zachari and Kristiano had gone to bed, he stayed up to watch Home Alone with his *yiayia* and *bapou*. Grandma and Grandad,' she added for Claire's benefit, 'my parents.' Nicolas said nothing. Claire nodded and waited and when Nicolas still made no response she went on, 'In situations where the children are a little older, as in your situation, we have looked to a shared custody agreement with the children remaining in their main family home, usually the main guardian, and splitting the time between both parents. This gives the children time with both parents and also gives the main carer time to re-charge their batteries.'

'For God's sake. The boys need to be with me. I'm their dad. I love them,' Nicolas cut in, angrily.

'And where have you been for the past year or so? You've been home late every night because you've been having an affair. You didn't want to be with your boys then did you?' asked Georgia, her eyes filling up. 'Sorry, but don't pretend to be the loving father now. It's too late for that.' Composing herself she turned towards Claire, 'What would that involve?'

'You would both have to come to an agreement but the court has a number of options which have worked for other families with children of similar ages as yours. So let's look at these as a starting point shall we?'

***

Thanking Claire for her support and understanding, Georgia burst out of the meeting room into the lobby. There were crowds of people hanging about now the day's session had got under way and she couldn't wait to get out. She pushed past three tall men and then around what looked like a Somalian family until she spotted Thalia and Andoni. They had moved from where she had left them sitting earlier. She ran over to Andoni and smiled the biggest happiest smile. She hugged him as she fought the tears welling up in her eyes.

'You okay Mum?' Andoni asked, pulling away from her. Georgia nodded and too afraid to speak she took his hand and followed closely behind Thalia who reached out behind her and gripped Georgia's free hand tightly.

Outside, the sky had cleared. Georgia made out the sound of bird song in the trees over the noise of afternoon traffic building up again along Ballards Lane. Glad to be out in the open air Georgia chatted with Andoni, upset he hadn't been called into the meeting.

'I was bored waiting all day,' he whined. Georgia sighed, a loud deep sigh of relief and then smiled at him. 'It's only just gone half past eleven. That's not all day,' she teased and then added, 'Look, that's a good thing, *agabi mou*. Dad and I have come to an agreement and I know you'll be pleased. I'll tell you all about it later, I promise, but right now let's go home,' she said, turning towards Thalia.

Nicolas appeared and offered to take Andoni for lunch. She had wanted Andoni to go back to school and Nicolas knew that. However not wanting to cause a scene she let Nicolas have his way, knowing too Andoni would like the treat.

'In that case you can pick up the other two from school and bring them all home at the same time.' Nicolas didn't argue even though she could sense his annoyance at being caught out at his own game and avoiding his stare she gave Andoni a quick kiss goodbye.

'Come on, you. Let's go home and put the kettle on,' said Thalia, 'you must be shattered.'

'Under-statement of the year, of the century,' said Georgia, 'but relieved babe, it's over. The woman was brilliant and you should have heard the way she reprimanded Nico...' she said, talking animatedly, as Thalia squeezed her friend's hand tightly.

'I love you,' Thalia said.

'And I love you,' Georgia said, every bone in her body tingling with something, something fizzy and bubbly. She felt super-human, energised, strong.

***

Walking back towards the house Georgia looked up as a black crow soared above her past the trees; its call pierced the blue sky. Thalia leaned into her but didn't say anything.

Georgia spotted Mark's van parked on her drive, the back doors open, jutting out awkwardly across the pavement. He pulled out the lawnmower, his tools scattered across the walkway. His face lit up as he saw her walking towards him.

'Hi.' He called out, banging the doors shut with a bang, adjusting his cap.

'Hi Mark.'

'I tried calling but no answer so I thought I'd take a chance.'

'That's fine, no worries.'

'You okay? You look upset.'

'No, just shattered. Need a cuppa. Would you like one?'

'Yeah, thanks.' He looked at her momentarily

holding her gaze for a fraction longer than he needed to. Her heart missed a beat. Her reaction left her confused and she put it down to being fatigued. 'I'll get on then.'

Georgia sat at the kitchen table while Thalia made three mugs of tea. Georgia took one out to Mark who had let himself in through the side gate and already cleared the lawn of the boys' scooters and bicycles and footballs. The whirring of the lawnmower and the smell of freshly cut grass filled the air as she walked across to Mark with his brew.

'This could be the last cut for a while. I'll see how the weather goes.'

'Oh right. Okay Mark. Just let me know when you're done with me.'

'Never. But I'll let you know when I'm finished here.' Georgia flushed again and went back into the house without responding.

Back inside, Georgia hardly said a word, the build-up of cumulative stress flooding out of her every pore. Her outer composure suddenly fell apart like a collapsing iceberg; she had only allowed people around her to see her coping but underneath she'd been crumbling. She felt a huge sense of relief, release, as she allowed her tears to fall unchecked. Thalia hugged her until she stopped eventually, nose and eyes red and sore.

Georgia felt everything untightening, her aching shoulders beginning to feel lighter, the numbness on the outside thawing.

'Thanks for being such a good friend Thal. You've been amazing.'

'And you're amazing too. Don't ever forget that. You're a coper, a doer. You'll get through all of this. I promise.'

As she sat looking through her divorce file she kept coming back to Mark's words. He was just being nice, she convinced herself. She looked up towards heaven, a faint smile on her lips. I need someone nice in my life she thought and then laughed out loud. She was being silly, not thinking straight. In fact, not thinking at all, she admonished herself. The last thing she needed was another man on the scene. Life was complicated enough; she was complicated enough.

Chapter Seventeen

'I'M SO SORRY,' Georgia said choking on her words.

'Look we knew this was coming. We will deal with it together Georgia,' said her mother and forgetting herself she burst out, 'The bastard. How could he have messed up this badly?' Her mother carried on wrapping Christmas presents, the mountain only marginally reducing each time she wrapped one. The kitchen table hid under an array of jumpers, board games, toiletries and books. With only a few days until Christmas her mum had exceeded herself yet again; presents not wrapped, Christmas cards still in the boxes not written let alone the envelopes stamped and addressed. Chaos consumed Georgia's space physically and emotionally.

'I know. But I have to tell the boys. Nico's not going to say anything, he's such a coward.' She reached over and held two edges of wrapping together so her mum could tape them down around a box of jumbo building blocks.

'You tell them,' said her father.

'But I don't want to look like the bad guy. They've been through enough and now to find out they've got a half-sister.'

'If he's told you they're spending Christmas together you have to tell them. They will meet her and they'll see the baby, *agabi mou*. There's no choice no. You can't keep delaying the inevitable…' Her mother let out a loud sigh.

'I know. But I need to be able to tell them without crying. I don't know if I can do it.'

'As much as it hurts us…you…the boys will be accepting…maybe even excited they have a little sister. They love children. Look how they are with Katia's two.'

'Really? I hope you're right. I feel so humiliated Mum.' Georgia broke down. Her mum hugged her and stroked her back, her tears soaking the front of her mum's blouse. Georgia's sobs abated and hearing a whimper she looked up to the threat of tears in her dad's eyes. He turned from her, his shoulders heaving as his whimper became an uncontrollable sob. Uncomfortable with displays of emotion he stepped away tapping her on the back just once before disappearing through the connecting glass doors into the lounge next door.

***

A cold January wind curled under the door of Café Buzz.

'I can't seem to hold onto the powerful strength I felt a few weeks ago. After court I felt a kind of bold happiness pushing outwards. I felt invincible,' said Georgia, as she took a bite of her pain au chocolat, the melted chocolate smothering her lips, the smell filling her nostrils as she chewed.

'So what's changed?'

'Me. I don't know. The baby. Knowing they're living together now. I can't see a future anymore.'

'Forget them…You've got the house, a job, the kids…Don't focus on his brat.'

'I can't help it. What's my life going to be like in a month, next year, in ten years' time?'

'You can't think like that Georgi. You have to focus on the here and now. The future will work out itself.'

'I'm trying babe. I really am.'

'Look with the court case over you have to get back into your routine of work and looking after the boys again,' said Thalia raising her voice slightly to be heard over the clanking of cutlery and crockery at the work station near them. She beckoned to the waitress and ordered another cappuccino for herself and another Earl Grey for Georgia.

'I can't do it. I'm breaking up slowly… like a completed puzzle you get fed up of looking at so you break it up, no longer caring about the time and effort you had to put in to reveal the picture. My life is just full of broken pieces, no tomorrow. All I can see is…broken pieces of tomorrow.'

'You've been dealing with a lot. You're physically and mentally exhausted but refuse to recognise it in yourself. Admitting it doesn't mean you're weak.'

'But I've always been the strong one. The one everyone can rely on and being the eldest everyone has always relied on me to do the right thing, especially my mum.'

'Well, you don't have to do that anymore. You're not on your own. Don't shut yourself away. Let people know how you feel. Let people help you.'

'I'm so lost Thal,' Georgia said, dabbing at the corners of her eyes to stop the tears. She looked down at the bright red of the serviette clashing with the smear of her green eyeliner. 'I'm crying all the time. Where's my life going?' She looked over at two workmen, the brightness of their fluorescent waistcoats mocking her feelings of hopelessness. The door to the café opened and another blast of freezing air whipped around her. A young mother with a double buggy pushed her way into the small café settling down at the table nearest the door. For a moment Georgia remembered the days she wheeled Zach and Kristiano in the tandem pushchair she borrowed from a friend. The new baby, about the same age made Georgia wonder whether Nicolas pushed her around in her pram like he used to with their children.

'Look you've got the boys. The court was on your side so that's a victory. That's something good in your life. And your job. You love your job.'

'My job's great but I'm missing something.'

'Look at this.' Thalia pulled out her phone and tapped away at the screen. Georgia took the phone from her and read the Facebook post.

'NEVER LET THE SADNESS

OF YOUR PAST AND THE FEAR
OF YOUR FUTURE DESTROY THE
HAPPINESS OF YOUR PRESENT.'

'That's beautiful,' said Georgia, tearing at her cooled chocolate croissant, now stretchy. 'I'm trying. I really am,' she said between chewing and taking a gulp of her tea.

'Do you still love him? Is that it?'

'No…yes. I don't know but I don't want him back babe. I know I deserve better.'

'So what's still nagging you, preventing you from moving on?' But Georgia couldn't speak for fear of looking weak and pathetic. Her pride hurt with the loss of her family unit. The embarrassment of her husband's infidelity; she thought he loved her as much as she loved him and yet he cheated on her. Nicolas lied to her, over and over again. Life had been good before. Their marriage had been good. Why hadn't she been enough for him? Her life had become a tumble-downed house of cards…bits everywhere, routine gone haywire…instability all around.

Georgia found her voice. 'He's being a shit about the divorce too. Won't admit he's had an affair and saying if I want the divorce then I have to say it's my fault.'

'Fucking pig,' said Thalia, a dark anger shadowing her eyes. 'He's such an arsehole. He really has no shame.'

'One Earl Grey and a cappuccino,' interrupted the

waitress as she put the drinks down with a clatter and swiftly removed their empty mugs.

'We're going to Barcelona. You and me. We both need a girls' holiday. You in?'

'Oh I don't know. I need to be here for the boys. I've got school…'

'We'll book over the next few weeks. A long weekend.'

'I'll let you know. Don't want to agitate Nico further and give him more ammunition against me.'

'All the more reason to come!'

Georgia smiled for the first time that morning.

***

Georgia, emotionally strung out, counted out her life in six and seven-week half term chunks. She made sure she spent as much time as she could with the boys before they went off to their dad's, sharing the holidays and half terms as agreed at the conciliation meeting.

Six months on, Christmas a long distant memory, the arrangement still bitter-sweet, Georgia often found herself upset without them. On edge, as she packed their bags, she would inevitably find something to argue about with one of the boys before they left. This made her mood even worse once the house became empty and void of all their chatter and running around. She felt guilty about everything from the boys moving from home to home to allowing her anxiousness to spiral into a row with them. She hated the boys leaving on bad terms and hated herself for allowing the situation to continuously upset her. Things were not good from a family point of view.

Over the first half of the year Georgia's relationship with Sean also began to deteriorate. Often late, he proved himself unreliable and increasingly had no money to take Georgia out. This irritated her. She didn't mind paying for the odd dinner but even his tube fare?

Attentive enough when they were together, she loved his insatiable sex drive, his longing for her and his creativity; sex on the stairs, the dining room table, on the couch…but other than having that between them she realised his immaturity, selfishness and anti-social behaviour riled her. He didn't like going out with her friends or mixing with anyone else. 'I love having you to myself,' he would say whenever she raised her concerns. 'We don't need anybody else, just you and me.' But Sean became more conscious of the fact the boys were her priority.

Georgia continued with their relationship. She liked saying she had a boyfriend. It made her less ugly, wanted. And although she was doing well at work and she had a good network of support around her and loving friends, she needed him to validate her, build her lack of inner confidence.

Chapter Eighteen

ONE SATURDAY EVENING in July, Georgia, content in the knowledge the boys were with their dad, looked forward to a night out at a bar and dance lounge in Islington. She knew she could party the night away to the resident DJ who always happily took requests and pleased the crowd.

Georgia waited for Sean at home. She agreed to drive, not minding being the chauffeur; she didn't need a drink to have a good time. She waited for over half an hour and killed time by unloading the dishwasher, putting in a white wash and folded the bath towels which had dried out on the wooden clothes horse on the patio earlier in the day.

She began to feel agitated. She checked her hair in front of the mirror and decided to put a diamante grip in it to stop it from falling in her eyes. Then she took it out again. She applied her lipstick hoping Sean would be with her soon.

Georgia looked at her watch; already nine o'clock. She decided to send him a quick text message.

```
R u on ur way babe? Xxx
Leaving soon, can't wait too c u my hot hot
babe x
```
His mis-spelling of to irritated her and over the next twenty minutes she texted him three times.

```
R u on ur way now? xxx
Guess u're on the bus and unable to get a
signal hence no response xxx
R u almost here? xxx
```

In the meantime, Jade and Paula texted asking where she was and saying she had better not be bailing out on them. Another forty-five minutes passed and Georgia began to lose her patience. She felt wound up and texted him again.

```
Sean, leaving now so c u there x
u know where it is x
```

Georgia drew the cerise line round her lips again to define them and then filled in with the Sexy Mother Pucker gloss with a hint of pink in it, topping up the lipstick she put on earlier. Her phone bleeped. She looked down and read the message.

`Forget it. I'm not coming.` And then a few seconds later.
```
It's over. Sorry.
What do u mean it's over? X
It's over. We're over. I wish you well
Georgia x
```

She read the texts and then re-read them. No way!

She tried to call him but his phone went to voice message. She couldn't deal with his childish behaviour.

Not tonight.

If u change ur mind see u there, OK? She sent the message and hoped she didn't sound desperate.

She grabbed her bag and jumped into the car. She revved it up and within thirty-five minutes she had parked on Essex Road, reversing expertly into a space she'd need a can opener to get out of again. She refused to let Sean's text spoil her night. Georgia gave the bouncer a huge wide smile as he held the door open for her. She flirtingly bid him a good evening and she walked straight into the bar, looking a million dollars and gloriously buoyant considering Sean's message. Her inner balloon elated again.

It took Georgia a few seconds to adjust to the dimness of the interior. Looking along the bar and from table to table she spotted her old school friend Alexia, standing at the far end of the curved counter, its highly polished wood panelling gleaming. Alexia almost always stood head and shoulders above everyone being over six foot with her heels on. Georgia waved but she caught the attention of a tall blond guy who waved back instead.

Probably thinks his luck is in…bloody hell,

she thought, that's all I need tonight. She pushed her way through the melee. The bar buzzed with an eclectic mix of young and old, drunk and not so drunk punters, women sipping at their drinks through straws and men swigging from their pint glasses. Some bopped and swayed to the beat of the live piano music as it cut across the throng of conversation, chatter and laughter.

Alexia gave her a huge hug and as Georgia stepped back she almost stood on Jade's foot who had appeared behind her with Paula.

'So glad you're here!' they both shrieked together.

'Sorry I'm late,' Georgia said to the trio and quickly introduced Paula and Jade to Alexia. 'Alexia's an old school friend. We've been friends since we were twelve. We used to go Greek Youth Club together on a Friday night as well. Jolening our tashes and the hair on our arms every few weeks. What a laugh. Why did we do that?'

'Because we're Greek girls with hair!' said Alexia laughing, pretending to be twirling her moustache. 'And at school we both fancied Mr White, our economics teacher.'

'And Mr Bernadelli. O Level Geography lessons were so good!' chimed in Georgia as her happiness-filled balloon floated further upwards.

'That's so funny,' said Paula.

'Yeah. We've all got those stories. Where's
Sean by the way?' asked Jade.

'Oh. He's dumped me, by text!' Jade, completely stupefied, didn't say anything, her mouth forming a big 'O' but no words coming out.

'What a twat,' said Paula. 'His loss babe, big time.'

'Complete and utter idiot! Fancy treating you like

that, you okay?' asked Alexia, with real concern in her soft brown eyes. Georgia could tell her exterior bravado did not fool Alexia.

'I will be once I've had a drink,' said Georgia. She waved at the barman who came straight over, much to the annoyance of another punter who had obviously been waiting to be served before her. But Georgia, uncharacteristically, didn't care.

'J2O please, orange and passion fruit if you've got it,' and then she noticed the guy who had waved to her earlier and as an afterthought added, 'and whatever the guy in the denim shirt wants.' She said it loud enough for him to hear her.

'Cheers!' he called out looking over.

'You're welcome! I'm celebrating!'

'Oh yeah, your birthday is it?'

'No, I've just been dumped by text!'

'Happy getting dumped day!' he called back.

'You are unbelievable,' said Alexia. 'How do you do it?'

'What?' said Georgia, taking a long suck of juice through her straw. The girls looked at her and then one by one burst into fits of laughter. Georgia joined in, the laughing infectious but her laughter soon turned to tears.

'Oh, babe. Come on. You'll meet someone better,' said Paula.

'And who drives a car and has his own house,' said Alexia trying to sound convincing.

'Yeah, I know,' said Georgia, dabbing at her eyes so as not to smudge her mascara. 'But I miss him already.'

'I need the loo. Come with me?' Alexia took Georgia by the arm.

Georgia weaved in and out of the growing number of people, keeping close to Alexia, who had passed her hand back to Georgia to hold onto. They shuffled past the white grand piano and down the stairs almost bumping into a couple who were entwined, leaning up against the wall in the stairwell. They need to get a room thought Georgia and let out a sigh.

The rest of the evening, more fun than she had hoped, passed quickly. Jade and Paula danced with her most of the night, the music played by the DJ blasted out across the bar. She knew the words and her singing left Georgia hoarse. After a long bout of dancing she collapsed on a leather sofa and checked her phone. The night's loud energetic atmosphere left her head banging and her feet screaming to get out of her high heeled shoes.

At home, she listened to the voice messages from Sean lying in bed, the duvet under her, too hot to cover herself. She had ignored his voice messages all night, reading only his over apologetic texts, enjoying the control she momentarily held over him but now she missed him. Georgia couldn't even make out what he tried to say as she listened to his drunken rambling about how she had misunderstood him and how he had been tired and how he loved her more than he had ever loved anyone in his life. Which she did believe because she knew he believed that.

With her bedroom window ajar she could hear the external commotion on the main road from the shisha bar and the latino dancing bar still trading even though 1am had come and gone. The house felt empty and she pricked her ears listening to every internal creak and strain of the old floorboards. Georgia fell asleep determined to keep control of the situation and to move on.

***

At school, despite Georgia's inner turmoil surrounding her break up with Sean, she received great news from her Head of Faculty.

'You've been awarded QTS status, Georgia. Congratulations.'

'Oh wow. That's brilliant. Thank you.'

'You've been one of the best PGCE and NQT students we've had in a long time. Thank you for all your hard work.'

'Well thank you for all your advice and guidance too. Team effort,' said Georgia embarrassed at the compliment.

'I wasn't going to say anything but you will be receiving a congratulatory email from your university course leader too as well as a special letter of recognition from the Deputy Vice Chancellor at Middlesex

University for your final module which has been externally moderated and received the highest mark possible.'

This made Georgia proud and as she pondered the news over a mug of tea in her classroom she realised she was a competent, clever woman who could live financially independently of Nicolas. She didn't need him and she didn't need Sean either. She had proven herself capable and worthy.

***

Padding around the kitchen still in her nightwear, Georgia made herself a cuppa and a slice of toast and wandered across the garden to her gypsy caravan hideaway, tucked in the far corner of the garden. One leg tucked under her and the other dangling lazily over the edge of the velvet covered swivel chair she sat at her little antique writing desk. She subconsciously twisted back and forth on the seat as she nibbled aimlessly at the skin around her index finger and then her thumb. Physically she appeared relaxed but the break up with Sean troubled her and deep down although she knew Sean was not the one for her she still missed him; he had filled a gap in her life.

She sat for a while enjoying the quiet yet missing the vibration of her phone with his texts. He had filled time with silly texts and sexy texts and romantic texts. She had liked the attention, something she'd never had with

Nicolas as there had been no mobile phones when they had first dated. But she smiled as she remembered the many phone calls lasting hours as she hid in her parents' bedroom talking to Nicolas from the second telephone extension. Her dad had been furious with the extortionate telephone bill. She never did admit to making all those calls but both her mum and dad guessed. Georgia knew from the way they looked at her.

The bright rays of the early morning sun reflected off the white painted wooden panelling of the caravan. Dazzled by them momentarily as they sliced through the single pane of glass, they created shafts of dust motes across the caravan highlighting the shelf of books on the opposite side. The faint rustle of leaves in the tall oak trees and the twitter of the finches and tits were the only sounds to distract her apart from the intermittent chugging of the tube trains coming in and out of Finchley Central Station, only the width of a small row of allotments and the access road to the station car park divided her garden from the railway lines.

***

The ringing of the house phone broke Georgia's concentration. She could hear it faintly in the background and knowing she would not get to it before it rang off she did not move. The answer phone will kick in anyway, she thought to herself. Within seconds her mobile rang. She looked at the screen – Thalia's name flashed across it. For a second she hesitated but then bent across and picked up.

'Hi,' she said with too much cheer in her voice. 'What are you up to?'

'Hi hun. I'm good thanks. I just wanted to see if you were around for a cuppa and a catch up? I've got lots to tell you. Not all good either...and we haven't seen each other for ages. I really need your advice...Where are you? Are you home? You never pick up your house phone.'

'Uh, yeah I'm home just doing a few bits and pieces you know what it's like. The boys have gone to their dad's, staying three nights, so any time's okay with me. But I'm not even dressed yet babe. What time did you want to meet up?'

'I'm not dressed either hun. Still in my onesie...no knickers on either. Shall we say about two? We could go to Med Blue.' Thalia laughed too loudly at her own joke about not wearing knickers.

Georgia ignored the comment about no knickers.

'Uh, yeah okay babe...why not? That's fine. Shall we just meet there...it's easier.'

'Yeah we can have a bite to eat too if you fancy it. Or grab a cuppa and a piece of cake...like we need it!' Thalia laughed down the phone again so loudly Georgia held the phone away from her ear.

'Yeah, okay, let's say half one for lunch,' said Georgia as enthusiastically as she could muster, bringing the phone back to her ear.

'Perfect. Byeee hun,' trilled Thalia, oblivious to the lack of mutual enthusiasm in her friend's voice. 'Can't wait!'

'Bye babe. See you there.' Georgia smiled as she pressed end call on her new mobile phone. She had waited for her up-grade to be available before replacing the damaged phone, so she avoided paying for a new handset. Sensible Georgia. The words echoed in her mind. That's what her mum had always called her but even now she still had her moments where she doubted how sensible or clever or intelligent she really was. Her broken marriage did not shout sensible Georgia or clever Georgia. To her, it shouted stupid, naïve Georgia!

Georgia knew it would be a full-on afternoon. That's something she could always count on Thalia for; fun, flirting and frolicking.

Her mobile rang and she picked up without looking, thinking Thalia probably forgot to say something to her.

'Oh, hello,' she said, coldly in response to Sean's voice.

'Hi,' he said warmly. She made no response wanting to make it as awkward as possible for him. 'About what happened,' he said. But again she said nothing. She waited for him to continue. 'I'm sorry. I don't know what came over me. I was tired from work and didn't fancy the bar in Islington.'

'Why didn't you just say instead of keeping me hanging around?' asked Georgia.

'I know. I should've said something. I'm sorry.'

'No. What you're sorry about is I went without you instead of driving round to your 'mother's' to beg you to not finish with me.'

'Now hold on a minute,' said Sean, but Georgia jumped straight in and stopped him mid-sentence.

'I won't hold on a minute. You couldn't stand the thought of me going out with my friends without you. So you finished with me by text!'

'I wasn't saying it's over. I just meant the night was over before it had even started.'

'Rubbish! And you know it. I've got to go,' she said. 'I'm going out for lunch.'

'With who? I want to see you.'

'None of your business!' and she cut the call. She couldn't believe it had taken him this long to call her! She secretly wondered what he really wanted and hated to admit it but she felt flattered he still thought about her. He obviously regretted his hasty decision to finish with her and this excited Georgia just a little bit.

She twisted round in her seat and gazed out of the caravan's open doorway back at the house and couldn't help noticing the long, ragged, gaping crack running horizontally upwards from the top of the kitchen window across the plaster. Like the cracks in my marriage and my relationship with Sean she thought and shivered involuntarily. Her gaze moved across the garden to the trellis above the fence, heavy with the weight of the overgrown clematis and honeysuckle entangled together just as her life had been with Nicolas and Roksana and Sean and his bloody mother. Fuck Roksana, she thought, getting wound up. And fuck Sean too. She shifted in her chair and thought literally that's what I want to do, fuck Sean.

***

Med Blue, a fabulous new place, had quickly become Georgia and Thalia's haunt after deciding on a whim to 'try something new' at the beginning of the year. With Christmas out the way and January dragging on like a cold, soggy sponge it had been a welcome place to hang out together.

As she swung her BMW into the car park she spotted Thalia's black convertible mini two spaces down. She smiled to herself. Always being on time was one of the traits she liked about Thalia as Georgia was a stickler for time-keeping too. She checked her lips in the mirror and outlining them with lip liner she added a clear sheen of her Sexy Mother Pucker gloss which she favoured for her day look. She gently rubbed her lips together, pouted and smiled.

Inside, Thalia waved at her from across the restaurant, already settled in a booth, sheltered with a bamboo screen from the other cubicles either side. Lit up by an old rusty fisherman's lamp hung low over the dark oak table it cast a subdued glow across the space and Thalia's face giving her an angel-like quality.

'Hi babe. Not late am I?'

'No hun just needed to get out the house.' They kissed each other hello, simultaneously clocking one of the waiters who kept staring over at them. They wasted no time ordering.

'The sticky sharing platter for two, a portion of bruschetta and the mixed olives please. And I'll have a freshly squeezed orange juice to drink. I like a bit of a squeeze,' Thalia said.

Georgia laughed.

'And I'll have a still water please. Not sparkling because the bubbles'll go straight to my head!' she joined in the banter, pulling at her white skirt which had somehow got caught up around her bottom as she'd slid into the booth showing more than just her shapely calves. They both fell about laughing as the waiter walked away obviously flustered.

'We've got him,' said Georgia. 'Or maybe it's me flashing my knickers!'

'I think it's gone right over his head babe!' Thalia said as she tried to stifle a second bout of giggles.

Georgia filled her in on Sean's incessant text messages and his morning call. 'Now he keeps coming back into my head. And I had an awful night's sleep last night, hardly slept. And I'm missing the boys.'

Thalia listened and nodded and made all the right

noises but Georgia could tell she wasn't engaging in the conversation. 'So what's with you?' Georgia asked steering the conversation. She sensed Thalia wasn't being the attentive friend Georgia was used to. 'How are things going with Phil?'

'Well I can't believe we get on so well.'

'So you're happy, yeah? I know in the beginning you were worried about his height, being shorter than you and him living in Manchester. What about his business?'

'I think it's okay. He's mentioned renting out his place and moving down to London. He does most of his business here anyway.'

'Wow things are moving fast then.'

'Well it's already been nearly seven months.'

'So why the glum face? What's wrong?'

'He's so good to me and loves the children. He's really patient with them.' Georgia noticed Thalia avoided answering her.

'I s'pose missing out on his own children growing up because of his divorce means he has a second chance,' said Georgia.

'I'm so glad I took a chance when Athena introduced me to him.'

'Well, she's been your hairdresser for so long babe if she'd got it wrong I would've been surprised. And he is her cousin after all so she must know him pretty well too.'

'Yeah, didn't think of that but you're probably right. She does know me. My mum and dad have met him a few times and they're both pleased I've met someone Greek Cypriot of course. My parents are not as liberal as yours.'

'Well mine never used to be. I always felt I had to marry someone Greek...never discussed openly but subconsciously ingrained while growing up.'

'Yeah, me too. Not sure what they'll say about his moving in eventually.'

'Moving in? It's early days babe. They'll get to know him in time and they'll be fine. There's no hurry,' said Georgia.

'I hope so. They'll expect us to marry though,' said Thalia.

'Really? Why?'

The waiter strolled over and placed the dishes of food down interrupting the flow of their conversation.

'Well living in sin and all that,' whispered Thalia as she peered across the waiter's arm. 'And they've always been religious. So it won't be long before they start about being Greek Orthodox and having to be married.'

'Do you want to get married again?' whispered Georgia back.

'To be honest I've not thought about it. I like having my independence. I'm queen of my castle now Tony is out of the way.'

'He's moved out?'

'Yeah. Last Friday. The divorce finally came through and off he went. Not a word or argument...Why are we whispering?' asked Thalia.

'You started it. When the waiter came over!' said Georgia raising her voice to its normal level again and laughing. 'Anyway…You didn't tell me. That's brilliant news Thal. You okay about it?'

'It's an odd feeling. I feel numb. I looked down at the paper and it didn't feel real.'

'That must be strange. I'm nowhere near yet…still stuck with trying to prove the affair.'

'You'll find a way.'

'Well it will definitely be down to me. The solicitor is a complete waste of time.' Georgia pierced an olive with a cocktail stick. 'She should be paying me,' she added, taking a chicken wing glazed in honey and sesame-seed. 'This is delicious. As always.'

'Yeah, I'm so hungry. My stomach's grumbling in protest at me not having breakfast.' Thalia cut into a thick wedge of bruschetta and forked it into her mouth catching two cubes of tomato in her hand as they wobbled off her fork.

Towards the end of their lunch, Thalia shocked Georgia as they sipped at their peppermint teas. She told Georgia Phil owed thousands of pounds, and being hounded by loan sharks who wanted their money. Rightly so thought Georgia but she didn't air her opinion out loud. She had already guessed there was more to why Thalia had instigated their lunch together. Their entire conversation inevitably building towards this thought Georgia.

'It's got to the stage where he's receiving threatening phone calls, text messages and he's sure he's being followed.'

'Oh my God! That's awful. I can't believe it Thal, it's like something out of Eastenders!' Georgia, fastidious about keeping the household accounts, now more than ever since being on her own had never spent what she didn't have. Georgia's parents had always instilled in her the importance of living within your means. Her mother and father were not materialistic although they enjoyed a comfortable, and some would say privileged, life-style. But Georgia knew they lived within their means and worked hard for what they had.

'There was a call on our house phone the other day and the caller asked for Phil by name. He actually said Phil. I thought how suspicious it was straight away 'cos no-one knows he's seeing me. I said there's no-one called Phil living here, thank God...but what if...one of the kids...or the cleaner...had answered the phone...I am just sick to the stomach with worry. I am so damn stressed! I don't know what to do.' Thalia looked over at Georgia. Her eyes begged Georgia for an answer.

'Well, what can you do? Have you got the money to help him? Is that what he wants?'

'I just don't know Georgi, I need to work something out. I've made an appointment with my accountant. I might be able to release some money to him, use the equity in the house.'

'You'd lend him the money? What makes you think he'd pay you back? I mean he can't pay the loan sharks which is why he's in this mess to start with Thal. Come on...don't get emotional about this. Think with your head not your heart, babe'.

'Well, I'm in it and I'm in it with him. We've been together long enough. He'll move in eventually. I can't just sit there and watch him be targeted like this. It's real...I'm scared...I've already said I would try to help him by releasing some equity in the house if I can. It's a fucking mess.'

'I wouldn't do it, Thalia,' Georgia repeated again. 'It doesn't matter how much you love him and he says he loves you. This is about your future security...financial security, the security of your children. It's their home too after all. God, think carefully, babe. I mean I know it's your choice and your life but must you get involved on a financial level?'

'Well, I am involved. I can't just sit back and do nothing.'

'And why has he not mentioned any of this before now?' asked Georgia.

'He thought he could handle it but business has not been doing well.'

'He's been seeing you for seven going on eight months! And how's he going to pay you?'

'He'll owe me a loan amount with a basic rate of interest instead of the daily 2000% or whatever it is,' she said, getting anxious.

'Well, do the maths properly and make sure he's bringing in what he says he is. What guarantee do you have he will continue to earn enough in the future. Ask for bank statements, some kind of proof,' said Georgia.

'I will hun. The accountant will advise me.'

The mood lightened when a couple of Polish guys on the next table flirted with them and offered them dessert. It finished the afternoon off on a high note for Georgia at least and Thalia, insisting on settling the lunch bill gave Georgia a big hug promising to keep her posted on the Phil situation. Georgia promised to do the same regarding Sean and they waved each other off in the car park, Thalia hooting as she sped off.

It had been a typical girls' afternoon out in the end with lots of conversation and laughing. But despite the meet-up Georgia felt extremely sad, lonely, isolated. She backed out of her parking space and paused as she adjusted her sunglasses and pulled down her visor to further shade her eyes from the big ball of Tuscan sunshine directly opposite her. She wondered whether Sean had tried to contact her again. She leant over to her white bucket bag slumped on the passenger seat. She pulled her mobile out after eventually finding it wedged between her school diary and her notebook.

Ten missed calls. Four text messages. All from Sean.

Message 1: Call me x

Message 2: Call me please. I miss you x
Message 3: Don't ignore me. Please x
Message 4: Pick up your phone x

She yawned. Her eyes felt sore and her eyelids heavy after being in the relative darkness of the restaurant for most of the afternoon. She decided to ignore him... at least for today. Let him wait...and wonder she thought.

Chapter Nineteen

'COME ON BOYS let's get ready for bed, eh?'

'Do we have to *mamma*? It's only…' Zach looked at his watch with an expression of pride spread across his face as he looked back up at her and said, 'twenty to eight.'

'Oooh my clever boy but I'm not changing my mind. We're getting up early tomorrow, remember to go strawberry picking so you don't want to spoil the day being tired and grumpy, now do you *agabi mou*?' said Georgia who had missed her boys being away for three days. She pulled Zach up from the sofa by the arm as he pretended to be all floppy. The other two, surprisingly, did not argue with her and they went straight up. Within a few minutes of brushing their teeth they were all tucked up in bed.

'That film was brilliant *mamma*, thank you.'

'You're welcome tired teddy,' said Georgia, tucking Kristiano into bed so he looked like a little sausage roll with only his head sticking out from under the duvet.

'I'm so glad you're all back home. Sweet dreams,' she called form the top of the stairs.

'Night night my darlings.'

Changed into a T-shirt and a pair of cotton shorts and with a bundle of dirty clothes in her arms, Georgia disappeared downstairs quietly. She programmed the washing machine to wash the load overnight. This extra chore reminded her of the altered family life and routine and the other downside of the boys spending time at their dad's; their dirty clothes always came back with them. However, despite the additional washing, she smiled overjoyed to have the boys back home. It wasn't home without them, just an empty house. She liked it full of life. She still hadn't got used to the emptiness of the house, of how lifeless it felt without them.

After loading the washing machine Georgia pottered about for a bit longer. She collected used crockery from the sitting room, wiped down the kitchen table, filled the dishwasher and put away the juice the boys had left on the kitchen counter back in the fridge. She ought to have swept the kitchen floor too but her legs were aching. She could do that tomorrow, first thing, before the boys were up, she decided.

***

Finally, in the sitting room she plumped up the cushions and folded the throws. Before settling back on the sofa, she took out her little basket of manicure bits from the dresser base which housed a multitude of possessions from DVDs, books, photo albums and board games. She pulled the footstool towards her and stretched out her tanned legs which had caught the sizzling summer sun. She held out her arms in front of her and noticed the warm sun-kissed glow on them too.

She began filing her nails, as she watched the last part of the ten o'clock news, chirpy at having met up with Thalia earlier in the day for a catch up. They hadn't seen much of each other recently and it had felt good being Thalia's listening ear and confidant. Despite Georgia's reservations, Georgia did not doubt Thalia had made her mind up to lend Phil the money and to him moving in with her.

She sipped at her mug of Fennel tea; scorching, she winced as she scalded her upper lip and the roof of her mouth as she swallowed. She took a bite out of a custard cream chewing slowly. She realised she didn't want to eat it though. She pushed the custard creams aside; a sign of real contentment. She would usually eat three or four of them with her cuppa, on the rare occasions the boys don't beat me to it, she thought. Her little lifeboat was on an even keel at last and despite everything she was peaceful sailing on the calm waters of life. Her boys were home and they had missed her just as much as she had missed them.

The mellow chime of the doorbell interrupted her manicure pamper session. Not expecting anyone she wondered who it could be. She got up from the sofa, and poised up onto the armrest. She leant over towards the window and opened the upper section of the wooden shutters. She peered out into the inky darkness but she could only see dark shadow there. Hesitantly she opened the front door, flicking on the light switch to the outdoor lanterns.

Getting over her initial shock, she gave Sean a half smile and rolled her eyes. She unlocked the porch door all the same, moving aside to let him in, all the while puzzling as to why he had come round.

'What are you doing here?' He stood casually with one hand tucked into his jeans pocket. She felt her heart thump in her chest. Was she excited? Or was it nerves?

'Hello to you too,' he said, taking a step towards her so he was no more than a few inches away, invading her personal space. 'Didn't you see my missed calls?'

'Uhh…no…I was out all afternoon…sorry,' she said, taking a step back to widen the space between them. She instantly felt annoyed with herself for offering him an explanation. After all they weren't going out any more even though he'd continued to make contact.

'What about tonight?' Sean said. His voice echoed across the silence, carrying up the stairs as he walked straight past her, across the hallway and into the sitting room.

'I've got nothing to say to you,' she forced herself to say, fighting the mixed emotions surfacing from within her.

'You could have responded to me.'

'I've been busy with the boys. They've been at their dad's and only got back a few hours ago,' said Georgia. Worried the boys would wake up and find Sean there she followed him into the sitting room and closed the door behind her.

'So?'

'I missed them. I wanted to spend some time with them. We watched a DVD, had hot dogs and popcorn,' she said, glancing at the last kernels still sitting in Kristiano's Scooby Doo bowl in the centre of the white-washed pine coffee table. She bit down on her lip, annoyed with herself for telling him too much, explaining herself. She always did that with Nicolas too.

'How exciting,' Sean said, sarcastically, twisting and untwisting the handles of the carrier he held, over and over.

'I wasn't asking you. And, it was actually, for me and for them.'

'Well, I thought we could make up. You know…' he said looking at her straight in the eyes, not wavering for a second. She stared back, feeling sick inside, and then as he relaxed his eyes flickered with what was it? She wondered; glint of mischief?

'Oh, did you?' she said, her heart racing, her palms moist with quiet anticipation. An odd mixture of panic and sexual attraction swept over her but again she didn't understand why. Was she pleased to see him? Was she willing to forgive him for dumping her? Was she still physically attracted to him? 'The boys are upstairs asleep. I'm going up too.'

'Yeah, course you are,' Sean said, looking over

towards her mug of tea, proffering the bottle of Baileys and a bag of Doritos he'd taken out of the carrier he'd been holding, his hands not quite steady.

'Yes. I was,' she said emphatically, standing her ground but blushing at the obvious lie. 'Anyway what's it got to do with you?'

'Look, I didn't want to finish on bad terms. Have a drink with me, one, and then I'll go.'

'I don't want a drink. I've got tea,' she said pointing to her mug of tea which she knew had probably gone cold by now. It sat there, incriminating evidence of her earlier fib, the lie resting on her lips.

'Yeah I can see that.'

'So there you go.'

'Well, have one small one with me and then I'll be off. It'll make me feel better.'

'Ten minutes. I'll get some glasses and then you can go, Sean,' she said, wanting to get out of the room, a suffocating blanket of ill ease washed over her, making her involuntarily shiver. She sensed a struggle in him. One drink she said to herself and then he can leave. One drink should appease him. I need to keep calm, need to keep him calm.

In the kitchen, Georgia didn't want to go back in. Panicking about Sean being in the house, she found it difficult to concentrate. Suspicion invaded her. Damn you Sean, she thought.

When she eventually came back with the glasses and

a bowl for the crisps, Sean had already taken off his jacket and kicked off his trainers, his crumpled white shirt hung loose over his Levis.

'Make yourself comfortable why don't you?'

'Thanks. I already have,' he said pushing himself comfortably further into the couch. 'No ice?'

'Oh, yeah...' She put down the bowl for the Doritos and the two glasses and automatically went back into the kitchen. She didn't want to get ice but needed to leave the room, a discordant note rang out through her thoughts.

In the kitchen, she wrestled with the ice cube tray which had iced over from being in the freezer for too long. All fingers and thumbs, she loosened the cubes under a spray of water from the tap and tried again. The pressure of her thumbs on the plastic forced ice cubes to spring out of their casement and fly into the sink across the granite worktop.

Back in the sitting room Georgia found the assertive voice she used in the classroom.

'So what do you really want Sean after all this time?' She noticed for the first time, since he'd walked in, dark circles under his eyes and sagging lines around his mouth. The light from the Tiffany lamp next to him highlighted every crease. His jaw set hard, had the faintest trace of stubble around it.

'So what do I really want?' said Sean. He sank into the back of the sofa, a cushion propping up his head and tapped the space next to him indicating to Georgia to park herself up close.

Georgia ignored his gesture. 'I'm guessing you're here to apologise for finishing with me by text...almost three weeks ago...' She dropped the ice cubes into the glasses, each clinking clearly, cutting the atmosphere building between them.

'Maybe...but not right now.'

'So what do you want?' she said, bending down to pick up the discarded carrier bag he'd left scrunched up on the floor next to the footstool. 'Because it's over. What we had is finished. You finished it.'

'I made a mistake.'

'Yeah, you did but I've got over it.' She felt her cheeks redden at yet another lie knowing too well she missed him. 'So what d'you want?'

'Just to see you, is that a crime all of a sudden?' he asked edgy, nervous. Georgia watched him as he kept swallowing, his Adam's apple bobbing up and down as he did so.

'No. Well yes, after all these weeks? And it's late.'

'It's not late. I've got Baileys for you,' he said again, nodding his head in the direction of the coffee table where he'd put down the bottle and the bag of Doritos.

'Thank you,' she said, not wanting to be rude. She reached over, just to give her something to do and unscrewed the cap of the bottle which opened easily. The bottle almost weighed less than she thought as she picked it up and it dawned on her it had already been opened. She realised how stupid she'd been not to have recognised how much he needed to drink before now. She had always fallen for his tales of no overtime at work and having to give his mum money for rent and food. He's not too different to his drunken Irish father, for God's sake, she thought. She recollected all the times Sean had poured out his heart about the stern father who drank and would make him clean out his pigeons in his pants and vest on the middle of winter, often waking him in the middle of the night yelling; pushing him out into the cold dark yard.

Georgia shivered and concentrated as she tipped the bottle; the smooth chocolate liquid flowed into her glass and she looked down at him.

'I'll open the munchies,' he said, getting up from his position on the sofa, his hands noticeably shaking as he pulled open the packet and emptied it into the bowl. Georgia noticed he spilled some onto the coffee table. He scooped them up shakily and crammed them into his mouth, bits of crisps sticking to his lips and a spray of crumbs scattering across the floor as he spoke with his mouth full. He wiped his palms on the front of his jeans to get the salt off his hands, not taking his eyes off her, standing one minute and then marching up and down in front of the fireplace the next. Georgia guessed he'd been drinking. She thought it explained his sudden manic pacing, his impromptu visit, agitation coming off him and filling all the space in the room.

She sat on the other sofa to get out of his way and

tucked her feet under her as she reached down and slipped off her slipper socks. She made every effort to look relaxed, but she sat too upright, as stiff as a sheet of MDF propped against the wall of a builders' yard. She took a sip of the Baileys, forgetting her mug of tea, trying to calm her jangling nerves.

'A new drama began last night. I recorded it…I was going to watch it,' she said, trying to make light conversation, but waffling on, speaking with uncertainty.

'Thought you were going to bed but don't let me stop you,' he said, pouring himself a huge measure and drinking it all in one gulp.

Georgia noticed his slurring words, just slightly, and his eyes looked glazed over.

Perhaps he'd already been at the Baileys himself and that's why the bottle had been so light before she'd opened it.

'Look, it's all well and good you wanting to make amends, coming over, but I'd planned an early night. On my own,' she added, looking straight at him. She felt strangely sorry for him. He wasn't a bad man; just unable to commit to anything, a relationship, a job. He had no drive, no ambition, unlike she who had ambition in abundance, she reflected. His voice broke into her thoughts.

'Well, I'm hardly stopping you,' he said, his posture now rigid, his hands clenching and unclenching by his sides, his knuckles white.

'Look, Sean, we're not going out any more. So there's no point you being here. What do you actually want?' she said agitated, yet trying to sound empathetic.

He took two determined steps across the room and moved over towards her. She fidgeted, nervous. He sat down, too close, almost on top of her feet but she pulled them up tighter towards her just before his weight settled on them.

'You,' he said, his voice husky, deep, low as he leaned in towards her, his breath heavy with the honeyed aroma of whisky. She had become familiar with that smell going out with him for almost a year.

'Look, it was great while it lasted. It's over. We want different things and I have to put the boys first. It's too late to go back. You must understand that, don't you?'

'I made a mistake. I was angry. It's not over. Come on, we were good together. We are still good together sweetheart.'

She ignored him turning away towards the television picking up the remote control resting on the arm of the sofa. The sound of gunfire blaring out from the TV invaded, the quiet of the dimly-lit room. She turned down the volume.

He shuffled up next to her, almost on top of her, again too close, claustrophobic. She pushed her legs out in front of her turning inwards to face him, an automatic reaction on her part to force him to move out of her personal space. It worked for a second and then out of nowhere he pulled her down roughly towards him in one move, until she faced up, staring at the ceiling. Catching her unawares, Sean's hands grabbed at her, pulled at her shorts, stroked her legs. Then he slid his hand under her T-shirt, groping her roughly, urgently.

'Look, we're not going out Sean. I'm not in the mood.' Georgia said incredulous, desperately willed herself to stay calm but overwhelming panic strangled her. She clumsily pulled herself up into a sitting position giving in to her unease. She flailed wildly at him.

'I'll get you in the mood, sweetheart. Come on…be nice…'

'Be nice? Are you serious?' she said, trying harder to push up into a sitting position.

'Calm down. What's with you, all narky?' he asked, his eyes narrowing, his jaw clenched.

'Calm down? Me? You're the one all pushy and expecting a fuck!' she spat at him.

'I thought that's what you wanted. Why are you playing hard to get?'

'Just get off me, will you?' she said, readjusting her shorts.

'You know you want it Georgia. You can't get enough of me.'

'Stop it.' She tugged desperately at her shorts, vulnerable and exposed.

'Or are you seeing someone else. Oh that's it! That's where you were this afternoon, out with your new bloke.'

He made a stabbing gesture with his finger.

'Don't be ridiculous. I'm not seeing anybody. I was out with Thalia.'

'If it isn't the boys it's Thalia. How can I compete with three boys and one fucking perfect woman? To hell with you! You're flipping me out!' His eyes full of fire, anger, he leaned his body in towards her and pressed down on her. She'd never seen him like this.

'I want you to go home. You're going to wake the boys up.'

'You really are something else you know that, telling me to go home. I had to get two busses to get here! I've been working all day, I'm knackered and it's not even the weekend yet! And you've been swanning around with God knows who. Do you think I'm a dick head?' She shrank back into the sofa to get away from his breath, his face in hers.

'I was out with Thalia. I've just told you that. Why would I lie to you?' Georgia tried to keep the desperation and panic out of her voice. Thinking of something to say to him, to placate him but a twitching smile took control of his face.

Georgia didn't know what happened next. All at once Sean jumped astride of her, his hands pinning her arms above her head. An overwhelming sense of panic rose within her, her breathing became wheezy. Her face felt flushed. He leaned into her, his weight pushing down on her, hurting her. He kissed her hard on the mouth and forcing her lips open, his teeth clashed with hers. He bit her tongue, his saliva choked her. He'd always been a sloppy kisser but it had never bothered her but now it disgusted her. She tried to move her head away, thrashing left and right. Desperately she tried to stop him, an animal-like sound coming from deep within her, but she couldn't engage her brain to do what she wanted, she couldn't free herself. Numb from the pressure of his grip on her slim wrists. Her bracelet dug into her skin under his clutching hands. Out of her depth, her nerves teetered on a knife edge. The boys were upstairs and she didn't want to wake them, to witness her like this, in this situation. Think, think, she kept telling herself over and over again, her eyes tightly shut and then open again, focusing on a forgotten piece of blue tack left on the ceiling above her, which had held up the snowy white paper chains she had made with Kristiano at Christmas.

Sean's face had become shadowed in a dark, wicked, glaze. He carried on, kissing her, roughly. With his right hand he held her, tightening his grip around her wrists. He pulled roughly at her shorts with his other hand. For a second he raised his weight off her, to get to her shorts more easily. The instant burning sensation, the pain she felt focused her thoughts to where his nails he had scraped her hard as he forced her shorts down below her knees. Georgia's head felt light and airy, fuzzy. The pit of her stomach contracted with spasms of nausea, her heart heavy with fear. Fuck, she thought.

The sound of a car pulling up, music blaring, stopped him. He pulled away momentarily. A confused expression crossed his face, as if he didn't recognise her. Georgia sighed, thankful for once the youngsters with their loud music and banter had parked outside her house. Normally she would complain about them parking across her drive to visit the shisha bar on the main road.

The loud bass booming against the windows distracted Sean. Georgia found strength from somewhere, a sudden burst of violent energy. She twisted free from his relaxing grip on her, lashing out with her right arm. She clawed at his face. He froze for a second. His vacant look stared back at her. Her blood froze in her veins as she saw his blood seep, trickle down his cheek. She followed his right hand as he touched the graze. Looking down at the specs of blood now on the tips of his fingers, his lips began to tremble as did hers. Horrified with what she had done to him, her eyes opened wide in shock.

'You bitch,' he said, slapping her hard across the face, his voice cold, his eyes hard as he stared at her. Georgia's only relief being he no longer had a grip on her other arm and the sensation came back slowly. She tried to move it, to ease the uncomfortable pins and needles, desperately shaking her hand about to get the sensation back. All the while the sting of Sean's slap lingered across her cheek.

'Sean,' she said. The usually soft hazel eyes looking at her were now the darkest brown, almost black, full of anger and something else. Something she didn't recognise. Fear consumed her; the look of someone unhinged, someone drunk, someone out of control stared back at her. She remembered as a girl the time she accidentally got locked in her grandparents' dark, damp cellar playing Hide and Seek with her two sisters and cousins. Terrified, she'd sat in the gloom for what seemed like an eternity until her *bapou* managed to unscrew the jammed lock.

She stood up, but Sean, too quick, pulled her back onto the sofa with an almighty tug. She reeled back hard, the back of her head hit the wall with a thud as she came down. She looked at the clock, its hands danced in and out, as if beckoning her.

She guessed she had been unconscious for a couple of seconds, maybe longer. She rubbed the back of her head, dazed. Her head heavy, frowsty. She tried to focus but everything swam around her.

She managed a pathetic, 'Sean?'

He just sat there next to her again, mesmerised almost and then he smiled, an odd crooked smile, kind of lop-sided. She couldn't smile back at him, her gaze fixated on the shaving nick on his upper lip. She kept trying to smile, to diffuse the situation, but she couldn't. Her heart thumped so loudly she could hear it over the TV. The quiet, calm Sean gone, now ferocious, silent. She began to cry, desperate for him to stop, thinking all the while she might never get out of this.

He lunged at her again and tore at her top, ripping it from the neck across to reveal her left shoulder and pink bra strap. She reached up to cover herself, conscious of her further semi-nakedness. He pulled at her strap tearing it away, her breasts fully exposed now. Her mind pictured her being raped. She began to sob more loudly, panic swallowing her whole. She forced herself to be quiet, conscious of her boys.

'Stop crying, Georgia,' he said, 'It's only a game.'

This was Sean. She thought she knew him. She concentrated on his face and forced herself to reach out to him slowly. But there was no connection there. He was cold, distant.

He undid the buttons on his jeans easily and nudged them down around his hips.

Georgia froze still. Panic rose within her, as fear for her boys, asleep upstairs, filled her mind again.

'No,' she managed, in a quiet terrified squeak. She barely recognised the voice speaking.

'Come on sweetheart, let's call it a final farewell fuck.'

'No, Sean.'

But he had already pulled himself out of his boxer shorts, on top of her before she had time to move away. Her head remained wedged between the back of the sofa and the armrest. He pulling at her knickers, the elastic pinged against her thigh leaving an uncomfortable sensation. Then, losing his temper, he ripped the delicate trim. She lay there frozen, terrified, full of panic.

The hypnotic ticking of the clock on the pine shelf, housing the Encyclopedia Britannica set, echoed loudly around the room in unison with her pounding heart. She stretched as far back behind her as she could and groped around with her right hand until she managed to grab the Laura Ashley table lamp. She hurled it towards him, all the while an agonising, guttural moan came from somewhere deep within her. But her arm, at the wrong angle and the lamp too heavy, hammered into Sean's shoulder as it missed his head completely.

The shade caught the side of his chin, disorientating him for a few seconds. She let go of the lamp, the glass base now cracked and splintered. It lay on the couch where she dropped it. She pushed him hard with both hands with all the force she could muster and catching him off guard she knocked him off the couch and onto the floor.

The resounding crack of his head shook her as it slammed against the coffee table's rounded corner. She jumped up, an adrenaline rush making her invincible. She grabbed the bottle of Baileys, her arm raised ready to lunge at him again when his sobs filled the room. She stepped out of her shorts and her knickers fell to the floor, her torn T-shirt hanging loose, drowning her. She just stared at him. She backed out of the sitting room, the bottle of Baileys still in her upstretched hand.

'Get out of my house, you bastard!' she forced

through clenched teeth. 'Now! Or I'll call those guys outside to sort you out!'

He seemed dazed. Shocked.

'I'm sorry. I didn't mean...'

'Now! And don't you ever come anywhere near me again.'

'Georgia, please, please. I don't know what came over me.' The dried blood from the deep scratches now mixed with his wet, salty tears coursed across his cheeks. Pink tear drops fell onto his white shirt and spread like ink blots as they merged into one another.

'I said get out!'

Sean seemed to come to his senses and he stumbled out of the room, tripping over the edge of the rug as he made his way out into the hallway. Georgia blundered towards the door and hovered there unsure of Sean's reaction. He turned towards her and she flinched, her arms crossed over her chest to cover herself. Sean said something, the words tripping over his lips.

'That wasn't me...I love you...sorry.'

***

Her whole body shook. Holding tightly onto her top to cover her exposed breasts, her head thumping and her heart banging in her chest she locked the porch door. She looked up, momentarily mesmerised by the moon shining down as silver as a new coin in the midnight blue of the summer sky. Her hand shook as she tried to get the key in the lock and needed the other to steady it. Gently she shut the front door behind her. She strained her ears to hear if the boys had stirred. Only the dull hum of the TV filled the silence.

Warren's words suddenly filled her mind...someone will test you...not themselves...they will be sorry...not bad. She couldn't believe how he could have predicted something like this. She couldn't stop shaking.

She walked heavily back into the lounge, dragging her feet, her body present but her mind lost, engulfed in Warren's words and what had just nearly happened. She grabbed the remote control, flicked the TV onto standby. She picked up her shorts, her knickers, lying shamefully on the floor, the seams ripped, the fabric torn. The image of delicate antique wedding lace, left to disintegrate after years of being stored in layers of tissue paper entered her head. She shook her head from side to side as if to focus herself. She rolled the underwear and shorts into a tight ball. She stared down at the material knotted up, like her body.

She winced in pain as she dabbed at the cuts on her hand. She couldn't feel any glass splinters, the cuts mainly superficial but the soreness pierced through her. She pulled the cashmere throw off the back of the sofa and wrapped it around her, shaking uncontrollably, a chill cleaving at her insides. All at once a wave of nausea swallowed her up. I'm okay she reassured herself as silent tears stung her eyes.

She all but managed to climb the stairs, avoiding the creaky one so as not to disturb any of the boys. In her bedroom, the door shut tightly behind her, she gave way to more wet tears. She curled over the toilet bowl in her en-suite vomiting, retching as her head and her insides rejected her thoughts.

More tears rolled down her face as she scrubbed herself in the shower with the back brush; her skin red and raw from the harsh bristles. The water ran cold but she didn't care wanting every imprint of him to wash away with the swirl down the plug hole.

As she lay on her bed the tears continued to flow with abandon. They trickled into her ear and her mussed up hair and soaked her neck. Her emotions flooded her unchecked and an outburst of heart-wrenching sobs followed. She stifled these with her face pushed into her pillow, not caring her mascara would stain the Cypriot *Lefkara* lace pillowcases, stitched by her *yiayia*, her only concern all the while being not to wake the boys, her beautiful boys.

The pain in her hand worsened, it throbbed and bled. She wrapped the corner of the throw around it more tightly to stem the bleeding. The back of her head hurt and a swelling had already developed.

She curled up in a foetal position. The bedside light, left on, gave her a comforting reassurance in the otherwise dark room.

Finally, she fell into a drowsy semi-sleep, thinking not about Sean and her ordeal but of the broken lamp sat on the floor where she had placed it carefully. She knew it could not be mended and had cried fresh tears remembering how delighted she had been when her mum had surprised her with the lamp only the week before. Because you deserve a treat her mum had said with tears stinging her eyes, full of emotion. She thought too about the bottle of Baileys and the uneaten Doritos on the coffee table, like a still life display in an artist's studio.

***

Georgia slept fitfully and woke up twice, her heart banging in her chest as she recoiled from her ordeal. The nightmare reality of what had nearly happened pierced her semi-conscious sleep, incoherent words confused her mind and sweat soaked through her. She couldn't but remind herself what had come to pass, admitting the chilling painful truth; Sean had actually attacked her. After everything he said to her, the intimacy between them. She couldn't understand him. She even blamed herself. She shouldn't have let him in.

The second time she woke from a restless, shadowy half-sleep she decided to get up even though an overwhelming sense of weariness consumed her. She guessed the time, early morning, not even five. She could hear the twitter of the blackbirds and jays in the tall trees opposite her house. The rumble of the dustcart and the banter of the dustmen outside broke across nature's unthreatening cheery sounds. It was collection day. She hadn't remembered to pull out her overflowing bins.

She stood up, her legs almost buckling beneath her, and tried to adjust to the early morning sun flooding the room through the still open Venetian blinds. She looked at herself in the small mirror she kept by her bedside table and a smudge of red broken veins across her cheek reflected back at her, her tongue felt sore and sticking it out she could see two cuts. She inspected her leg but the scratches were mainly superficial. Her hand however throbbed, as did her head.

She wandered down to the kitchen still wrapped in the throw and filled a glass of water from the tap. She took a gulp swallowing three paracetamol, knowing two wouldn't do a thing.

She had to act quickly. The boys would be up early excited about the strawberry-picking treat she'd planned for them, and she didn't want them to suspect anything. She forced herself to go into the sitting room and tidy up. She picked up the lamp and placed it on the hearth out of the way for now and with the handheld hoover sucked up the bits of glass on the sofa and on the waxed floor boards. She gently shook out the edge of the rug for any errant bits of glass. She threw the two glasses away not bearing the thought of having to drink out of them again. She emptied the bowl and plumped up the cushions on both the sofas careful to arrange them as she normally would. She didn't want the boys to pick up on anything.

Upstairs, she showered again. The hot water splashed all over her as she viciously scrubbed herself with her body brush, using all of her exfoliating shower wash. She let the water flow over her, careful not to touch her head which had come up in a bump now. She lathered the ends of her hair; the steamy water almost choking her, taking her breath away.

She put on a pair of cotton jim-jams and rolled up her torn top and tattered shorts from the night before into a tight ball before putting them into her bedroom bin with her bra and knickers set too. She hid the blood-stained throw in the bottom of the overspill laundry basket of her en-suite, knowing the boys would not come across it in there. She brushed her teeth, careful not to make her tongue bleed; the side of her mouth sore and her lip bruised.

Finally, she shut out the sun rays and got into bed, grateful again for the soft downy pillow under her head and the crisp cotton duvet around her. She hugged herself tightly and within minutes she fell asleep. But her sleep was a haunting one, punctuated with images of Sean, pulling at her clothes, slapping her, grabbing at her underwear. She turned and thrashed until she woke herself up, wringing in perspiration, her pillow damp from her wet hair now mingled with the smell of sweat; terrified, sweet. She tried to swallow but her tongue seemed to be stuck to the roof of her mouth, dry and furry.

Groggily she reached over to the bedside table and poured the last of the water from the carafe. It was warm, having been there for two nights, but it gave her some relief. She didn't respond to the buzz of her mobile as two new messages come through.

She lay across the bed, partly covered until she again found her way back into sleep, uneasy and troubled, lost in the nightmare all over again. But she knew the real story after all. That it happened. And it lived on in her head.

Chapter Twenty

'*MAMMA, MAMMA* WAKE up,' called Kristiano, bouncing on her bed, on his knees.

Georgia, roused from her half-sleep, opened her eyes.

'Good morning *agabi mou*,' she said, reaching out to caress his bare legs.

'When are we going strawberry picking?'

'Soon, my darling,' she said pulling him close and giving him a big sloppy kiss on the cheek. 'Aren't your brothers up yet?'

She prayed and prayed she would get through the day; going with a teacher from school who she didn't know too well would make it more bearable she hoped. It meant she could hide behind her smile and not worry about last night's nightmare being found out. The land line rang downstairs and thankfully Kristiano shot off to answer it. She smiled at his cartoon character slippers making his feet look huge.

A few seconds later he called up. '*Maaa-mmaaa*! It's *yiaaa-yiaaa*.'

'Coming one minute,' called Georgia quietly as she got out of bed. She swallowed but the taste of Sean filled her senses and she gagged. She slowly pulled on her upside-down cardigan and pulled her hair up into a messy half-bun half-ponytail to keep the curls out of her eyes.

She padded down the stairs in her bare feet and then remembering the splintered glass ran back up to slip into her pink slipper socks.

'*Kalimera mamma.* How are you?' she asked.

'*Kala agabi mou.* How are you?'

'Fine Mum thanks. Just getting up and then we're meeting one of my friends, a teacher from my school, who's got two little boys. We've arranged to go strawberry-picking.'

'That's nice. It's a lovely day. I've already been for my walk this morning and I was really sweating by the time I got home.'

'Yeah, it looks bright.'

'Make sure the boys have their sun hats and put some sun cream on them too, Georgia *mou.*'

'Yeah, I will, Mum.'

'And how are you really? You're not still crying over Nicolas are you? Or Sean? You have to move on. I know it's difficult but things can't go back to how they were.' Georgia knew her mum referred to Nicolas.

'I'm fine Mum, honest.'

'Well, how can you be after everything he's done to you? You can tell me how you're feeling you know. I am your mum.'

'Yes Mum, I know. But I'm not upset. I'm getting on with my life, with the boys. I've got planning to do for school in September. Thalia and I are planning a few days in Barcelona…'

'Well, don't bottle it all up.'

'Mum, I'm not. Look I have to go, the boys want their breakfast and it's already nearly nine,' she said, glancing at the clock and trying to stay patient.

'Okay. Have a lovely day. Love you. And remember what I said.'

'Yes Mum, I will. Love you too.

'Bye darling.'

'Bye, bye,' she said absent mindedly as she tried to shake off the thunderbolt of a shiver whipped through her and hit her straight in the heart with all the force of a staple gun.

Tears welled up and she began to cry. She squeezed her eyes tight to stop more tears from coming but she couldn't. Hearing the boys thumping down the stairs, arguing about something or other, urged her to pull herself together.

'Stop arguing boys,' she called out wearily, 'or we won't go anywhere today. I'm not in the mood.'

'It's not me. It's Zach,' answered Andoni.

'I didn't say it was you, did I Andoni? I just said stop arguing.'

'I don't want to go stupid strawberry-picking,' he argued back.

'Then don't even come. I can drop you off at *yiayia's* house and you can spend all day trimming beans with her from *bapou's* allotment.'

'I'm not doing that.'

'Then come with us and stuff your face with big fat strawberries,' she said, pushing the door to the sitting room open. Her eyes felt sore but she felt more in control of her emotions now knowing she couldn't break down in front of them all. The younger boys didn't notice a thing although Andoni looked over at her with a perplexed expression a couple of times. She grabbed him and hugged him tight, holding her hurt hand away from him and fighting back the floods of tears threatening to fall again.

'Mum, you're squashing me,' he said.

'Yes I am. I love you,' she said, forcing the tears not to fall.

'I love you too Mum,' he said as he wriggled free of her embrace.

***

Breakfast was the usual chaos, toast crumbs everywhere, knives covered in sticky jam, the Nutella jar covered in dribbles and streaks of chocolate. She sent the boys upstairs to get dressed while she loaded the dishwasher. She listened to them arguing again and, drawing on every ounce of energy, she stopped herself from yelling at them.

'Mum, it's Sean calling on your mobile,' said Andoni, proffering the phone to her, out of breath, having just charged down the stairs. She heard him jump the last three steps to land in the middle of the hallway rug with a thump.

Georgia froze, leaning against the dishwasher for support.

'Mum!' he repeated as he came into the kitchen.

Georgia stood there chilled to the core. The phone rang off.

'And what's happened to your hand?' he blurted out.

'I cut it on the lamp. I knocked it over last night and picked it up not realising the glass had cracked,' she lied, avoiding his stare.

'The new one?'

'Yes, the one *yiayia* got me.'

'Dad always said you were clumsy,' he said innocently.

'Did he now?' she teased.

'You can't tell *yiayia*, Mum, she'll be so upset with you.'

'I know. I won't tell her if you don't.'

'I won't Mum.' He turned and shot up the stairs.

'I'll go out and buy a new one,' she whispered, but he didn't hear her.

***

Her mobile rang again, twice. Georgia tugged at the knotted curls which had fallen from the band in her hair. She stood rooted to the spot, mobile in her hand, rocking her upper body back and forth. She felt on the outside looking in on herself. Somehow she managed to get to a chair before her legs gave way. Her head suffocated her in a hot cloud of smoke. She couldn't see anything. It took a few moments for her mind to clear and her memory as the images of Sean flashing in front of her, over and over again, like a recorder in painful slow motion.

The phone rang again. She looked down and pressed 'ignore'. It was Sean again.

She sat there for maybe five, ten minutes willing herself not to cry again, her head still banged and her hand still throbbed. She ignored all his calls and deleted his messages. In the end she put her phone on silent.

***

The couple of hours at Parkside Pick Your Own farm could not have gone any slower. Georgia had arranged to meet up at half past eleven and she pulled into the gravel make-shift car park and turned off the engine at exactly 11.28am. They scrambled out of the car straight away, the sun beating down on them through the tinted windows making the temperature far too hot to sit in the car.

Georgia hadn't known the farm existed despite having driven past its entrance to go to the garden centres at Crew's Hill a couple of times before. Set in greenbelt countryside and not far from Enfield in North London, the farm stretched back as far as the eye could see. Breathtakingly beautiful the light breeze which came off the flat, open land blew the clinging cobwebs clear from deep within her, restoring her mood and refreshing her outlook.

Her friend turned up ten or so minutes after, apologizing for being late, her two children, hanging onto her skirt, both hiding behind her.

'Don't mind these two,' she said. 'They'll warm up soon enough.' Georgia already regretted the day out. Her head was frazzled.

They made their way towards a huge farmhouse building, a huge barn with peeling curls of black and white painted walls, which had clearly seen better days. Georgia's boys ran ahead following the rough driftwood 'WAY IN' signs hanging with bits of frayed rope on nails hammered into the side of the tall oak trees. Eventually these led them to the main entrance on the other side of the building. The children each took a basket, they listened impatiently to the rules of the farm from the lady with a polka dot apron embellished with two strawberries, one pink and one red, and then ran off. Andoni trailed behind them unenthusiastically, dragging his trainers across the dry earth. Her friend's children were still hanging onto her side like little leeches.

'I'll go on ahead with them Georgia, if that's okay? Once they've come out of their shell I'll come back for a chat,' she said.

'You go ahead, hun,' said Georgia, relieved she wouldn't have to hold a conversation with her. She had no energy and no inclination to be around people, either. She wanted to disappear, into thin air, and return as the old Georgia before the attack in a time machine.

Georgia's boys were delighted picking their own strawberries, and Andoni soon found some untapped eagerness too. Each holding onto their own basket, the boys went off into the fields full of rows and rows of strawberry plants heavy with big juicy bright red strawberries, resting on clumps of soft golden barley straw. Georgia dawdled behind them admonishing them every now and then for demolishing more berries than they were putting in their baskets. She reminded them they were breaking the rules about eating the produce but her voice had no severity to it and the boys, picking up on this, just carried on popping one after the other into their mouths.

Just then her friend, walked towards Georgia, one of her children propped up on her hip, the little blond head buried into her mum's shoulder.

'I'm going to have to go. I'm so sorry,' she said, her face full of genuine sorrow.

Regrettably for her friend, but fortunately for Georgia, the child had a fever and the day out had to be abandoned. She apologised profusely to Georgia for having to leave, calling goodbye to the boys. Zachari waved to her from where he stood some fifteen feet away, before kneeling back down in the dry earth furrows and diverting his attention back to the task at hand. The other two boys remained oblivious, too distracted by their freshly picked produce.

Georgia knew they were not purposefully being unfriendly; they were too busy running a 'who could pick the biggest strawberry competition' between them. Georgia had suggested it to keep them occupied, a way of injecting some enthusiasm into Andoni who, naturally competitive, always wanted to be the best and better at everything where his brothers were concerned.

'Wow, look at this one,' Georgia heard him exclaim, 'I'm going to be the wi...nner!'

Georgia glad to be in the fresh air and open countryside breathed a sigh of relief not having to make polite conversation any longer. Strangely her thoughts crept back to when she used to stuff her ears with cotton wool to block out her *bapou's* snoring, wedged between him and her *yiayia*, during sleepovers with them. By morning she couldn't wait to get up and out of bed and used to offer to buy extra supplies of milk or bread for breakfast just to get some fresh air and to stretch her limbs.

While the cashier weighed up each of the boys' baskets Georgia bought two packets of homemade rose-tinged meringue cases and just at the last moment grabbed a jar of chocolate dipping sauce remembering how the boys had almost eaten all the Nutella at breakfast in the morning. The boys picked up a Calypso orange pouch each. Georgia paid with her credit card and they walked over to the picnic area, the boys thirsty and Georgia wanting to sit a while. The boys sucked up the juice faster than ever and then went off to play on the big steel climbing frame which looked like a higgledy-piggledy mishmash of bars all at different levels.

Georgia sat on a wooden stool, shaped like a mushroom and carved out of an old tree trunk, her face tilted up towards the sun, her eyes closed as it intermittently disappeared behind soft wispy clouds. Every few minutes she opened her eyes to look over at the boys and to check on the time.

'Excuse me. I think this is yours,' a tall blond guy with a tattoo of a mermaid on his forearm said to her, handing her credit card back.

'Oh yes, thank you.'

'You left it in the farm shop.'

'I'm all over the place today,' she said, her voice quivering as she burst into tears.

'Hey, no harm done.'

'Sorry,' she mumbled, her voice barely audible, her heart pounding in her chest.

'You okay?'

Georgia just nodded, her head bowed down in embarrassment not daring to look up, tears streamed down her face. She desperately tried to stop crying and rubbed at her nose with the back of her hand.

'If there's anything I can do...' he trailed off, handing her a scrunched up tissue, 'It's clean. I promise,' he said.

'No. I'm fine,' she said. 'Thank you.'

'You sure? You don't look okay. Look I'm not going to get involved and my mum's always telling me to keep my nose out of other people's business but…you don't have to put up with it,' he said hesitantly, his voice dripping with sympathy, his eyes resting on her bruised face. He reached out clumsily and squeezed her arm, before strolling back towards the barn. Georgia sat motionless, still feeling the pressure of his touch on her skin long after he'd walked away.

She stayed there, her head bowed, until her tears dried up. Bloody hell, how embarrassing she thought, I'm behaving like a victim. She pulled her compact out of her make-up bag and touched up her powder foundation in an attempt to cover the evident bruise. She dabbed at the make-up around her eyes, noticing the bruising had spread close to her eye too, giving the impression she had a smear of purple-blue eye shadow around her eye like those catwalk models who wore wacky wild make-up. She did the best she could to camouflage the bruising and then called out to the boys.

'Come on boys. It's nearly two o'clock.'

'Not yet *mamma*,' called back Kristiano.

'We're having fun,' shouted back Zachari, hanging upside down on the bars by his legs and waving his arms around.

'You just be careful!'

'Oh Mum it's so easy,' he called back, his hair flopping into his face as he pushed himself back and forth. Georgia watched him sway and then move his grip from one bar to the next as he swung across to the other side of the frame where Kristiano clapped loudly.

'Well done, honey!' she called over to him.

'Watch me, *mamma*,' called Kristiano.

'Okay and then another ten minutes and we're off.'

'Okay,' they called back in unison.

Andoni sloped over, the three years he had on Zachari clear to Georgia from his body language; his rounded shoulders and scowly expression shouted boredom.

'Have you had a good day, *agabi mou*?'

'Yeah Mum. Are you okay?'

'Yes darling. It's so hot, I'm getting a headache.'

'What did that man want?'

'Oh, I left my credit card in the shop. He just came to give it to me.'

'And how did the lamp break?'

'I just dropped it honey. I'm so frustrated with myself.'

'Is that why you're crying?'

'Yeah, I'm just being silly. Come here give your mum a hug.'

'I love you Mum,' he said.

'I love you too. To the moon and back,' she said, fighting the tears. Georgia remained seated on the wooden stool and Andoni bent down to her. She pulled him onto her lap and they hugged each other tightly, the early afternoon sun beating down on them, as they sat there entwined, love passing from one to the other, like one of those Willow Tree mother and child sculptured figurines.

***

Eventually, the boys were ready to go. Georgia grabbed a few pages of newspapers from a pile stored in a wooden container made from pallets, on the side of the car park, and lined her boot with them.

'Be careful, boys,' she said, 'I don't want strawberry stains everywhere.' She helped them place their cardboard baskets carefully in a row before banging the boot shut.

Stopped at the traffic lights, Georgia glanced down at a message from Katia.

```
Hi babe. Do the boys want 2 come over 2nite
?
Kids making pizza. Come and join in. Plenty
2 go round xxx

Brilliant x thanks babe x will drop them
off in half an hour x love u xxx

Love u 2 x
```

Georgia weaved in and out of the late lunch time traffic. She had her front window rolled down all the way and the breeze rushed round the car cooling her down. Facing towards the open window, the whipped up air blew Zacahri's fringe across his eyes. Georgia looked down again at her mobile vibrating in the storage section between the two front seats, behind the gear box, and picked it up. She put the phone back face down. She didn't open the message from Sean.

'Aunty Katia has a surprise planned for you tonight. She said you can all go round and stay the night,' she said, a bit too cheerily.

'Yeah,' said Kristiano.

'We can have a Wi tennis tournament,' said Zachari.

'What about our pyjamas and stuff?' asked Andoni.

'We'll pick up everything you need now on our way and then I'll drop you off,' said Georgia.

'Do I have to go?' Andoni asked.

'Not if you don't want to honey. You can stay home with me.'

'Do you think Aunty will be upset if I don't go?'

'Of course not, the other two are going anyway.'

'I'd rather stay with you *mamma*,' he said, reaching over and squeezing her hand. Georgia squeezed her eyes tight so the welling tears didn't fall. She looked straight ahead, hiding behind her sunglasses. She couldn't say anything. She knew if she tried to speak the tears would come pouring again.

BROKEN PIECES OF TOMORROW

***

Within forty minutes, she dropped off the boys and made an excuse not to stop for a cuppa saying she needed to go Tesco shopping but instead drove straight home. She felt relieved the boys were spending the night at their aunt's. She desperately needed time alone, to think about what had happened the night before. Andoni would be no trouble. He would probably be on his PS2 and so wouldn't need too much attention. The thought of him being in the house comforted her as she dreaded being home alone, uneasy, jumpy in her own space.

She threw open the french doors of the dining room, in an effort to cool the already stifling hot room but more warm air pouring in from the south-facing garden engulfed her. In her neighbour's garden a playful squirrel jumped between the branches of the lush trees and softly fluttered the leaves, sending a shower of moss and mint confetti floating downwards. They landed gently on the shed, its asphalt roof curled up at the edges like the crusts of sandwiches left out too long at a children's party. She took in a big breath of hot air, glad for the peace. Andoni she thought was no doubt plugged into his PlayStation, in the throes of his FIFA match upstairs.

Georgia walked back through the dining room running her fingers over the English Oak dining table. She wandered into the kitchen. She took a glass from the antique pine shelf above the sink and took out a bottle of

Evian from the fridge. The cold water running down her throat made her shiver. She thought about the events of the night before and wondered, for the first time, whether she should report what happened. What if she hadn't stopped him? What if he had raped her? Her mind filled with questions, scenes playing and then re-winding only to play again in her head, over and over again. She poured another glass of Evian and snapped two paracetamol tablets out of the blister. Her head began to throb again and she reached up to touch the raised bump. She winced as she felt the bulge; the pain raw and harsh. Then she retched. Sick splattered the back of the kitchen chair and the floor. She tried to re-compose herself choking on her vomit but she lost the battle against her grief as the tears fell hot and plump down her face exploding like the little water bombs the boys liked to throw.

She grabbed a tea towel and soaked it with hot water from the kitchen sink. She wiped her mouth and mopped the chair. She rinsed the cloth through a couple of times before she'd scooped all the sick up. She opened the windows and hoped the stench would dissipate before Andoni had a reason to come downstairs. She stood listening for footsteps on the stairs, nothing. Thank God Andoni had not heard her retching above the cheers of the football commentary. She went upstairs, calling through his half-open door.

'I'm going to take a shower.'

'Okay, Mum,' he called back. She could tell he

wasn't listening but for once she was grateful for his lack of focus. She didn't want any more questions. She didn't want to think about anything.

The water couldn't come fast enough or hot enough over her. She forced the last dollop of exfoliating wash into her hand and then closing her eyes she scrubbed hard in an effort to cleanse herself. She wanted every invisible imprint of Sean to disappear.

In her bedroom, she looked at herself in the mirror. Her face appeared puffed up and she had a bruise coming up across her shoulder. She changed into a white strapless summer dress she'd bought from Zara the summer before, discarding her clothes in the laundry basket. She put on a light cotton-silk mix cardigan with three-quarter length sleeves to hide the mauve blemish and ran some serum through her hair after towel-drying it.

Downstairs, she placed an-online shopping order with Tesco and paid the highest price for delivery wanting to get her order as soon as possible - £123.43 with savings of £7.50, and a delivery charge of £5.00. Happy days, Georgia thought to herself, the tears silently falling as they left salty streaks in her cleavage.

***

In the end, the boys stayed at their *thea's* house for another two nights; their aunt glad to have them. Georgia's boys, being older than her two meant she could get on with her household chores. The boys were her sister's free babysitters. Everybody was gratified with the arrangement including Georgia who was relieved to have the time to herself. Andoni spent most of the following day playing football with his school friends in Victoria Park, popping back home once for another bottle of water and then a second time for some money to buy an ice cream from the park café. The second day he went to the local shopping centre Brent Cross to buy a pair of trainers and kill some time with a couple of friends. Georgia gave him an extra fiver to buy McDonald's for lunch too.

That third evening, sitting in front of the TV watching an episode of Eastenders, Georgia decided to pull herself together and to face up to what had happened. The soap's storyline had been seriously depressing recently. Georgia tutted at the screen; Dawn and Gary had found each other again and had sailed off on a canal boat. Georgia willed herself to not look back. She had to look forward to what life was now going to bring her. That's what she was going to do. She had a lot to be thankful for. She had her boys, a roof over her head, a good job and lots of family and friends around her. She knew life just had to get better. There was no way she was going to let Sean drag her down.

***

Over the next week or so, Georgia focused on work and

compiled her Schemes of Work and planned resources for her lessons ready for September. She signed onto the Times Education Supplement website which gave her access to hundreds of great resources which she easily adapted to her school's exam specification. The TES helped her to work smarter not harder.

Georgia consciously focused her pent up anger and frustration and channelled these into something positive and productive. It kept her mind off what had happened, nearly happened, at least in the day but at night broken sleep haunted her with images of Sean, on that terrible night, his constant text messaging and all his calls. The nightmare seemed endless.

***

Back at work, after the summer holidays and having passed her Newly Qualified Teacher period - NQT - Georgia proud to have achieved her Qualified Teacher Status - QTS - enjoyed the stability of her routine. She re-balanced her emotions, feeling calmer, happier and stronger as time went by. She didn't tell anyone about her ordeal and brushed off Thalia's questions about Sean. Thalia gave her a quizzical look. Georgia knew Thalia wondered why she was being adamant about not speaking to Sean or meeting him. But despite the barrage of communications from him Georgia stood firm.

She closed Sean and all thoughts of him tightly away

into a vault she created in her mind's depth. She visually turned the key in the padlock. She vowed never to think about any of it again. At least this is what she tried to do.

Chapter Twenty-One

PULLING ONTO THE drive, after what seemed like an interminable day at school, Georgia glanced over and waved to her gardener in the front garden of her neighbour's house, tugging at some weeds. She watched him tug hard, his muscles pushing through the white T-shirt he wore, the late sandy summer sun bouncing off his mousy brown hair.

'Hi Mark,' she said, as she got out of the car, balancing a pile of coursework folders. Awkwardly she tried to hold onto her handbag too, which had slipped off her shoulder and pulled heavily at the crook in her elbow.

'Here, let me get those for you,' he said, scooting over. He came to her rescue just as she almost dropped them all.

'Oh, thanks Mark. Are you doing me today?' she asked.

'Yeah, if you want me to. And ya garden.'

'Oh…umm…' she mumbled, completely flustered by his reply.

'I tried calling you last night to let ya know I'd be around, but there was no answer. Where were you, then?' he asked, with a cheeky grin on his face.

'Nowhere, I was definitely home. Might have been in the shower,' she said. 'Anyway, knock when you're done. I think I still owe you from last month,' she said.

She turned the key in the lock of the porch door and dumped her bag there. As she turned round she almost knocked into him. 'Whoops, sorry,' she said unusually flustered and embarrassed.

'Where d'ya want these?'

'Oh, that's fine thanks.' She reached for the folders, her cheeks flushed crimson.

***

An hour later, Georgia toasted a pitta bread and prepared a salad for dinner with feta cheese, as she relaxed in her loungewear from The White Company. About to take a mouthful of salad a tapping on the glass of the front door forced her to put her fork down. She froze. Instantly, her heart constricted and panic rose within her. Then remembering it would be Mark she opened the door.

She paid him what she owed him, embarrassingly making up the £24.00 with loose change from wherever she could find it. Conscious of keeping him waiting at the door, she rushed around the house collecting odd coins from the kitchen drawer, her bedside table and finally her ten pence piece jar at the back of the dresser cabinet.

'Sorry to keep you Mark,' she said, out of breath. 'And sorry for all the coins.'

'Not a problem. You could'a left it till next month.'

'Actually I might have to ask you to stop coming, money's a bit tight right now,' she said.

'No, don't do that,' he interrupted, 'look I'll call over every six weeks if it'll make things a bit easier for ya.'

'Are you sure? That might be better for me since I'm only earning a measly teacher's salary,' Georgia said. Painfully embarrassed she wore no bra, she tried to politely cut the conversation short.

'So where're the boys?' he asked, clearly not taking the hint.

'Oh, they're having dinner with their dad and coming home later,' she said.

'Nigh' off, is it?'

'Actually we're not together anymore so they see him once a week and every other weekend.' Tears welled behind her eyes.

'Oh, I'm sorry. I thought I hadn't seen 'is car on the drive. Oh, I'm really sorry Georgia. I didn't mean t'upset ya. Look, d'ya want me to come in? D'ya wanna talk?'

'No it's fine, thank you. The divorce papers came through this morning. It's a bit raw that's all.'

'I'm so sorry.'

'Anyway I'd better get in. It's getting cold.'

'That's tough. How're the boys? Bet they're gutted.'

'They are. It's been hard on all of us. But we're getting used to things now…new routines...'

'What happened?'

'Long story. He was seeing someone. Seeing them for a while actually.'

'That's awful. I'm so sorry Georgia,' he said again.

'Yeah, well. I just have to get on with it.'

'Let me know if you need anything. You've got my mobile number.'

'Yeah, I will.'

'You take care and I'll see ya soon.'

'Okay, thank you Mark. You too,' said Georgia.

'If you need anything,' he repeated.

'Thanks. I'm fine,' Georgia said and she pulled the porch door closed, turning her back on Mark, tears stinging her eyes.

Back inside, she thought about her situation. A single mother with three children. Who on earth would be interested in her? Why would anyone be interested in her? Not long term anyway…Sean had been…what had he been? She thought he'd loved her, thought he cared for her but in the end…she involuntarily shook off a shiver. No. No-one would be interested in her and bringing up three boys. Baggage, that's what men would say. And men like that she wouldn't want to be with…she'd learnt the hard way. She'd given all her energy, her youth and love to Nicolas and look how that had turned out. If she and the boys, their life, hadn't been enough for him then how would it be enough for someone new? Someone without any history between them?

She spent the rest of the evening thinking, thinking, thinking. She needed to pick herself up and make a plan. She couldn't keep on drifting. Drifting didn't get you anywhere. She went over Warren's haemorrhage of words and names; 'big bold gold letters, bright and flashing spelling out the name David', the initial N, the letter T. She came back to the same thought every time, who could David be? She didn't know anyone called David and yet Warren insisted he existed in her life.

***

At work, the following day, Georgia lunched with the usual crowd of teachers. They gathered round the mishmash of tables pushed together, to form a dining table of sorts, in the staff room. Listening to the surge of laughter and conversation, Georgia drew deeper into herself until her face choked up, turbulent emotions engulfing her.

'You okay?' asked Stella, the Spanish teacher.

'Yeah, sorry I'm fine,' she lied, feeling bad because Stella had been genuinely welcoming and supportive since she had joined the school and Georgia had enjoyed the ease with which they both got on, had the same sense of humour.

'You don't look fine,' said Reece. 'We don't work in business just for the fun of it Georgia. I'm your friend as well, you know that, don't you?' he continued, looking a bit embarrassed as the words tumbled out replicating one of those agony aunt sessions on This Morning.

'No. I'm okay, really. I'm just in a bad place right now. You know, at home, not work.'

'Well, we're both here for you,' said Stella gently,

looking over at Reece, who shrugged his shoulders in a gesture of confusion.

'I'm just hormonal,' said Georgia and left it there.

'If you ever want to talk I'm here for you.' Stella tapped her on the hand.

'Me too,' said Reece, 'even if I don't know what hormonal means,' he winked at her and leaning across the table he tried to hug her but didn't quite manage to across the width of the table.

'Thanks guys, both of you. I'll be okay.'

***

The rest of the day went by quickly but Georgia felt she was on the outside looking in, not present. Her Year 10 class got on with their coursework on the different functional areas of business, which was a blessing, as she had no patience for their usual misdemeanours and, picking up on her mood, kept their heads down. The Year 11 class continued with the research she had set the previous lesson on stakeholder groups for Waitrose and their level of influence on the business's operations.

'Fuck you. You piece of shit!' She looked up from the front of the class where she had been checking through her emails to catch one boy throwing a chair across the room towards another.

'You dumb arse!' Jason retorted.

'That's enough,' said Georgia calmly.

Both boys ignored her. Within seconds three other boys jumped out of their seats at their computer terminals.

'Fight! Fight! Get in there!'

'I said that's enough! Mohammed, Emmanuel, Tarik sit down right now,' Georgia said with such severity in her voice they didn't argue. She took four wide strides over towards Jason and Roberto. 'Roberto pick up the chair. How dare you! What would your mother say if you were throwing her furniture around the living room at home?' she took a deep breath and turned towards Jason. 'Language like this is unacceptable. Outside. Now.' Her voice almost a whisper, cut through the hush in the room. 'The rest of you get on with your work while I sort this out. And. Not. A. Word.'

***

During the next hour, allocated as Planning, Preparation and Assessment time, PPA, she planned her lessons for the following week. She always prepared ahead and it meant if she had an off-day she didn't fall behind or put herself under unnecessary pressure.

As she went through her Schemes of Work and mapped out her lesson content her mind drifted back to what Warren had told her. Nicolas continued to harass her. Sean did too as she woke with Sean's dark twisted face in her mind's eye most mornings. She fought with the turmoil of emotions surrounding both Nicolas and

Sean. She had to get Nicolas out of her heart and Sean out of her head. She took a big breath and then exhaled slowly trying to calm herself. The tension built up and pushed uncomfortably on her aching heart and squeezed her head. She could sense another headache coming on.

There was a knock at her classroom door and before she responded Craig stepped in.

'Hi,' he said. 'I saw you upset at lunch time. But I didn't want to butt in. What's wrong?' She burst into tears again.

'Everything's a mess, Craig.'

'Why? What's going on?'

'You don't want to know.'

'Come on Georgia. Try me.'

'I don't know really. Everything. Nicolas's being horrible to me. Sending me texts all the time, criticising me and saying I'm a bad mum, he's poisoning the boys against me telling them it's my fault we split up and he still loves me. He says this is my fault because I won't have him back. The boys are confused. I'm tired. I'm running around trying to hold it all together and then there's Sean…he…he…' Georgia, ambushed by a swell of emotion mid-sentence, shook.

'Hey, come here,' he said, reaching out to hug her. 'It'll be alright, you know, you'll get through this.' She pulled away awkward of their closeness and took a step back.

'Thanks, Craig,' I'm just tired, I guess.

'Well, relax tonight.'

'I can't. I've got Kristiano's Parent's Evening tonight and then I'm seeing Zach's Deputy Head about this blasted Anger Management Programme for him too. There's no time to relax.'

'Well, just go with the flow. The boys'll pick up on it if you're stressed and it'll make things worse.'

'They couldn't get any worse, seriously,' she said, just as the bell indicating the end of the school day rang across the empty classroom, momentarily interrupting their conversation. She heard sounds floating up the corridor; scampering feet, doors banging, the shrill voice of a member of staff, a boy swearing.

'Has something else happened? With this Sean guy?'

'No...' she hesitated.

'You sure?' he asked, with genuine concern.

'It's nothing honest.'

'I don't believe you.'

'I can't tell you, Craig. I'm sorry.'

'Come on. A trouble shared is a trouble halved or whatever it is they say,' he said, looking her straight in the eyes. Georgia didn't budge. She stayed silent, her fingers twirling the ends of her hair. 'Tell me when you're ready,' Craig eventually said.

'Maybe,' she said, relieved he'd let it drop.

'You going straight home now?' he asked, changing the subject.

'Yeah, why?'

'Can I get a lift?'

From that day onwards Georgia often gave Craig a lift as far as the traffic lights opposite the road leading down to Finchley Central Tube Station. It had become their routine since the first time he'd asked her for a lift and she didn't mind his company. She was happy to have someone to talk to about her day and to share her days' experiences with. School continued to be full of 'situations' and she had underestimated the impact the children would have on her.

Only two weeks before, one of her Year 10s had admitted hurting herself. Georgia had to involve the school's designated Child Protection Officer. Dealing with it had taken up all of her lunchtime; the student had to make a written statement and Georgia had to contact the girl's parents and organising follow-up meetings. At the end of the same week Georgia broke up a fight at the bottom of the staircase between three boys and two girls, which ended up in her getting elbowed in the stomach by one of the boys, albeit accidentally, but it left her vulnerable and tearful.

On another occasion, while on break duty by the tennis courts, she asked a student to pick up an empty drink can he had kicked across the court and he had yelled abuse at her. She had simultaneously felt violated and humiliated by his reaction towards her request and had taken the abuse personally. The incidences were emotionally draining and talking to Craig helped her put things into perspective. His logical way of looking at things didn't allow him to get emotionally entangled. He was a good listener and although comfortable around him she couldn't bring herself to talk about what had happened with Sean even though Craig asked again. She kept thinking back to Warren's reading and the name David too. It played over in her mind. Could he be the man Warren talked about? Could Warren have got the name wrong?

Chapter Twenty-Two

IT WAS AN unusually beautiful warm Saturday afternoon towards the end of September. Georgia wondered where the past year, since she gained her QTS, had gone. On one level she thought it had flown by but on another it had been a tough year.

She looked up into the blue clear sky, sunglasses shading her eyes, her oversized T knotted to one side just below her thigh. A noisy engine sounded and she looked over from her drive to see Mark's van pulling up.

'Here, let me help ya with that,' he said, calling over as he slammed his door shut.

'No, don't worry. I've nearly finished now,' said Georgia, conscious of how dishevelled she looked, her hair tied up in a messy top knot, no make-up on. She could feel the perspiration running between her cleavage and reached up to wipe her forehead and upper lip.

'Won't take me a minute. Where's all this come from?' he asked, grabbing a huge piece of cardboard. He tore it apart, his muscles showing through the scruffy Umbro T-shirt he wore. She noticed too, the tattoo of a bird with a Latin inscription around it at the top of his right arm.

'Two new wardrobes for the boys. It's taken me all morning to put them together.' She reached up to wipe her brow again.

'On ya own?' he asked.

'Well they were partly built. Only had to put the door and the sides on. The drawers were already made up.'

'Brains and beauty, eh?' he teased, the creases around his blue eyes deepened as he smiled at her.

'Not sure about that but I've put them together at last and they look great. The boys'll be surprised when they get back.'

'You should've said. I would've helped ya.' He picked up another sheet of packaging and tore it effortlessly lengthways, as if merely tearing a sheet of paper in half.

'I've done them, now. But thank you.'

'Bet it took ages didn't it?'

'Nearly three hours,' said Georgia. 'But the delivery men took them upstairs for me which saved me lagging them.'

'So the boys are with their dad?'

'Yeah, til Sunday night. It's what we have arranged so we all stick to the routine.'

'Hard, though, I'm guessing?' He looked straight at her, stroking his arm and shifting his weight from one foot to the other.

'Yeah, it is. But it's probably hardest for the boys so I'm not going to feel sorry for myself.'

'Good for you. And kids cope don't they? What are you up to tonight then?'

'Nothing really.'

'Look, do you fancy going for a drink, if you're not busy?'

'Oh, thanks Mark. But, I'm up to my…eyes…with planning …you know, for my lessons next week.' She felt light-headed, finding it difficult to articulate what she wanted to say.

'You work too hard.'

'Well I can't just sit back and relax. Not yet. I need to prove myself.'

'Give me ya mobile number and I'll text ya later. You might change ya mind.'

'No really. It's fine.'

'I was gonna ask for it anyways…don't always get through on your land line, you know, to tell ya I'm coming for the garden.' Georgia tapped her number straight into his phone and passed it back to him, his fingers brushed against hers.

'So you're staying in tonight?' Mark asked again.

'Me, myself and I with a cuppa and a bag of marshmallows.'

'Marshmallows, eh? Really pushing the boat out.' His playful grin touched his eyes.

'Yeah lots of sugar, no fat.'

'Sounds good to me.'

'Anyway what are you doing round here on a Saturday?' she asked.

'Neighbours owe me for three months and then there's a lady down the road who wants a quote for her trees to be cut back.'

'No rest for the wicked, eh?' said Georgia, smiling, as she threw the last bit of card into the skip on her neighbours' drive.

'No, you're right there. Is he alright you using his skip?'

'Bit late asking now. But yeah, Derek said it's fine. He's a kind man. Him and his wife actually. They were ever so sweet one time when they heard Nicolas yelling at me. God knows what they thought was going on. Winnie came over after he'd stormed out to check I was alright.'

'No way! He didn't hurt you did he?'

'No, not really. Not physically anyway. Just frightened the boys and smashed my vase I found splinters of glass everywhere for days...'

'No way! That's bad.'

'Well, he's not around anymore.'

An awkward silence fell between them after the easy, relaxed chatter and Mark looked at her expectantly which unnerved her.

'Well thanks for your help, Mark, I'd better get back in.'

'You do that,' he said, smiling straight at her.

***

Georgia spent the afternoon preparing her business

lessons for the following week, five A Level lessons on the different responsibilities of Human Resources, three Year 10 lessons on interview skills and preparing for an interview and three Year 11 lessons on cash flow and break even.

In the kitchen, she flicked on the kettle and pulled out one of the baskets in the base of the larder. After working for almost four hours, exhausted, her head aching and her brain frazzled, she found some cream crackers and took a bite out of one. She felt hungry but the dry cracker stuck to the back of her throat and sides of her mouth. She reached over to the butter dish on the iron wall shelf. She smiled as she remembered what a joy it had been when the french antique shelf had finally arrived after weeks of waiting.

The mug of tea energised her and she spread some cream cheese across a couple more crackers making them much more palatable and enjoyable.

On the granite worktop her mobile rang loudly, breaking through the unusual silence. She reached over not recognising the number but picked up anyway.

'Hello,' she said.

'Hi Georgia? It's Mark.' She recognised his voice immediately. 'I think I left my work notebook on your driveway wall this morning.'

'Oh, I didn't notice,' she said, 'let me take a look. Hold on...' She ran out. 'Can't see it...oh wait...found it,' she said, 'in Derek's front drive, wedged behind the big planter with weeds growing out of it.'

'Oh, thank God. I'd be lost without it. All my customer contact details and price plans are in there.'

'I'll hold onto it for you.'

'Well, if you're still gonna be home, can I pass by later?'

'Uh, yeah no worries.' She walked back into the house as she ended the call.

***

Georgia sat in the back garden catching the last of the day's rays. By half five, the chill touched her as the temperature dropped and she came in to have a bubble bath. Something she hadn't indulged in since before she had the boys.

She swirled the orange bubble bath under the running hot water and then she sank back into the deep tub, the fluffy lathery bubbles almost spilling over the roll-top edge. She nestled into the bath cushion wedged behind her head, closed her eyes and thought about the boys and how they were coping with their new routine. She hoped the Anger Management Programme would help Zachari control his temper and his shouting and screaming.

His behaviour had become increasingly difficult to cope with and Georgia sometimes thought Craig's suggestion of seeking out some sort of therapy for her too wouldn't be such a bad idea. She was coping on the outside but on the inside guilt wracked her. She hid the emotional wreck she had become after what happened with Sean. She constantly chastised herself for being so stupid, so naïve.

Her mind wandered back to her PGCE course and how it had thrown her into a busy hectic routine, different to the extreme, to what her married life had been like. The course had been a welcome distraction, giving her a focus away from the anguish of the pending divorce and associated trauma. She hadn't even been overly angered, more accepting, in the end, of her fate. Everyone, her mum, her sisters, Thalia, kept asking her why she wasn't angry and she couldn't tell them. Maybe because she knew she had to hold it together, to get through the course and be strong for the boys. Maybe because she realised being bitter would only hurt her, hurt her more than it would hurt Nicolas. They'd had fourteen years of marriage together. They were just kids when they'd met although at the time they knew what they both wanted. She now had to accept their relationship had reached its expiry date. Like everything in life nothing lasts forever, she thought.

She immersed herself in the bubbles with her eyes closed. The music filtered through her ear buds on her iPod shuffle, sitting on the window sill above her and she thought about her life and what could have been and what could now be. She remembered being the eighteen-year-old Nicolas asked out and how ecstatic she had been to have got noticed by someone. Her mum had always introduced her to friends as 'my clever girl' and her sister as 'my pretty girl'. Looking back, over her life, this had subconsciously pushed her to make the decisions and choices she had made. Everything she did hinged on her being successful, proving her cleverness, intelligence, capabilities. Her looks always came second. She didn't have real confidence in herself. Hiding behind her cleverness gave her the outward confidence everyone saw. Over the years she had learnt to capitalise on this using her intelligence to somehow deflect from her lack of looks.

Playfully scooping up the bubbles in the palm of her hand, the aroma of lemon oil and orange peel tickled her nose. Georgia blew them away. She thought how far she had come in such a short space of time. As a qualified teacher with a full time job, in a position to keep the boys with her, Nicolas's efforts to take them away and tarnish her good character would unlikely be successful.

She shook off a shiver as she remembered what he was like after they got married and she had the boys. He became controlling, criticised everything she did from the way she cleaned the bathroom to the way she bathed the boys, from the way she washed up to the way she drove the car. Slowly, slowly, year after year, he had chipped away until her confidence was gone. She realised too she must have been depressed at various times during her marriage, after her first miscarriage when he said he didn't blame her but it was plain to see in his eyes; he thought the loss of their baby had been her fault.

Then he blamed her again when she fell pregnant after Kristiano. Nicolas said how three was a crowd but four would be a disaster. He put her under so much emotional and mental pressure she convinced herself she had gone on to lose the baby because of it and she'd cried her heart out. And now the bastard had fathered a girl with someone else. The irony of it all was sometimes too much to bear. And the arrogance of him wanting her to take the child on after everything he'd put her through. He was manipulative and deceitful to the core.

She shivered and realised the water had become almost cold. She pulled out the plug to let some of the bathwater drain away before topping it up; the scorching water splashed in. She took the exfoliating sponge from the metal caddy and scrubbed, gently at first and then more vigorously as if to scrub away all her invading thoughts.

She stood up, rinsed away the last of the bubbles off her and climbed out wrapping herself in the bath sheet, warm from the heated towel rail. She wished life always felt this cosy and safe.

No sooner had she thrown on her silk kimono, her mobile rang. She lazily reached over to the Laura Ashley cabinet and picked it up.

'Hello,' she said.

'Hello, Georgia. It's Mark.'

'Oh hi.'

'Are you home?'

'Uh, yes…'

'Open up then? I've been ringing the doorbell for ten minutes.'

'Have you? I didn't hear you.' She padded down the stairs, her hair dripping at the ends. 'Here,' she said, handing him the notebook which she had left sitting on the antique pine unit in the hallway. 'And sorry I didn't hear you I was in the bath.'

'You're a lifesaver, thanks.' Mark said, his piercing blue eyes locking with hers.

'You're welcome,' she said, looking down at her pearly-pink pedicured feet, blushing.

'Well I'll say goodnight then. Leave you to your marshmallows.'

'Good night Mark.'

***

The next morning, up early, Georgia vacuumed the house and opened the front door to run the hoover hose over the Victorian porch tiles. There was something wedged into the letter box. She eased it out of the clasp of the metal plate. There was a note taped to a packet of marshmallows. She screwed up her eyes in concentration, trying to place the writing, she'd seen it somewhere before.

'You're sweeter than candy
You make me feel randy
Right to my core
Wanna know you more'

M x

Georgia realised, immediately she saw the initial M, that Mark had posted it. She came over all hot and flustered. When did he post them? Was he here now? Was he being genuine? Was he after one thing now he knew she was no longer with Nicolas?

After her initial panic, as she drank a mug of earl grey and despite her underlying inner turmoil, she smiled as she read through his note again. She thought how sweet the note was. She opened up the bag and popped one of her favourite candy treats into her mouth.

Naughty but nice she thought.

Chapter Twenty-Three

THE WEEKS TURNED into months, and as the days waned and the October nights closed in, the trees shed their crisp copper leaves which eventually fell to the ground creating a crunchy auburn carpet underfoot. A chill began to pervade the air as the temperature dropped and Georgia found herself flicking on the heating manually earlier and earlier in the day until she gave in one weekend and adjusted the timer to her usual winter settings.

***

At school her work colleagues tried to make light of Georgia's dental appointment later that morning but little they said lightened her anxiety.

'You'll be fine,' Craig said as he ran some documents through the photocopier.

'Well, I'm not so sure. I hate the dentist at the best of times.'

'You won't feel a thing. Once the injection takes you'll be in numbness heaven,' said Stella, puffing out her cheeks.

'That's just it Stella, I don't usually have an injection. I just brave the pain.'

'You truly are wonder woman!' said Stella, 'I knew

there was something more than just books in your store cupboard.'

'Ha ha, if only you knew…'

'Well, there won't be any pain with the injection you divvy,' said Craig.

'You're not helping Craig! I'm still nervous.'

'Of course you are but they know what they're doing. They're specialists,' said Stella.

'Well, the dentist I saw for the initial consultation was lovely, really young too.'

'There you go. Lie back and fantasise,' said Stella, giggling loudly.

'Some fantasy, lying there with my mouth wide open while some cold gadget is rammed into it.'

'Exactly,' said Stella, giggling so loudly the new administrative assistant gave them both one of her matronly looks as she squeezed past them to get to the laminating machine. They rolled their eyes at one another and in unison Stella and Georgia shrieked with laughter.

'Women,' Craig said. 'You're all mad.'

***

Sitting in the reception area of the North & Jones Day Dental Surgery an edgy Georgia waited to be called in for her treatment. She had not stopped thinking about it all morning and had worked herself up.

She flicked on her mobile and played her word game

for a few minutes before reaching up for one of the magazines, COUNTRYFILE, stacked neatly in the wall rack above her head. She leafed through the articles, none of the feature stories igniting any interest…The countryside at war, Taking a Trip back in Time, Nature in July, Damsels & dragons. This last one caught her attention. She had been developing the school's nature reserve and pond area through the new extra-curricular club she had set up with one of the geography teachers. *'High summer is dragonfly and damselfly time, when the sun revs up these supercharged insects and the air above ponds*,' she read. Looking out of the tall arched window she took in how wintry the afternoon had turned already, the sky a heavy lead grey of low rain clouds. She pulled her jacket tighter around her, a cold shiver running through her. She made a mental note to take her duffle coat out of the spare wardrobe and air it. She would definitely need it now.

'Mrs Josephides?'

'Yes.' Georgia looked up.

'We're ready for you now.'

'Wish I could say I was ready for you,' said Georgia, smiling uncertainly at her from her seat. She stood up and closing the magazine she put it neatly back into the rack.

'You'll be well looked after,' the dental assistant said, giving her a half smile full of kindness.

'Good luck,' said the elderly gentleman who had been sitting motionless, opposite her, in the only armchair in the waiting area, his snaggle-toothed smile warm and gentle. He leaned forward heavily on his walking stick, its brass top shaped like a duck, his body an amorphous bulk of tawny tweed, his coat overly big for him.

'Thank you, you too,' said Georgia, noticing the dark purple veins protruding from his weathered hands, speckled with age spots, a wedding band shining out against his dull skin.

Georgia followed the dental assistant, already a few strides ahead of her, down the long corridor which smelt of peppermint. She didn't rush to catch up with her, being in no hurry to start her inevitable treatment.

'Good afternoon,' said Roger, as she walked into the treatment room.

'Hi,' said Georgia and zipping up her handbag she placed it on the empty work surface nearest the door. The fresh peppermint smell in the room cleared her nasal passages, its aroma quite overpowering in the otherwise damp-smelling room.

'How are you today?'

'Really nervous. I've got myself into a panic thinking about it all.'

'There's nothing to worry about. You'll be just fine.' He smiled sympathetically.

Georgia got comfortable on the blue leather dentist's chair. She pulled her jacket tighter around her and buttoned it up. She took the pair of protective glasses handed to her by the assistant and adjusted them to fit under her soft long curls. As the chair reclined, so she was facing up towards the ceiling, almost flat, she closed her eyes not wanting to see the hypodermic needle and crossed her arms in front of her; her hands together, her fingers intertwined.

'Comfortable?'

'Yes, thank you,' she replied, her eyes still tight shut, her mind trying to desperately bring up an image of one of her happy places to focus on as she opened wide.

'Just a dab of numbing gel on the inside of your mouth,' said Roger. 'I'm going to be working on the lower left side today.'

She blinked a response with her eyes. As she lay there waiting for the strong peppermint gel to take, she saw something from the corner of her eye. She averted her gaze across and stared. Stuck on the coving was a piece of blue tack. Panic consumed her instantly, tears streamed from her eyes and filled her ears.

'You okay?' asked the young girl, assisting. Roger quickly took out the little stick with the gel on it she'd been biting on.

'Sorry, yes. I'm just so nervous. How embarrassing,' Georgia said, wiping the tears away with her fingers simultaneously from both eyes, as she edged them behind the plastic lenses of the goggles to catch the still falling tears. She took a tissue from the square box held out to her and dabbed gently trying not to smudge her mascara and mopping up the tears around her ears and down her neck.

'That's fine. You're doing great,' said Roger.

'I feel really silly. I'll have no make-up left by the end of this,' she said, waffling on in an effort to mask the panic and her embarrassment.

'You'll be fine,' he reassured her again.

'Thank you,' said Georgia. She closed her eyes but her happy place was gone. She tried to stop crying, but the tears kept coming. She kept thinking about the blue tack and didn't even feel the injections going in. The blue tack had taken her back to that dreadful night.

Almost forty-five minutes later Georgia, back in an upright position sloshed her mouth out with the pink champagne-coloured antiseptic mouthwash. The porcelain turned bright red as she spat into it, careful not to dribble. She dabbed at her mouth, with the scrunched up tissue she had blown her nose into earlier, the sponginess of her lips tingling. Desperate to get out of the consulting room, sudden claustrophobia strangling her, she thanked Roger and his assistant and quickly left the room, carelessly banging into the door jamb.

At the reception desk Georgia waited impatiently to pay for the privilege of having her gums and teeth prodded, scraped and poked. She felt like a freak, the sensation of the anaesthetic alien to her. The whole left side of her face was numb from her chin all the way up to around her eye. Her gums felt red raw from the deep non-surgical procedure she'd gone through. She rummaged around in the bottom of her hand bag to get her Gucci wallet. She tried to keep her patience as the receptionist finished one call and picked up another straight away without even acknowledging Georgia, who was standing in front of her.

'North & Jones Day Dental Surgery, good afternoon,' she trilled down the phone. Georgia hopped from one foot to the other, desperate to kick off her high heels, her legs aching terribly, her mouth and the side of her face numb, when something on the mid-day news caught her attention.

'A drink driver from Cricklewood has received a seven-year sentence after killing two passengers in an 80mph crash...'

The local newscaster's bobbed hair framed her pretty face as it reflected the hazy autumn light filtering through the tall buildings around her. Georgia thought the lightness seemed incongruous with the dark message she delivered with such seriousness.

'That's £230.00 Mrs Josephides. How would you like to settle?'

'Cash.' Georgia bit on the inside of her mouth as she spoke, the numbness alien to her. She counted out the £20 and £10 notes onto the desk. She'd been saving for the past three weeks to pay for the first of four sessions she needed. 'It's all the stress, darling,' her mum had said to her when she had told her about her referral. Georgia miscounted because she was trying to catch the rest of the news story. She scooped up the notes and started again, twenty, forty, sixty…two hundred, two twenty, two thirty. By the time Georgia looked back at the screen, the weather girl was pointing to the north of England where there were images of heavy rain clouds scattered across the map behind her.

***

Wednesday came round too quickly again and the boys were at their dad's. What with work and juggling the boys it seemed life was rushing past her without pausing. Nicolas kept to the agreement as per the court's directive to have them overnight, once a week. Georgia had grown to enjoy the mid-week break and space their absence gave her. Sometimes she would mark school books or read her Country Living magazine, which was delivered monthly. Other times she was more energetic and caught up on domestic chores, wiping down skirting boards or clearing out the clothes the boys had outgrown from their wardrobes and chests of drawers. Occasionally she would go out for dinner with Thalia or her PGCE peers who she had continued to keep in touch with.

It was one of those rare Wednesday evenings where she was glad to be at a loose end, with no set plans for the evening, and after a lazy snooze and read her latest novel,

Chocolat, on and off for a couple of hours. She then decided to make herself a mug of soothing black tea with cinnamon sticks and cloves.

Georgia flicked on the TV with one touch of the remote and something subconsciously urged her to switch channels to the BBC London News. The pain of her dental treatment niggled at her as the anaesthetic began to wear off. She tipped back her head swallowing two ibuprofen tablets, with a swig of her herbal tea, having topped it up with cold water from the tap to cool it slightly. She sat on the rug, her knees tucked up under her chin, the couch giving her back some support. She rarely sat on either of the sofas any more unless she had company. Trying to ignore the niggling ache in her lower jaw now the local anaesthetic had almost worn off, she sat there, annoyed at herself for still being jittery and nervous when alone in the sitting room. There was no way Sean was ever going to step foot in her house again, she assured herself.

The shrill ringing of the house phone cut across the silence of the house.

'Georgia. It's Mark.'

'Oh, hi Mark. How are you?'

'Good thanks.'

'Thank you for the marshmallows. That was really sweet of you.'

'You're welcome. Look are ya around tomorrow?'

'I'm out most of the day but I didn't think you were

due for another two weeks but I can leave the side gate open for you.'

'No that's not why I'm calling…'

'Oh?'

'I wanted to see ya…ask ya out…'

'Out?'

'Yeah. Go out for a drink, the two of us. We get on don't we?'

'Yeah of course we do. But I've got so much on right now Mark.'

'Well, you can tell me when you're free.'

'I'm busy all the time with work and the boys…you know…'

'Well perhaps we can have a cuppa together next time I'm over?'

'Yeah. Of course we can.'

'And about the marshmallows…'

'Yeah?'

'I hope you saved some for me.' She could hear the smile in his voice now, the blue of his eyes dancing as he spoke to her.

'Uh no…sorry…' She giggled nervously. 'But I'm sure you could buy some more.' She felt bold hiding behind the phone. She heard him sigh and she exhaled slowly too conscious her breathing was fast.

'Okay, well I'll see you soon.'

Georgia ended the call, flattered he had asked her out and yet anxious about getting involved with him. As she slurped some more of her tea something on the TV caught her attention. Georgia turned up the volume; her eyes wide and her ears pricked to take in every word of the news report.

'A drink driver from Cricklewood has received a seven-year sentence after killing two passengers in an 80mph crash. Sean O'Donnell, 33, gave a lift to two colleagues when he swerved round a lorry losing control. He smashed into a tree and bus stop, killing Daniel Jones aged 28 who died at the scene and Thomas Broadmore aged 30 who died two days later in intensive care.

O'Donnell, driving while on a three-year ban, was one-and-a-half times over the drink-drive limit when tested two hours after the crash. He pleaded guilty to causing death by dangerous driving, driving with excess alcohol and failing to comply with his disqualification terms.'

Georgia's concentration faded in and out. She couldn't take it in.

'Oh My God!' she blurted out, her heart pounding.

Was she relieved or in shock? Sean? She couldn't believe it. She struggled with her emotions. She never ever wanted any harm to come to him. He had been a troubled soul but she never ever thought he would have been capable of this, be so stupid. She recognised the crash scene as being very close to the hotel they used to go to. Had he been thinking about her? She thought about his texts; erratic, desperate in tone the last few times she had read through them.

She reached for the telephone to call her mum. On hearing her mum's voice, Georgia broke down.

Chapter Twenty-Four

GEORGIA WOKE NIGHT after shadowy night in a pool of sweat, her eyes swollen with fear. Her nightmares got worse and she kept seeing Sean standing over her, the shadows in his eyes dark, cold, something unnatural radiating from them. She heard his voice; his insides sounded like they were twisted, he was hurting and she felt his pain, saw it in his naked eyes. Grief pulled at her, dragging her deeper into the abyss of confused emotions; relief he was locked away, grief he was not the man she thought he was, sadness at the frailty of life, shock at his behaviour towards her in the end.

In the day questions ran around in her head; could it be he had been trying to block out the pain of what he'd done to her? Of what he had become? Had he been going back to one of the places they had passionately made love? Could she have prevented this from happening? Why hadn't she noticed he was unwell all the time she went out with him?

Slowly, as time passed, she learnt to be kind to herself again. The nightmares abated, and when she dreamt she woke with no recollection of what had filled her sleep. She began to adjust to the bleak reality of what had happened and she returned to what was her life now; work, home, the boys.

***

Nearing Christmas, she remembered back to September when she and the boys had planned an A-Z of days out or fun things to do together. They had all contributed ideas and agreed they would randomly work their way through the list and do everything before the end of the school year.

She recalled how the list had taken over an hour to compile, with disagreements, tears and tantrums to the point Georgia almost abandoned her 'brilliant' idea until the boys promised to behave.

The list, neatly written out on a piece of A4 lined paper, taken out of Andoni's Arsenal notepad, was attached to the family calendar with a butterfly peg. The bright magenta clip clashed with the red edge of the December page.

A – Arsenal match
B – Baskin Robbins ice cream DONE
C – Cinema DONE
D – Drive through McDonald's
E – Elstree Aerodrome
F – Father Christmas
G – Growing sunflowers
H – Hamleys
I – I Spy
J – Jogging round the park
K – *Kiofdethes* with yiayia and bapou

L – Lemon chicken (*bapou's*)
M – Play Monopoly
N – Dinner at Nando's
O – Origami
P – Planet Hollywood
Q – Quiz night DONE
R – Roast dinner with Yorkshire puddings and gravy DONE
S – Swimming DONE
T – Tennis in the park
U – Go somewhere on the underground
V – Visit a museum
W – West End shopping
X – X marks the spot treasure hunt
Y – Yoyo competition with mum
Z – Zoo

Andoni ticked off 'H' and 'W'. Georgia also planned to surprise the boys by taking them to Planet Hollywood for lunch.

By the time they all got ready it was gone eleven o'clock and Georgia clamped her lips to avoid swearing as she watched the 82 bus accelerate away from the bus shelter.

'It's Andoni's fault,' said Zachari.

'No it's not. You're the one who took ages doing your laces,' said Andoni.

'Well it doesn't matter now. Zach you are super doing your laces on your own. Now let's run into the sweet shop and get some drinks,' she said to deflect their bickering and because she didn't want to be standing at the stop for the next twenty minutes.

In the newsagents the boys took their time deciding which drink they wanted and Georgia sent Kristiano back to the chiller cabinet to change his choice twice.

'No, you know you're not allowed fizzy drinks unless it's a special occasion.'

'Well, this is,' he moaned.

'It's not a party, dog breath,' said Zachari.

'That's enough foul language.' Georgia gave the elderly lady standing in the queue behind her an apologetic look before turning her back to avoid the woman's clear wrath of disapproval.

'Quickly, or we'll miss the bus again.'

They just caught the next 82 bus. Georgia waited a few seconds before alighting so she could catch her breath. The boys flew ahead of her, and Georgia's pause allowed a woman with a buggy to reach the bus before the driver closed the doors.

Georgia swiped her Oyster card, waved bye-bye to the toddler in the pushchair and climbed up the stairs to the top deck calling to the boys who had rushed ahead and clambered up the narrow stairs one after the other. Zachari and Kristiano unsteadily made their way to the rear of the bus, holding onto the seats to stop themselves from falling over as the bus lurched forward unexpectedly. They launched onto the back row of seats, rolling around having the whole area to themselves. They knelt up and facing out the back window called out noisily, pointing, playing some sort of game.

'Behave boys,' said Georgia, already beginning to regret her decision to spend the day in town with them. She'd forgotten how energetic they were and how tiring working full-time was. Glad the Christmas break was ahead of her she felt herself relax.

'What are you playing?' she asked, trying to put some bounce and warmth back into her voice.

'Spot the Mini,' said Zachari. 'We made it up.'

'How d'you play that then?'

'Uh, you know minis, the cars? Well when you see one, it can be parked or driving around you shout 'mini'.'

Georgia joined in for a while peering out of the grimy window pane. The boys were so competitive she quickly tired of the bickering between them and opted out preferring to sit with her own thoughts.

Andoni tutting, moved from where the boys were messing about to a seat two rows in front. He took out his Nintendo from his pouch, bowed his head. Georgia imagined the deep concentration etched on his face. Since starting secondary school he had grown up. She tried to think back to what it was like to be thirteen but could only remember rolling up her school skirt at the waistband to make it shorter. Georgia smiled at the fond memory and took out her mobile phone, shuffling over towards the window to let a teenager sit down next to her. The bus was filling up and she looked over towards the boys who had quietened down, bored expressions on their faces. Georgia checked her phone. No messages. But then Sean was gone now. Who else would text her?

They alighted the bus at Marble Arch, along the side entrance of Selfridges and Georgia was reminded just how packed the pavements became as she looked around and saw a sea of bodies moving in all directions and at different paces.

'Andoni, you hold onto Zachari's hand and I'll hold Kristiano's. It's really busy being a Saturday so concentrate on where I'm heading and stay close *agabi mou*.'

'Do I have to hold his hand, he's such a baby.'

'Right, I'll hold onto them both, you follow me. Don't you dare lose us,' she said.

Georgia re-adjusted her envelope bag across her shoulder shifting it under her left arm. 'Right, hands,' she said to the younger boys gripping them tightly. Off she marched determined not to be slowed down by the heaving crowd of tourists and holidaymakers, meandering along like the Lazy River ride in the water park, they had frequented when holidaying in Cyprus.

She caught fragments of conversation as she weaved in and out of the crowd. When she heard Greek, she was tempted to say, '*Yeia sas.*'. But knowing the boys would ask why she was saying hello to people she didn't know when she had brought them up 'not to speak to strangers', she said nothing.

Navigating their way down Oxford Street was a struggle and the boys kept bumping into the back of people making up the busy city sprawl.

'Try to look where you're going boys,' she said.

One shopper, holding a huge suit bag, shoved past Kristiano, almost knocking him over had it not been for Georgia's tight grip on his hand. Zachari complained he was hungry and wanted to go to McDonald's.

'We're not going to McDonald's,' said Georgia, exasperated by his whinging.

'This is so boring. Dad always takes us to McDonald's,' joined in Andoni.

'Well, maybe you would like to go and live with him permanently!' she yelled, regretting what she'd said the moment the words came out. 'Sorry, darling. I'm tired. Look, I had a surprise planned for you for lunch. Somewhere you haven't been before but if you guys want to go to McDonald's then McDonald's it is. What shall I have?' She hid her disappointment at her plans for lunch at Planet Hollywood not evolving. It was, she thought to herself, about the boys having fun today.

'Yipee!' yelled Kristiano. 'I want Bob,' already trying to guess what his Happy Meal toy would be.

'You can have a McChicken Sandwich meal, with medium fries and a milkshake,' said Zachari earnestly.

'Come on then,' she said, already quietly relieved she didn't have to get to Haymarket now; her feet ached in her suede boots, not used to wearing flat footwear since starting work.

Meals ordered the boys grabbed a handful of ketchup and BBQ sauce portions from the service counters and half the straws from the dispenser. Georgia counted out four napkins and a few spare and they pushed their way past the now long queue to the staircase leading to the downstairs seating area. She had hoped it would be less busy on the lower level but was quickly disappointed. They stood around for a couple of minutes and then a woman with a young boy indicated she was leaving. Georgia thanked her and awkwardly lowered the heavily laden tray onto the table with a clank; the weight of it had made her wrist ache.

Kristiano jumped up with joy when he discovered his free toy was Gallaxhar.

'I haven't got him,' he yelled, forgetting he had wanted Bob. He pulled at his rubbery legs and twisted them back and forth discovering his head lit up, a little light shone through his big elongated forehead, like a purple beacon.

The McDonald's experience wasn't as awful as Georgia had anticipated and she actually enjoyed her meal it having been a long time since she had eaten McDonald's or taken the boys. She kept her patience as Kristiano dropped a huge dollop of ketchup all down his top. Zachari got his sleeve covered in ketchup too when he reached over to pick up his milkshake and got the open portion stuck to his elbow.

'You two are such messy pups.' Georgia dabbed at the stain with a napkin she soaked with water from the bottle in her bag. 'I'll have to shout it out when we get home,' she said, tutting at them both. Zachari proceeded to knock his milkshake over. The lid popped off spattering a big splodge across the table and into Andoni's lap opposite him.

'You idiot!' Andoni yelled at Zachari.

'It was an accident. Calm down,' Georgia said through clenched teeth. 'Most of it is on the seat between your legs.'

The situation was diffused by Kristiano who, bending down to pick up an errant portion of BBQ sauce off the floor, found an unopened Happy Meal Toy.

'It's Bob!' he yelled ecstatically, as he pulled open the blue packet, his cherubic face glowing.

'He's a bit goofy looking,' said Georgia.

'*Mamma* he's the best, look,' he said showing her the blobby shaped creature with one googly eye protruding from the top of his shapeless form. Kristiano wound him up with the little key at the back. Bob glided across the table.

'Aren't you lucky?' said Georgia giving him a hug and wiping his mouth clean of ketchup.

***

Back in the nippy cold biting at their faces, Georgia quickly found her bearings and meandered towards

Hamleys, the boys ambling ahead of her. Thankfully Regent's Street wasn't as busy as Oxford Street, the Christmas street lights brightening the already fading light. Georgia adjusted to the noise; screeching taxis, noisy double decker tour buses filled with tourists, the chatter of smiling shoppers out for the day.

'There's Hamleys!' Zachari pointed with glee to the bright red banners across the front of the store, fluttering gently in the light breeze. 'Come on *mamma*,' he said tugging on her hand and endeavouring to pull her forward and run ahead of her, but Georgia held onto his hand tighter than ever.

In Hamleys shiny decorations and Christmas wreaths covered the walls and gigantic Christmas baubles in red, gold and green hung from the ceiling giving the store a warm glow. The boys were overexcited and wanted to visit every floor, including Andoni which pleased Georgia. She watched as they disappeared like mice behind shelves and cabinets stacked high with puzzles, board games, computer games and stuffed oversized bears and animals.

'It's like Christmas already.' Zach wanted everything he saw, from the special edition monopoly, the Pokemon Nintendo game, remote control tank…he went on and on, picking things up, grabbing everything he saw and generally messing up every display he came across. Zach and Kristiano were evidently excited and Georgia felt a deep stab of regret as she recalled family visits they used to have to Hamleys on Christmas Eve with Nicolas. She couldn't escape the fact the boys' lives had been shattered by their father's affair. Thankfully they can still laugh and smile, she thought. Georgia felt a surge of love reach out to them from deep within her and she vowed to never ever let them down.

Georgia reminded them all they could only spend what they had. She took out the list from her purse and read out loud, 'Andoni, you have £35.00, Zachari £40.00 and Kristiano £15.00.'

Andoni, pulled at Georgia's arm to follow him, and they all stood amongst a dozen or so other shoppers, mostly foreign, watching the Marvin's Magic Box of Tricks demonstration. Andoni was the most fascinated by what he saw, asking questions, wanting to touch the props. The young shop assistant, probably a student working to pay towards his huge university fees Georgia guessed, beckoned Andoni to step forward. The young man leaned over the black clothed bench in front of him and pulled a gold chocolate coin from the pocket of Andoni's T-shirt. Andoni beamed with wonder. Then he shuffled a deck of cards, an ordinary looking set to the untrained eye of course.

'Pull out a card,' he said to Andoni. 'Look at it. Remember it. Put it back into the deck, anywhere you choose.' He spread out the cards like a Japanese paper fan. Andoni concentrated hard, unfazed by the on-lookers around him and did as he was asked. Within seconds the promoter shuffled the cards, put them into four piles and asked Andoni for a number between one and twelve.

'Nine,' said Andoni in a clear booming voice. Georgia could see how he was clearly enjoying being the centre of everyone's attention.

Counting out the cards, the demonstrator tapped the ninth one and before turning it over asked Andoni to name his chosen card.

'Ten of hearts,' he said. As the card was turned, there in front of them all, was the ten of hearts.

'Wow, that's brilliant,' Andoni said. Everyone around him clapped. The small crowd began to thin out saying thanks as they dispersed, making room for those stood behind them to step forward for the next magic display.

Georgia jostled through the melee of shoppers still standing around the magician and searched for her two younger boys. She saw Zach and called out to him to come to her. She grabbed his hand. She looked around, low down, between skirted and trousered legs but couldn't see Kristiano.

'Can you see your brother?' she asked Zach. 'Andoni?'

'No,' they answered in unison. She moved further into the crowd. A wave of anxiety choked her. Her eyes flitted from one spot to the next, scanning, scanning, scanning the whole time. She looked for a member of staff. The heat rose within her. She felt hot and flushed.

She pulled at the front of her jacket to cool herself.

Georgia's eyes darted around the store frantically as she described Kristiano to the shop floor assistant. Her hands pulled at her hair nervously as shoppers glanced in her direction.

'He's only six years old. He's got dark brown hair. Cut short. His name's Kristiano. He was right here a minute ago…'

'I'm sure he hasn't gone far Madam. I will alert security.'

'Security? Oh my God…why? Do you think someone's taken him?' She looked at Andoni who was shaking his head in disbelief. Zach's lashes were heavy with tears as she looked down at his hand gripping hers.

'No. It's just a precaution.'

'Please just find him.'

Georgia felt the sting of tears behind her eyes and she willed herself not to cry, to stay in control. He would be somewhere playing with a game or something…something… Her head felt heavy and her breathing was short, sharp, shallow. She closed her eyes in an effort to stop the surroundings from caving in on her. Her legs buckled and in slow motion she dropped to the shop floor in a crumpled heap. All she could envisage was Nicolas's face with an accusing look across it. How would she explain this? She could hear Zach sobbing now, Andoni calling out his brother's name in panic. She could sense people crowding round her. She became increasingly agitated and claustrophobic. She couldn't breathe and grabbed at her throat, clutching at her neck. She struggled to open her eyes, everything a blur around her. A dark figure bent over her and she could hear a woman talking...in Italian... she felt herself losing consciousness, felt a warm pudgy hand grab at her arm.

'*Mamma*, what's happened?' Then she passed out.

***

Guilt forced its way into her and although exhausted, Georgia eventually gained her composure. She martyred on with the shopping trip not letting the boys out of her sight for a second. Andoni spent most of what was left of his birthday money unsurprisingly, on a Marvin's Magic Big Box of Tricks set, looking at the range available and coming to a decision after much thought and consideration. He didn't part with his money easily and it took every ounce of patience for Georgia not to rush his decision.

Zachari chose a huge, realistic-looking, rubberised Dinosaur which made a roaring sound and glowed in the dark. Georgia was not impressed with his choice but respected it was his money and all she wanted was to get out of the store. While standing in line to pay, her panic abating, she thought about the Dinosaur Zachari had chosen which might mean she could switch the upstairs hallway light off at night now, since Zachari would still not sleep in darkness. Kristiano bought a Star Wars Lego set, Georgia giving him the extra £5.99 he needed to buy it without hesitation wanting to get out of the store as quickly as possible. She avoided the gaze of some of the shoppers around her embarrassed about fainting and even more so about losing her son.

Kristiano was the easiest to please and the guilt she felt for losing him in the store had already settled heavily on her chest.

Finally, out of the store, each carried a Hamleys bag, Zachari struggling with the huge carrier as he dragged it along the ground. Georgia thought how Andoni, again, was growing up fast as he looked back, a pace or two ahead, worry etched across his pale face. Georgia felt a pang of guilt about fainting and ruining her time with them, she already dreaded Nicolas's reaction. Damn she thought…that's all I need. She hoped the boys wouldn't mention it and she tightened her grip on Kristiano's hand.

The bus ride home was long and tiring, heavy rush hour traffic slowed their journey and the bus pulled in at almost every stop along the way. The only free run was through Finchley Road and along Swiss Cottage where the bus lane was clear and the bus made no stops for anyone to get on or off. Shops, houses whizzed past her in a blur.

The boys were grouchy and she knew it had been a long day for them too. Checking the time, she was shocked it was coming up to twenty to seven. Kristiano, complaining he was tired, snuggled into her and she shifted wrapping her arm around him, the weight of his head on her lap comforting as he dropped off. He fell asleep holding onto his Hamleys bag. She uncurled his fingers from around the handles and wedged the bag between her feet on the floor. As they approached their stop, she roused him. As floppy as a limp lettuce leaf, he held loosely onto her hand as he followed her down the stairs. The other two filed down the road towards home, not speaking.

Georgia entered the house, slipping off her shoes and tucking them into the corner behind the 'homework basket' where the boys kept their school books. She switched off the alarm as they came in, tapping the code in; the date of her honeymoon with Nicolas. She'd wanted to change it for ages but hadn't got round to finding the instruction manual and a wave of warm heart-wrenching nostalgia hit her for a moment, forcing her to catch her breath.

'Bath, dinner and bed,' she said to the boys who didn't argue.

In the kitchen, she heated through the *louvi*, prepared the night before, and straining it to get rid of all the water, she dished the beautifully clean white black-eyed beans her aunt had sent her from Cyprus, into a big bowl. She drizzled them with olive oil and squeezed over fresh lemon through a tea strainer to catch the pips, before giving them a toss with two serving spoons. She rustled up a tuna salad with spring onion and fresh coriander and cut chunks of *goulouri*, straight into the bread basket, lined with a natural linen fabric.

'Come on boys,' she called up the stairs, but the boys ignored her. She ran up the stairs, picking up the boys' discarded trainers which were thrown in a jumble at the bottom of the stairs. Zachari and Kristiano refused to have a bath but Andoni had been quick and was already stepping out of the shower. She pulled Kristiano's pyjama top down over his head as soon as he stripped out of his clothes.

'Wash your face and hands, darling,' she said to him, and to Zachari, who continued to ignore her. Andoni was chasing Zachari up and down the length of the landing, trying to grab his dinosaur off him.

'Enough, now!' said Georgia, 'let's get downstairs to eat and then beddy-byes it is for you all.'

'Not me Mum,' said Andoni. She gave him one of her serious but not too serious looks which he recognised as meaning 'you can stay up a bit longer'.

They sat down round the kitchen table. Andoni ravished everything off his plate, Zachari picked out the tuna chunks from the salad complaining he didn't like the green bits and Kristiano chewed the bread chunks scattering sesame seeds everywhere, his tiredness masking his appetite as he ate nothing more.

Eventually, with the boys tucked up in bed, physically and emotionally spent apart from Andoni who was on his PS2 console, Georgia sat alone. The quiet of the house enveloped her and the usual comfort it gave her didn't come. She was lonely.

Chapter Twenty-Five

'I CANNOT KEEP what you have just told me confidential,' Georgia said softly, leaning in a little closer to one of her sixth form students.

'But I don't want my parents to know.'

'I have a duty of care. I have to meet my responsibilities as per Child Protection guidelines. As your teacher I must share this information with our school designated Child Protection Officer.'

'Who?' asked the girl, her voice quivering.

'Mr Stephens. He will know what the best way forward will be so the school can support you while meeting all its responsibilities. Our priority has to be to make you safe.'

***

Later that afternoon, Georgia recalled the disclosure made to her and shivered. The girl's boyfriend was forcing her to go to parties and making her feel unable to say no to drinking which had led to something quite disturbing the night before. No-one should ever be made to feel like they owe anybody a part of them let alone to someone who makes them feel used and dirty. Georgia's personal experiences came flooding back and the pile of marking she planned to do lay in front of her, unmarked.

She hoped Mr Stephens moved the case forward, as promised. He mentioned contacting the girl's parents and the police too. It was out of Georgia's hands now but she still couldn't help but wonder how the girl was going to cope with her parents knowing.

Sitting quietly in her classroom Craig walked in with a bunch of papers and a highlighter.

'Can we go through the Year 10 end of year data together?'

'Uh, yeah of course. Give me two minutes to finish this.'

Craig walked over to the classroom window and Georgia watched him as he looked out across the still grounds of the school.

'I'm all yours.'

'Straight in? No playing hard to get?' he teased.

Those words instantly made her freeze...playing hard to get. Sean had said the same words to her and suddenly she was shaking as nausea strangled her. She held onto her stomach and doubled over.

'Bloody hell. Georgia! What's wrong?'

'Sean attacked me. He nearly...nearly...' Before she knew it Craig was cradling her in his arms. He didn't say anything, waiting for her to calm down.

Eventually Craig let go of her and tilted her chin up towards him. 'You have to tell someone...when did he...?'

'Ages ago...nearly eighteen months ago. I can't tell

anyone. I'm so ashamed and embarrassed. I let him into my life, my home…I'm such a fool. No wonder Nico left me…'

'Look you have to report this.'

'No. It's over. He's in prison serving time for killing two people while drunk driving. He can't touch me again.'

'Then get some help to cope with the trauma. Oh Georgia. I'm so sorry.'

'No. I'm fine. It's just what you said about playing hard to get…that's what he said on the night before he…he…attacked me.'

'I'm so sorry. I didn't mean anything by it.'

'I know. It's okay. I'm okay now. Sorry.'

'Shall I get Stella?'

'No please. Please don't say anything to anyone Craig. Promise me?'

'If that's what you want.'

***

It was February half term and Georgia was glad to be getting away from the increasing pressures of work. Craig had been attentive and kind at work and even though Georgia found it a bit stifling she appreciated his genuine concern and was glad it had been him she had finally confided in.

Georgia and Thalia were on a European trip together

in Barcelona. It was a real treat because Thalia's life had taken her one way and Georgia's had taken her in another. Thalia, now divorced, was building a new life with Phil in it and Georgia concentrated on making a living to provide for the boys, her confidence and drive getting her noticed at work. Her teaching career seemed to be the perfect fit for her and the head teacher recognised her drive, commitment to the students and loyalty to the school. Georgia was quickly promoted to Deputy Head of Year for the Sixth Form within a year of gaining her Qualified Teacher Status.

It was a huge achievement in such a short space of time and she relished in the recognition she got. She enjoyed the dimension the new position added to her role as a teacher and enjoyed building relationships with the older students. The relationships she built were on a different level to those with the lower year groups. She was dealing with young adults who shared their hopes and dreams and disappointments and fears with her. She discovered students opened up easily to her. Perhaps it was her worldly-wise demeanour and openness about her own experiences at work and as a mum encouraged this but she also knew deep down she wanted to help others. She had persevered through life's rough edges and it had changed her. She knew how difficult it could be and wanted to give something back.

***

Both girls were excited to be leaving the ordinary day-to-day hum-drum of life behind as they flew off on their adventure, an escape, in anticipation of something more exciting. They were celebrating Thalia's birthday and although Georgia had reluctantly agreed to go away with her, she was glad she had.

In Barcelona, the late afternoon was still holding onto the warm temperature of the day and the low sun gave the city a romantic glow, a mystic semblance. After checking into the Meliá Barcelona Sarriá Hotel, Georgia and Thalia, having freshened up took to the streets and walked to the city's main tourist attractions; Paseo de Gracia and La Pedrera, and Sagrada Familia and Parque Güell.

The hotel was perfectly located in the thick of the action and within walking distance of all the places warranting a visit. The main thing was they were spending time together and allowed them time for the heart to heart conversations missing recently back home.

'I could do with a drink,' said Georgia, the heat, the closeness of the atmosphere stifling her, making her breathless.

'Let's find somewhere busy where we can have a laugh.'

'Find some men, you mean.' Georgia knew too well what still made her friend tick even though she was now in a relationship.

'Well, who else can we take the piss out of?' she laughed.

'So bloody true, babe,' joined in Georgia, her laughter a welcome tonic after the last few months of being scared of her own shadow, of her own blind stupidity and naivety.

'This looks buzzy.'

'This looks like men only.' Georgia looked towards the café bar Thalia was pointing to which was overflowing with only men, at first glance.

'Perfect,' said Thalia, already making her way over, big purposeful strides, her legs as long as a giraffe's in her three-inch wedge sandals.

'Bloody hell,' said Georgia, more to herself than to Thalia as she skipped to catch up, holding onto her sunhat which the light breeze threatened to blow away.

They sat down, at a table for four, Thalia facing the main walkway and Georgia facing back into the canopied seating area outside. She picked up a menu and choked, the laughter catching in her throat.

'What?' said Thalia.

'Shall we order a cocktail?'

'Yeah, we could but why are you laughing?'

'Look,' said Georgia passing her the cocktail list, still chuckling away.

Sex on the beach – Vodka, crab berry juice, liqueur, peach, orange juice

Pina Colada – Crème de cock nut, pineapple juice, Rum

Mojito – Lime juice, Rum, Sugar, Syrup, Soda water
Tequila Sunrise – Tequila, Grenadine, orange juice
Cosmopolitan – Crab berry juice, Lime juice, Cointreau, Vodka, lemon
Blue Barcelona Lady – Gin, Curaçao blue, Lemon juice
Barcelona Alexander – Cognac, Cream, Crème de Cacao

It didn't take long for Thalia to spot the spelling mistakes. They both roared with laughter.

'Ladies, can I get you anything to drink,' asked the stocky dark-haired waiter with the white apron which looked like it was giant-sized.

'Can you tell me what crab berry juice is?' asked Thalia, serious as can be, Georgia choking into her handbag, pretending to be looking for something, anything, to avoid looking up. She desperately tried to keep the laughter in but failed miserably, choking on a squeal as it burst out of her.

'This is a small red berry,' he said.

'And the cock o nut?'

'This is white and hard on the outside,' he said.

Thalia and Georgia both erupted, like volcanoes, their laughter punctuating the quiet hum of conversation around them.

'Welcome to Barcelona!' managed Georgia, still not daring to look up at the waiter, who was now looking rather dumb found and a little embarrassed around them.

'I will come back,' he said, taking the overflowing ashtray and walking off.

'Yes, you "cum" back,' said Thalia.

***

Their bill paid, they both walked side by side, the silence between them comforting, like a favourite blanket with a familiar smell is to a new born baby. Each knew how far the other had come and equally knew nothing would ever take away the journey they had made together. The sun was low in the sky now and the city bustled with a second surge of life. There were men in business suits and women spilling out of an office block, some in pencil skirts others in less formal wear like linen trousers and summer dresses covered in pretty flower prints and stripes.

'What are you thinking, hun?' asked Thalia.

'Nothing really. Everything. I mean look at us Thalia. Who would've thought years ago we'd be in Barcelona, both divorced, me with a new career, you with a new man…it's crazy. We've come so far and yet sometimes I don't feel I've moved on emotionally from Nico, not properly. Sometimes I think I still love him…'

'Oh, darling. You're amazing and love doesn't just go away. It was different for me. Tony crushed my love so there was none left in me. But you. Your situation was so different. You loved Nicolas. I remember how you had him on a pedestal. But you'll meet someone else and be in love again.'

'It's not even that babe. It's my family unit. I've lost it forever. The boys are like little gypsies, back and forth, week in week out. This isn't the life I wanted for them. I wanted more. I had big dreams. We had big dreams.'

'And he smashed them up, hun. Not you. You remember that.'

'I know. But what if I realised earlier. What if I had been a better wife?'

'Georgia, you listen to me. You did nothing wrong. He's an idiot. He thought he could have his cake and eat it. Well life isn't like that.'

'I feel so messed up sometimes, babe. So…lost. I don't know where I'm heading, my life's compass is just going round and round.'

'You're not fucked up. You're on a different journey hun across new oceans. New beginnings Georgi, come on, cheer up, we're in Barrrr-the-lo-na!'

They both giggled at her silly Spanish accent and decided to find somewhere to have some tapas and sangria. Georgia felt the first of an adrenaline rush.

***

Sitting across from Thalia, Georgia felt content. Thalia was the one who had kept her going through everything and she was the one who really knew her.

Having chosen random dishes from the tapas menu Georgia filled her plate with a spoon of everything; *patatas bravas, tabla serrana, bombas, calamares fritos, gambas pil-pil, chorizo, almendras and espinaca*. Each little terracotta bowl or dish filled with delicious food from olives and spinach to chilli prawns and meat and potato balls. Georgia savoured every mouthful; all the flavours feeding her taste buds like she hadn't eaten for days.

'Absolutely delicious,' she said, through a mouthful of fried squid ring and fried potato cubes in a tomato sauce.

'Almost as good as meze.'

'Here's to a new working compass.' Georgia raised her glass of sangria and clinked it with Thalia's.

'And some beautiful new oceans,' said Thalia, smiling.

They took their time eating and even ordered a couple more dishes before ordering their desserts. *Arozz con leche* turned out to be a rice pudding and the flan wasn't a flan at all as they'd guessed but a crème caramel, served with a little shaker of cinnamon to sprinkle over the top.

'It's been a great first night, Thal,' said Georgia stifling a yawn, her appetite satisfied and the day's travelling catching up with her.

'Of course. Why wouldn't it be? We always have a

great time wherever we are.'

'I know. But tonight was lovely. I don't feel so heavy, so out of my depth anymore.'

'You were never out of your depth hun. You just forgot how to swim!'

'Yeah, I s'pose you're right, babe.'

'To swimming,' said Georgia, raising her glass again.

'To armbands,' laughed Thalia, slurping the last of her Sangria through her straw.

***

The break was just what Georgia needed and she took comfort in Thalia's presence and bonded with her; real friends. Some things would never change, thought Georgia. She smiled as she looked out of the plane window as she bumpily landed back in the UK.

Chapter Twenty-Six

HER HEART HAD ached telling them about what their dad had been up to. All sitting on her bed after dinner Georgia explained what he had done in a kind way which wouldn't paint him as the monster she now saw him as.

'But he says he loves you still, *mamma*,' said Andoni earnestly.

'But loving someone when you are an adult means you stay with them and love them always. Your dad has loved someone else.'

'He's sorry. He told me.'

'But it's too late *agabi mou*,' she said, looking round at their little faces.

'When you are all older and you have girlfriends and wives you will understand this better. Look, who's your best friend?' she asked Andoni.

'Josh,' he replied straight away.

'Well, imagine Josh did something to upset you. Then he promised he would never ever do that again. But then you found out he'd done it again. How would you feel?'

'I'd be really angry. I wouldn't want to be friends with him anymore.'

'Why?'

'Because he's lied. I wouldn't believe he could lie to me. He's my best friend.'

'Well, it's kind of like that with me and your dad now. He has been sleeping, having sex, with someone else for a long time when he made a promise when he married me to love only me,' she said, the tears streaming down her face. She had reached out and pulled Kristiano close into a hug and Zachari had moved in and snuggled up against the soft mound of her belly. They all cried together for what felt like forever but had only been a few minutes, Andoni stroking her hand gently as he cried too.

She half-heartedly packed the boys' bags for their weekend stay at their dad's which came round too quickly still and went by equally slowly.

'Mum, I don't want to leave you,' said Andoni, holding her hand tightly. She packed the last of their belongings into the oversized sports holdall which was bursting more with what the boys wanted rather than needed for the weekend.

'I know honey, but I'm out tonight. Aunty Thalia is having a party so I'll be having lots of fun. Don't you worry about me.'

'But we're always unpacking and packing, forgetting things, losing things, being late for school…' he whined.

'Look I will text your dad and ask him to double check you have everything before you come back on Sunday night, darling, okay?'

'It shouldn't be like this…we should be living together in one house, one happy family…' he said, looking away, fighting the tears welling up in his eyes.

'I'm sorry but this is how our life is now. I know it's hard. It's hard for me too,' she said guiltily. Georgia was thinking about the affair. Nothing would have stopped Nicolas from doing this to them. If it hadn't been that *boudana* Roksana then it would have been some other tart, she was now sure. Nico had been stupid, weak and he had been flattered by Roksana's attention. Stupid, stupid man, she thought. 'We will all be happy again,' she said, trying to convince Andoni just as much as herself. And she wondered when that would be as she fought against the all-consuming sadness seeping through her.

***

Despite her sadness Georgia had been looking forward to Thalia's house party all week and Thalia too was just as excited, texting her often in the week leading up to the event

```
Flowers ordered picking them up on Saturday
x
Got the most gorgeous smelling candles
today x
Spoke to the DJ
All set
Music will be brilliant so get ur dancing
shoes on x

SO excited
what r u wearing? X
```

```
Am I doing the right thing?
Phil moving in?!!!
```

Georgia replied each time with ecstatic oohs and ahhs when they spoke and lots of heart and smiley face emoticons when she texted. Georgia reassured her despite all her previous doubts about Phil, yes, him moving in was a great idea and Thalia and Phil would be happy together and they texted right up until the day of the party.

```
This is ur forever after babe x be happy x
love u! xxx

Love u too x
See you tonight xxx
```

***

Jade and Paula were also coming to the party with Georgia. Both girls had met Thalia a couple of times at Georgia's for a natter and a cuppa. Thalia was pleased her friend had found some new girls to hang out with, especially since her relationship with Phil had become more serious and as a result, coupled with Georgia's full-time teaching job, had been spending less and less time with her. Georgia was delighted Thalia had invited them too as it meant she wouldn't look too conspicuous arriving with no man by her side.

She still missed Nico and thought about him. She still

thought about Sean too but in a confused, detached and unemotional way. Sean had made her feel special but she knew the relationship had been going no-where and walking away, in the end, had been the only grown-up thing to do. She couldn't blame herself for his reaction to that and his attack on her. She knew that now. She had to protect herself and her boys from pain. The pain of her marriage breaking down, she knew, would never be matched by anything.

No man, however much she thought she loved him, would ever hurt her as much as Nicolas had. The pain was still as authentic as ever and her heart tumbled at the emotional turmoil she couldn't help but feel when she thought about him. He was her children's father after all. They had both loved each other once.

Georgia shook herself out of her reverie, the hot water spraying over her as she showered, the steam engulfing her, making her light headed. She stood there for over twenty minutes letting the water run over her. As she telexed, her thoughts wandered to her night out. She lathered herself with the Champneys Exotic Retreat, a birthday present from Jade. She squeezed and bent back the end of the tube managing to get the last squirt out into the palm of her hand.

She moved away from the shower spray and taking in the smell of ylang ylang and sandalwood, she ran her hands over her wet skin, building up a rich foam. The aroma was sensational. She was turned on. Her skin felt smooth and young again; toned as a result of her weekly half hour swim.

She began to probe and caress the most sensual part of her. She felt her nipples harden, her body tingle. She stroked her throbbing button, hot and moist. Lost in the moment she teased until she found release; the sound from her lips a high pitch, full of emotion. Her legs shook and her knees buckled. She slid down the tiled wall into a sitting position, her knees tucked up against her. The water ran over her for a few more minutes and then she eased herself up, her legs still weak. She rinsed off what was left of the creamy lather and stepped out of the shower, roughly drying herself before entering her bedroom, leaving a trail of wet footprints across the stripped floorboards.

She took her time getting dressed and delayed putting on her make-up until the flush across her face died down. She checked her Facebook account on her laptop, Jade and Paula had helped her set it up recently. Sitting on her bed, the pillows all plumped up behind her, she browsed through the only two messages, from the girls, both saying how much they were looking forward to the party. She put the laptop to one side and stood opposite her dressing table mirror. She looked at her reflection and smiled. She pulled on a pair of knickers and rummaged around in the deep drawer for the matching bra.

Her phone vibrated. She rolled across the bed, to the other side. Planting her feet firmly on the floor she reached for her phone. It was a text from Mark.

```
Hiya, gorgeous Georgia.
```

Mark? Who was Mark? Gorgeous Georgia? Oh my God, she thought. Mark? Mark! Her mind went into an electric frenzy like an overloaded fuse board. Did he genuinely think she was gorgeous? She tried to backtrack over their conversations at the front door and on the front drive over the years. And more recently. Had she ever given him the impression she was interested in him? She didn't think so and hesitated. If she responded it would be giving him the green light she was open to more. More? More of what? She wondered. On the other hand, if she didn't she would come across rude, superior maybe, which wasn't true on both counts. She decided to text him back and became aware of her heart racing.

```
Hi

What are you up to tonight?

Going out to a party. U?

Nothing much. Been working all day.
Quiet nite in, then?

Yeah. Can I text u later or are u going to
the party with ur boyfriend?
```

She hesitated. Bugger it. He can text. Why not? There's nothing wrong with that, she thought. It's only texting.

`Yeah, course u can. And no, not going with my bf.` Georgia texted back.

***

Arriving at Thalia's at half past nine, she felt excited, goose pimples on her arms and the hair on the back of her neck standing up alert, as if waiting for something to happen. She kissed Thalia on both cheeks and gave her a big hug, then gave Phil a quick hug too, as he was passing through the small hallway carrying a pile of coats and jackets.

'I'm just taking these upstairs, darling,' he said to Thalia.

'Okay, thanks,' she said, and then addressing Georgia, 'He's been on the go all day helping me get organised, moved the furniture around, unpacked the food shop and even helped arrange the flowers,' beamed Thalia.

'That's great. I'm thrilled for you both. Good luck!' She handed over two bottles of Pinot Grigio to Phil, now back downstairs, and a small gift bag to Thalia. 'Something ditsy for you cos I love you and I know this will all be brilliant.'

'Thanks Georgi. This is it, no turning back.'

'You won't have to turn back babe. If this is right for you, then it's right.' Georgia turned to Phil who was now holding Thalia's hand, 'Don't you ever dare let her down.'

'I won't,' he said, slightly taken aback by her forthright manner. 'I know what a good friend you've been to Thalia and I want you to know I love her too. I promise I won't hurt her.'

Georgia was equally taken aback by the earnestness of his response. 'So let the party begin!' she trilled deflecting the conversation.

'Whoop! Whoop!' chimed in Thalia as both she and Georgia threw their arms into the air.

Jade and Paula were already there and Georgia gave them a wave as she made her way into the lounge. Both shifted from their wallflower poses and hugged her.

The DJ and dining room table were positioned at the far end of the room. The buffet under the window looking out onto the lush green garden, full of purples and pinks and yellows. The DJ was set up against the adjacent wall, opposite the french doors, which opened onto the raised decking.

Georgia gasped as she took in the beautiful ambiance of the lounge; bright fresh flowers in huge glass vases stood at different focal points around the room adding colour to an otherwise plain room. Candles of different heights gave off the light scent of white jasmine and orange, strategically placed on the window sill, side tables and on the mantel piece, their flickering flames casting a warm glow across the room. The only other light came from the DJ's set of disco lights punctuating the dimness in time with the music.

Hugging each other they laughed at the fact they were all wearing something red. Georgia had a pair of bright red high heels on from Dune, red fishnets and a denim skirt layered with a white chiffon blouse.

'They're wow,' said Jade. 'I want a pair!'

'Your top's fab too,' said Georgia to Jade who was wearing a halter neck top in a bright silky fabric and then looking at Paula 'and you've got your red jeans on. Very sexy.'

'We're like the best of the Spice Girls or…'

'The Three Degrees,' interjected Georgia, laughing and wondering whether the younger girls, in their early twenties had a clue as to who The Three Degrees were, but they didn't comment both too busy giggling.

They made their way back into the kitchen, where all the bottles and cans of drink were lined up neatly along the kitchen worktop and plastic cups were stacked up high, again neatly, along one end. Georgia poured herself a vodka and lemonade, plopping in a couple of ice cubes which she scooped out with her fingers from the huge metal bowl taking pride of place amongst all the drinks. Jade popped open a raspberry flavoured cider and Paula filled a plastic pint cup with ice before splashing it with a generous amount of vodka and then topping it with coke. It frothed up quickly and spilled over the brim of the cup and onto the kitchen floor. Georgia grabbed some kitchen towel and bent down to wipe it up. 'This is going to be a hell of a night,' she said.

'Why's that then?' she heard a voice behind her and looked round.

'Hello! How are you? I wondered whether you'd be here,' said Georgia excitedly, standing up from her squat position on the floor where she had finished mopping up the coke.

'How are you? I haven't seen you in ages. Thalia has kept me up-to-date with your new career and stuff. You look great.'

'So do you,' said Georgia, leaning in to hug Thalia's first cousin, Athena, who Georgia had got to know and like over the years.

'These are two friends of mine, Paula and Jade. We studied the PGCE together.'

'Hi, nice to meet you both,' said Athena.

'You too,' they chorused, smiling and then loudly said, 'Cheers.' The girls clinked their plastic cups together with Georgia's and drank, Paula almost taking down half her pint glass in one go. Mario, Athena's second husband, walked into the kitchen just then and Georgia did the introductions all over again while Mario introduced one of his oldest school friends to the them all too. The kitchen getting tighter with lots of guests grabbing at the drinks bottles and reaching across for cups and ice and mixers was uncomfortable to be in so the three girls shuffled towards the lounge.

Georgia thought the DJ was fantastic. He played so many of the R 'n' B artists she loved as well as the oldies from the seventies, eighties and early nineties and Georgia being Georgia got the dancing underway. Her mum had often told her how her paternal grandmother had been a beautiful dancer and Georgia had taken after her. Georgia remembered her *yiayia* as they danced together on Georgia's wedding day back in 1993, Georgia in her flowing ivory dupion silk wedding gown and her long flowing veil trailing to the floor. Her *yiayia* had held tightly onto one corner of the *mandili*, Georgia held onto the handkerchief's opposite corner and as they turned moving around the dance floor the handkerchief had got twisted tighter and tighter bringing them dancing closer together. Georgia remembered hugging her *yiayia* after the dance, full of emotion. Georgia danced losing all her inhibitions. She knew she looked good and knew men looked her up and down. She felt in control and she could feel the music in her, not just hear it and feel it on the outside, but feel it to her core, like it was a part of her.

Jade and Paula danced too and Paula was brilliant at shaking her booty as Jade put it. They laughed, and drank and flirted with a couple of Phil's mates. Georgia was on a real high, flirting shamelessly and determined to have fun. She didn't drink anything else, just a shot of vodka and lemonade but it was enough to give the impression she was tipsy which suited her fine. She was in control.

After dancing through a number of tracks straight, Georgia put her hands up in protest and sat down on the couch pushed up against the wall, behind the door. The candle had gone out on the side table leaving the corner in semi-darkness. Georgia surveyed the room, waving across to a couple of Thalia's neighbours she recognised and two of Thalia's other cousins, Luca and George. She eased her bottom up off the seat and slipped her mobile phone out of her back pocket. As she settled back onto the couch she stared down at it.

Message 1: `Hiya sexy`

Message 2: `Having to much of a good time 2 text then r ya?` Georgia noticed his incorrect spelling of too and shuddered remembering Sean.

Message 3: `Bet u look hot tonight. What r ya wearing?`

Message 4: `Can't stop thinking about ya`

Jade and Paula came and flopped on the couch either side of her.

'Who's that?' asked Jade.

'Uh no one…'

'Is it the boys? Are they okay?' asked Paula.

'It's my gardener,' blurted out Georgia.

'Your gardener?'

'Yeah, he's asked me out twice and now he's texting me.'

'No way, when did he ask you out? You never said. Blimey Georgia, you really are a man magnet, aren't you?' said Jade, 'Isn't she Paula?'

'Yeah, I wish I had men throwing themselves at me like you,' said Paula, 'are you going to go out with him?'

'I don't know. He's my gardener. It feels weird, maybe even a bit sleazy. My mum and dad wouldn't approve that's for sure.'

'I know what you mean,' said Paula. 'My parents want me to marry someone educated, an accountant, a solicitor, a doctor…'

'Yeah, I know. How can I introduce my gardener as my new boyfriend?'

'Gosh, Georgia that would be really awkward, wouldn't it? I mean how long have you known him?'

'Over seven years I think, but that's not the point. I can't even bring myself to say gardener. That's snobby isn't it?'

'No it isn't. You have to have standards, babe,' said Paula.

'Yeah, you do, but you can still text him and flirt and have some fun. No harm is there?' said Jade, giggling, 'and you're a free agent. Do what you want.'

Georgia read through the texts again out loud. She looked up from Paula to Jade and back to Paula again and laughed and within seconds, all three of them were leaning into each other in fits of laughter, their hollering punctuating the split second silence between tunes. Georgia held onto her stomach as she bent forward. 'I'm going to wet myself.' She snorted loudly which set them all off again uncontrollably. They carried on laughing for a few minutes, tears streaming down Georgia's face, Paula repeating Georgia's I'm going to wet myself? but as a question which threw them into hysterics again not really knowing why they were actually laughing which made it even more hysterical.

'I'm starving,' said Georgia, holding her side, the laughter finally subsiding, 'I didn't have anything to eat tonight, did you?' she said, changing the subject completely, trying to compose herself.

'No,' the girls answered in unison, as they wiped tears from their eyes, exchanging knowing looks with each other.

'Help yourself to food ladies,' said Thalia, right on cue, 'I don't want any leftovers.'

'We will, thanks, hun. It's great tonight, Thal. You pleased?' asked Georgia.

'Yeah, I am but there're always the last minute drop-outs full of excuses, which is so annoying.'

'Yeah, but your main party girl is here,' said Georgia. She grabbed Thalia's hand pulling her towards the centre of the room to dance just as 'We Are Family' by Sister Sledge came on. Jade and Paula jumped up and before they knew it there was a group of about ten dancing and singing their hearts out. Georgia looked over at the DJ who winked at her.

'Man magnet! Man magnet!' teased Jade, having clocked the wink from the DJ.

'Enough!' said Georgia, but deep down inside she was flattered and flattery did get some people somewhere. For a split second she thought of Nico. Had it been like this with Roksana after being with Georgia for so many years? Her mind went back to Mark and his text messages, she pulled out her phone, a twinkle of mischief crossing her face. Where's the harm? she asked herself. I'm in control here and I'm single.

```
   Hi she texted, looking hot like u'd never
believe!
   Oh yeah bet u r
   So?

   So I'm thinking about ya

   What r u thinking?

   How sexy u r

   And?

   How I wanna make ya feel

   Oh yeah?

   Make ya wanna scream
```

```
Oh yeah?


Make u cum
```

'Shit,' Georgia said out loud. She laughed nervously and then apologised to those around her. She felt her body temperature jump a few degrees even though an open window at the far end of the room let in a chilly waft of night air.

In the kitchen, she poured another drink this time mostly lemonade, as there was literally a teensy weensy drop of vodka left in the bottom of the now empty bottle. She had to drive home anyway and was only drinking to be sociable. Jade and Paula glugged the drink like it was a competition but she reminded herself they were almost half her age. Just then, Jade came bundling in with Paula.

'What's happened?' Georgia asked, her eyes wide with horror.

'She's drunk,' said Jade.

'Sensible Paula?'

'I feel sick,' mumbled Paula, her head flopping forward, her hair covering her face.

They hoisted her into a chair and Georgia grabbed the black liner from the kitchen bin just in time for Paula to throw up into. Jade pulled Paula's hair back to avoid getting it covered in bits of half-digested food but her jeans were not so fortunate.

Thalia looked on unimpressed and walked out.

Georgia recognised anger in Thalia's twitching, agitated face.

'Oh darling,' Georgia said, trying to console Paula as she burst into tears and blabbered on, apologising.

'She's been drinking since five o'clock while we were getting ready,' said Jade, looking a bit embarrassed and trying to justify the situation.

'Look, I think we should clean this mess up and get her a cab home,' said Georgia, soaking a cloth under the tap and trying to sponge the sick off Paula's jeans.

'I'm staying at hers tonight so I'll have to go with her,' said Jade. 'We've already got a cab booked for between one and half past.'

'Okay. Another half an hour or so. Water's what she needs now.'

'I am here, you know,' piped up Paula, her face ashen white and her eyes flushed red and teary-stained, splatters of sick pebble-dashed her front.

'Look, you'll be fine honey.'

'We'll go home together as planned,' said Jade, rubbing Paula on the back, 'just take small sips of water and breathe.'

'I'm so embarrassed. Where's Thalia? I need to say sorry.'

'She's fine. I'll tell her you're sorry. Don't worry about that now,' said Georgia, knowing full well Thalia was not impressed with Paula's performance.

'Let me get rid of this outside.' Georgia knotted the

top of the bag and went out by the kitchen door. It was chilly, and yet she welcomed the sharp coolness around her. She took another look at her phone; Mark again.

```
All OK?

Had a bit of an accident

Oh yeah? Got u excited did I?

Ha ha! friend from uni was sick

Oh dear

She's going off home in a cab

So u will be all alone will ya?

The party's still going

Not tired?

No

So you've got staying power have u?

I have

Prove it

I will

How?
```

```
Will text u wen I get in
```

Back inside, Jade and Paula were putting on their coats and saying good night. Georgia gave Jade two Tesco bags, one inside the other, just in case Paula was sick in the cab.

'Goodnight, Mummy Georgia,' said Paula.

'Night hun and look after her.'

'I will,' Jade said, running after Paula who was already half way up the drive, unsteady on her feet, even though she was holding her high heels in her hand.

'And text me when you get in!' called Georgia after them both.

***

The party carried on. There were still at least twenty people milling around, sitting on the bottom of the stairs, standing chatting in the kitchen and a couple smooching to some Lionel Richie song in the lounge. Georgia grabbed a cup and filled it with Evian. She was thirsty, dehydrated; probably too much vodka and not enough food. Food! She remembered she still hadn't eaten anything. She wandered into the lounge. The dining table, still laden with over flowing platters of party nibbles but also strewn with half empty plastic cups, scrunched up napkins and half eaten plates of food teetering in haphazard piles.

She picked up a paper plate and piled it up with chicken satay skewers and a dollop of gloopy peanut sauce, two samosas of some kind, a handful of hand-cooked crisps and a few dried up carrot sticks.

'What shall I play for you?' asked the DJ, beaming across at her.

'Anything dancy, Rihanna, Beyonce, Neyo, Chris Brown, you choose,' she said, smiling back at him.

She walked round the couple who were still entwined; the girl's arms around the man's waist and his hands open, groping her bum. Georgia sat down on a chair adjacent to the fireplace. She picked at her food, her stomach rumbling all the while but nothing satisfied her confused appetite or state of mind.

The rest of the night, she danced with Phil and Thalia and a couple of his mates and then, her feet aching and screaming to get out of her high heels, she tottered off towards her car to drive home, having scooted round and discarded most of the rubbish and empty bottles into two big refuse bags for Thalia, before saying goodnight and apologising for Paula being sick.

***

Pulling up onto her drive, the wall lanterns throwing a bright light across the paving stones, she turned off the engine and sat for a few minutes, the key still in the ignition. It had been a great night. She had enjoyed herself and smiled at the thought of Paula being sick. Silly girl, she said to herself. She text Jade to check they were both okay, having realised she didn't get a home safe message from her.

```
Hi girls x you both ok? Xxx

Yes darling. All ok. U? x

Just got home x had a great nite! Xxx

We did too. Paula is knock out! X

Good she needs to sleep it off x

Yeah lol x

Knackered too x speak in the morning? xxx

OK. Night hun x

Nite nite x sweet dreams xxx

Love you x

Love u more   xxx
```

***

Safely indoors, Georgia forced herself to cleanse, tone and moisturise her face. She plugged her phone in to charge. She padded across the bare floorboards of her bedroom to the en-suite and brushed her teeth. Turning the light out, she released the cord to her blinds, letting them drop shut. The street lights were eliminated in an instant, her room thrown into complete darkness. She climbed into bed, wriggled under the duvet, rubbing her arms to warm herself up, remembering Mark's texts. She leaned over to her phone and pulled hard on it so the charger pinged out of the back of it. Lying in bed, she read through the texts again, smiling.

She eventually dosed off until the mobile vibrating in her hand roused her into wakefulness.

'Hello,' she said, in a sleepy half-awake voice.

'Hello you. You asleep?' said Mark.

'I'm semi-conscious,' said Georgia, pulling herself up into a slouchy sitting position, as she re-adjusted the pillows behind her, alert to the sound of his voice.

'Thought you were going to text me?' His husky voice aroused her.

'I did didn't I? What's the time?'

'Nearly half two.'

'So early enough to be talking and late enough to be…naughty.'

'Oh yeah?' he said.

'Oh yes,' she responded warming up. 'So now I'm awake let's not waste any time.'

'Not tired then?'

'No…not…tired…at…all. I want to be naughty…' she teased, her voice gaspy, sexy, sultry. Her body tensed with excitement.

'Yeah?'

'You just relax and enjoy the ride.'

'Really, now?' he said.

'Really. Put your phone on loudspeaker.' Georgia did the same.

'Why?'

'Because you're going to need both hands free...'Georgia switched her mobile to hands free too.

'Oh now you're talking.'

'Lie back...imagine me.'

'I'm imagining alright...you're so sexy you know that?'

'You're feeling horny, eh?'

'Like you I'm guessing,' Mark whispered.

'Oh, yes,' she said, laughing, a little out of control. She wondered what he was thinking but didn't care.

'Yeah. I can hear excitement in ya voice,' he said in a deep sexy voice.

'Excitement?'

'Yeah. What have you got on?'

'What have I got on?'

'Yeah, what are ya wearing?'

'My nightie. Why?'

'What's it like?'

'It's strappy, it's blue with cream stripes, a baby doll. What are you wearing?'

'Boxers.'

'Take them off,' she commanded, taking back control.

As she talked to him, telling him what to do, where to touch, Georgia moaned and surrendered too. He was totally hers. But she got lost in the moment too. Aroused from her fingertips down to her painted toes, she threw all caution away. Not thinking about what she was doing with this man who tended her garden. And finally she let go and felt the warmth of her inner moistness spill over her fingers and down onto her bum cheeks. Gasping, she couldn't say a word. Mark told her over and over again what a gorgeous amazing woman she was while she let out a quiet moan, wave after wave of sheer pleasure drowning her over and over again. Finally, with no energy left, she lay there, her heart racing, her pulse loud in her ears.

Mark continued talking to her. He said he'd had a great night. He waffled on about wanting to see her the next day. Georgia reached over, fumbling for the phone no longer on the pillow where she'd left it. Stretching out her hand she eventually found it. She flipped off the speaker phone and managed a breathy goodnight, not agreeing or disagreeing with his intention to see her, and ended the call.

She had never ever done anything like it before and couldn't believe quiet cockney Mark had just given her the most spine-tingling orgasm ever and he hadn't even been there with her. She wondered what Thalia would say. She wondered what anyone who knew the 'old' Georgia would say. I am taking control of my life, she said out loud. You had better be listening Georgia, you are going to have way more fun being this way.

***

Georgia woke early. She was unusually hot and couldn't work out why. Then she remembered. She got up and put on the dimmer low and pulled on her nightie, discarded somewhere near the bottom of her bed. Her legs were clammy. She threw the duvet off her. She reached for her mobile. It was 5:18. There were also two unread messages.

> Message 1: `U r amazing x`
> Message 2: `Good night gorgeous Georgia. Sleep well x`

Chapter Twenty-Seven

IN HER NIGHTWEAR, loosely wrapped in her silk kimono from The White Company, Georgia ran out across the drive to throw out the two bags of rubbish. The spring breeze rose in a gust around her, tangling her curls and blowing them across her face. The sun peeked out of the clouds, sending splashes of warmth across the drive. As she ran back to the porch someone called out her name. She turned round. Mark was climbing out of his van parked on the other side of the neighbour's drive.

'Good morning,' she blurted pulling her blossom robe tighter around her. She tugged at the collar to cover her half-exposed shoulder.

'Wondered when you'd be up.'

'Did you now?'

'Thought I'd get over here before the football traffic on the North Circular builds up, big match today.'

'Oh, right.' She took the bunch of variegated blush roses from his hand and thanked him.

'Have you had breakfast yet?'

'No. I can't face anything.'

'Shall I make you a cuppa?'

'Ah, thank you,' she said leading the way back into the house and into the kitchen.

Georgia filled the kettle and flicked on the switch. The kettle gurgled as it warmed up.

'That's noisy,' he said, as she pulled out a chair tucked under the kitchen table and sat down, careful to keep herself covered.

'Yeah, that's Dualit for you. My old kettle was never this noisy.'

'So how are you?' he said, leaning towards her, his eyes bright and glossy.

'Fine thanks,' she said, embarrassed by his rapt attention and conscious of how they'd been with each other only a few hours ago. She blushed – the re-run of last night flashing in full colour across the wide screen of her memory. As Georgia got up Mark put his arm out indicating for her to stay where she was.

'I'll make the drinks. Just tell me where everything is. Tea or coffee?'

'Tea please I don't drink coffee.'

'You okay?'

'Yeah, course.'

'About last night. You were amazing Georgia.'

'Right.' Her voice cracked with emotion.

'And I hope you're not embarrassed. I'm not.'

'Well, I don't want you to think I do that sort of thing all the time. I've never done anything like that in my whole life. I don't know what came over me. I wasn't even drunk.'

'Good. I'm glad you weren't drunk,' he said, looking straight at her. 'Sugar?'

'No thanks,' she said, looking away, the heat

blushing her cheeks all over again.

She watched him stir two teaspoons of sugar into his tea. He carried both mugs over to the kitchen table and Georgia got up to get some biscuits from the larder.

They carried on chatting for a while longer.

'Just like that?' asked Georgia gob-smacked with the revelation of his announcement.

'Yeah, basically.'

'And how do you feel?'

'Relieved. She's been a right cow for the past eight, nine years, maybe longer. I don't know what I ever saw in her. We got married young. But I'm fine really. The divorce is the next step.'

'I had no idea. And the children?'

'They're pretty upset. Both crying all the time. It's hard on them, poor loves. Are yours alright?'

'On the outside maybe, but not on the inside. I have nightmares thinking about how they really feel sometimes.'

'Well you're a great mum. You're always doing something for them. I've seen how ya dote on 'em. Run around doing everything for 'em. You're unbelievable. And your cooking always smells delicious.'

'My cooking?'

'Yeah, I smell it from the front door when I come to collect what you owe me sometimes.'

'Oh right.'

They chatted for another half an hour or so, Georgia

relaxing a bit more and enjoying his easy, calm nature and his sense of humour. She laughed out loud more than once at his recollection of antics he and his brother got up to when they were younger and in turn she told him about some of the scrapes her two sisters and brother had got into growing up too. They laughed together. Georgia was surprisingly comfortable in his company as he appeared to be in hers.

'Well, it's about time I should be making tracks.' Mark looked up at the washed blue shabby chic style clock above the alcove which housed her range. Georgia didn't encourage him to stay any longer. She didn't want anything happening face-to-face. Last night was one thing over the phone but not now. She hadn't even brushed her teeth yet.

She followed him out into the hallway and he took three paces towards the front door, his hand on the door handle. He hesitated for a split second and then turned round to face her head on.

'Look, I really like you,' he blurted out, 'and I know you've knocked me back before, twice,' he added smiling, 'but what do you say to going out for dinner one night?'

'I don't know.'

'I'm on me own. You're on ya own. Where's the harm. I think we'll get on great together.'

'And if we don't? I'll have to look for another gardener,' she joked in an effort to lighten the mood.

'If we don't get on I'll do your garden for the rest of time, no charge.' He winked at her and her heart did a little flip, heat spreading through her like hot steam from a jacuzzi.

'Really now.'

'Yeah. Scout's Honour.'

'You were never a Boy Scout,' she teased.

'I was, 1st Walthamstow Scouts, every Thursday and once a month we did an away trip. I loved the scouts. Mum did too, she was glad to get rid of me.'

'Look, I don't know.'

'Say yes. The summer will come soon and I don't want to be on my own. Do you?'

'No, I s'pose not.'

'Is that a yes then?'

'Yes.'

'Brilliant and thanks for the company, Georgia, and for last night.'

'Uh, yeah. Nice to see you Mark,' she said unable to look him in the eye at the mention of the night before again.

'I'll call you, text you.'

'Okay. Bye,' she said, a hurried tone to her voice.

'Bye,' he said, and he leant in towards her, brushed his lips on the side of her cheek and gave her the lightest, gentlest kiss as his hand, as light as a summer breeze, squeezed her arm. A tingling wave shot through her and she found herself not wanting him to go.

'Look, I know you're probably busy and stuff but do you want to stay and we can go and have lunch somewhere?'

'Wow, yeah. I'd love that.'

'Okay. Can you find something to do for a bit while I go and shower and get dressed.'

'Yeah. I need to chase a couple of customers for money. See you in half an hour or so?'

'Perfect,' she said smiling, her heart fluttering like a butterfly in her chest.

Closing the door behind him Georgia was consumed by a strangling panic. What on earth was she doing? This was ridiculous. She had to call him and say she'd made a mistake. Upstairs she picked up her mobile from the dressing table and scrolled down her contacts list for Mark's number. She clicked on it and then hesitated. He might think she's lost the plot. Damn! She really was a stupid cow sometimes. She sat staring at his number for what seemed like ages and then a new message flashed across the screen. She opened it up. It was from Mark. That was it. No turning back.

***

Lunch at The Orange Tree in Totteridge was hectic. The pub popular amongst the local residents had recently been refurbished in a mix of traditional décor with a twist of fresh modern fixtures and fittings bringing it bang up to date. Georgia and Mark shuffled past a group of noisy thirty-somethings and stood by the bar. Georgia rubbed her hands together nervously and shuffled from one to the other to soothe her aching feet. The pub's car park was chock-a-block and they had parked some distance away.

'What d'you want to drink?' Mark asked.

'J2O please. Any mix will do.'

Mark eased his way nearer the bar pushing his way between a tall bleached blond woman who looked like she'd had a few too many sessions under a sun lamp and a younger guy who looked like he was just old enough to be allowed in a pub.

Georgia hung back and surveyed the bar for a couple of empty seats or a table looking like it might be soon vacated by its occupants. She spotted a waiter putting down a small plate with a folded bill on it at a round table by the open fire. She leaned over the shoulder of a woman and tapped Mark on the shoulder indicating to him she was going to stand over the other side of the bar. She squeezed past a body builder type with bulging muscles stretching his shirtsleeves to the max and then past a family all dressed up for a celebration. The girl with them of about ten years old held onto a heart-shaped helium balloon with Happy Birthday printed across it in silver letters.

Georgia stood looking across at Mark. It was warm standing in the vicinity of the log fire even though the logs had turned to mainly ash, and the heat, combined with her jangled nerves, was making her hot from the inside out. She eased her jacket off and re-adjusted her bag over her shoulder.

Within a few minutes the gentleman sat at the table, took a final swig of his pint, finishing it off.

'You can have our seats now, darling,' he said.

'Sorry. I didn't mean to rush you. It's mad busy in here isn't it?'

'We're done so the table's yours darling,' he said, winking at her.

'Thank you so much,' said Georgia.

The well-groomed woman with him said nothing. She stood up, clutching her Louis Vuitton handbag and Georgia noticed her fingers adorned with two gold rings, one with a shiny diamond. Perhaps the woman didn't like him addressing me as 'darling', Georgia thought.

'Thanks again,' said Georgia taking his seat. She moved the empty glasses to one side of the dark mahogany table and draped her jacket on the back of her leather tub chair. She surveyed the pub from where she was sitting, noticing one of the mini spots above her was out and further along there were another two bulbs not working.

Mark sat opposite her, opening his legs and extending them either side of the table's pedestal foot towards Georgia's seat.

'This is a great pub,' he said. 'Never been here before.'

'It's one of our meeting places, me and the girls and I bring the boys sometimes as a treat,' she said.

'Very classy,' he said, picking up his pint and holding it up ready to make a toast.

'Yeah, I s'pose it is,' she said, picking up her bottle of juice. She poured half of it into the glass after she'd spilled the ice cubes into one of the used glasses she'd pushed to the side.

'Cheers,' said Mark.

'Cheers.'

'To new beginnings and happier endings,' he said.

'I'll drink to that,' she said, tears welling in her eyes.

'You okay?'

'Yeah, just a bit emotional, missing the boys, tired from last night, tired of all the upheaval and constant barrage of everything coming at me…sorry. Yeah, I'm fine.'

'I'll listen to anything you wanna say. Anything you wanna talk about, Georgia. You know that don't ya?'

'Thank you, Mark. I'm fine. Sorry...'

'Don't apologise. You think that's emotional? I've spent the last decade sleeping with one eye open not knowing what that mad cow of a wife was gonna do to me.'

'Oh no. I didn't realise things were that bad.'

'Manic depressive most of our married life, she was, and so things were never good in our house. She was always going off on one and her moods would go on for weeks, months at a time.' Georgia looked into his eyes and saw loneliness, desperation. 'Anyway, that's enough of.'er an' all. What're you doing for the summer?'

'The boys will be with Nicolas.'

'So you're on your own?'

'Oh no. I'm going to visit a friend in Canada. I'm going to stay with her and her husband and three children.'

'It's going to be a full house then?'

'Oh yeah, and then my sister Theresa's coming from Lincolnshire. She has three children and Katia, my other sister has two. She'll stay with me for a few days. But we're used to lots of family, being Greek.'

'Did you say Lincolnshire?'

'She lives on the outskirts of a village up there.'

'It's nice that way. We was near there years ago with me mum and dad, visited Lincoln Cathedral. Beau'iful place but I didn't appreciate it at the time. Found it boring, moaned all the way there, the whole time we was there and then all the way back.'

'Oh, no.'

'Yeah, I know. Poor Mum I drove her mad with me whining.'

'It's nice up there. The boys love going for the weekend and especially in the school holidays, all those big country parks...'

'Bet they do. They've got a lot of energy ain't they?'

'Yeah and they miss their cousins so we spend proper

time together when we visit.

Just then a waiter came over and cleared the empty glasses.

'Can we have a menu when you're ready mate?' said Mark.

***

Lunch was delicious. Georgia ate everything on her plate bar the rind of fat from her roast pork and a couple of parsnips. Mark took big mouthfuls, complimenting each one. Georgia giggled at him, commenting how he was like an advert for the place.

'Wow. Amazing meal.' He patted his stomach through his shirt. He leaned towards her and emptied the last of his bottle of cider into his pint glass, his hand brushing hers as she reached for her drink.

'The food is great here. Service was a bit slow though.' She waffled on trying to ignore the electric current his touch had ignited in her.

'Well we weren't in a hurry,' he said, reaching over and taking her hand in his.

'I really like you Georgia. I know you've had a hard time. I know you're scared. I can see it in your eyes. I'm not gonna be the guy who hurts you again. I'm gonna make ya happy.'

'That's a bit heavy, Mark,' she said, uncomfortable at his open display of affection. She fought the flutter of panic rising within her. She looked round checking if anyone was listening now the bar had quietened down and the lunch time rush had subsided.

'I'm being honest with ya. I've liked you from the minute I saw you in 2001. You were amazing then and you're amazing now.'

'2001? The only thing I remember from 2001 is the news about the Twin Towers collapsing, all those thousands of people dying. We'd moved into the house a few weeks before. I remember the electrician coming in mid-morning, mid-afternoon, and telling me. I was horrified. I'd been up those towers a few years before. I couldn't believe it. I cried my eyes out.'

'Yeah I remember that too. Shocking. But 2001 was a great year for me cos I started doing ya garden. I remember the white top you was wearing and your infectious smile as you looked over at me.'

'Really? I don't remember…' she trailed off, embarrassed.

'I do. I remember it like it were yesterday and I remember that feeling in my stomach and somewhere else too.'

'And here we are,' she said, not knowing what to say.

'Yeah. Here we are. Glad you were forward and asked me out for lunch,' he teased. 'Feel like the luckiest bastard in the world right now.'

***

She drove back from her sister's house, swerving round corners and slamming on the brakes as she approached the traffic lights far too fast. She had the music blaring but it excited her, enlivened her. This was either going to be great or it was going to be a huge slap across her face. Sexting was one thing. Lunch in a pub was another. But meeting up for dinner was kind of serious and quite another thing altogether. It was two weeks before her holiday to Canada.

Georgia had gone round to her sister's to help out with some of the preparations for her 'Big Fat Greek BBQ' the next day. She'd told Katia all about Mark and she thought Georgia should go for it.

Chapter Twenty-Eight

AT HOME, SHE dashed up the stairs two steps at a time, leaving her discarded cardigan in the hallway with her bag and her suede boots, left there in the same abandoned way she always told the boys not to.

Having brushed her teeth, she decided to change her top. She squeezed on her caramel stretchy one with the spaghetti cross-over straps at the back and then threw on her lacy brown short-sleeved blouse over it. She buttoned up the front leaving the two top buttons undone, revealing her cleavage. She checked herself in the mirror. There. She was almost ready. Looking at her watch she had fifteen minutes before Mark was due to arrive and so she touched up her make-up, being careful not to smudge her mascara as she added another thick line of deepest brown eyeliner under her eyes and brushed on a sparkle of 'Summer Sun' eye shadow over her eyelids. Last, but not least, she defined her lips with the velvet beige liner and filled in with her usual Sexy Mother Pucker gloss.

Just as she was taking her chocolate brown leather jacket from the wardrobe, the doorbell rang. Her heart missed a beat and the feeling of being out of her depth washed over her.

'Hi,' he said, as she let him in. 'You look absolutely gorgeous.' He pulled her into him, and kissed her on the lips. A full blown kiss, not once, not twice, but three times, his tongue caressing hers in a way she had never been kissed before.

'Hi,' she gasped, as she pulled away, a tingling sensation running across her chest and down between her legs. Georgia looked up into eyes brightest blue; a blueness deep and never ending like the line where the sea merges into the sky on a summer holiday.

'Sorry. I just had to do that. B'n thinking about you all day.'

'Gosh, that's really taken me by surprise. You don't waste any time, do you?' she said, her voice quivering.

'I've wanted to do that ever since lunch the other day. Well, from seven years ago.'

'Seven years ago?'

'Yeah. From that first moment you asked if I could do your garden, I said to myself, that's the woman I want to be with.'

'But you were married then,' Georgia said, incredulity in her voice.

'Yeah, I was. But looking back I hadn't had any fun with her for a long, long time. It was already dead between us.'

'How sad,' said Georgia.

'Not sad. It's the best thing that's ever happened to me. You are just gorgeous, d'ya know that?'

'Stop it. Shall we get going?'

'Yes. Your carriage awaits,' he said, sweeping his arms exaggeratedly toward the front door and the drive beyond. The smile on his face lit up his whole face and revealed two dimples in his cheeks she had not noticed before.

She pulled on her leather jacket, buttoning it from the middle down and slipped on her boots, leaning up onto the hallway wall so as not to lose her balance as she bent down to zip them up. Letting him out of the house ahead of her, she punched in the alarm code and followed him out. He had already opened the passenger door to his black Astra, and being careful not to flash her knickers, she lowered herself into the seat admiring the sky streaked with magical pinks and purples.

'I imagined you picking me up in your white van,' she teased.

'Na, no way. The van's for work. And you deserve the best.'

'Ooh aren't I the lucky one?

So where to?'

'D'you like Indian?'

'My favourite.'

'So let's head towards West Hampstead.'

'Wherever you say, gorgeous Georgia,' he said. She gave him directions to an Indian restaurant she knew and had eaten in many times with her sisters and cousins in the past. She was happy he was glad to go wherever she wanted to. He talked non-stop all the way there, pausing only to confirm the route, being in unfamiliar territory.

Their evening passed and Georgia laughed too much,

attracting the attention of other diners in the small, compact restaurant, but she didn't care, even when a woman gave her a sideways glance. She felt totally comfortable with Mark. He was easy to talk to and she realised there had been many conversations between them over the years standing in the porch doorway, in the back garden or by the side gate. She felt as if she knew him. They laughed at the same things. He complimented her all the time and Georgia lost count of how many times he used the word gorgeous. She had not forgotten the session after Thalia's party either, but parked it somewhere out of her conscious mind, for now.

After too much food and too much laughter, Mark asked for the bill. As he took out his credit card and placed it on the silver tray which also held two after dinner chocolate mints she noticed the initials on the card, D. M. Richards. Her heart missed a beat. Could the D be David?

'What's the D on your card stand for?'

'Oh it's for David after my grandfather. But everyone calls me Mark.'

'Your middle name I'm guessing.'

'Yeah. I was always Mark at school to avoid confusion with another boy called David in my class so it kinda stuck so I just carried on using it.'

Georgia smiled to herself and thought back to her reading with Warren. He had been so sure David was already in her life; David was Mark. Her heart danced in her chest sending flutters through her.

After the clammy warmth of the restaurant the cool summer air hit Georgia as they made their way back up the hill towards Hampstead Heath to where the car was parked.

Suddenly a man came stumbling out of the shadows towards them wearing a sludge-green and brown overcoat, his lips clenched around the stub of a cigarette. He made no motion to move out of their way and swayed unsteadily a few feet from them. Georgia could smell the sweat and dirt coming off him; the pungent whiff of rotten apples, sweat and alcohol.

'Miserable sinners,' he slurred at them. He raised his hand, knuckles cracked and blackened, clutching a bottle of cider which spilled onto the ground in front of them.

'Watch it mate.' Mark protectively pulled Georgia behind him, away from the grilles on the shop windows where the man collapsed. The man stared at them unflinching through grimy eyelashes, a trail of smoke wafted up in front of him.

'Sinners. All of you.' He straightened up only to lose his balance and fell back onto the cold pavement beneath him, up against the store front. He let go of the bottle which rolled away a few feet.

'Yeah, yeah…' said Mark under his breath as he hurriedly pulled Georgia away, who looked back towards the man intermittently.

'Is he okay?'

'He's drunk Georgia. Let him sleep it off. Poor bastard.'

'Oh my God. I didn't see that coming,' said Georgia, breathy, when they were far enough away to slow their pace.

Mark stopped abruptly under the glow of light spilling from an old fashioned street lamp. He looked her in the eyes and pulled her to him. Georgia almost crashed into his chest, as he drew her closer. He kissed her on the lips. She tasted the chocolate after-dinner mint on his lips.

'And I didn't see that coming either,' she said, looking up at him, her eyes filling with tears from the icy wind blowing across her face, her cheeks red.

'I've had one of the best nights out in a long time.' His fingers twiddled with her hair and then his hand brushed the back of her neck, caressing her there, sending electric currents through her. 'Let's get you home. You're shivering.'

'I'm okay. He just shook me up a bit,' she said. He pulled her closer into him. His body heat warmed her through and made her smile as they walked up the hill together.

'He's harmless. Unlike those...that top makes your boobs look amazing, you know that? I couldn't stop staring in the restaurant. You are just so gorgeous, Georgia.'

'Stop it...but thank you,' she said going redder.

'Don't thank me. It should be me thanking you.

Sitting across from you all night. I've been in heaven.'

In the distance behind her she heard the faceless, homeless man shouting the same obscenities, his words carried on the night wind as it picked up and she shivered again.

On the way home, Georgia was much quieter, she was already wondering whether to invite him in or not when he interrupted her thoughts and made the decision for her.

'I'll make you a nice cuppa when we get in. That'll warm you up.'

'Ah thanks.'

'Perfect,' he said, leaning over. He gave her leg a gentle squeeze, ran his hand up and down her inner thigh. Georgia felt her heart pumping, her pulse racing. Was she scared or excited? She couldn't work out what she was feeling.

***

At home, Georgia took off her jacket and sat on the bottom of the stairs to pull off her boots; they were tight and awkward to remove, but she managed to take them off, albeit getting herself a bit flustered in the process, before Mark emerged from the downstairs toilet.

'Do you still want a cuppa?' he asked.

'No, not really. I'm tired.'

'Look, you can say no if you like but I thought I could

stay the night and then go out tomorrow morning to collect some money owed me round this way. It'll save me going back to Enfield and then coming back tomorrow. Is that okay?'

'Oh, uh…look I'm not sure Mark. I've had a lovely night but…'

'I'll get up and make you breakfast in the morning, if you like. I'll run over to Tesco and get whatever you fancy,' he said, standing over her.

'Sounds great but…I'm… not ready for anything…'

Mark bent down and planted his lips on hers. He took her breath away; kissed and caressed her all over, her neck, her décolletage, her cleavage.

She didn't remember getting into bed or him getting in next to her. But she remembered the slow gentle sex. He made her feel safe. He kept going and each time she thought he'd say goodnight to her she found herself lost in swallowing sensation as he made her moan over and over again, until spent, gone, he whispered in her ear, 'You amazing, gorgeous woman. I am never going to give you up. Not ever.'

'Good night David,' she whispered. Georgia felt safe. She felt protected. She knew this man had come into her life for a reason. May be he would stay…maybe he was passing through…but she knew he would care for her the way she deserved and the relief, the realisation she wasn't alone, overwhelmed her. Maybe she didn't have to face the future on her own.

Silent tears of joy rolled down her face as she could finally fit together her broken pieces of tomorrow.

The End

Author Bio

Born in London to Greek Cypriot parents Soulla Christodoulou spent much of her childhood living carefree days full of family, school and friends. She was the first in her family to go to university and studied BA Hotel & Catering Management at Portsmouth University. Years later, after having a family of her own she studied again at Middlesex University and has a PGCE in Business Studies and an MA in Education.

Soulla is a Fiction author and wrote her first novel Broken Pieces of Tomorrow over a few months while working full time in secondary education. The novel has been nominated for the 2017 Reader's Choice Awards. She is a mother of three boys.

She is a compassionate and empathetic supporter of young people. Her passion for teaching continues through private tuition of English Language and Children's Creative Writing Classes.

Her writing has also connected her with a charity in California which she is very much involved in as a contributor of handwritten letters every month to support and give hope to women diagnosed with breast cancer. One of her letters is featured in a book 'Dear Friend', released on Amazon in September 2017.

She also has a poetry collection, Sunshine after Rain, published on Amazon and is releasing her second novel, The Summer Will Come in March 2018 which has received an endorsement from William Mallinson, Author and Historian. Her current work in progress is titled Trust is a Big Word and will be her third fiction novel.

When asked, she will tell you she has always, somewhere on a subconscious level, wanted to write and her life's experiences both personal and professional have played a huge part in bringing her to where she was always meant to be; writing books and drinking lots of cinnamon and clove tea!

Thank you!

It is with a grateful heart that I thank you for reading my book.

I would love it if you would keep in touch and invite you to connect through any of my social media platforms.

I look forward very much to welcoming you and hope that you continue to support me on my writing journey as I will support you too in any way I can.

The world is a big place and there's room for all of us to be successful, so join me and let's enjoy future happiness and success together as we celebrate achievement hand in hand.

With much love, Soulla xxx

Other books

The Summer Will Come

(Historical Fiction)

Set in 1950s Cyprus, EOKA, British rule, and the fight for Enosis where two Greek Cypriot families, living in different villages on the island, are coping with the unpredictability of this fractious time.

Circumstances over a five-year period push both families to escape to London where, as immigrants, they struggle to settle, face new challenges, trauma and cope with missing their homeland's traditions and culture.

Both families' lives cross paths in London and it seems that happier beginnings could be theirs. But at what cost?

A story of passion for a country in turmoil, family love, loyalty and treachery and how, sometimes, starting over isn't always as imagined.

> 'A racy, gripping and fluently written novel, which brings to life the unfortunate realities of Britain's occupation of Cyprus.'
>
> - William Mallinson, former British diplomat, Professor of Political Ideas and Institutions, Universita Guglieml Marconi, and author of *Cyprus: A Modern History*.

Sunshine after Rain

(Poetry)

A collection of thirty poems inspired by old sayings and phrases. Many of us have grown up listening to our parents and grandparents saying them, our teachers and friends.

Included in the collection are poems written around a number of different themes and ideas including: hope, love, happiness, disappointment, beauty, struggle, resignation, joy, life, nature and of course that most British of all things, the weather!

Social Media

soulla-author.com
soulla-author.com/blog
twitter.com/schristodoulou2
instagram.com/soullasays
facebook.com/soullabookauthor
uk.pinterest.com/asceducational

Book Club Guide

A Book Club Guide for Broken Pieces of Tomorrow is available via my website so please take a look.

soulla-author.com

I hope you enjoy discussing the story with your friends and family.

Book Review

All reviews are welcome so please take a few minutes to leave yours.

If you're not sure what to include in a book review then you can look at some helpful tips, available on my website.

soulla-author.com

Thanks again for taking the time to read and review my book.

Printed in Great Britain
by Amazon